Óna Crainn

An Ancient Secret - From the Trees

Books by:

Robert Leiterman

The Bigfoot Trilogy:

The Bigfoot Mystery – The Adventure Begins

ISBN: 0-595-14175-7

Yeti or not, Here we come! – Bigfoot in the Redwoods

ISBN: 0-595-26561-8

Operation Redwood Quest – Search for Answers

ISBN: 0-595-30513-X

Other natural history related books:

Great Valley Grassland Adventure

ISBN: 0-595-20302-7

GOJU QUEST – A Martial Artist Journey

ISBN: 0-595-34185-3

Either One Way or The Otter

ISBN-13: 978-0-595-38218-7

Óna Crainn

An Ancient Secret - From the Trees

Robert Leiterman

iUniverse, Inc.
Bloomington

Óna Crainn
An Ancient Secret - From the Trees

iUniverse books may be ordered through booksellers or by contacting:

iUniverse
1663 Liberty Drive
Bloomington, IN 47403
www.iuniverse.com
1-800-Authors (1-800-288-4677)

ISBN: 978-1-4697-4469-8 (sc)
ISBN: 978-1-4697-4470-4 (e)

Printed in the United States of America

iUniverse rev. date: 01/12/2012

I dedicate this novel to all of us who believe.

The fairy stone:
Find a stone that the river has bored, like a hole through the center of a seedless gourd. Hold it up high so the eye could see through and if you believe, there might be an ancient fairy looking back at you.

Acknowledgements

I would like to thank the following family and friends for the last eight years of this project: **James Leiterman**, (my big brother for his unyielding support) **Erik Leiterman** (my nephew and # 1 fan), **Butch** and **Shirley Russell** (for assisting on this and other projects), **Betty Lee** (for taking the time), **Eric Rowland** (my lifelong friend and supporter for taking the time to read almost every novel I have written), **Ed Cushman** (a talented artisan who has helped my with other projects in the past), **Tom Yamarone** , (my good friend and fellow adventurer & Squatcher who has helped me on several journalist projects), **Jerry Olesen** (fellow parishioner and friend), **David Sopjes**,(fellow martial artist), **Richard Gunn** (patient friend), **Andrew Scotti** (retired park ranger, friend and adventurer), **Kim Nickles** (friend and coworker), **Nancye Kirtly** and **Rick Dowd** (fellow artisans, supporters and friends), **Sandra Warade Baca** (a retired teacher, for being a friend and taking the time to support me on this and other projects),or anyone else I may have forgotten to mention, during my frantic search for notes, for their enthusiastic support and editorial review on this and other projects. I would also like to thank **April Leiterman** (my very talented daughter) for drawing and designing the front and back covers of this book. Lastly, I would like to give thanks to my **Na síogaí** loving daughters **Corina** and **April Leiterman** for without them; I probably would have written about trolls, gnomes and ogres instead of fairies. I would like to thank my wife **Regina** for her abundant wildlife knowledge and better grammar and spelling, for her patience and helpful suggestions throughout my writing phases, and for giving me the time to stumble through the woods looking for inspiration and answers. I am very grateful for her support on this and many other writing projects. By giving me time to write, she has taken more of the burdens of family life onto her shoulders, a dept that I may never be able to repay.

I give a special thank you to my children, especially for those who have stumbled along besides me through the darkest portions of the forests and the others who have yet to do so. May they be inspired to take a closer look and examine nature's mysteries with an open mind and caring, understanding heart. I hope the enjoyment of this and my other books: **The Bigfoot Mystery**, **Great Valley Grassland Adventure**, ***Yeti or not – Here we come! Operation Redwood Quest***, ***GOJU Quest – A Martial Artist's Journey***, ***Either OneWay or The Otter***, and ***Óna Crainn An Ancient Secret – From the Trees*** Will inspire and encourage them to participate in many adventures of their own. It is especially to my family and their many adventures to come that I dedicate this work.

Introduction

You ask the average person about fairies and they smile amusingly. You tell them that you've seen them during your last visit to the forest and they raise an eyebrow or two. Let's face it; most people in this country have a bit of trouble buying into the existence of fairy folk "**Na síogaí**" pronounced (Na shee-ogh-ee) or an assortment of other Celtic fairly tale creatures like *bean sí (ban shee), puca (pook-ah), gruagach (groo-ug-ukh), leipreachán (lep-rukh-awn), leannan sí (lan-awn shee),* and *cailleach (kal-yukh).*" A quick translation leaves you with Fairies, Gnomes, Ban shee's, Hob, Hairy goblins and Witches haunting children's nightmares worldwide. By no means are these all of them. No, the list of legendary creatures is extensive. Go ahead, pick any environment in the world and a culture has got a name for the critter that inhabits that nitch and no doubt does something bizarre that would easily tie them into fairy people. A considerable percentage of the Irish, Scottish and Welsh population still entertain the idea that *Na siogi* may still occupy their ancestral lands. They've been living with this legendary mythological folk tales a lot longer than we have.

Evidently, these immortal, human like, mythical beings range in size anywhere from the very tiny flower fairies to great stone divas large enough to control the weather. With a size range that broad, SciFi hits like James Cameron's *AVATAR* , a modern version of the animated hit *Fern Gully* and Disney's *Tinkerbell* fit right in there. Whether they're twice the size of a human or the size of a humming bird, it all seems to work. Outside of Tinkerbell, some of the common threads of the fairy line are the possession of magical powers and the ability to change the seasons as well as the aspects of weather and nature. They move swiftly and blend into their environments. They seem to like the color green and live on hills, under water, woody dells, caves, and to them hollow trees become doorways to different realms. (That could explain why were having trouble confirming the existence of cryptids like Bigfoot and the Loc Ness Monster.) They love to eat fruit, make shoes and bows, steal house hold items (Which explains a lot like … like why we can't seem to find things.), and enjoy music, laughter, dancing and fighting under the moonlight. Apparently they hate insects and reptiles. You see, they aren't so different from us in many ways. In their worlds, every flower, leaf, and blade of grass has a story to share and the wind whispers ancient secrets into the ears of those who listen. There are lessons for us in every forest trip that we take. This should give you a new meaning to the phrase *stop and smell the roses.*

Fortunately for me, my job gives me an opportunity to spend a considerable amount of time in the outdoors, ancient redwood forests to be exact. And as you know, there is no shortage of huge ancient trees, lush groundcover, dark shadows and huge hollowed trees in an ancient redwood forest. If there were ever a place you would expect to find fairies, it would be there.

So … while on your forest travels have you ever heard the music, the distant conversations near the creek, or the strange laughter? Have you ever seen the darting shadow that seemed a little too big for a bird? Have you ever had that feeling that you weren't alone? Smelled the orchids when there weren't any to be found? Have you ever passed through sections of the forest that made you either feel happy or sad? Have you ever lost something only to find it in the strangest of places? Have animals ever walk right by you and acted like they hadn't seen you? Have you ever taken that one photograph that had that face staring back at you from the shadows? (I believe blob shot is the term.) Was it an optical allusion? Were they shadows playing on your imagination? Have you ever found a flower sitting on your things awaiting your return when you were only gone for a moment? (A buddy of mine swears by this one.)

I have. Were all of these things a coincidence helped along by a health imagination of the unknown? I don't know about you, but the thought that there might be things going on in the ancient forests of the world that we know nothing about makes life that much more interesting. Do you believe in fairies … **Na síogaí** (*na shee-ohg-ee*)? What have you got to lose? My fascination with the fairy folk came to a head on April 19 2004 when I finally managed to organize thoughts into words. Enjoy the book and I hope to see you in the woods.

Act 1: Circumstances

Chapter One

Out of the Storm

Another flash of blinding blue light illuminated the dark shadows of the ancient forest and the ear-piercing rumble that immediately followed shook everything to its core. Dark purple clouds turned the January day into night. Like the four other girls who stumbled along in front of her, Fionna paused momentarily to regain her balance, rest her shoulders and legs, and let the blue spots fade from in front of her green eyes. Shuddering as the icy rains raced down her neck and bit deeply into her pale skin, she peered through her long leaf-and-stick-tangled hair that hung, lifeless, over her face, almost as if it did not belong to her. Once beautiful, her auburn hair was now dark, dirty and unkempt, a reflection of her mood. She was too exhausted to care.

Fionna's body instinctively shivered to keep warm. She watched her breath drift up and disappear into the strange darkness. It hadn't been that long ago that the sun was shining, the cool air was dry, crisp and refreshing, and the birds were serenading anyone in the forest who would listen; the spirits of the group were high. She and her friends had been determined to take a winter backpacking trip into Roosevelt Redwoods Park, through one of the largest remaining groves of ancient redwood giants in the world. It has been said by those who spent time in this coastal woods during the winter when the weather was good, the experience of solitude was incredible and the scenery, spectacular. But if Mother Nature decided to seek vengeance, intruders would be guaranteed one of the most miserable experiences of their lives. Once the rains came crashing down, it could be days or even weeks before they stopped.

For four glorious days, the little band wandered among the sun-filtered giants until a sudden drop in pressure brought gusty winds, overcast skies and early morning drizzle, heralding the arrival of a series of Humboldt County storms. On top of the persistent damp and building winds, they had to dodge the falling debris that showered from the tops of the groaning trees. Knowing their luck had run out and that they had expected too much from the unpredictable weather of California's North Coast, the girls packed their gear, broke camp, and accepted their fate. Their goal had been to spend five nights in the forest, one night for each member of the group. But one night short of their goal and with fifteen rough, soggy miles left to cover, they sought to end their adventure early.

With water cascading down her entire body, Fionna's tired muscles screamed stop, rest, but her brain argued that she needed to keep up with the others. This strange exhaustion seemed to pull her further and further away from the others. If separated from the group, she was sure she would become lost and inevitably take her last breath in this remote wilderness. Confused, even though on some level she knew it was walking that generated life-sustaining warmth, she stopped, marking time with violent shivering and wandering thoughts, the first indications of hypothermia. She knew that if things didn't change, she would no longer be able to control her movements or her actions.

In her otherworldly state, Fionna could barely hear her friends over the angry winds that whistled through the tops of the trees and the icy rains that noisily pelted their gear. "Let's take a break," the firm, familiar voice screamed in her ears. It was Mary, Fionna's childhood friend and, as far as she was concerned, the most sensible person on the expedition. Mary had become her guardian, seeming to always look after her.

Thankful moans from the group joined the sounds of the winter storm as all the figures but one huddled together for safety and warmth under the drip line of the trees. With obvious dread, the others gazed up at the torrential waterfall splashing through the gap in the upper canopy of the forest. Fionna tried to focus on the silhouetted figure of a stocky girl lumbering toward her.

Fighting to control her chattering teeth, Fionna forced a smile in the direction of her concerned friend. Through Fionna's blue rain parka and pants that were guaranteed to protect her from the icy rain, her skin was drenched to the bone. As the raindrops pelted her face with every sporadic gust of wind, her thoughts drifted to the girl moving toward her.

They met by accident, colliding in the lunch line and leading to a food smashed mess on the cafeteria floor. Mary was the new girl in school that a few of the more popular girls labeled 'tomboy' and a few other words that angered Fionna every time she heard them. They hit it off immediately. When Fionna first looked into Mary's embarrassed face, she saw a kindred spirit and a person in whom she could confide. Mary was headstrong and determined, two qualities Fionna knew were recessed within herself. She had finally met a friend she knew she could count on.

The shadow in pink rain gear moved towards her. "Are you okay?" Mary's voice reflected her honest concern.

Fionna nodded her head, causing drops of water to spray in all directions, forcing her friend to smile. "Yeah … just a little cold, tired and cranky."

"Aren't we all!" Mary nodded towards the rest of the group. "We should join them … there's warmth in numbers. Besides, Jinn's got enough hot air coming out of her trunk to warm us all," she laughed at her own comment.

"I'll be right over," Fionna promised.

"Don't take too long." Mary gave her a kind wink and returned to the group.

Fionna sighed as she shivered uncontrollably. It took cherished energy to control her shudders but she knew she would have to pretend. Once she joined the group, they would all know that she was getting sick and with her feeling the way she did, things could only get worse. She could already hear Jinn blaming all of the group's discomfort on her sickness. She cursed her sickness. She cursed Jinn. The weight of her backpack dug deeply into her petite shoulders and neck. Sharp pains radiated from her every muscle. She struggled to stay focused on two things as she fought the panic that welled up within her, conserving energy and trying to catch up with the others would be a priority.

Whether they were willing to admit it or not, her being sick wasn't the worst of their worries because they were hopelessly lost in the wilderness of ancient and mysterious trees. Though Jinn, the group's self-appointed leader, wouldn't agree, they had been lost for the last two hours. Fionna took in her surroundings. By the looks of the unforgiving forest, the place was a land where humans hadn't spent much time, or for that matter, maybe none at all. Under normal circumstances, the adventure of discovery would fascinate her but this time all she really wanted was dry clothes, a kind words and a warm bed.

Fionna's weary eyes cautiously searched the shadows around her. Their meandering path had taken them into a clearing of ferns through a maze of fallen trees, some eight feet in diameter. The moss hanging from the bark and branches took on mysterious shapes and when exposed to the angry winds, and creeping shadows the shapes appeared ominously lifelike. Every silhouette had the potential to be a stalking creature awaiting its opportunity to pounce. The towering tops of the swaying trees made sounds she never thought possible. She constantly reminded herself that the regular crashes she heard in the forest around her were only branches giving up their fight with gravity and not legendary creatures stalking their every move. The howling winds spoke to the forest as it whistled through the tops of the trees. Every once in a while she thought she understood its warning; they should not have been where they were. Leave they would, but only if they knew where to go.

A white light flashed, bathing everything in its sudden rays. She counted the seconds until the thunder rumbled through the forest. "Seven seconds!" she whispered to herself. "It's getting closer." The very thought of it made her quiver and her heart race. She didn't like thunderstorms.

Her thoughts continued to quicken … *First, they were outrunning the rain, but now the lightning.*

Summoning the last vestiges of strength, she jogged toward the others, splashing through puddles and was quickly engulfed into the huddle. She saw the fear and concern in their eyes too, it wasn't comforting to know that she wasn't the only one who felt the way she did. She caught the other girls cautiously searching the shadows, the whites of their eyes reflecting the ambient light. The storm cells had turned day into night. The girls backed into each other, forming a natural defensive circle like prey animals on the plains. She should have found comfort in the fact that she wasn't the only one afraid and unsure of the path they had chosen, but she didn't. It was because of them that she was in this predicament. Another flash of lightning with a rumble of thunder following six seconds later. Louder and closer, the vibrations rose up from the ground and rippled through her pack. The thunderhead was moving their way and they were exposed.

Fionna glared at Jinn, her thoughts flashing to the other's unilateral decision. It was Jinn, the self-appointed leader, who suggested the short cut through the ancient forest. Despite Mary's and Fionna's protest, the others followed Jinn into the thick foliage. Early on, they decided not to split up, and so far they had stuck with it. Good or bad, right or wrong, they were in this together, all five of them.

At first they followed a series of deer trails that traversed the hillside, winding their way through giant ferns, incredibly huge redwoods and, in some places, dense ground cover. At first the travel was easy but soon the route became more difficult as the barely visible path wrapped itself around the side of a mountain. Committed to their choice, they pushed on, believing that their discomfort was temporary and that the forest floor would open back up like it had when they first left the marked trail. Their choices went against all of their outdoor training, but like many bad choices, it seemed right at the time.

Fionna balanced herself with the girls' shoulders as she squinted towards the tops of the towering trees that were complaining loudly as they waved back and forth against the sky. She imagined them begging to be spared the fate of the others that were ripped free and lying on the ground. Here, she felt the unnerving effects of the wind's power as it swirled and danced around her. The vegetation pulsed in rhythmic waves as each gust made its presence known. The raindrops stung her face. A storm much like this one had passed through years ago and started a chain reaction by toppling one huge, shallow rooted tree into the next, much like dominos carefully placed to fall in sequence, and inevitably ripping an opening into the forest canopy above.

She returned her gaze to the fallen trees, staring at their massive, finger-like root-balls that stuck fifteen feet into the air like appendages reaching up from the ground. Every winter, the huge holes in the forest floor from which the giant trees had been torn free were transformed into deep, fern-lined ponds. Young trees, ferns and huckleberries took advantage of the soil that still clung to the massive roots of the fallen monarchs. These growths were the weakest links that affected the entire balance of the forest and needed the support of the fallen giants. She saw some similarities to their own feeble condition. The wildness suddenly overwhelmed her. Before them lay a jumble of huge, trees and staring into the dense, debris-strewn forest, she feared that nothing human had ever passed this way before.

Another flash illuminated the panic-stricken expressions of the faces around her as they huddled together for warmth and security. Fionna welcomed the small comfort, the first she had felt in hours. It felt good.

Fionna saw the worried look in their eyes. At first she thought it was due to the obvious; they had violated one of the basic rules of wilderness travel and not stayed put once they had realized they were lost. But when she saw that all eyes were on her, she struggled to hold back her panic. They knew she was not well and she knew the last thing they wanted to deal with was a sick member in their group.

They stared at her for a moment with pity before any of them spoke.

"Are you okay? You look terrible!" Mary yelled from under the brim of her rain hat and over the pounding rain. Her voice quivered with concern and fear.

Fionna nodded, but knew her face revealed the lie. She hoped they would not be able to read her expression in the dim light.

Mary reached up and touched the side of her friend's face with her dirty fingers. Fionna immediately felt the warmth of her hand and closed her eyes.

"Fionna, your face … it's so cold!" Mary exclaimed as she shot an angry glare at Jinn. "We shouldn't have come this way. You picked one heck of a shortcut!"

Betsy, a chubby short girl, reached up and also touched the side of Fionna's face, as if to confirm it for herself. "She is …"

Fionna watched the rain pour off the rim of the girl's cap and then drip down her face.

"What are we supposed to do?" Jinn whined as she threw her hands into the air. "Just sit here and wait for the storm to stop?"

White light streaked across the purple sky, silhouetting the tops of thc trees and momentarily stunning everyone in the group to silence. Each silently counted the seconds until the wave of thunder reached them.

Four seconds went by before the ominous sound sliced through everything around them. A couple of the girls shrieked at the sound of the pulsating thunder. Its power radiated through everything; they could even feel it through their clothing.

"I hate this," Nikki, a tall slender girl announced. "It's less than a mile away!"

Betsy reached up and grabbed the girl's hand. They squeezed together, forcing a tighter circle.

"This rain hasn't let up since we started heading back," Jinn said. "One more day was all we asked … just one more day." She looked towards the heavens as if asking for mercy and closed her eyes to protect them from the powerful drops. They bounced off her exposed face, ran beneath her parka hood and dripped off the strands of blonde hair.

"We should have stayed on the trails," Mary lectured in her *I told you so* voice as she stared directly at Jinn.

"You didn't have to go this way, you know!" Jinn avoided eye contact as she continued to look up into the downpour of rain. Her posture rang of arrogance and her voice was heavy with sarcasm.

"Oh yes, we did; we agreed to stay together … remember?" Mary exclaimed. "All for one and one for all!"

Jinn shot her a nervous look just as another blue flash stunned everyone to silence.

Only two seconds went by until a clap of thunder, sounding as if it were shot from the guns of a battleship, attacked all around them. They covered their ears, squatted closer to the ground and huddled tighter together. The gasps that followed were absorbed by the storm.

The resulting static in the air caused Nikki's hair to stand straight up.

"My goodness! Saint Elmo's Fire!" Jinn exclaimed as she pointed at Nikki and beyond. An eerie bluish glow, a halo framing Nikki's static strewn hair and terrified face, emanated from the old metal frame of Nikki's backpack.

Panic stricken with their group cohesion finally broken, everyone dropped to their hands and knees and frantically scrambled through the ferns and organic duff towards the safety of the nearest huge log. Betsy and Jinn crawled in the opposite direction from Nikki who slipped, unnoticed, headfirst into one of the smaller of the root hole ponds. Moments later she rolled back out of it and staggered towards the edge of the nearest log. Mary pushed Fionna along towards one of the ends of the huge log.

There was no doubt in their minds that the storm cell was directly overhead. Warnings raced through their minds; they knew what was going to happen next. They had read about it in their safety manuals.

Stay out of clearings, away from metal objects and tall trees. *What about tall people wearing metal packs?* Fionna panicked when she realized that they were in the heart of a forest, surrounded by the tallest trees in the world, and believed that one of her group had already been marked by the god of Thunder as his next intended target.

With an incredible show of ferocity, a wall of bright blue light engulfed a grove of ancient trees across the clearing from where they lay, a half a football field distance away. A deafening crack rolled through the earth like a shock wave from a detonated bomb. Fionna felt the vibrations pass through her. The blue flash blinded her; the smell of ozone, dirt and conifer filled her nostrils. She felt a strange wave of heat against her face and hands. Cowering on the ground, she was momentarily deaf, blinded and disoriented.

Fionna fought her urge to panic. It took a moment for the spots to clear from her eyes and the sound to return to her ears. But she didn't need to see or hear to know that the storm had peaked; she felt the lessening vibrations through her body. As quickly as it had raced in and hurdled over them, the storm vaulted away.

One by one, the group rose to their feet and silently looked around, cautiously searching for anything unusual. There was an audible sigh of relief when they saw that Nikki had been sparred.

The sound of distant thunder rumbled; its intimidation waning.

Mary was the first to speak. "Wow! What a rush!"

The winds had died down and the rain was only a drizzle. The once dark and intimidating clouds were only tinged with gray. The sound of water droplets falling from the saturated forest dominated the clearing.

"It's almost gone!" Nikki exclaimed with delight, her face splattered with mud, her hair no longer standing on end. "Is it finally over?"

"It's about time," Jinn sighed. She unsuccessfully attempted to brush the mud from her once blue rain pants and parka and straightened up her brimmed hat.

Despite the change in lighting and the absent gusty winds, something else was different. Fionna was the first to notice. "Look at that!" Her voice crackled with discovery and awe as she pointed beyond the huge log they had used for cover during the storm toward the far side of the clearing. She swallowed nervously. She couldn't believe how close they had come to being struck by lightning.

One by one, their heads turned in the direction Fionna was pointing.

A distant rumble caused Nikki to flinch and look around.

They quickly located the mutilated tree with its top third missing. The rest of it looked as if it had been twisted like a licorice stick and then peeled apart. Strips of the thick blackened bark curled down from its sides. A pillow of smoke steamed out of the top and from the full length of the back.

"I smell smoke," Mary said.

"It's no longer the tallest tree in the grove." Fionna sadly whispered. She didn't know why but she felt a tremendous loss for the monarch.

"You got that right," Jinn agreed. "Tall today, short tomorrow … no harm intended, Nikki."

"None taken," Nikki sighed. "What about the burning tree?"

"Won't really matter, the rain will probably put it out. It's pretty wet." Mary explained. "We probably couldn't get a fire going if we wanted to."

"But, where is the top; where did it go?" Nikki asked, using her hands to talk. "Did the lightning incinerate it? And to think we were this close to the whole thing … this close to being blown to bits!" Her voice reflected her frightened mood.

Mary took off her pack and started to climb up the side of the eight-foot redwood log that blocked her way. She got halfway up before she slipped against the saturated dark red fibrous bark, "Hey, give me a hand why don't you!"

Nikki and Betsy scrambled forward to help but stopped when Jinn spoke up.

"What are you doing?" Jinn asked. She crossed her arms in disapproval.

"What do you think! I just want to see something. It's hard to see anything over these logs and ferns. Come on, give me a boost, then I can wedge my fingers into the gaps of the thicker bark and pull myself up the rest of the way."

Jinn nodded to the other two girls as if giving her approval to help. Betsy laced her fingers together for a foothold, while Nikki and Jinn pushed against Mary's backside with their hands and shoulders. Laughing as they scrambled for balance, they were suddenly working together as a team again.

"Easy Amazons!" Mary chuckled. "Got it!" She scrambled the rest of the way up onto the eight-foot diameter log as the others took a couple of steps back to watch. "Piece of cake," Mary yelled with glee.

Jinn just shook her head. "What do you see?"

Nikki and Betsy smiled without saying a word as they waited patiently.

The redwood leaves sticking in Fionna's hair gently tickled her face in the breeze. She untangled them from her hair and let them fall to the ground. It was then that she noticed the sweet scent of flowers permeating the air. The smell seemed to be coming from beyond the maze of ancient logs that formed a corridor deeper into the forest. The smell relaxed her and made her shivering stop. As she deeply inhaled the sweet and pure fragrance, she was overcome with the need to follow, to find its source. She didn't understand but the message was clear … she was being summoned.

"Do you smell that?" she asked Betsy, the girl standing next to her.

"Smell what?"

"That sweet smell, like flowers … I think it's coming from that way." Fionna pointed in the direction they were heading before the thunderstorm brought their caravan to a halt.

Betsy raised her head and sniffed. She looked at Fionna and shook her head. "All I smell is rain, trees, mud and smoke. Why would we smell flowers, nothing blooms in a redwood forest!"

"Are you sure you don't smell the flowers?" *How could she not smell that?* Fionna wondered, the aroma overwhelming her senses.

Betsy looked at her strangely. "Yes, I'm sure I don't smell any flowers!"

The other girls just looked at her. One by one, each stuck her nose into the air and shook her head.

"Mary, what can you see?" Nikki asked, turning her attention back towards Mary who was still astride the fallen log.

"This is one heck of a forest. There are quite a few downed trees; man, it's like a maze. The route we were taking seems to be the only direct one through this mess." She pointed in the direction they needed to continue. As she looked back towards the charred pieces of the shattered tree, she noted the red and tan wood fragments and branches that were spread throughout the area. "Nikki, the tree wasn't incinerated, it was blown to pieces … it's pretty incredible. You should see this!"

"Can I go up next?" Betsy pleaded as she looked around her for assistance to get up on the log that dwarfed her in size.

"No," Jinn protested, "we don't have time for this. We should take advantage of the calm in the storm. This is probably the only break we will get on this trip."

"Fionna is too sick to go anywhere!" Mary argued as she looked back towards her friend.

"We need to get out of here, and the sooner the better!" Jinn commanded.

"Jinn is right." Fionna spoke up. For the first time in a while, her voice sparkled with confidence.

Jinn looked surprised, as if she never expected Fionna to agree with anything that she had to say.

"But you're freezing to death, you …" Mary started to argue, but realized that arguing with her strong willed friends would be useless. "Are you sure you know what you are doing?"

"I'll be all right as long as we keep moving." She pointed towards Jinn, "She is good with a map and compass."

Mary gave her a disbelieving glance.

"I promise, I will be okay." Fionna paused for a moment before she spoke again. "Do you smell any flowers?"

Mary raised her eyebrows as she gave her friend a questioning look.

"Do you smell any flowers?" Fionna repeated.

"Flowers?"

Fionna nodded.

Mary took a deep, exaggerated breath and then coughed. "No, but I sure do smell smoke. Why do you ask …?" She stopped suddenly, looking in the direction of Fionna's flowery smell. "Wait, do you guys hear that?" She cupped her hands behind her ears and tilted her head.

"What is it?" Fionna asked excitedly.

The others looked on with great interest. They also cupped their hands around their ears to help funnel the sound.

"I'm not sure but I think I hear water." Mary sounded as if she doubted her own ears.

"Right … they call that rain!" Jinn forced an unconvincing laugh.

"I don't hear it." Nikki complained as she looked back towards Fionna. "Do you?"

Fionna shrugged her shoulders. "Evidently, I only smell flowers."

"Water … like a creek?" Jinn quizzed. She now seemed focused on Mary's every word.

"No, bigger, like a cascading river," she yelled back.

Jinn smiled as she excitedly tore off her pack and dug out her map and compass. She seemed to be re-energized. "I think I know where we are!" She unfolded the coated map, anxiously spread it over her pack and followed her suspected route with the bright red fingernail of her index finger.

The others huddled around with excitement. Mary looked down expectantly from where she stood on the log, her hands resting on her hips.

"We must be here." Jinn brushed the droplets of water from the map with the back of her hand and confidently tapped on the location with the pad of her finger. "This is the biggest creek on this side of the mountain. It's got to be it." Her eyes widened as she retraced their steps with her extended pinkie to the point where they left the trail. "We're four miles into this. Once we cross this creek, let's see … that leaves us with less than two miles of cross country travel before we intersect the trail here." She followed it again with her index finger. "From there, it will be a walk in the park, so to speak." She smiled as if she had solved all of their problems. "When it is all said and done, we will have cut more than ten miles off our trip."

"Are you sure?" Mary asked.

"Come down and see for yourself; where else could we be?" She shrugged her shoulders. "There aren't that many fast moving creeks around here."

Chapter Two

Indecision

Mary nodded as she felt a spark of hope surge through her. Good news was what she really wanted to hear. With her friend's failing health, being almost killed by lightning, being hopelessly lost and bombarded by relentless rain, they were due for a positive change. *Any change was good … it couldn't get any worse*, she thought.

Being careful of the slippery bark, she inched to the edge of the log's curved surface, lay on her belly and slid feet first over the side. After a moment of free falling the four short feet to the forest floor, her momentum carried her into a graceful backwards roll. When her feet hit the ground, she immediately got up laughing. Her pink, Gore-Tex rain hat fell off, exposing her short dark hair. She snatched up her hat and walked over to where everyone was huddled over the map.

"That was quite a ride," Mary laughed.

"I'll bet!" Jinn looked up, smiled, and pointed to the map. "Here is where we are and here is where we need to be."

The group slid over to make room for Mary.

Mary filled in the open spot and peered at the rain-coated map. It took a moment for her eyes to adjust. The droplets of standing rain and duff had blurred some sections of the map and magnified others. She looked off toward the surrounding trees, as if trying to confirm her bearings. Her friends' anticipatory looks unnerved her; they were waiting for her to agree that they were no longer lost. They might have followed Jinn's leadership but they also valued Mary's judgment. She felt sudden pressure on her tired shoulders to make things right. She listened carefully as Jinn spoke.

"That creek … the one you must have heard is in that direction, right?" Jinn stood up and pointed her compass toward the trees ahead of them, holding it out for Mary to see. She used her other hand to help explain.

The others silently listened.

"Up until this point, we have basically been traveling in a southeasterly direction, keeping the mountain to our right and the valley to our left. So, if all this still makes sense … we should be right about here!" Jinn knelt down and tapped the long red nail of her index finger onto the spot, knocking mud onto the map. She immediately shifted her attention to her nails and began picking them free of dirt.

Some things never change, Mary thought. "If your manicurist could only see you now, she wouldn't be happy." Mary smiled as she smeared the mud across the map with her hat. "Good as new." She motioned towards Jinn's hands. "By the way, that's why I keep mine short."

"I thought it was just something tomboys did," Jinn retorted, making an attempt to appear non-confrontational. Her eyes never left her own hands.

Mary grinned, keeping her thoughts to herself. She returned her attention to the map for a moment to study the detail. They were in a natural clearing that wouldn't be on any maps. But the angle of slope and topography matched the contour lines on the map. The position of the creek made sense. It was a creek, not a river, made to sound larger by the heavy, rain swollen and saturated conditions. She nodded in agreement and stood up. "Jinn's right." It sounded funny hearing those exact words coming from her own mouth. The thought made her smile.

Jinn stopped picking at her nails and confidently gazed at everyone, as if she had just been redeemed.

Mary rose to her feet, walked over to Fionna and motioned for her to follow to a spot just out of earshot of the rest of the group.

Jinn and the rest of the girls stared at them as they walked away.

Mary heard them mumbling but didn't really care whatever it was they had to say. She ignored them and turned toward her friend. Gently, she implored, "So, how are we really feeling?"

"Much better, thank you."

Mary reached up and touched the side of Fionna's face with her fingers and then gave a welcomed sigh. "At least you're not freezing anymore."

Fionna smiled. "No, it's like it just went away … I think it has something to do with the flowers …"

"What Jinn says makes sense for once." Mary interrupted. "She is right. Once we make it over this creek, the rest should be … well, at least easier than what we have gone through so far."

"Did you really hear the creek?" Fionna's eyes expressed her excitement.

Mary nodded. She suddenly remembered what it was that her friend had said. "Did you really smell the flowers?"

"Yes, yes I did … didn't you?" She pointed her hand up the trail.

Mary breathed in deeply, exhaled and let it drift away as mist. "No, I don't but I also don't hear the creek anymore either."

They laughed and looked back over towards the group. The group was watching them closely.

"If you ladies are about finished over there, we need to get going," Jinn whined.

Mary held up he hand, asking for more time.

Jinn moaned in response, "A minute is about all we have to spare."

Mary ignored her and continued to talk quietly with her friend. To Fionna's delight, Mary rolled her eyes. "I can't believe she still thinks she is in charge of this fiasco. Being in the group the longest and having two out of four votes doesn't make it unanimous." She paused a moment to let out a heavy sigh, "So, do you smell the flowers right now?"

"Yes, I do. I don't know how to say this but they make me feel better; it makes me want to follow them."

Mary knew that Fionna behaved strangely from time to time, but this was a bit different. Trying to hide that fact from her friend, she sniffed the air again but smelled nothing except the aroma of an organic rich forest and the aftermath of the relentless rain. She wondered if her friend was still scratching the surface of hypothermia.

Fionna glanced over at the rest of the girls to see if they were listening and then back to her friend. "I know this must sound strange."

"You've got that right."

"... But it is almost as if it is calling me … asking me to follow," she whispered.

"The *smell* of the flowers is *calling* …"

Fionna grabbed Mary's arm and nodded. "You have to trust me on this one. How long have we been friends?" Her green, expressive eyes burned right through Mary.

Mary could tell that she was deadly serious. "About four years," she stammered. She was seeing a new side of her friend, a side that made her a bit nervous. She wondered if the stages of hypothermia were much farther along than she had previously thought.

"Have I ever lied to you or misled you?" Fionna's voice sounded desperate.

Mary's thoughts raced to find an answer. "Well, not that I'm aware of."

Fionna glared at her.

"Well, no," Mary corrected.

"Then, there is no need to start now is there?"

Mary stared at her a moment. "You're serious, aren't you?"

"Dead serious."

Mary tried to read her body language. She had never seen this side of Fionna before. Her friend no longer seemed to be the timid little mouse she once knew. "Then we should follow your nose." She forced a smiled and thrust out her hand, "All for one, one for all?"

Fionna returned her grip, "All for one, one for all."

"Well, what's it going to be, girls?" Jinn's impatient voice interrupted.

Both looked in Jinn's direction. Mary picked up her pack and put it on.

"Fionna," Mary spoke in a soft voice, barely audible over the light falling rain. "Let's keep this our little secret for now, okay?"

"Sure!"

"That's my girl," Mary said as she patted her on her back and encouraged her towards the rest of the awaiting group. "Let's not tell our faithful leader everything."

"It's about time!" Jinn mumbled under her breath as she uncrossed her arms.

"I see what you mean," Fionna whispered to Mary.

"Lead the way," Mary motioned with her hand in the direction of the distant creek.

"With pleasure!" Jinn smiled as she threw on her pack with a grunt. "I believe if we follow this maze of logs, they should take us to the creek. When we get close enough, we will probably hear it before we see it.

"No doubt," Mary agreed.

The procession of five weary backpackers weaved in and out of the lush fern covered logs in a tight single file. Once they were out of the clearing, the forest darkened and closed in around them. The vegetation again became tall and dense. The hanging moss took on inexplicable shapes and the shadows danced around them. Mary brought up the rear, but spent half her time looking over her shoulder in the direction they had come. Where they had been suddenly began to look better than the direction they were heading, a passage into an unknown void.

In the back of her mind, hidden from all, she hoped that crossing the creek would be easy but, deep down, she knew it probably wasn't in the cards that were being dealt. By no means had this been an ordinary day.

♦ ♦ ♦

The thundering sound of the creek stopped Jinn in her tracks and the two girls following stumbled into her.

"Geeeeeeeez … how about a signal or something!" Nikki protested. "This place is creepy enough."

"Shhhhhhh … I hear it … quiet, listen," Jinn barked in a harsh whisper. "The creek … I hear the creek. We're very close."

Everyone stopped and listened. One by one, they expressed their excitement as they recognized the familiar sound. Fionna found herself smiling. At least one of the group's two senses had been confirmed. Their ears were working fine but what about their sense of smell. *They should surely be able to smell the flowers by now*, she thought. Fionna breathed in deeply. The smell was stronger than ever. She looked back towards Mary.

"Mary, how far up would you say?" Jinn's voice quizzed from the front of the group.

"Hard to say," Mary replied, "with the trees and landscape and all, an eighth, quarter mile at most." She shrugged her shoulders.

"That's my guess as well," Jinn agreed.

"Do you smell them?" Fionna whispered towards her friend, her eyes pleading for confirmation.

Mary shook her head no. "Sorry, nothing. Let's get going." She gestured towards the rest of the group.

Fionna turned around to see that the group had started up again, this time at a faster pace. They had opened a ten-yard lead and were disappearing into the forest. Fionna picked up her pace; she didn't want to be left behind. She panted as she brushed past the tangles of hanging moss and weaved between the forest growth. The sound of the cascading water echoed alongside the face of the mountain and into the recesses of her mind. The others' walking pace suddenly became a jog. They pulled a strange strength from their earlier fatigue as they scrambled towards the call of the water. It was now a race to see who got there first.

Fionna caught up to Betsy who was only a couple of steps ahead of the long legged Nikki before Mary blasted past them all as if they were standing still. They elbowed each other as they weaved through the forest with Jinn and Mary leading the charge.

Fionna couldn't believe how the call of the water had overwhelmed their every thought. It screamed louder until its thunderous echo was all she could hear. She skidded to a stop on the heels of the two-silhouetted figures that blocked her path. Her heart pounded as she gasped for breath.

Below her lay a mist-filled canyon that almost completely obstructed their view of the creek below. Towards her left, the canyon faded into the shadows of the mist shrouded forest. Towards her right, it ate away at the steep rocky face from which fell a cascading waterfall. A rainbow stretched across its base. Thick moss grew across the rocks, nourished by the clouds of mist that appeared a permanent fixture of this beautiful place. She breathed in the moist air. She couldn't believe it; the flower aroma was stronger than ever.

Fionna watched the others' excitement of discovery fade to concern but it took her a moment to realize that they had another problem on their hands. The very creek they were searching for had trapped them; there was no place to go except back from where they had just come or to venture in the direction of the creek, hoping for a place to cross. As scary as the second option sounded, she knew the group would opt for it. Anything sounded better than walking all the way back to where they had first left the trail.

Amazed and disappointed, they searched for answers as if they were working an algebraic equation. The river screamed in their ears as it echoed off the face of the cliff. The mist formed into beads of water on their face and clothes, mixing with their previous soaking and causing an uncomfortable chill.

Nikki and Betsy glanced at Jinn and Mary, both looking desperate. They stood close together for warmth and comfort. Their hopes now rested in the hands of the one that they chose as their leader.

Jinn walked to the edge of the canyon, turned away from the two of them, and stared down at the base of the falls. Fionna could not tell if she was seeking space to think or a place to pout. She thought she heard some sniffles and couldn't tell if those were tears that ran down her face or the mist that accumulated on everything around them.

Her friend Mary silently stared down at the river, as if making it a point not to look in Jinn's direction.

Fionna wondered how this once well-organized, experienced

collection of young women had turned into this, a group beaten by the elements and the ruggedness of the terrain. They no longer enjoyed the beauty and the winter solitude they had expected to experience in the mountains. Maybe they had experienced enough. Maybe they should have stopped after the fourth night, but tradition was tradition after all. *All for one … one for all!*

She had been invited at the last minute, changing the number of their group to five and forcing them to make it a five-night affair. *Maybe the whole thing was really her fault.* The thought raced through her mind. She felt tears build in her eyes and a lump develop in her throat. Then, the smell of the flowers reminded her of other things.

"The flowers," she mumbled to herself. It was like the voice in her dream that told her to go on the trip. She felt her body shudder at the thought that she was supposed to go. She was supposed to be there; they were supposed to be there the fifth night. When she looked down the canyon, she caught a strong whiff of the aromatic flowers. It forced her to smile. It warmed her insides; she no longer felt sad. Again, she felt a strange compulsion to follow the smell of the flowers.

Down the creek, the mist swirled in and out of the shadows, giving the forest an eerie look, but she didn't care; for some reason, that didn't scare her anymore. She couldn't explain it but somehow she knew the smell of the flowers would protect her and her friends. She walked past Mary and toward the unknown. *Maybe it was her job to get the group safely across the canyon.*

Mary reached up and grabbed her arm. "Where are you going?" she yelled over the thundering falls.

"There is a way across," she smiled. "Don't ask me how I know but I just do!"

Mary stared at her a moment before she spoke. She squinted into Fionna's face as if trying to read something that wasn't there. "Does this have anything to do with the flowers?"

Fionna nodded.

After another silent pause, Mary turned towards Jinn, cupped her hands and yelled back towards the group. When she had their attention, Mary motioned that they were going to scout for a crossing. Jinn waved them on and turned away.

"Okay, your lead but watch the canyon edge," Mary lectured.

Fionna smiled in return and followed the edge, being careful not to slip on the slick rocks and sponge-like moss as she navigated through the huge ferns and around the trees. The thunderous sound of the falls faded and the sounds of the surging creek below began to dominate the forest sounds. She traveled only about fifty yards before she stopped. Blocking her path was the base of a huge fallen redwood that stood a head taller than her. To her left, about ten yards away, lay the massive, upended root ball of the fallen monarch. Ferns and moss clung to its spindly, finger-like roots. Below them was a cratered pond filled with clear, emerald colored water but, most importantly, off to her right, the rest of the huge log extended out above the canyon and into the mist and rain.

As if on cue, the mist momentarily cleared enough to reveal that the huge log had extended the entire width of the canyon. The six-foot diameter redwood log reached thirty yards across the gap, while thirty feet below the fast moving waters of the creek zipped through the canyon.

Fionna smiled; she could not hold back her surprise. "Told you so!"

"It's like a bridge!" Mary exclaimed as she stared in awe. "It's incredible."

Fionna unhooked her waist belt and let her backpack slip off her shoulders and onto the ground. It felt good to have the weight off her back. She felt as light as a feather and as agile as a cat. Without giving it a second thought, she used the deep, soft louver bark as hand and foot holds and gracefully climbed onto the log. Her lungs filled with the sweet smelling flowers. "They smell incredibly beautiful; we must be very close."

"Wait!" Mary protested as she fumbled with the removal of her own pack. "Stop … I'm going with you!" Her voice was on the verge of panic.

"I can do this … this log is wide enough to ride a bike on."

"It is slippery and shrouded in mist; you should take it slowly," Mary lectured.

"See you on the other side," Fionna shrugged, extended her arms out for balance and walked into the growing mist. Seconds later, she had disappeared from sight.

"Wait!" Mary yelled again as she scrambled up the side of the log and pulled herself onto its flat surface. She paused a moment to regain her balance. Her visibility was suddenly reduced to fifteen yards and was getting worse every second. She could barely make out the faint blue silhouette of her friend. She swallowed hard and followed. Every step she took was now slow and steady. She no longer looked ahead; her thoughts were focused on the careful placement of her every step.

Fionna slowed once the mist obscured her view of the other side of the canyon. Everything around her turned gray, then white. The cool mist filled her lungs, the droplets of water dripped down her face. She shifted her gaze to her feet to make sure every step was where it was supposed to be. About halfway across she stopped to regain her balance; the huge log bounced with her every step and that of her friend. The further towards the middle Fionna traveled, the more the log seemed to come alive. Staring at her feet was now making her dizzy. She stopped every few steps to regain her balance and her nerve. No longer feeling light and in control, she wavered on the verge of fear. Fionna wanted off the log.

She felt her friend's every movement and finally yelled for Mary to stop. Hearing her friend's voice over the rushing water below brought her a strange comfort. She dared not look back for the fear of falling had now become a reality. "I suddenly don't think it was a good idea to cross on this log," Fionna screamed. Her voice quivered with fear. She stood there staring at her feet with bent knees, still keeping her hands out away from her sides and her elbows tucked in tightly for balance. "Everything is spinning."

"Close your eyes and don't move. I will work my way to where you are," Mary offered.

"No! Stay where you are. Give me a minute. I just need to pull myself together long enough to make the rest of the trip."

"You're probably about halfway across; the log is more flexible in the middle."

"No kidding!"

"Are you sure …"

"Yes, I can do this," Fionna tried to reassure herself.

"Do you still smell the flowers?" She knew her friend was trying to help take her mind off of her situation.

Fionna had forgotten all about the flowers. She slowly breathed in. The smell of moist flowers was still there. "Yes. Do you smell them?"

"Okay then, keep thinking about the flowers?" Mary ignored her question. "Use them to help get you across."

After a moment of silence, Fionna responded. "Okay!" Her voice wasn't very convincing. "Think of the flowers," she mumbled to herself. "Think of the flowers."

She took a few more baby steps and then a couple of longer ones. As if in response, a gentle breeze began to blow. She felt it push the hair around her face. It tickled. She reached up and wiped the moisture from her eyes. The breeze turned into gusts and the log began to shake. She squatted in a lower stance and gripped the log tighter with her feet. She felt the muscles in her legs tighten.

The wind began to whistle through the tops of the trees. She shivered; she didn't know if it was from the chill in the air or from the strange feeling that now seemed to crawl under her skin. The trees began to creak and moan under the strain. She felt the push and pull against her body.

"What's happening?" Fionna screamed.

"I don't know; stay focused! Let it blow over; wait for it to stop!" Mary begged as she continued to walk the length of the log in the direction of her friend.

Fionna could no longer wait for the winds to die down or for whatever it was to stop. With her eyes full of tears and her ears full of strange sounds, she dropped to her knees and began frantically to crawl the rest of the way across the log.

To her, the winds first began to sound like moans, then like voices. They were sounds she had never heard before. The sounds brushed past her as they danced around. She gripped the slippery log even tighter to keep herself from being pushed over the edge. But the tighter she held on, the stronger the wind attempted to push and pull. Her fingers throbbed and her lungs burned.

"Leave me alone!" She screamed.

A chill surged through her as the wind whispered her name. Her foot slipped and her knee slammed against the log. Her hand could no longer support her weight and her face collided heavily with the log. The smell of duff filled her lungs. She lost her grip and balance. Suddenly but slowly, she felt herself slip lifelessly over the side of the log. The sound of the creek and the wind were now one. The fragrant flowers suddenly became stronger. A sweet voice whispered into her ear Ó*na Crainn* … Ó*na Crainn*. Then everything went black.

Act 2: Discovery

Chapter Three

The Search

"Fionna, where are you?" Mary screamed through her dirty, cupped hands. Her voice was no longer loud and confident and her eyes were filled with tears. "I'm sorry, I'm so sorry … it was my fault!" Her voice cracked as she sobbed. Exhausted, she fell to her knees, toppled to the forest floor and curled into a ball.

Under any other circumstances, the scene would have been touching. But in the cold mist of the ancient forest, miles from the nearest park facility, it tugged frightfully at the heart of the tired thirty-five year old park ranger. His blue eyes watered as he fought back the lump that suddenly appeared in his parched throat. He tried to swallow but noisily cleared his throat instead. He felt such sympathy for the sobbing young teen near his feet, as she poured out her emotional frustration over the lack of success on their three-day search. His rugged features softened as he failed to hold back his own frustration and for the first time in a while, he was at a loss for what to do.

He dropped to one knee, balancing his pack on his back and started to lay a comforting hand on the girl's shoulder, but at the last second he decided to remove his green ball cap instead. He vigorously ran his fingers through his dark, thickly matted hair, wiping the sweat from his forehead with the back of his hand before slipping the ball cap back on his head. In frustration he closed his eyes, turned away and took a couple of deep breaths to calm himself. He opened his eyes and silently focused on the scattered clouds in the distance. He watched the mist swirl around the tops of the trees. The heavy mist was dissipating. The light rain had stopped for the moment. The thought brought a weak smile to his lips. "It looks like the weatherman finally got it right." His voice sounded forced. "I think we might see some sun today after all!" He shifted his uneasy gaze between the young teen and Susan, the tall ranger who stood next to him. Her braided red ponytail hung through the back of her green, park service ball cap and down across the right shoulder of her green rain parka.

"You think?" Susan responded, sounding less convinced. "If that man finally gets it right, it will be a first."

He motioned toward the young girl, pleading for the middle-aged woman to take over. It was obvious that he was uncomfortable dealing with Mary's roller coaster of emotions. He wasn't very good at being sensitive and he knew it.

Searching for missing persons was nothing new. Throughout his ten years as a park ranger, he had plucked the unfortunate souls of many from jagged cliff faces, turbulent rivers and dark, isolated forests. Visions of their individual faces garbled his thoughts like distant memories. The ones he found, dead or alive, he returned to their awaiting families and friends and to their endless questions of how and why. The ones he never found always baffled him the most, their disappearances still a mystery. The blame shifted between the elements of nature, the mountain's rugged and unforgiving topography, and the scavenging animals. The 100,000-acre park was massive, rugged, and isolated enough to keep her secrets and protect her mysteries.

Susan squeezed his shoulder gently as she knelt down beside him. He felt the emotional warmth within her firm grip.

"Okay, Mr. Tough Guy!" she teased.

As Paul looked into her caring eyes, he felt a heavy burden lift from his shoulders and work its way down to his tired legs. He nodded and stepped away from the heart-wrenching scene. He knew Susan would be able to turn the situation around and make some sense out of the chaos. She was good with people; a little callous at times, but she had a warm heart for the sensitive side of things.

He surveyed the surrounding hillside and then let his gaze drift up the path of the creek. The depressing gray mist had momentarily parted; faint rays of sunlight struggled to penetrate through the clouds. The beauty warmed his heart and he was glad for the well-deserved break in the weather that would soon be theirs. Magically, the clouds parted and twilight rays of light floated down, like illumination from heaven onto the distant grove of magnificent trees. The forest glowed invitingly with golden hues. It was then that he smelled the sweet fragrant flowers. He closed his eyes and filled his lungs with the moist, aromatic air to determine from which direction it was coming. He was surprised that the sunlit grove appeared to be its source. Never before had he ever smelled anything so mouth wateringly sweet.

♦ ♦ ♦

This time, Mary accepted the embrace from Susan and allowed herself to be held; she no longer shied away when touched. The contact around her shoulder felt comforting. Uncontrollable emotion poured from her body in shuddering fits and sobs. Her thoughts flashed to those last moments with her friend Fionna, nearly three long days ago, just before she slipped off the log and into the misty void below …

… There was the scream, then the splash … and then nothing but the powerful sound of the cascading water as it tumbled down the rugged canyon. She ran recklessly down the length of the log, disregarding her own safety and slid to a stop half way across. Realizing how close she had come to joining her friend in the void, Mary crouched, gripped the log tightly with her arms and legs to prevent herself from falling. Her heart pounded in her chest and ears as she screamed her friend's name in vain. Hearing her plaintive wails, the other girls ran to the edge of the canyon. Through fits of sobs she explained that Fionna had fallen from the log. Their haunted expressions of disbelief reflected in their wild-eyed gaze. They too shrieked Fionna's name into the misty canyon below but the unsympathetic torrent only carried their voices downstream.

As if choreographed, there was a moment when they all simply stopped screaming and just stared at each other in disbelief, as if they finally realized that screaming was hopeless, that there was nothing else they could do. Her best friend, Fionna was gone, taken by the merciless river that carved the depth of the canyon before them. For the longest time, they stood there not knowing what to do as they wept and shivered in the cool mist.

Surrounded by an ancient forest, connected to civilization by a lone log, span across a canyon like a bridge connecting two worlds, they needed to go get help. Surprisingly, to Jinn's credit, it was her who first pulled herself together enough to rally them for help. She retrieved pieces of clothing from Fionna's pack and stuffed them into a plastic bag to be used by search dogs. It was Jinn who convinced her to leave Fionna's pack leaning against a tree in case she returned. It was Jinn who marked the trail for the rescuers return, and it was also Jinn who safely lead them down the deer trails and off the mountain at a coyote's pace. She had gained a whole new respect for Jinn.

She shouldered the burden of her own pack and reluctantly followed the rest of the distraught backpackers across the log and down the game trail. She remembered pausing momentarily on the log above the swirling mist that she would return for her.

Jinn's grueling pace took them back to the trail in less than an hour. A couple of hours later, they stumbled onto the trailhead, as the darkness engulfed the exhausted, beaten foursome. Twenty more minutes brought them to the doorsteps of the ranger station. Their expressions had said it all. In a matter of moments, they had turned the calmness into chaos.

Fulfilling a promise, exhausted and worried, she joined the search the next morning to lead a couple of the rangers back to the edge of the canyon.

They arrived at the canyon crossing before noon. The forested mountain peaks were shrouded in dark clouds. The filtered sunlight cast shadows across the canyon. The crossing log sat ominously above the dark canyon. The cascading creek echoed louder than ever.

When she first arrived, she remembered sliding her pack from her numb shoulders and let it topple noisily to the forest floor and then staggered to the edge of the canyon. The two rangers just stood there exchanging glances as they watched making sure she stayed clear of the canyon edge. Secretly she hoped her friends pack would be gone, that would have meant that there might have been a chance that her friend was still alive. But her heart sank when she saw the pack sitting exactly where they had left it undisturbed.

She screamed for Fionna until she dropped to her knees from exhaustion. The only reply she heard was the echo of her own voice until a nearby great horned owl returned her call with a cry of its own. A chill ran the length of her spine and caused fingers to tingle.

Owls weren't supposed to sound off during the day. Something had to be wrong. Owls were believed to be the harbinger of death and disaster. She wondered if this special bird was sharing a message about her friends demise or mistaken the darkened day as night. She wanted, in the worst way, to inhale the fragrance of the sweet flowers Fionna had talked about, but all she could smell was the rain soaked forest. The relentless rains had started up again.

They carefully used the log to access the other side of the canyon to retrace her and her friends earlier steps. Their efforts only brought back sad memories. When they came up empty handed, they returned to the canyon crossing and followed the canyon edge down stream as far as they safely could. When the topography became too hazardous to navigate, they returned back to the log crossing and spent the night along the edge of the canyon with plans to continue searching again at first light when they were fresh. The rangers said they knew of a place where they could access the canyon down stream to search there as well. To her that only meant one thing, that the odds were working against them finding her friend alive.

The thoughts saddened her, but she tried to hold it together. What was she to do? The weight of the whole ordeal was bearing down on her shoulders. If only she were faster, if only she had stayed next to her friend, if only she could have smelled the flowers. *Why couldn't she smell the flowers?* The tears flowed freely, her body shook with every sob.

She heard the first of the heavier rain drops pelt the tarp. She felt a gentle arm rest on her shoulders but turned and stepped away towards her tent without saying a word. She did not want to be comforted. She regretted behaving the way she did the first night; she only wanted to be left alone in her own self pity, alone with her thoughts and concerns. She wanted to burden the blame.

Two days of trudging through the dark rain forest passed by as a blur, the second day much like the first. Searching during the day and burning their lanterns throughout most of the night. Miles of dense forest searched, her nightmarish memory of cross-country travel renewed. The rains returned, but not with the force they experienced on that last miserable day of their trip. Instead, the steady drizzle soaked everything. It was the continual movement down the mountainside that kept her warm enough to function. She insisted that they keep the rest breaks short; the rangers reluctantly relented. They had followed the canyon down the side of the mountain but had not seen any sign of her friend. Farther down the mountain, the canyon walls spread out away from the creek, forcing Mary and the rangers to deploy ropes to gain access to the valley bottom below. Near the valley floor, the forest became even thicker; the trees seemed to grow larger and taller than any she had ever seen before. Even the lush ground cover and ferns took on tremendous size.

Paul and Susan looked on in awe. She was surprised that neither of them had ever seen this part of the mountain before.

They silently followed the creek downstream as they searched. All of their hopes were fading with each passing hour...

"Do you smell that?" Paul's voice interrupted Mary's meandering thoughts.

"Smell what?" Susan quizzed.

"Flowers!" Paul's tone sounded as if he doubted himself.

Susan inhaled deeply and then glanced inquisitively back at Paul. "All I smell is this rain forest, the very same one I've smelled for the last, oh, let's say …" she looked down at her watch, "46 hours, 23 minutes and 22 seconds!" Her sarcasm was obvious.

"Then, I suppose you haven't noticed the piece of heaven over there either," Paul nodded his head towards the rays of sunlight. She followed his gaze and sighed as her eyes fell on the breathtaking sight.

"So, that's where you have been hiding over the last couple of days, sweetheart," Susan said as she playfully shook her finger in the direction of the sun. "I'm a little disappointed in you!"

"Don't chase him away now with insults," Paul teased.

"Him! Didn't anybody tell you that Mother Nature is a she not a he?" Susan countered with friendly banter.

Mary perked up when she first heard the mention of flowers. Her thoughts flashed to her friend; Fionna had also talked about the flowers. She saw Paul nodding towards the far end of the narrow valley and Susan following his gaze. The sight of the sunlight brought a smile to her face. She tried again but all she smelled was the rich organic aroma of the dampened forest. *Why am I not able to smell the flowers?*

"Fionna also spoke of flowers!" She squeaked barely loud enough for anyone else to hear.

"What's that?" Paul quizzed without taking his eyes off the illuminated forest.

Mary tried to read his reaction. "Before Fionna's … accident," she found herself forcing her words, "she talked about following the smell of the flowers."

Paul turned his inquisitive eyes towards her, "Flowers?"

Mary nodded and scrambled to her feet, "Yes, Fionna talked about smelling flowers. She said the odor was growing stronger right up until the log crossing." Mary watched him narrow his eyes as if concentrating on her every word. "I think she was following the smell of flowers!"

Paul silently looked at Susan, then Mary and back to the ancient grove. "Did you smell the flowers that day?" His eyes searched deeply into hers.

Mary shook her head. She felt her friend's loss again.

"Do you smell them now?" Susan asked, beating Paul to the question.

Mary shifted her gaze to Susan. "No, but I wish I did," she added with disappointment.

"Paul, do you have an uncontrollable desire to follow your nose?" Susan teased.

Paul grinned.

"God help us," Susan sighed.

"Are you ready?" Paul looked directly at Mary. "To find your friend?"

Mary smiled.

"Then it's decided, we will search over there. Call it a hunch, call it a beacon, call it whatever you will. It's as good a place as any to resume our search," Paul's said confidently.

He turned and started walking in the direction of the feathered rays of light that illuminated the forest below the mist. The others anxiously filed in behind him. First Mary, then Susan. Mary felt her heart pounding harder in her chest. She didn't know why, but she felt that wherever they were going, it was definitely a much nicer place than where they had been.

Chapter Four

Na síogaí (Na Shee-ohg-ee)

Unlike a rainbow that always seems to stay just out of reach, the light grew brighter and even more beautiful as they approached. Paul picked up his pace as if afraid that the sunshine might disappear. He thought of naming the rays of light and smiled. He would keep that opinion to himself for now.

Knocking the water droplets from the rain soaked ferns with his arms, chest and legs, Paul weaved his way through the narrow path. *After all, wet was wet,* he thought. He glanced over his shoulder ever so often to make sure that Mary and Susan still followed closely behind. At least that was what he kept telling himself. There was something very unnerving about where they were going.

His trained eyes searched for signs, an indication of any recent disturbance in the ground cover. Every creature but humans seemed to know of this special place. He wondered if the fox, deer, bear and even the secretive, misunderstood mountain lion that used this isolated trail were watching them right now. He could imagine a medicine man of the Sinkeyone, the First Nations People that once called this ancient forest their home, using this very trail to reach this very spot to gain inspiration and pray for guidance. This charged his imagination, giving him the chills.

If Fionna had actually traveled through the area, where are her footprints? Where is the sigh that she had. He stopped and looked down at the moist ground in the direction he had just come. He stared in surprise, there was virtually no sign that he had even passed through. The thick layer of organic material and duff had absorbed his every foot impression. He forced himself to move forward, farther down the game trail, struggling to shrug the notion that they were traveling blind. For the first time during the search, negative thoughts began to creep into his mind. He was well aware that there was the chance that they might never find her in the forest. If in fact she had hit her head and drowned, which was a great possibility, her lifeless body could become wedged in among debris or submerged logs, held in place by the fast moving creek. If that were the case, she wouldn't be recovered until early summer when the power of the water released her remains. The family would have no peace until then. He force those negative thoughts out of his mind.

He stopped and looked up river for a moment in the direction they had come; he closed his eyes, trying to shut out his discouraging thoughts. With his eyes closed, the sound of the creek was very distinct and the aromatic flowers filled his lungs … *orchids*, he thought.

He opened his eyes to the dark, dreary mist that shrouded the forest around him. He was reminded again how unusually strange this place was. The rays of sunlight seemed to have sheltered only this very spot. *But the orchids that bloomed in the redwood forest bloomed in the spring and none were as aromatic or as powerful as this*, he thought. The fact that, like Fionna, he was the only other one in their group to smell them added a strange twist to things. He felt an unusual bond to Fionna, a person he didn't even know. For many searches, it had been his responsibility to review the victim's personal information to get a better understanding of the *subject.*

Fionna was shy, quiet, with an unspoken loyalty to her family and friends. Based on information from her parents and those who knew her, she didn't have any problems at home or at school. She had an appreciation for the outdoors and never took risks. But strangely, during the latter part of her trip she stepped out of character. On the last day, they said she was sick, constantly shivering, possibly hypothermic, slowly succumbing to the bone chilling cold. And then, according to Mary, after smelling the flowers, she acquired a renewed strength, an uncontrolled desire to find their source. He felt that now. The thought made him shiver again.

He turned back towards the warmth of the sunlight and continued down the game trail. He had an inexplicable feeling that the girl was still alive. But, why? *How?*

There was the inclement weather plus the physical injury she most likely suffered from her fall. The longer she was out in the wilds, the greater the chances were that she would not be found alive or in some cases, found at all. As far as he knew, s*he might already be dead but, for whatever reason his gut told him no.*

As Paul approached the grove of trees, they seemed to grow in size. At a distance they looked like all the other trees in the ancient forests but as he walked among them, their immensity dwarfed him. His eyes silently traced the thick grooves of the cinnamon colored bark as it spiraled up into the upper canopy. He squinted into the brightness of the filtered sunlight that reflected off the droplets of rain. They looked like diamonds weaved into a latticework of green, brown, and gold. The lowest branches started hundreds of feet above the rich greens of the assortment of fern and sorrel that covered the forest floor. The trees appeared to be older than any others that he had seen in his wanderings. The moisture danced in the rays of light, forming intense beams. Fallen trees lay as logs, their sides now their tops, their spindly, upended roots, rising fifteen feet above the forest floor like an old man's gnarled fingers. A garden of ferns and clover blossomed on the charred and weathered wood and cold, emerald colored ponds filled the craters that were once occupied by the root balls of the trees.

Standing above the meadow of lush ground cover like silhouettes in the shadows were the blackened, charred remains of trees that once stood guard. Deformed and scorched by ancient fires, they refused to fall; their ghostly remains still standing as centurions over the remaining giants. They formed a stark contrast between life and death.

Obviously, this section of the forest had escaped the devastating landslides and major fires that had altered the valley over the last thousand years. The natural disasters had reached the flanks of the grove but had not entered its heart. This was special, much different than all the other groves he had seen.

"Wow!" Susan's voice sounded loud yet muted in the strange, deafening silence. "This is definitely something new," she spoke in a low, reverential tone.

Paul grunted and nodded in agreement while Mary looked silently on.

There was a curiousness about the grove. Though the game trail they were following had taken them away from the sight of the creek, they could still hear the muffled, distant sounds of the cascading water. The effect brought Paul a needed sort of comfort as the aromatic orchids pulled him along in the direction of the creek. He cut through the meadow of clover ground cover and aimed for a huge burned out snag to his left. He worked his way towards the edge of the creek. As tired as he was, Paul was still conscientious about reducing his impact on the delicate plants of the forest floor.

The others silently followed, their eyes searching in every direction.

As he was walking past the huge blackened snag, he heard a squeak like whistle and the buzzing of little wings. He stopped and quickly focused in the direction of the sounds, hoping to catch a glimpse before the source was lost among the trees. Out of the corner of his eye, he caught the shadow of something small and dark just as it disappeared. At first he thought it odd for a hummingbird to be in the forest at this time of year but he suddenly realized that what he saw was much too large to be a hummingbird. He stopped, turned his head and squinted into the rays of light. He eyed the length of the snag. Whatever it was, was gone. He shivered with an unexplained chill. His mind raced as he tried to figure out what he had seen.

"What's up?" Susan whispered.

Paul jumped at the sound of her voice. He hoped she hadn't noticed but she did; he caught her smiling.

"I don't know … I thought I saw something!" he answered defensively, his voice low.

"Like what?" Susan looked at him surprised.

"A big hummingbird?" He shrugged.

"Humming bird?" She was fighting back a teasing smile. How big?" Her eyes now reflected her curiosity.

Paul turned his attention back towards the snag, "The size of a robin!"

"You sure?"

Paul nodded.

"You still smell those flowers?" She teased.

"Orchids!" Paul said so matter-of-fact.

"Now, they're orchids? Why are you whispering?"

Paul gave her a serious look. He suddenly felt the need to defend himself. He continued to speak softly, "First, I don't know what I saw but I know I saw something. Second, I don't know why I smell the *orchids*," he emphasized the word, "but I do. Or why the drive is so strong to follow. Third, neither you nor I have ever been here before, or for that matter, even known that this grove existed. And fourth, for some reason, and don't ask me why I know this … if we're ever going to find Fionna, it's probably going to be in a place like this."

He stared at her a moment before he turned and headed for the creek, no longer being careful where he stepped. He stopped momentarily to whisper over his shoulder. "You coming?"

"Now, that was strange!" she mumbled just loud enough for Paul to hear . She stared at him, blankly, and then turned to follow.

Paul no longer waited for them; he trudged along toward the sound of the creek that grew louder in his ears. He knew that Susan could use her tracking skills to find him and if that didn't work, she could always raise her on the park radio.

Just before he reached the creek, he thought he heard whispers and then the buzzing of wings. He looked around but saw nothing. He felt the unnerving chill again, it was like we was being watched. He stopped and yelled, "Fionna!"

He listened but all he heard was the sound of the creek as it rolled over rocks and around logs. He wondered if his mind was now playing tricks on him as well. He knew that some people claimed they heard voices coming from creeks and rivers. It was the human imagination; the way the water echoed off the rocks or the way the breeze moved through the trees. Then, there was the First Nations lore about the little people who inhabited the shorelines of creeks and rivers. He kept telling himself that they were myths and legends, children's stories told around the fires at night to keep the little ones away from the hazards of creeks and rivers. He needed to keep moving, he couldn't let his thoughts spook him.

Just as he was about to take a couple more cautious steps, he again heard the sounds of faint whispers, this time louder than before. *They're close*, he thought. It seemed as if they, whoever *they* were, were following the creek. He called Fionna's name again through cupped hands and quietly listened over his panting breath for a reply. He heard the nervousness in his own voice and the pounding of his heart in his ears.

The rhythmic whispering continued. He felt the chill again. This time, he could almost make out the words. He feared that the flow of the water through the forest was carrying his desperate calls down the creek and away from the sounds of the mysterious voices. So, he climbed along the shoreline in the direction of what was beginning to sound more and more like human voices. Scrambling over logs and crawling through the ferns like a desperate man, he felt a spark of hope rekindle in his heart. The sounds of the voices grew louder and clearer but he was stunned when he realized that he didn't recognize the language.

"This is too weird," he mumbled to himself.

As he scrambled towards the top of a moss-covered boulder, the buzzing of wings and the voices on the other side abruptly stopped. He froze, clinging to the rock. The weight of his pack was now noticeable against his shoulders. He strained his ears for a moment but the muffled conversation never returned. The smell of the orchids was now overpowering. His grip on the slippery, mossy handholds was giving way. He tried to reposition his weakening hands in the tiny cracks, but he could no longer cling to the boulder. Instead, he slid ten feet back down the rock without even a panicked cry for help. His hands, knees and chest dragged against the abrasive surface. When his feet hit the ground, the momentum carried him backwards and he tumbled backwards into the undergrowth. He lay there for a moment, surprised. It was foolish to attempt to climb the slick boulder, with or without a full pack, and he knew it. The drive to seek and find was much too strong; he needed to be careful. When all seemed to be in order, he took a deep sigh and raised his head towards the top of the fifteen-foot boulder, squinting into the sunlight.

What he thought he saw sent a wave of goose bumps down his

spine. A little person, about the size of a robin, was sitting on top of the boulder, back-lit by the filtered rays of sunlight, a golden hue around its tiny silhouette. Motionless, it stared down at him with big expressive, curious eyes. At first he wondered if he had hit his head in the fall. *How can this be?* Without taking his eyes off the figure, he ran a hand through his hair. *No tenderness … no deformities … and no blood. He hadn't hit his head. If not his head, then was it his mind?*

"Ó*na crainn...*" echoed faintly over the water. The sound came from the shadows to his left. He turned and looked but could see nothing through the ferns that obstructed his view.

He heard the buzzing of wings, this time from the top of the boulder. When he turned to look back the tiny figure was gone. *Did I imagine it?* He wondered. The rays no longer seemed as golden; the sunlight no longer seemed as bright. He could smell the rain on the breeze, the tops of the trees began to sway again. Some creaked and groaned sorrowfully in the building winds. The storm front was back. The patterns were consistent, winds before the rains. The heavier the winds, the more precipitation. He knew it would be only a short time before sheets of rain once again darkened the sky, making life miserable.

He first rose to his hands and knees and then pushed himself up to his feet. The process was harder than he expected. The fatigue of three long days was setting in. He felt a strange need to search the nearby shadows. He turned and headed in that direction, putting the waning low angled sunlight to his back and the blending shadows in front of him. *There had to be someone there.*

"Fionna?" he murmured.

"*Na síogaí (Na shee-ogh-ee).*" A faint whisper filled his ears.

"What?" He crashed through the ferns in the direction of the female voice. This time, he was determined that what ever had made the voices was not going to escape. Five strides brought him to their source.

Below him, snuggled among a bed of ferns lay a young teen. Her auburn hair was matted and dirt, her clothing soiled. Her rain parka and one of her shoes were missing, most likely the result of her swim in the creek's powerful current. Snuggled in a fetal position, she lay almost motionless, except for the slow rise and fall of her chest.

Paul felt an uncontrollable joy surge through his body. "Fionna," he yelped in a voice he didn't recognize.

He knelt down beside her and gently shook her shoulders with his trembling hands. She mumbled something he couldn't understand.

He took another quick glance towards the surrounding forest, they appeared to be alone. The voice of the young teen was nothing like the one he had heard. Paul refocused his attention on the victim in front of him. He ran his hands down the sides of her arms, torso and legs looking for any other obvious signs of trauma. The purple and yellow coloration of an old bruise on the side of her forehead appeared to be the only signs of injury. Her head wound had already begun the process of healing.

"I'm Paul, the park ranger, you're going to be all right!" He hoped the patient could hear and understand that help had arrived.

He turned and yelled in the direction of the rest of the group. "Susan, Mary, come here quickly. I've found her. I've found Fionna!" He heard the quiver in his own voice. "I found you!" he whispered. He pulled out his radio and attempted to notify his dispatcher of the welcomed news. All he got was radio silence; he couldn't even hear the repeater engage. He cursed the fact that they were in a dead spot. But that no longer seemed to matter. The lonely sounds of the cascading creek and the wind moving through the trees was all he heard at first.

Then he heard Susan and Mary hurriedly making their way through the forest; they were almost upon them. Their heavy breathing and excited conversation echoed through the forest. He turned back towards the boulder just as the last of the sunlight disappeared behind the clouds. He inhaled the rich aroma of the ancient forest but something was different; he could no longer smell the flowers. The orchids were gone.

Act 3:
The Ripple Affect

Chapter Five

Fairies of Cottingley

Paul stared at the moving shadows on his television screen as he nursed his fourth beer. The figures on the screen spoke but their voices didn't register. His thoughts drifted back to the ancient forest, back to Fionna. It was unusual for him to use the victims name instead of calling them, injured party, missing person or victim. There had always been a disconnect, a separation. It was safer way to emotionally deal with the parties involved.

It had been a week since the rescue, although he viewed the three-day adventure as more of a search than a rescue. It wasn't like Fionna had been trapped on an inaccessible ledge or anything like that. She had been lying comfortably in a bed of clover with no indication of how she had gotten there. A mystery that still baffled him. Then, there was what he heard, what he smelled, what he felt, and strangely enough … what he had seen … *or had he?*

Once Fionna was found, they hauled her out on a lightweight, collapsible litter designed for that very purpose. After consulting the map, they decided the path of least resistance was to parallel the creek down to one of the larger rivers in the park. They tried their park radios along the way but, as expected, they couldn't get out. The forested canyon blocked the radio waves.

"Jeez! The service around here sucks … remind me to change carriers when we get back," Susan complained, in her unique sarcastic way. The thought made him smile. Even Susan's trusty cell phone didn't work. They had no choice but to use the litter themselves and carry her out in the rain.

It was late afternoon with no more than a couple of hours of sunlight left before the long winter shadows cloaked them in darkness. With headlamps glowing in the mist, they struggled over the moss-covered rocks and downed logs as they made their way, keeping the sounds of the creek to their left.

Even though the air was cold and wet, he was pleased at having found the proverbial needle in the haystack; Fionna, the missing sixteen-year-old. Mary's constant mumbles and whispering tones echoed off the rocks and trees as she stumbled along exhausted, one hand on the edge of the litter and the other caressing her friend's. An eerie silence overwhelmed the group but the forest chattered on with a voice of its own. A great horned owl hooted its haunting cries as the wind blew through the tops of the trees, causing them to protest mournfully as they swayed to the uneven rhythm of the storm. The symphony came to crescendo with the occasional branches that broke free and crashed loudly to the ground in the growing darkness. The rain constantly dripped onto the saturated forest floor and left concentric rings in the beams of their headlamps on the surface of the water that pooled.

Deep in their own thoughts, they shuffled along, zombie-like, on their descent, stopping only long enough to check Fionna's vitals from time to time. Thankfully, the results were always the same, stable and resting soundly. While Paul handled the medical checks, Susan tried to contact the outside world, first by radio, then by cell phone. However, they soon reached the point when disappointment was expected as if it in itself were part of the adventure.

Two and a half hours into their descent, their park radios came to life in scratchy, intermittent voices; the first welcomed voices in nearly three days. They looked at each other stunned. In unison, the rangers abruptly lowered the litter to the ground and scrambled for their radios. Susan was responding before Paul had even gotten his out of his pack. He remembered her wink and her raised thumb as she spoke excitedly into the mike. He shared her success with renewed energy; they were no longer alone.

An inflatable Zodiac was waiting for them in the darkness where the creek met the main river. There, they turned Mary and their charge over to the rescue crew, who floated them to the nearby overlook and then to the waiting ambulance. From there, Fionna was driven to the hospital in Springville. Another job well done.

She still remembered after loading Mary and her unconscious friend onto the inflatable Zodiac, they watched until the group disappeared into the darkness, swept away by the angry river current. Strangely, he felt a familiar bond with them; he fought the urge to go along. Mary tried to wave but quickly grabbed onto the rubber raft for balance as they were gripped by the edge of the current and pulled down the silt filled water. He returned her wave in the darkness until Susan nudged him on the shoulder.

"Don't get too attached, you'll never see them again." He knew she was right. He saw the pride and satisfaction in her eyes; he felt the same within himself. Mary was a young lady devoted to her friend; Fionna, a stranger with whom he felt an inexplicable bond. They had brought the teens back safe and delivered them to their parents. The mystery of Fionna's disappearance was believed solved, but he knew differently. For him, he felt this mystery had only just begun.

Paul smiled again when he thought about that moment. He saw everything clearly as if he were there again in the dank forest. He instinctively looked around the room to see if anyone had noticed the tears that appeared on his cheeks but realized that was silly when he remembered he was alone in his living room. It was late, his wife and his young children had already gone to bed. Unable to sleep, he stayed up to watch a PBS special but the people on the television screen were talking in barely audible voices. He had turned down the volume so he wouldn't awaken his family. He let his thought drift back to the present, back to the program.

"We call them *Na síogaí (na shee-ohg-ee)* or fairy folk." The man's heavy accent reflected his Irish upbringing. "There ar' good an' bad, but there is one thing fer sure...they love te' meddle in everyone's affairs!"

"Na shee-ohg-ee?" Paul whispered, repeating the familiar phrase. He felt a chill run down his spine and his fingers tingled as he gripped the chair to keep himself from falling out. *He had heard that word before … but where?*

He searched his memory as he patted around for the volume control on the cluttered table next to him, his eyes not leaving the screen, his ears straining to hear the sound. The balding, elderly gentleman in the gray tweed coat and black turtleneck continued to speak. His bushy eyebrows shadowed expressive eyes that told of his excitement about the subject. Behind him lay the ruins of a medieval castle; its fractured gray stone stood in stark contrast to the tall green grass and open fields that caressed the valley beyond. There was no doubt he was in Ireland.

Paul turned up the volume. The man's voice boomed with a Gaelic accent as the camera zoomed in on a faded black and white photograph that he held delicately in his wrinkled hands. Paul's focused on the photograph; the remote slid out of his trembling hands as he remembered where he had heard the word. A chill surged through him. With surprise and bewilderment, he was mentally transported back to the misty rays of the ancient forests where he had seen the very same thing before.

A miniature figure of a young woman with delicate features and pointed ears sat on the extended index finger of a normal sized child, like a bird perched on a branch. Fragile transparent wings spread out from its back and glistened in the sunlight. The two figures in the photograph gazed at each other as if they were both amazed by what they were seeing.

Paul felt his heart pounding in his ears and nervous perspiration building on his brow. "No, this can't be!"

As if the television announcer had heard his protestations, the Irish voice boomed, "Yes … the Fairies of Cottingley. First published in *Strand Magazine* in 1920 by Sir Arthur Conan Doyle … the very one who wrote the *Sherlock Homes Mysteries.* T'was in the spring of 1917. Elsie Wright age 15 an' Frances Griffiths age 10 talked of fairies they claimed te' 'ave played with in the glen outside of the Yorkshire village of Cottingley. None believed 'em so they decided te' prove it. Ye' see, young Elsie borrowed her father's camera an' took pictures of Frances posing wit' the fairies, that's her ther' in the picture." The old man pointed at the obvious. "They later took a picture of a gnome too! Over the next three years, they took three similar photographs. The girl's mother was so convinced that there was somethin' te' this fairy thing that she started attending lectures on the subject. Twas' during one of these lectures that she decided te' mention the photograph her daughter had taken te' Edward Gardner, a leading Theosophist. He, in turn, shared it with a photographer friend of his."

The man laughed heartily before he continued. "It didn't take long before the existence of the photograph reached the news. Ye' see, unlike today, back then many more Irish people believed in fairies; they also spoke Irish, our traditional language. They shared the stories with their children and grandchildren. Ye' know, I smile when I hear in the news that farmers won't cut down the oak trees that are in the middle of their fields; they just plow around 'em so as te' not upset the fairies. The highway people, when putting in roads, will move the road, not the trees. They say they want to keep the trees but there is more te' it than they ar' willing te' admit. They say they don't believe in the Irish folk lore of *na síogaí (na shee-ohg-ee), bean sí (ban shee), puca (pook-ah), gruagach (groo-ug-ukh), leipreachán (lep-rukh-awn), leannan sí (lan-awn shee)*, an' *cailleach (kal-yukh).*"

The old man paused a moment before he explained. He saw the announcer wasn't following. "Ye' know, Fairies, Gnomes, Ban shee's, Hob an' Hairy goblins, Witches, Fairy lovers an' the like. They say they don't believe, but they remember the old stories." He laughed. "The *piseoga (pish-ohg-sh)*, the superstitions, still flow through the blood of the honest Irish man an' woman. Most won't go near a *lios (lis)*, a fairies' mound, at night." He smiled and pointed toward the announcer. "I see ye' know what I am talkin' about."

They both laughed. Paul found himself laughing too. It felt good to laugh. He didn't know if he was laughing about the attitudes of those involved or his own mixed feelings on the subject. He heard his wife's muffled call from the back room, asking him to turn down the television.

"Honey, you've got to come see this!" He yelled back. He barely heard her muffled reply before shifting his attention back to the television.

"The negatives wer' sent te' the experts at Kodak," the old man continued. "They couldn't find any signs of fraud or tampering. So, over time, Doyle accepted the fact that the photographs might 'ave indeed been real an' published his article. For sixty years, the photographs were studied an' debated, some finding it hard te' believe that fairies existed in the twentieth century.

"In the 1960's, new techniques were used te' examine the photos … they said the lighting on the fairies didn't match the lighting on the girls … the wings of the fairies didn't show blurred motion like they thought it should have. By 1977, a historian and book illustrator by the name of Fred Gettings, said that he had uncovered drawings, from a 1915 children's book written by Claude A. Shepperson, that matched the Cottingley fairies! It seemed strange, don't it, Shepperson's pictures of the fairies and Doyle's story titled *Bimbashi*, all printed together in the same book. But neither of them wer' to put it together until five years later!" He paused for a moment before continuing.

"In 1982, the controversy started up again. This time, a man named Geoffrey Crowley, the editor of the *British Journal of Photography* claimed the pictures had been re-touched. In 1985, Elsie Wright an' Frances Griffiths, now in their late 70s an' early 80s, confessed that they had staged the photographs. That the fairies they had photographed wer' paper cut outs they had propped up with hat pins."

The sweet, rhythmic sounds of the Irish flute and the steady beat of the bodhran began to blend and build, creating a nostalgic mood.

Paul felt a strange sort of anger flash through his mind. "How could they have led people on for sixty years?" he mumbled under his breath. He flashed back to what he had seen and heard. "There is just no way!"

His wife walked up behind him and laid a gentle hand on his shoulder before she sat down next to him."

He flinched.

"A little jumpy, aren't we?" she teased. "So, what is so …"

He hushed her quiet.

The Irish voice continued. "They said they did it te' play tricks on the grownups who made fun of the fairies. They were surprised that they wer' taken so seriously even if it weren't te' goal they wanted te' achieve." The old man folded his arms and slid the aging framed photograph under one of them. "Despite their fakin' the photos, they still believed in fairies. They went te' the glen te' watch 'em. Now that they swear te' be the honest te' God truth. And I believe 'em. The fairies do exist, ye know! Every myth an' legend has its roots in reality. The problem is, most of us don't live in reality. We live in a world that we have created fer' ourselves. An', when we take a moment te' step out of that world, we enter one that we ar' no longer prepared fer'."

Paul's throat tightened and became dry. He was moved by what he had heard. It wasn't a coincidence that he had stayed up like he did and stumbled upon the late night special. He didn't believe in luck or coincidence; his experiences had taught him that. He placed an arm around his wife's shoulder. "Those were fairies that I saw in the park that day, I'm sure of it now."

"How much have you had to drink?"

He saw the confused look in her eyes and felt her starting to pull away from him.

He held her tightly and pulled her closer to him. He realized he had a lot of explaining to do.

He needed to talk to Fionna. It was all much too strange. The last he heard, she was still in a coma, recuperating in the children's wing of a local hospital. Her mother, thankful for their rescue of her daughter, promised to call him as soon as she awakened. He didn't know how to explain it but he knew that he was expecting a call very soon.

Chapter Six

The Awakening

Paul paused momentarily at the wide, solid wood double doors to catch his breath and calm his nerves. Above the doors, a sign indicated *Children's Ward*, a place that had been Fionna's home since she arrived a week and a half earlier. He cleared his throat and tried to shake off the awkwardness of the moment as he took one last glimpse at his mirrored reflection in the small, rectangular window in the door. He removed his regulation-felt Stetson hat and attempted unsuccessfully to flatten the brown curls at his temples. A nervous, uniformed park ranger stared back at him from the small mirrored window. He tried to swallow but his throat felt dry. He coughed again to clear it. He started to place his hat back on his head but thinking differently of it, he held it in his hand. He looked around to see if anyone was watching. No one was. The other people sitting in the chairs down the long hallway appeared to be busy with thoughts of their own.

A hospital was never a happy place. He had been here many times before to follow up on accidents and crimes or to collect statements from parties involved. It wasn't unusual to see uniformed peace officers walking the halls of the emergency room. But, here, at the opposite end of the hospital, it must have been curious indeed to see one stalking the hallways of the Children's Ward.

He pushed open the doors and walked down the hallway. Paintings of dinosaurs and horses decorated the walls. The smells of cleanser and disinfectant no longer dominated. He smelled cotton candy and licorice. The hallway looked more like a living room than a waiting room. The people who sat on the couches looked up and smiled at him as he walked by. He returned a pleasant nod and continued toward the front desk at the end of the hall. The occupants here seemed a bit more at ease, a bit more permanent. A child in colorful pajamas and slippers with no hair on his head looked up at him, obviously excited to see his uniform.

"Mommy, mommy, a policeman!"

Paul felt compelled to stop.

The boy pushed himself up and walked towards Paul, looking him over closely.

"Actually, I'm a park ranger. I work at Roosevelt Redwoods Park," Paul said, dropping into his teaching mode.

The child squinted first at Paul's face and then at the holstered handgun on his hip, pausing a moment before pointing to the weapon. "But you have a gun!"

Paul nodded. "Yes, park rangers carry guns. We're the policemen in the parks."

The young boy stared at him for a moment as if processing what he had just heard. "Do you have any cards?"

"I might … let's see." Paul reached into his top pocket and pulled out a pocket sized cardholder, removed a photographed trading card he had especially made for that very purpose and handed it to the boy.

The young boy anxiously read the card before he spoke. "You're a park ranger!"

"Yes, I am." He heard the ring of pride in his own voice. "So what is your name?"

"Robert," the boy looked up and smiled. "But you can call me Bobby." He held the card in the both of his hands as if it were priceless. "I bet I'm the only one of my friends who has a ranger trading card." He looked up at Paul again; his eye's beaming as if he had a brilliant idea. "Could you give me another card to trade with my friends?"

"Bobby!" His mother warned.

"No, it's okay," Paul laughed. "Yes, Bobby."

The boy's eyes lit up.

Paul reached in his pocket and pulled out a couple more cards and offered them to the child.

"Wow, thanks!" he exclaimed as he accepted the cards with great delight.

"Thank you, ranger," the mother said. "It's all he thinks about these days. It's what helps him through it all … thank you!"

"You're quite welcome." Paul felt his throat tighten. He forced a smile. "See you Bobby." He gently rested his hand on Bobby's head. He was surprised by how smooth it felt.

The boy nodded and hurried back to his seat. "See you around, ranger. Thanks for the cool cards."

"You're welcome." At a loss for anything else to say, Paul walked further down the hallway toward the reception desk. He fought the urge to feel sorry for the child. He didn't want it to show.

When he reached the reception desk, he stopped. Painted horses and balloons sat on the counter. The whole reception area looked as if they were celebrating a birthday.

"Whose birthday?" Paul asked. He still felt the tightness in his voice.

"Everyone's!" said the portly, middle aged blonde woman. "We celebrate life here every day. These children experience enough sorrow in their lives. It is probably the only pleasant experience they will have during their visit." She lowered her voice. "They're much too young to understand what life is dishing out to them. But yet, very brave."

Paul gave her a bewildered look.

"That was very nice of you to do what you did back there," the lady behind the counter smiled.

Paul nodded towards Bobby and started to ask a question but she cut him off.

"Cancer … was in remission. It's been two years. I don't think things are looking up for that little guy." Her voice sounded so matter of fact. As if reading Paul's thoughts, she continued, "They are pretty incredible, these children," she nodded towards the children in the hallway. "Beyond their innocence, they know that things aren't right, yet they seem to embrace life. There are a lot of Bobby's in here. It's tough to see." She paused for a moment, cleared her throat before she continued, "It's good to see visitors; they enjoy the visitors, you know."

He reached up and firmly shook her hand, "Name's Paul."

"Sally," she cleared her throat again and looked at his name tag. "So what can I do for you, ranger …. Behaaaaneeee?"

"It's actually pronounced Behaan … but you can call me Paul … I'm here to see Fionna Brien."

"Oh yes, Fionna … she said you would be coming."

Paul raised his eyebrows.

"Yes, strange that one," Sally laughed. "She said you rescued her from the forest?"

Paul returned the smiled. "Yes, Ranger Sheatham and myself … a three day affair." Paul tried to downplay it. "Her mother called me this morning. Said she was finally awake. I needed to put the finishing comments in my report." That wasn't the whole truth but he didn't want to say too much. He certainly couldn't tell the nurse that this moment was all he had been thinking about for the last week and a half.

"She came out of her coma the other day," the nurse rambled on. "Looks like she is going to be fine … we will be keeping her a couple more days for observation, of course. She had a nasty bruise on her head. She may have suffered a concussion … she doesn't seem to remember how she got it." She pointed to her head. "What happened to that poor girl?"

"She went backpacking in the park with some friends."

"In the middle of winter … what were they thinking?" She sighed, reflecting her disbelief.

Paul shrugged his shoulders and continued. He enjoyed the winter solitude in the park. He had no problem understanding why someone would do that, but he decided not to take the time to explain. "The weather had gotten bad and they decided to take a short cut. While crossing a log, she slipped and fell into a raging creek. It took us three days to find her."

"My goodness, I didn't know. That poor child!" The nurse glanced over her shoulder towards the row of curtain separated rooms.

"Has her friend Mary been here?" Paul changed the subject.

"Yes, you just missed her by a half hour or so, very nice young lady … to go back and help search for her friend."

"She is indeed," Paul shifted his gaze down the hall. "A very good friend."

"Fionna's in room 117, fourth door, or rather the fourth curtain opening on your left. Her mother should be in there with her."

Paul looked back and nodded thanks before he turned and headed past the counter.

"Hey!" Sally's voice echoed.

Paul stopped and turned.

She nodded towards the little boy on the couch in the lobby area,

"Don't be such a stranger around here. They enjoy seeing a new face as much as the next."

Paul nodded as he turned towards the boy. "He hasn't seen the last of me, I promise!"

The nurse nodded.

Continuing down the hall, his mind flashed to the phone call he received earlier that morning. It was Fionna's mother, her excited voice boomed over the other end. The sound of someone whose life had turned for the better. "She's been asking for you all morning! Can you come?" The thought fascinated him. *How could Fionna have known who he was?* When he reached the closed curtain, he took a deep breath, cleared his throat and said, "Knock, knock!"

"Come in," a woman's voice said from behind it.

The curtain slid open before Paul had a chance to push it open. He felt the excitement build within himself. He was greeted with smiles.

"Ranger Behaan, thank you for coming!" The attractive brunette walked over to greet him. She firmly shook his hand and then gave him a warm embrace. Her action caught him by surprise. "I'm Anna Brien, Fionna's mom." She turned back towards her daughter. "Fionna has been asking for you ever since she woke up. Come in, come in!"

Paul stepped toward the center of the room.

His eyes met Fionna's as she sat up in bed. Her bruise was no longer noticeable.

"Hi, remember me?" she asked.

"Yes, I do … good to see you're awake." Paul suddenly felt awkward. He nervously played with his hat in his hands, hoping his body language didn't give away how he felt. "How are they treating you around here? How's the food?"

"Very nicely, thank you."

"How do you feel?" Paul asked. He walked up next to the bed

and leaned towards her to exaggerate the act of inspecting her forehead. "The bruise on your forehead seems to be gone."

When he leaned close, she quickly wrapped her arms around him and gave him a tight squeeze, almost pulling him off his feet. He barely saved his Stetson from being crushed. He was caught off guard a second time.

Her mother laughed, "Take it easy there, Fionna."

It seemed like the longest time before she released him.

Once released Paul instinctively took a couple of steps back and looked his hat over. Nothing was damaged. He wasn't going to be taken off guard a third time.

Fionna noted his surprise. "Sorry about that, I wanted to say thank you for rescuing me! Mary told me all about it!" Fionna's voice was filled with excitement. "I am glad you came."

Paul nodded. "I need to ask you a few questions … for the report."

"Okay! For the report," she replied, enthusiastically.

Paul asked what she remembered about her accident. She reviewed their trip, rambling on about the shortcut they had taken, the dense forest, the fierceness of the storm, the dreaded rain, and about finding the log. Beyond that, she said she couldn't remember. Paul read her expression, noted the change, and knew she wasn't telling him everything. For some reason, she was holding back, keeping secrets. He decided not to push her. There was always another time; he had enough to finish his report. He stared quietly at her for a moment before thanking her and backed away from the side of the bed to escape another one of her bear hugs. He extended his hand to her mother.

"Mom, could I talk to the ranger in private?" Her voice had suddenly become serious.

Paul looked strangely in her direction. He wondered why the sudden change of heart.

"Well, all right, I guess," her mom answered. "I'll wait out in the hallway." She reluctantly walked out of the room, quietly letting the curtain fall behind her.

Paul nervously fidgeted with his hat again as he watched her leave. He listened to her footsteps fade away. She was walking towards the front desk.

Fionna was first to interrupt the uneasy silence. "Mary told me you smelled the flowers!"

He nodded and took a couple of steps closer to the bed.

"So … you smelled the flowers too?" She sighed, playfully.

"What?" Paul looked up into the green eyes that were burning holes in him.

"They were so sweet and strong, weren't they? It was almost as if …"

"Yes, they were pulling me along," Paul interrupted. He suddenly felt a draft.

Fionna shifted her gaze between Paul and the curtain. "They led me to the log … and then into the creek," she spoke again after a moment of silence. "What do you think they mean?"

"They?"

Fionna narrowed her eyes and stared at him a moment before she spoke. "The fairies … I know you saw them too! They live there in that ancient grove."

Despite his promise to himself, her frankness caught him off guard yet a third time.

Paul felt a strange surge of excitement and exhaustion flow through him. *How could two people experience the same dream?* His mind raced back to the forest, back to the strange voices, back to the figure that sat on top of the boulder.

"Maybe you should sit down," Fionna nodded to the chair that sat next to the bed and night stand. "Your looking a little pale. What I'm about to tell you is very strange indeed but I know you'll believe me. You're part of this whether you want to believe it or not. I've been asked to help and I believe so have you." She cleared her throat.

He stared at her stunned, mouth half open.

"Please sit," she pointed to a chair near the wall, "before you fall over of something."

He reluctantly dragged the chair closer to the bed and plopped down noisily, spinning his hat nervously in his hands.

"I haven't told my mom and dad or talked to my grandma about it yet. I'm not supposed to. For right now, at least, I'm only supposed to talk to you."

"Me! Why me?" He could hear the surprise in his own voice.

"Because you are supposed to help me," she stated as if that should have been obvious.

Her words echoed in his head. Somehow, he knew she was right. He felt a strong bond between them. It felt good to sit, much easier to listen and comprehend. He crossed his legs and placed his Stetson on one of his knees as he hung on her every word trying to make some sense out of it.

Chapter Seven

An Irish Tale

Fionna let her exposed calves dangle over the edge of the bed and readjusted the floral patterned gown around her knees. She stared at her pink painted toenails a moment before she looked at Paul.

She was pleased by the fact that the color of her toenails matched the pink floral patterns in her gown and accentuated the paleness of her feet. She bubbled with excitement as she rubbed her feet together. She had so much to tell. *Would he believe her*, she wondered. She had to trust him. The voices had told her that he would. The expression on the ranger's face when he found her was still etched in her memory. He cared about helping people. The fairies said that he was the one who would help her. Now, she had to explain it all. She brushed her bangs out of her face, rested her hands on her knees, crossed her feet and nervously swung them back and forth as she spoke.

She watched as Paul fidgeted, moving his hat from one crossed knee to the other. He eventually folded his hands in his lap, leaned back into his chair, and patiently listened. His eyes never left Fionna‘s.

"Did you know that I'm the fifth generation of Irish born in America?" she asked finally. "My mother is fourth! And my Grandma ..."

Paul nodded his head, "Is third?"

"Yes, my name use to have an Ó in front of it ... used to be Ó'Brien. But somewhere along the way they lost the Ó and decided that Brien was good enough." She watched Paul's reaction. He raised his eyebrows, which meant he was listening to what she was saying.

Paul smiled before he spoke. "I think maybe the Ó is missing from Behaan as well. I kind of like the sound of that Ó."

"It's Irish, you know!" her voice quivered.

"I do believe you're right."

She blushed with a great big smile and fidgeted with the fabric around her knees. "You know, none of this is a coincidence. Things happen for reasons. Our paths are picked for us ... all we do is follow them. Many people live simple lives but some are asked to do wonderful things."

Paul refolded his arms across his chest and gazed at her inquisitively. She knew she needed to get to the point.

"This is what I was told," she began without explaining by whom she was told. "In the mid-1800s, the Great Potato Famine caused people to leave western Ireland in droves. They were starving to death and some believed that the world as they knew it was coming to an end. Believing that England was part of the problem, many of them came to America for a new start."

Paul nodded.

She looked down at her feet. "Evidently, my family left Ireland in 1847 for America. They left many of their possessions behind, items that they could easily replace wherever they ended up. They didn't want to leave the Ireland they loved but felt they had no choice. They took the important things like their family bibles and personal items and …" She looked toward the curtain entrance, then leaned forward looking at him directly. "There is more to Ireland than meets the eye. Their myths and legends run deep in their culture, you know."

"So, I've heard," Paul sat up in his chair an leaned forward, remembering the television special. She knew he was listening carefully.

"Are you familiar with the term na síogaí (na shee-ohg-ee)?" She pronounced it with an Irish accent.

She watched his mouth drop open. She knew right away that he was.

"Fairies used to live in the forests of Ireland but, evidently, some of my ancestors brought them over to America," she spoke quietly as she nodded towards the window, "and, eventually, to the ancient redwoods."

"B-b-but h-h-how?" Paul stammered as if he didn't want to believe what he himself had seen.

"My Great, Great, Great Grandmother smuggled them over the ocean to their new home on the East Coast of America and my Great Grandmother brought them to the ancient forests of Northwestern California. They have been here for more than a hundred years. They have been hiding in that canyon for years." She pointed out the window. "It's one of the last place untouched by man. They said there were other places like it all over the world!" She gave him a puzzled look, "Why do you think my grandmother never mentioned it to me?"

Paul narrowed his eyes and slid his fingers together. "I don't know … how do you know all of this?"

"They told me."

"There is that *they* again!"

"The fairies, of course, silly," she smiled. "They said that my family accepted the responsibility to be their guardians years ago." She spoke with great pride. "It is a big responsibility, you know."

"... And your mother?" He pointed towards the curtain opening. "What role does she play in all of this?"

"She doesn't know about any of it. Evidently, I'm not supposed to tell her."

"She doesn't know! You're not supposed to tell?" he interrupted.

"It's a family secret," she shrugged, shifting her gaze towards the door. "The fairies are concerned about the ancient trees … they heard their cries for help." She looked back into his eyes. "I believe that we've been chosen to help."

"We've … How? All of the trees in the parks and reserves are protected. What makes you think you can do what many others have tried and failed to do … protect the ancient forests on private timberland? People with more clout than you or me have been trying for years! They win a few battles but ultimately lose the war!" His voice was loud and pointed.

Fionna spoke calmly, "My grandmother will be home from her vacation in a few days. She must know about the fairies."

"Let me guess … the fairies told you!"

She nodded. "That will make three of us who know."

"Three of us? Why are you telling me this?" He quizzed in a much quieter voice.

"Because, whether you like it or not, you're supposed to help too! Don't you feel it? You have also been chosen. Think about it, What have you seen? What have you felt? What have you smelled? Your senses don't lie." She spoke plainly, "It's your job to protect the ancient trees, is it not? It's your job to protect everything in the forest … right!"

Paul tried to regain his composure. He ran his fingers through his hair and quietly settled back into his chair. She could tell he was thinking about what she had said. “So, how do you plan to do all of this?”

Fionna fluffed her pillows and smiled. She had a plan, one that nobody would ever expect.

Chapter Eight

Confiding in a Friend

Paul leaned back in his chair, his fingers laced behind his head, his boots resting on the edge of his desk. His groggy mind finally relaxed as he silently gazed at a picture that hung on the wall of his office. An unidentified man in a park ranger uniform was fearlessly crossing a huge redwood log that spanned a thirty-yard wide, creek-carved canyon. Beyond him lay a lush, ancient redwood forest. The immensity of the log dwarfed the man in tan and green who appeared to be brave and adventurous. But Paul knew better; the man on the log was him. It had taken him a while to work up the nerve to make the crossing and stare macho-like into the camera. He remembered how nervous and dizzy he felt the first time he tried to cross on the log.

He smiled when he thought about it. It was only on a dare that he even walked out there.

Every time, he had looked directly at his feet, the log appeared to spin and his balance was jeopardized. He learned to look down the log, his eyes set at 45 degrees and breath, to stop the spinning.

About halfway across, the log bounced under his every step. He froze and waited for the swaying and bouncing to stop, too scared to close his eyes. Then, there was the breeze that pushed on his shoulders, forced him to stop and regain his balance. He remembered the comforting, shrill call of the osprey that glided unseen among the tops of the trees. He knew a nearby nest overlooked that section of the main river. He remembered drawing strength and courage from its inspirational call and the incredible feeling of pride and success when he finally made it all the way to the other side. He could imagine Fionna experiencing similar sensations when she crossed her own log.

The day he crossed his log, he understood why people took risks in the outdoors; it gave them a strange power, a feeling of invincibility, a possible understanding of how our ancient ancestors must have felt when they lived in the wilderness. It was hard to explain, but there was a strange bit of magic in nature; he had always felt it. *So, why was what he experienced in the heart of the forest so hard to believe?* His mind drifted to Fionna's secret, which was now his as well.

"Reminiscing, are we?" Susan playfully teased.

Paul sat up in his chair, slipped his booted feet off his desk and let them fall noisily to the floor. He looked at her, started to say something but stopped.

Susan was looking at the several pictures that decorated his wall. "I especially like the one with you doing a handstand on top of the boulder." She nodded towards the photo, her eyes never leaving the wall.

"Don't you ever knock?" His eyes followed hers to the picture and he laughed, "I almost fell off just after they snapped that photo."

"Good thing you didn't."

"Yeah, it would have been hard to explain … How could this accident have been prevented!"

Susan joined him in a heartfelt laughter.

When Paul looked back at her, he saw she was concerned.

"You mind if I sit down?" she asked.

Paul noted the caring tone in her voice. "Oh, not at all. I was just …," he started shuffling papers around his desk.

"Catching up on some shut eye, yes, I know." She noisily dragged a chair over to the edge of his desk and plopped down heavily with a exhausted sigh. She then leaned back and dropped her hands along her side. "Is everything okay?"

"Yes, why do you ask?" His tone said it wasn't.

"Oh, well, because ever since we went after that teen in the woods, you just haven't been yourself. You've been, well, strange." She raised her eyebrows like she always did when she knew more than she let on. "It's been more than two weeks … I have never seen you like this before."

He shrugged and looked off towards the wall.

She waited a moment before she continued, "There is that *wall look* again … why did you go back to the hospital? I'm pretty sure you could have gotten everything you needed with a phone call. That's why they invented cell phones." She flashed him her cell phone and then slid it back into her pocket. She then narrowed her eyes, interlaced her fingers, leaned towards him and rested her elbows on her knees. "Hey, aren't you a little too old for her?" she teased. "What is there … what, a 19 year difference. Not to forget to mention your already married and the fact that she's … sixteen!" She emphasized her lat word.

Paul turned towards her and frowned. Most of the time he liked Susan's sense of humor but today …. He started to say something but she cut him off.

She held her palms out towards him, "You know I'm just kidding, right! Come on, help me out here. I'm your partner, the one who puts up with you, remember … through thick and thin and all that stuff!"

He picked up a clear crystal agate from his desk and fumbled with it in his fingers as he stared down at it.

"Well, what do you say, ranger? I'm not going anywhere until you tell me. You at least owe me that much."

He looked at her out of the corner of his eye. He saw her raise her eyebrows and tilt her head, the stubborn streak accenting her face. Her expression made him smile. "Okay, you win."

She nodded, "And …?"

"Did you smell the flowers?"

"Paul, we have gone over this already. No, I didn't smell flowers."

"Did you see or hear anything unusual?" Paul's voice began to quicken.

"No!" she was suddenly sounding impatient. She spoke as if she were talking to a little child. "I saw the usual, lots of rain, rugged canyons, dark, dark forests," she shook her head, "with very little sunlight … did I mention the rain?" She held her hand out in front of her and measured an inch gap between her thumb and index finger. "Oh yes, and we went to a place in the park that neither of us have ever been to before!"

"That's right!" He noisily tossed the agate onto his desk, walked over to the door, looked down the hall, closed the door behind him and walked back to his chair and sat down next to her.

She watched his action with surprise.

He slid his chair closer and leaned towards her, "Yes, a place that neither of us have ever been to before," Paul whispered.

She recoiled at the strangeness of his behavior.

"So, what exactly do you want to know?" Paul asked.

She grabbed both of his wrists, turned his hands palm up and felt for his pulse.

Paul didn't resist.

"It's lie detector test time!" She leaned towards him and stared into his eyes, looking carefully from one eye to the other. "So, Ranger Behaan, why did you go back to the hospital? Do I need to remind you that you are under oath, Ranger Behaan!"

Paul laughed at her silliness.

"Paul I'm serious!"

"Okay … okay." He knew exactly what she was doing. She was turning her body into a lie detector. If he were lying, his pulse and eyes would be the first to give him away. He knew this was the only way to convince her that there were strange things going on. He spoke calmly so she could easily follow. "I went to the hospital to get her statement … and to talk with her."

"I understand the part about getting her statement, which you could still have done over the telephone. Nothing a good cell phone couldn't fix. But to visit her a second time … why did you need to go back a second time? You know the rules, once we do our jobs, we cut them loose. We separate; we don't become attached. We don't get involved. It's better that way. Isn't that what you taught me? Get as far away as you can … run and hide if you have to." She slowly released one of his arms, slid her hand away from her body and then ran her fingers through her hair to exaggerate her point.

"But, this is different, Miss Prosecutor!" Paul exclaimed.

"Different … how is that so, Mr. Defendant?"

Paul nodded towards her hands.

She shook the hair out of her face and readjusted her grip on both of his wrists.

"You ready?" Paul exclaimed.

"As I will ever be!"

"Because she smelled the flowers, the same ones that I smelled and the same ones that led us both to that part of the forest."

"Why did you ask me if I heard anything unusual?"

After a momentary pause, he answered. "I heard voices," he mumbled.

"You heard what?" her voice inquisitive. "You sure it wasn't the river; you know the river can …"

"Yes, I know but it wasn't the river," he cut her off. "They were voices, Gaelic voices."

She wrinkled her nose.

"The voices led me to a huge boulder so I climbed the rock to see who or what was on the other side. I almost made it to the top but I slipped, lost my footing … fell the rest of the way back to the ground. Good thing the forest floor was soft and forgiving."

"That explains the scratches on the both of your palms."

Paul nodded, "But, when I looked up … at first, I thought it was the same huge hummingbird that I saw earlier." He paused a moment, noting the disbelief in her eyes and that her grip around his wrists was no longer firm. She was trying to understand.

"I saw a fairy, sitting there on the top of the rock. Oh, yes, it was a fairy alright!" His voice quivered and goose bumps ran the length of his body. He suddenly found himself back there, lying in the ferns. "It was beautiful. Its wings glowing in the rays of sunlight. It just stared down at me. At first I thought I must have hit my head or something … it stared back at me for the longest time, motionless. It wasn't until I heard Fionna's mumbling coming from the nearby ferns that I turned away. When I looked back, the fairy was gone." He stopped talking and stared at his friend, begging for her to believe.

She released both of his wrists and sat back in her chair. He didn't know what else to do so he continued to speak. "I followed the smell of the flowers and found her … just like she was when you arrived." He shook his head, "It was strange … as soon as I found her, I stopped smelling the flowers and stopped hearing the voices. The clouds came back and the rains continued. Don't you see, the whole scene was like a beacon guiding us to her … guiding us to that very spot!"

"There were no tracks," Susan mumbled. Her voice sounded as one of discovery. "How did she get there?"

Paul shrugged his shoulders. "Yeah, weird. The soil wasn't that great for tracks, but we should have seen something. It was as if she was put there … don't you understand, carried over and placed. Strange … it was like we were all meant to be there."

She nodded and looked towards his wall of pictures. He could tell that she was now in deep thought, most likely reviewing that day in her own mind.

"It gets weirder," Paul cautioned.

Susan looked back at him.

"At the hospital, after the interview, she asked to speak to me in private. She told me that she was fifth generation Irish American. That her Great, Great, Great, Grandmother smuggled fairies to America from Ireland to save them from the potato famine. They were eventually released here on the West Coast." He nodded at the wall. "Released into the ancient redwoods. Evidently, at a place in the park that we work, in a place where no one goes." Susan was hanging on his every word. "The very same place we were drawn to."

"My God, do you believe her? Sure she didn't bump her head?" Susan tried to force a laugh. Confusion and disbelief were etched into her face. "For that matter, are you sure you didn't bump yours?"

Paul smiled at her attempt at humor. Both situations had indeed happened. "As odd as it sounds, I think I believe her."

Susan became strangely quiet and stared off at the wall.

"So, you with me on this one?" Paul asked.

"I'll probably regret this, but what is it that you need me to do?"

"I don't know, but I'm sure we'll find out soon enough. There is one other thing."

"Like?"

"We shouldn't tell anyone."

"Yeah, or they'll think we're crazy!"

Act 4: Antiquity

Chapter Nine

From the Trees

The sun shone brightly under the upper canopy of the ancient redwood forest; its warm rays of February notably contrasted the weather of nearly three weeks ago. It hadn't rained for five days. Anyone who spent time behind the redwood curtain knew that even the sunshine plays an integral part in winter weather. It was these breaks between the powerful storms that allowed the forest inhabitants, plants, animals, and humans, to put their lives back together and prepare for the next series of storms. Once the low pressure settled in, the clouds accumulated and the rains began to fall, the pattern sustained itself. All who made this area their home knew that without the winter rains, they wouldn't have the beautiful forests with the tallest trees in the world. Not everyone stayed; the first few major storms of the season weeded them out and sent them packing to sunnier, warmer parts of the state.

Paul was not born and raised in the forest he now called home. It grew on him like the moss that grew on the sides of the trees and shaded rocks. He learned to love the beauty and the magic of the redwood forest. He also learned to enjoy and appreciate the beauty and solitude of winter. Thus, when Fionna asked if he would escort her and her friend Mary back to the place she was found, the thought excited him. He too wanted to go back to what he was now calling the magical forest; there was much to investigate, much to learn.

His fellow ranger, Susan, led the group of four on what she was calling *The Quest*. The end of her ponytail hanging across the top of her green daypack shone in the low angle sunlight. Following closely behind her were Fionna and her friend Mary, the reasons they had returned to that part of the forest.

When Fionna first suggested that they go back to the place, the same place he encountered the voices and fairies, Paul didn't know what to say. He was still having difficulties placing his role in this strange adventure. *You're part of this, you know*, Fionna's voice echoed in his mind. *We must return to the forest as soon as possible. Once in the ancient forest, I will know what to do next. So many are counting on us!* Her plaintive tone and the excitement and sincerity with which his new friend spoke forced him to agree. She had been released from the hospital only the day before and he had to make special promises just to convince Fionna's mother to let her go on the trip. She was entrusted to his safety for a second time and now here they were. In a way he was glad he no longer smelled the flowers … orchids, heard the voices or saw the fairies. He wasn't so sure he wanted to experience any of them again.

When he spilled his guts to Susan that day in his office, he was surprised that she believed him but relieved that she did. Now, he wouldn't have to carry the burden on his own. As strange as it sounded, he slept better after that first visit with Fionna at the hospital. He never believed how powerful support and understanding were until that day.

Susan caught Paul looking at her. "What?" she yelled back to him.

Paul raised his hands into the air, "How lucky can we get?"

She playfully put her index finger up to her lips and then pointed towards the rays of sunlight. “Not so loud, they will hear you!” She gave him a wink and continued up the overgrown trail.

Paul smiled as he followed along, bringing up the rear. The grove was only a couple of miles and less than an hour away.

♦ ♦ ♦

Unlike their miserable, silent descent out of the mountains three weeks earlier, Mary and Fionna chattered away like the teenagers they were. While Paul and Susan talked about the mountains and their work, Mary and Fionna covered anything and everything with a lively, youthful bounce in their steps.

Mary was excited about being back in the mountains with her friend. When Fionna shared the incredible story of the mysterious mountain, she was skeptical at first but when Paul added his own experiences, she had no other choice but to believe. *How could two total strangers experience the same thing?* In a way, she almost felt cheated that she didn’t get to see, hear and or smell the mystery on her own. Her glance darted back and forth among the tops of the trees and into the dense growth of ferns, in search of anything unusual, as she walked, talked, and listened. If she acted like she was oblivious to everything around her, she thought, she would be sure to catch an off guard glimpse of whatever it was that lived in the forest. So far there was nothing. The closer they got to the mysterious grove, the more she found it harder to believe.

She heard the small birds scamper as the group cautiously approached, most likely the winter wrens that curiously followed them from the shadows. The more older snags and trees they found the more woodpeckers and flickers they saw. The hammering and calls of the pileated woodpeckers became louder and more common. She wondered if martens, a fox-like weasel thought to be either extinct or extremely rare, still inhabited this section of the forest. Only two sightings had been verified in these mountains over the last fifty years, a concept of time that to the teen seemed to be forever. Mary knew there were concerns that the ancient redwood forest ecosystem was endangered but, here in the park, those worries no longer seemed justified. Everything seemed as it should be, wild, dark and beautiful but she was glad she wasn't alone.

As she followed closely behind Fionna, Mary reflected on how strange the last three weeks had been. Fionna wasn't the same timid person she used to be. She now glowed with an aura of confidence and an abundant knowledge of fairies and the ancient forest. It was all weird but Fionna was still her best friend. As a matter of fact, their friendship had grown in the last three weeks, possibly a consequence of feeling she had lost her friend forever.

Fionna made her swear not to tell anyone what she was about to hear. She told her about her adventure in the canyon, her encounter with fairies, that she was fifth generation American Irish, that her Great, Great, Great, Grandmother had done the unthinkable. She had smuggled fairies into this country, into this forest. As far as she knew, they were watching her right then and there from the shadows. She found herself walking closer to Fionna, spending more time watching the surrounding forest than where she was placing her feet. She stumbled along and forced herself to talk and laugh. She had heard that fairies were mischievous and not trusting of humans, probably for good reason. History had not changed; man still tried to conquer everything. It was in his nature.

She smelled the air and let out a disappointed sigh. The rich organic aroma of the forest filled her lungs; the forest sounds filled her ears. So much she wanted to smell the flowers, to hear the voices, to see the creatures … to get a better understanding of what they were doing there. Her friend had never said exactly why, only that it was important that they came.

♦ ♦ ♦

"Susan, we need to stop here," Fionna said, her voice barely a whisper.

"What?" Susan panted as she suddenly stopped, looking back towards her and the rest of the group.

Fionna smiled, "We are at the edge." Her voice sounded sweet and excited.

"We're at the edge of the world!" Susan grumbled. "Beyond it lies smells and sounds from another realm that none of us seem to smell or hear." Her attempt at being funny fell on deaf ears. When no one laughed, she shrugged her shoulders and walked back towards Paul. "So what next … we're not even close to that grove!"

"She's calling the shots," Paul shrugged. "We have no choice but to believe."

"In fairy tails? I believe I'm a bit too old for that. So we're taking orders from an imaginative sixteen year old!"

"For the moment," Paul said.

Fionna took off her daypack, let it fall to the forest floor, closed her eyes and took in a deep breath. She tried to shut out the doubting voices of her friends. She really couldn't blame them; it was all so crazy, so different. She took in another breath, this one even deeper. To her delight, there it was, ever so faint. She breathed in again; this time it was more pronounced, more detectable. She looked back at everyone and smiled, her eyes sparkled with excitement. She was surprised to see them staring at her, wonder and curiosity notable across their faces.

"Well?" Susan asked, "What's up?"

"The flowers … they're back."

Fionna saw the doubt in Mary and Susan as they inhaled, turning their heads and moving around to improve their ability to smell. Moments later, disappointment spread across their faces as they shook their heads no. Fionna could tell that, despite Susan's sarcasm, they desperately wanted to believe; they really wanted to smell the flowers. "I'm sorry," she said and she was … sorry for them.

"I do smell the forest," Susan exclaimed as she wiped beads of sweat from her forehead with the back of her hand.

Fionna looked at Paul and was relieved when he smiled back. She knew that he also smelled the flowers. She returned the smile before she turned toward the forest, took a few steps farther down the path, sat down, closed her eyes and tilted her head back. She tried to eliminate all of the thoughts racing through her mind. She listened to the muted conversations of her friends' fade into the sound of her breath and the slow beating of her heart.

The voices appeared, faint at first like they always did, then they became clear. They were excited; they were close. She opened her eyes and searched the surrounding forest. The smell of the flowers was so sweet, she could almost taste it. She stood up, took a few more steps and stopped. She felt chilled, yet warm. The feeling was familiar; her eyes carefully searched the forest again. This time she saw something, the movement of a branch, and heard the buzzing of an insect among the winter forest sounds. She squinted into the rays of sunlight. She thought she saw a shadow dart behind the base of a huge tree. She felt warm all over. "I think they are here!" she whispered. She looked over her shoulder to see the others straining their eyes in the light.

Fionna turned back towards the forest, closed her eyes and listened. The voices spoke again. They thanked her for coming and shared their disappointment with her for bringing the two others.

"They are my friends … we will need their help," she protested, her voice barely audible to those behind her.

Just the two of ye', the voices whispered. *The weapons ar' scary an' dangerous … we will be waiting.*

As quickly as the voices came, they faded into the sounds of the forest. Fionna stood up and walked back to the others. She saw their curious stares. “They don’t like the guns,” she said in a soft voice. She stared off towards an old burned out snag. “They are really not needed here.”

“What?” Susan exclaimed annoyingly in a harsh whisper. “They? I’ve got news for you, we wear the guns!” Her voice rang of anger as she looked at Paul to reinforce her stand. “They are part of our ...” She stopped in her tracks when she saw Paul taking off his gun belt and stuffing it into his already full day pack. “What are you doing?”

Paul replied, “As I am asked … I think they will be fine in our packs. Think of this as an interpretive program.”

Susan stared a moment, trying to understand her partners irrational decision. She shook her head and started to take off her gun belt as well. “I sure hope you know what you are doing!”

“Me too!” Paul answered.

“Oh, that’s comforting!”

“They only want the two of us right now,” Fionna frowned. “Sorry Mary … Susan!” She shrugged. She read the disappointment on her friend’s face.

“What?” Susan looked up to see Paul handing her his heavy pack.

“It seems that the two of you will be staying here,” Paul was straightforward.

Both Susan and Mary protested.

“Please … you will get your chance soon enough,” Fionna pleaded.

Susan reluctantly snatched the pack. “Right! To protect and to serve!”

“Be back soon,” Paul said before he followed Fionna into the forest.

Susan looked on in disbelief as the two disappeared into the forest. "Did you smell, hear or see anything?" she asked Mary.

Mary shook her head. "I wish I had."

"Yeah, that goes for me too," Susan nodded. "Me too!"

Chapter Ten

Change of Heart

They sat in silent protest for what seemed nearly an hour, each deep in her own thoughts. They leaned back to back, facing in the opposite direction, a trick Susan learned long ago to make her stay in the forest more comfortable even though she sat head and shoulders above Mary. For the moment, neither of them really knew what to say to the other.

Both were still bothered by the fact that they were left behind to sit and wait. They ran the gamut of individual thoughts, each trying to put the mystery together. Although they were sitting in one of the most beautiful forests in the world, they no longer saw beauty; they saw only mystery and confusion.

When Mary looked down at her watch, it was 1:00 p.m.; they had been sitting there for less than ten minutes. It had taken the group almost three hours to hike there. The days were getting longer, which meant more light for their return trip. She reflected on her trip three weeks ago when this whole mess started … the rain, the wind, the darkness. When she looked up, she felt the warmth of the sunshine. The two worlds seemed so different; it was hard to believe they were in the same forest.

Then, there it was, faint at first, but stronger. It filled her nose, her throat and then her lungs. It felt sweet, comforting, and she was overwhelmed by a desire to follow.

"I can't believe it!" Mary exclaimed, overwhelmed with excitement. "Do you smell that?"

Susan shook her head, "Smell what?"

"It's the flowers. I smell the flowers!" Mary jumped to her feet and turned in the direction Paul and Fionna had disappeared.

Susan had to catch her balance to keep from rolling backwards. "Now you, too! What's with this flower stuff?"

Mary snatched up her and Fionna's pack, slung both of their straps over each shoulder, and started to walk quickly into the forest.

"What in the … where are you going?" Susan quizzed.

"That way!" She answered with a nod of her head and a quick gesture of her hand. "I have to follow! I think I'm supposed to follow!"

Susan scrambled to her feet and dusted off the seat of her pants with her hands. "Then, that is the way we need to go." She effortlessly snatched up her and Paul's pack. "Lead the way!"

Mary smiled, turned and walked briskly in the direction of the aromatic flowers. Breathing heavily, heart pounding in her chest, she tried to fight her excitement.

♦ ♦ ♦

Fionna zigzagged through the forest as she followed the concentrated aroma of incredible flowers. Paul followed in amazement. His throat was dry and his fingers tingled. He could feel that they were getting closer but to what he wasn't quite sure. When Fionna stopped, it was only long enough to catch her breath and to refine her direction of travel.

She never looked back, only stared straight ahead. She looked so small compared to the trees. This section of the forest seemed untouched by fire and landslides; it was virginal and pure. The deeply grooved bark and immense size spoke of the trees' age. They lacked blackened fire scars that told of a dramatic past. Traveling through the grove was like traveling back into time. He heard the woodpeckers, the ravens, and the distant sound of the creek. He saw small shadows darting through the tree tops and dense ground cover. He wanted to write off the shadows as birds but he knew better. He had seen those fleeting silhouettes before. They now seemed to mirror his every movement. He couldn't tell if they were there to guide, to follow and observe, or to stop them from entering. He didn't get the warm welcoming feeling he expected. For the first time, he became nervous and feared for his and Fionna's safety. He instinctively felt for the butt of his handgun and then suddenly remembered he had left his holster and his pack with Susan, a decision he now regretted.

Paul didn't recognize the landscape; it was unlike any section he had seen before. He looked over his shoulder to memorize patterns in the terrain but, to his surprise, everything looked the same. He purposely broke the ends of the fronds and thrust the toes and heels of his boots into the ground cover to leave signs. Then, the sudden, familiar chill overwhelmed him, like he was being stalked, pursued by an unseen predator in the shadows. He looked towards Fionna and knew he wasn't alone in feeling things just weren't right; she was having the same concerns.

He had no idea what they were going to find in the shadows. He heard the echo of voices and saw the flashes of what looked like several more small birds paralleling their route and encouraging them on. There appeared to be even more shadows paralleling them than before.

Fionna traveled with a sense of purpose until she looked back over her shoulder towards Paul, abruptly changed direction, tripped and fell. She rolled across the ground and came to rest flat on her back, panting heavily.

When she didn't get up right away, Paul hurried over to her. He was surprised to see her staring wide-eyed and speechless into the upper canopy directly above them, her eyes filled with fear and wonder as they fixed on something high above their heads. All she could do was slowly raise her hand into the air and point. She let out a gasp he could barely hear. He didn't need to understand the words to know what they meant. They had visitors.

Paul felt it too, a nervous tingle plus a sudden surge of impending doom, numbness about his fingers and toes. He didn't have to look up to know they were being watched, surrounded. He could feel it. Its presence was all around. He was almost afraid to look up.

♦ ♦ ♦

"Slow down, girl!" Susan panted as she struggled along. "This isn't a race, you know!" The two packs no longer seemed light; the weight of the gun belts, batons, radios and extra rounds over each shoulder were wearing her down. "Can we at least walk fast instead of jog? Have mercy on a middle aged woman," she whined.

Mary heard her complain, but felt the compulsion to hurry. She didn't know how long the smell of the flowers would last. She didn't know if it was a warning or an invitation to join. All she knew was that her thoughts translated it as a request to follow.

"We need to catch up," she panted.

"Yes, but the need isn't that great. They can take care of themselves!"

Mary ignored her and continued at a brisk pace; she figured they would be running into the rest of their group at any moment.

"Maybe I didn't explain myself very well. Mary, slow down!" Susan commanded.

Mary stopped for a moment to catch her breath. Her chest heaved as she panted heavily. She slid the packs off her shoulders. Once her load was lightened, she noticed the soreness in her legs and shoulders. Susan plopped ungracefully, with packs and all, onto the forest floor. Once on the ground, she lay on her back with her knees bent as she gasped for air. "I'm getting too old for this!" Susan panted. She looked towards Mary, "Thanks! You don't know what this means to me!"

Mary nodded, "Sorry I pushed the pace, I couldn't help it …"

"I know … the flowers!"

Mary nodded, "Don't you smell them?"

Susan shook her head. "I wish I did, but … I'm more concerned … about breathing right now! I wish … I understood what this was all about."

Mary looked in the direction of the forest and listened. She heard the distinct *caw* of a raven echo from above. She looked up to see a pair fly overhead, the air whistling through their wing tips as they weaved in and out of the trees. She knew the call was for them. It was like, *we see you*, and then they continued on their way, disappearing from sight. She liked ravens; they stayed for the winters, not letting a little rains chase them away. She listened to their wing beats fade into the forest and heard the final distant *caw;* this time she could imagine them saying, *goodbye … good luck*!

The hammering of a woodpecker on a tree echoing nearby drew her focus. *Pileated woodpecker* traced her memory. They were the birds of the ancient forest. The biggest woodpecker on the west coast. The bright red feathers on the tops of their heads found their way into the traditional regalia of the local First Nations.

Listening to the forest and the distant breeze reminded her of why she liked coming here in the winter.

"Is that the creek I hear?" Susan asked as she sat up and looked around. She swiveled her head in an attempt to determine from which direction the sound was coming.

"I thought it was the wind!"

"Nahhh … it's the creek, I'm sure of it!" Susan said knowingly. She climbed to her feet, cupped her hands behind her ears to improve her hearing and slowly spun around in a 360-degree circle. She stopped halfway through her second circle and nodded. "There, the creek's that way."

"How do you know?"

"Years of training and lots of luck!" Susan laughed uncomfortably, "And …"

She stopped, wrinkled her eyebrows and her mouth dropped open.

Mary noticed something was different about Susan's behavior. "What's wrong?" she asked, staring in the direction Susan was looking.

"It's in the same direction as the flowers," Susan spoke softly. "I smell the flowers … I really do smell the flowers!" Her voice rose to an excited pitch. She started to give Mary a hug but quickly turned it into a firm grip on both of her shoulders.

"So, what are we waiting for," Susan said. "Time's a wasting, we're not getting any younger."

The faint sound of a yell broke the forest silence.

They looked at each other, each of them heard it. Without saying a word, they grabbed their things and sprinted in the direction of the voice. Mary felt an urgency to hurry and she knew Susan felt the same.

Chapter Eleven

Position in the Circle

Paul forced himself to look up slowly. Nothing could prepare him for what he was about to see. He caught a flash of what appeared to be shiny, translucent wings. His ears funneled what sounded like a half dozen robin sized hummingbirds revving up for flight as they positioned around him. He snapped his head in their direction. He felt chilled to the bone. "My Goodness, look at them!" escaped from his lungs in a coarse whisper. He slowly stood up straight and turned to face the closest one.

They hovered a few feet closer, squaring off as if preparing for a fight, then abruptly stopped. In the updraft of their wing beats, their long white hair waved above their oversized pointy ears. Their big eyes looked angry, their weathered faces stern, their tiny chest and arm muscles rippled under their skin-like suits. They wore rough, fibrous looking pants and sandal-type shoes.

Paul was speechless. He opened his mouth, but nothing came out. His legs and arms felt heavy, his head dizzy. Fear was the only feeling he recognized. He suddenly felt as if they were somewhere they should never have been. He tried to give a warning cry to Fionna but his voice no longer worked. His mind no longer seemed to function; it was shutting down. He knew he was succumbing to fear.

One of the angered figures uttered something; Paul recognized the language as Irish. Against the seeming protest of a few of the others, the figures dove towards Paul's face with lightning fast speed. Paul reacted quickly by stepping backwards out of the way and waving his arms as if he were shooing away a barrage of angry hornets. His movement tumbled him backward over the top of Fionna and then into the surrounding ferns. He rolled back onto his feet, assuming a fighting stance, his hands clutched tightly into fists. He gasped for breath and moved closer to Fionna. He felt supercharged as the adrenaline flowed through his body. He swiveled his head and turned in anticipation of the next attack.

He heard eerie dwarfish laughter and turned to face another that attempted to charge. Two more moved in to meet the challenge. He suddenly felt surrounded by a pack of bullies looking for a little afternoon fun. Paul felt another surge of adrenaline as he tried to meet the next challenge. He couldn't believe it; angry fairies were attacking him in the middle of the ancient forest.

"*Ní hea* (nee hah) … No!" a loud, reverberating voice echoed among the trees. "Ye' ar' te' leave them be. Now!"

The fairies stopped in their tracks and gazed angrily back in the direction of the voice, their looks unnerving. It was then that he realized that there was an even mix of graceful looking males and females.

Both he and Fionna followed their gaze.

Fionna slowly rose to her feet and stepped forward. "It is them!" she whispered.

"I see why I was asked not to bring my handgun; there would be a few less of these pests around right now!" Paul mumbled to Fionna, as he watched the reluctant fairies widen the circle around them as if almost in response to his threat. Their angry eyes never left the two humans. Paul reached up and rested a hand on Fionna's shoulder to prevent her from moving too far away from his side.

A silver bearded fairy, larger than the others, flew out from behind a tree and hovered above a huge, moss covered log. He was dressed like the others but had added a long sleeveless coat made of fibrous redwood bark, which hung to his knobby knees like a medium sized skirt. With his pudgy arms across his chest, the curious creature looked them up and down for a moment before gently landing on the mossy portion of the nearby log. He stepped out of his sandals and dug his oversized toes into the dark green moss with a sigh. He then stuck out his chest, folded his hands behind his back and let his opalescent, delicate wings droop.

Paul blinked as if he were in a dream but nothing had changed; it was all still there. It was for real. His hands still balled into fists, his stance still bladed.

"*Tá fáfilte romhat go hÉirinn (taw fawl che row-at go-hay-run)*," the little creature said joyfully in his Gaelic accent. "Welcome te' me' Ireland." The little old man bowed deeply.

His voice reminded Paul of that of the munchkins in *The Wizard of Oz*. He fought back a confused smile.

"*Táim buíoch díot (taw-im bwee-ukh jee-ut)* … I am grateful to ye."

Fionna gracefully returned the greeting with a curtsey, genuflecting nod of her own and then took a few steps closer, slipping out of Paul's stunned grip.

Paul stumbled along to stay with her. "You speak and understand Irish?" he asked in a surprised voice.

She ignored him.

"I am sorry fer ye troubles," the elder fairy gestured to the younger ones that now busied themselves a short distance away.

A few of the others still gave the two suspicious glares with most of their attention focused on Paul.

"Yes, I know, not all fairies are good," Fionna said. "Many are mischievous … most don't like humans." She directed her comment to Paul without taking her eyes off of the diminutive creature on the log in front of her.

"No kidding," Paul mumbled under his breath. He felt drained. "Who would think something so small could be so, so … dangerous!"

"Dangerous, ar' we," laughed the miniature man.

Some of the other fairies joined in with the forced laughter at Paul's expense.

Paul glared back at them. "Evidently, they understand English just fine," Paul whispered to Fionna without taking his eyes off the others.

The elder fairy quieted the others with a wave of his stubby hand and then flew slowly to within a couple feet of Paul's face. He looked deeply into his eyes as if searching for something.

The old fairy's actions surprised Paul. He flinched and he found himself moving backwards, his hands brought closer to his own face.

The group laughed again.

"An Éireannach thú (un ayr-un-ukh hoo)? Ar' ye' Irish?" the oldest fairy asked.

"Yes, he is," Fionna answered.

"Is that so?" The old man laughed and gestured his hands to the rest of the group. "Sea (shah), yes, as quiet as a cat he is!"

The others laughed heartily.

Paul glared in the direction of the laughter. He was getting quite tired of the arrogance of these little creatures.

"Sea (shah) yes, but as bold as a lion I see," the older fairy whispered with a heavy Gaelic accent.

Paul snapped a quick glance back in his direction. *Was that a compliment*, he wondered. He nodded appreciatively, surprised by what he had just heard.

"Séamus is ainm dom (an-um dum) … my name is Séamus (Shay-mus); I am the fairy leader in this here forest." He gestured his hands at the surrounding trees.

Paul started to give his name but was cut off by a wave of the aging fairy's hand.

"We know who ye' ar,' Mr. Behaan!" he raised an eyebrow at Paul.

Paul gave him a strange look.

"The likes of ye' ar' nothing new te' this here ancient forest. It isn't by chance that ye' ar' here."

Paul's thoughts flashed back to his many visits to the ancient groves, his mind searching the shadows for a familiar form. *Had these swift darting creatures been mistaken for birds?*

The old fairy flew backward towards the log and gracefully floated down on to the delicate moss. He took another deep sigh as he wiggled his toes in the moss. "Ye' ar' here te' protect the forest," he stated, watching Paul closely.

Paul nodded. He didn't know what else to say. He still had trouble believing that all of this was really happening.

"Ye' ar' a guardian of the forest, by choice, ar' ye' now? Ye' may think ye' hav' chosen this profession of yer's. But ye' ar' wrong!" He paused a moment to let his words sink in. "'tis has chosen ye'." He laughed. "In a strange sort of way, ye speak fer' the trees." He gestured again to the surrounding forest.

Paul looked around and saw that the other fairies no longer looked aggressive; they were hanging on the elder's every word. They no longer hovered in a defensive circle. Some sat on logs; others sat down on low-lying branches.

"We hav' lived here fer' many years. We hav' done what we can. Now we need yer' help."

Paul could feel all of the little creatures peering down at him.

"We hav' a plan and we need the both of ye' te' carry it out," he continued. "Ye' humans continue te' cut down the ancient trees like there is no tomorrow and there may not be; very soon, the only ancient trees tha' will be left will be in parks an' preserves. That will not be enough!" His voice exploded in anger, "These magnificent groves ar' shrinking te' only remnants of what they once were. Ye' must understand … they ar'n't just trees!" His voice became passionate. "They make an' filter the air we breathe." He tightened his stubby fingers into a fist, "They hold the fog that drifts in from the ocean. They create their own weather, ye' know. Of course, ye' know! When ye' remove the ancient trees, the moisture disappears, it becomes dry, it affects the weather … it loses the very thing tha' keeps them here."

Paul knew well enough that the old fairy was right. People needed the timber, *but did they really need to harvest the 400 year old trees?* Concerned people attempted to pass bills through the legislature to protect the ancient trees on private lands but even if it worked, would it be enough? Even if they only harvested trees less than 300 year old, some day in the future, the ancient trees would eventually give in to gravity and topple to the forest floor. With no replacements, the ancient forest would cease to exist. A variety of aged trees, including younger trees as replacement trees, required protection. It would be the only way to preserve the ancient ecosystem, to have aging trees forever on lands other than public lands.

Only two percent of the ancient coastal redwood forest ecosystem, of its original range of two million acres, remained in public trust. Fewer than that remained in private hands. To accomplish protection, there would have to be a major change in timber harvesting philosophy. Large area clear-cutting, the taking down of all the trees in one section and the problems associated with it, would have to become a thing of the past. On the other hand, areas that had once been cleared for farms hundreds of years ago were being reclaimed by the forest. If left alone for a couple of hundred years, they would take on the characteristics of ancient forests. A proven fact that there was always hope.

The weather in the coastal mountains was already changing. Paul noticed over the last couple of years that the summers looked and felt drier, that the trees looked more stressed by late August than they used to look by late September. Even though they had normal rainfall, the rivers were running low. Some of the old timers claimed they had never seen the rivers this low before. The ground water wasn't being replenished properly. Paul had observed an increase in clear-cutting surrounding the north coast parks. No one had any idea of what was happening; could they dare tie the timber harvest into the changing weather patterns. He had friends in the timber industry … he had friends who were environmentalists. Was he now going to have to choose between his friends and the trees?

"If the humans could only realize the importance of these ancient trees … the power these trees hav'... their ability te' heal the mind, heart an' soul! Sea (shah) yes, would they look at them differently?"

He directed his speech to Paul.

"I would like to think so," Paul stammered. "Given a good enough reason not to cut them down might do the trick but it would have to be worth their while financially. They run a business and can't afford to leave the best of their timber standing because we ask them to. They need a greater incentive."

"Greed! Humans hav' not changed," grumped the elder fairy.

"Doesn't mean they can't or won't," Paul said.

The old fairy looked at the others and then back to Paul and Fionna; he wrinkled his eyebrows as if he had a secret to share. "What if they wer' convinced that by leaving the ancient trees standing, they could heal their bodies, minds an' souls."

Paul looked anxiously at Fionna, “What do you mean?”

The fairy pushed his toes carefully through the moss before he answered, “Tis’ tha’ simple, some of the ancient trees ar’ endowed with power. When they ar’ no longer attached te’ this earth, their powers an’ energies ar’ shared with those who ar’ left. With each passing of an ancient redwood, the remaining trees become stronger, more powerful … powerful enough te’ heal.”

Paul shook his head. It was all too much. Fairies in an ancient redwood forest … trees that could heal!

“Ye’ think those flowers ye’ smell ar’ from us? Ní hea (nee hah), no,” Séamus shook his head and gestured his hands towards the forest. “It is the trees that call ye’ te’ service. We ar’ only here te’ protect them. Ye’ see, we need each other.”

Paul gave him a stunned look; he again felt overwhelmed.

“Sea (shah), yes,” Séamus nodded, “ye’, the trees hav’ called us into service, one we cannot fail. I believe ye’ will find what ye’ ar’ looking for over there.” He pointed his weathered hand in a direction that paralleled the creek. “An’ so, it has finally come te’ this!”

Paul could smell the flowers. He sensed the sadness in the aging voice. The reluctant creature was being forced to do something he never thought he would ever have to do, being forced to work with humans. The trail secreted information that only fairies knew … all of this was in the park where he worked. Myths and legends ran deep in the park folklore. Voices, moving shadows, balls of light, legendary Bigfoot and fairies, none of it taken seriously. *Boy … were they ever wrong*!

“I will truly miss these simple pleasures tha’ the ancient forests hav’ shared with an old fairy’s tired feet!” Séamus added as he gently stepped back into his sandals.

Both Paul and Fionna followed his gaze. Before them lay a deer path through the towering ferns and the clover-like sorrel. The sound of the creek reverberated off the huge trees.

"Why do it?" Paul blurted out, his voice breaking the calm silence.

"Paul!" Fionna stared at him in disbelief.

The fairy elder turned and focused on Paul. The wrinkles ran deep around his eyes and across his face. They reminded Paul of the growth rings of an ancient tree. At that moment the creature that stood before him had more in common with the ancient forest than he could even imagine.

"Why would you do this?" Paul asked again, this time his voice calm.

"Te' save what remains … te' protect the future fer' all." He gestured to the forest with both hands. "This is a special forest...it holds the power te' heal the mind, body, an' soul."

Paul looked around but all he could see were the usual huge trees, giant ferns, and lush ground cover. He heard the babbling of the creek. Somewhere a distant woodpecker hammered against an old snag in search of a meal. The air smelled of the moist forest but also the mysterious flowers that he had once thought belonged to fairies. Paul pieced together the fairy's response and reviewed the chain of events that drew him to the forest. The health of the forest meant the health of mankind. Despite what people might think, one could not live without the other; they were tied together with delicate threads. As the size of the ancient forest shrank, so did the magic of being in and among them. He still felt the magic; he knew it was here. It was here that many came to escape their problems and worries; it was here that they satisfied the primal need for solitude and the self-reflection that only a wilderness could provide. It was also here where some people came to take their lives and end it all. It had not been that long ago when man had looked at places like these in a much different light, with reverence, fear, and a desire to understand.

The fairies knew and in desperation they turned for help to the very species that was destroying it. It was an honor and an incredible responsibility that had been entrusted to them.

The fairy gazed tenderly at Fionna and gestured down the deer trail.

"Follow the path, 'twill take ye' te' what ye' ar' looking fer'."

Fionna looked into the shadows.

The fairy fluttered its delicate wings and rose above the moss-covered log. "Ye' know what ye' need te' do … ye're Great, Great, Great Grandmother would be so proud." The fairy smiled.

Fionna nodded.

"May the luck of the Irish be with the two of ye' an' yer' friends! We'll be around!" The elderly fairy winked, "Visitors!" He nodded in the direction of the oncoming noise.

A sound of crunching debris under foot was abruptly coming their way and when they turned around, the fairies were gone.

Chapter Twelve

Seeing is Believing

A loud voice echoed through the shadows of the trees from the direction of the creek.

Susan grabbed Mary's shoulder and stopped her. "That scream was close!" Mary pulled away and sprinted in the direction of the sound. Susan followed. Mary's heart pounded in her chest. The scream sounded as if it had come from just around the next bend.

After about a dozen steps down the narrow path, a bird-sized shadow streaked noisily in their direction. They leaped out of the way to dodge the blurred figure as it went streaming past, unwilling to yield an inch. Mary held her breath as she fell on her hands and knees, almost tripping over the cumbersome daypacks.

As they threw themselves out of its way, their eyes followed the silhouette into the shadows. Its buzzing sound faded into the sounds of the forest; Mary couldn't believe what she had just seen.

Susan was the first to break the uneasy silence, "Did you see … what I thought I saw?"

They fixed on the location where they had last seen it, neither willing to turn her head. The adventurous part of Mary wanted it to come back, to reappear, but the rest of her wanted it to go away. "What do you think you saw?" Mary's voice cracked. She couldn't believe it either. She was sure it wasn't a bird because it had a face, arms and legs.

"I'm not sure," Susan whispered, "but I know it wasn't a bird … at least not one that I'm familiar with. Somehow I don't think it's on the park's bird list! This is too weird … let's get moving before we see something else we're going to have to try to explain. Frankly, I don't think you really want to know what I'm thinking. Jeez! I don't even want to know what I'm thinking."

Mary saw the concern and confusion etched across Susan's face. Her hands tingled and her heart pounded in her chest. She was feeling spooked, big time.

"Come on!" Susan said as she turned and continued to jog in the direction she thought they needed to go. Her voice contained an urgency that neither wanted to talk about.

Mary followed closely behind. They took turns glancing over their shoulders as they crashed through the ferns and weaved around the huge trees and downed logs. She really didn't want to see whatever that was again.

Two minutes later, they heard muffled conversation and Paul's familiar voice. They picked up their pace. Mary suddenly felt a great desire to be with the others; safety in numbers was all she could think about, maybe Fionna could explain what it was she just saw.

Just as they barged onto the edge of a small clearing, they saw two more of the bird-sized silhouettes dart noisily off to the side and disappear into the shadows. Neither of them stopped to take a second look; they already knew the figures were exactly like the one they saw earlier.

Mary was relieved when she saw both Fionna and Paul standing next to a huge log. She leaned forward and crashed noisily in their direction, fighting the urge to call their names. Even if she wanted to, she couldn't; she was panting heavily, struggling to breathe.

When Mary and Susan reached the group, they dropped their packs and bent over, gasping for breath. Their eyes searched the shadows.

Paul and Fionna stared at them.

"You found us!" Fionna exclaimed happily.

Regaining her composure, Susan could no longer wait; she wanted answers. "What on earth is going on around here? People that look like birds. Birds that look like people that force you off the trails! The forest smells like flowers! I believe the two of you have some explaining to do!"

"You smelled the flowers?" Fionna asked.

"Yeah, yeah, yeah, I smell the flowers …" Susan looked at Fionna and forced a smile and then returned her pointed gaze to Paul. "What's up with this?" She panted.

"Congratulations, welcome to the club," Paul gestured his arms towards the surrounding forest. "You are now members of an elite club that's current human enrollment stands at four but the forest membership is yet to be determined."

Susan stood up, put her hands on her hips and looked around, her anger turning to confusion.

"Did you see them?" Fionna asked Mary.

Mary gave her a blank stare.

"The fairies … did you see the fairies," her voice quivered with excitement.

Mary felt a strange tremor start at her neck and worm its way down her spine and into her feet, immediately followed by a tingling sensation in her toes. "Fairies?" The confused words tumbled from her parched throat.

"Yep! And they need our help!" Fionna announced.

"Oh, that's good; for a moment there I thought you said that a bunch of fairies needed our help!" Susan's sarcastic humor relayed her nervousness. "Because we all know, that *Fairies*," she accented the word, "are a figment of someone's imagination … mythological creatures created to keep good little Irish boys and girls honest and well behaved."

"So we thought …" Paul said, his voice sincere. "But evidently there is a little bit of truth to it."

"A little bit!" Susan exclaimed as she pointed to the shadows. "Ahhhh … holy cow, I can't believe this!" She pushed her fingers through the front of her hair and closed her eyes for a moment before she spoke again.

Mary watched Susan's expressions alter through the phases of understanding, first disbelief, denial and then acceptance.

"So," Susan asked, "what is it that we need to do and why?"

Mary listened intently as Paul explained all that had taken place over the last few weeks. He recapped how they had been selected and why. And that the smell of the flowers came from the trees that had asked for their help. It made sense. The trees couldn't move to protect themselves so this chosen few were to become their arms and legs. As a child, Mary had believed that unicorns were real and that she had the power to catch one. She still remembered the devastating day she was told that there were no such things, that they were the stuff of fairy tales made up to entertain little boys and girls.

Evidently, fairies weren't real either! And if all of this were really happening, then … maybe unicorns were possible … a strange chill rippled through her every muscle as her thoughts ran wild. She envisioned herself riding through the trees mounted on the white horned beast. Then, as quickly as the first, another dark, unsettled feeling drifted in. *What about witches, goblins and trolls? If fairies indeed existed, then so could they!* She found herself glaring uncomfortably into the shadows. She struggled to pull her thoughts back to the subject of ancient trees and the fact that they had been chosen for a quest.

Chapter Thirteen

The Ancient Tree

The aromatic flowers overwhelmed Fionna. She couldn't take her eyes off the inviting rays of light that angled down from the upper canopy; they danced in the mist as they illuminated the narrow trail, giving the surroundings a storybook beauty. It was like they had been dropped into a chapter of *Grimm's Fairytales*.

The path threaded itself through huge sword and chain ferns as it weaved past gigantic downed logs and the occasional snag, indicating that the ancient grove wasn't invincible. Like her's, the tree's lives were finite. Even though the coastal redwood could live to be over 2,000 years old under the right conditions, the average age in most ancient groves was about 600 years. The majority of these trees were huge at the base and almost deformed looking towards their tops. Their multiple branches clawed at the sky like thick, weathered fingers. High above their heads, the branches were big enough to support a city of fairies. Periodically sticking out of the ground fallen, branchless trees, some as much as two foot in diameter, protruded ten feet out of the lush growth like skeletons. It took her a moment to realize that they were branches that had fallen from the tops of the huge trees and embedded themselves deeply into the ground. Broken free by the powerful winds, not much different than those they experienced that stormy night. The thought gave her a chill.

Thickly louvered cinnamon colored bark spiraled up the length of the trees. Their bases grew extremely thick and bulky as if the trees had created their own burls to have a place to sit. In some places, fires of long ago had darkened the richly colored bark, turning sections into charcoal that still blackened hands and clothes if touched. On others, the fires had eaten into the living trees leaving dark caves at their bases, now used as homes for bats, hibernating bears and a multitude of other creatures. At first glance, the fire scars could be thought of as recent but after a closer look, there were obvious signs of healing. The bark was growing back over the scars. Time had healed the forest. She wondered if time would heal the forest again but suddenly felt saddened when she realized that time was actually working against them. Time was what the trees were running out of. Based on the number of giant logs she had seen strapped to the trailers of logging trucks, she could only guess that the increase in the cutting of the ancient coastal redwood trees was signaling the end of the major groves outside of the protection of parks. She felt the urgency of what they had been asked to do.

She no longer heard Paul's voice; she hadn't since her mind drifted off into the forest. At the far end of the clearing, the rays were shining brightest on a huge twisted tree about a hundred yards away, soaring behind a mammoth of a downed log. To the right, a deer trail led them around the edges of a fern-lined pond that had once been the root hole of the downed log blocking their way.

The late afternoon sunlight glowed golden brown around its edges. She could feel its inviting warmth. *That's it!* The flowers smelled the strongest in that direction. The thought made her feel good. She pushed the unnerving thoughts out of her mind.

Without saying a word, she turned and started walking towards the trees. She had momentarily forgotten about the others; all she could focus on was the tree.

"Where is she going?" Mary pointed to Fionna's departing figure.

Paul sighed, "Get your stuff, evidently the bus is leaving."

Susan handed Paul his pack. "It's about time. I'm glad someone knows where she is going," she said as she prepared to follow Fionna, Mary in tow.

Paul stared into the shadows of the ancient forest, trying to capture the essence of the moment. He shrugged, tossed his pack over his shoulder and followed the others.

Fionna followed the deer path to the right as it skirted the edge of the small pond and curved to the left, following the length of the log as it braced through a gauntlet of colossal ferns. Warmth flowed through her as she approached the gigantic tree. The ferns at its base glowed with golden hues. The moisture in the air danced in the beams of sunlight. The aroma of flowers was sweeter than ever.

"You are the one," she whispered only loud enough for herself to hear. At ten yards away, she stopped, dropped to the seat of her pants on a bare patch of moist duff and stared up at the tree. Its base stretched up into a ceiling of green. As her eyes scanned the trunk all the way into the upper canopy, the width seemed unchanged. She strained her ears in the winter silence and listened for the sound of water. Moments later she heard it. The sound of drips coming from the tree. She felt the tingle of success.

Susan stopped behind her and dropped her pack to the forest floor.

"It's so … beautiful," Susan whispered loudly enough for Fionna to hear.

Fionna turned to meet Susan's surprised gaze, "This is the one … this is the tree we were supposed to find."

Mary and Paul abruptly braked behind Susan as if there were an invisible line drawn in front of them. Each smiled and exchanged glances as if they had discovered a magical place. Fionna was overcome with peaceful happiness.

"This is the place," she whistered, suppressing a giggle. "This is why we are here."

"To stare at this tree?" Susan had lost little of her cynicism. "I do have to admit this place is well worth the trip … look at that thing. Now, that is one gnarly-looking old tree!"

"Fionna, how do you know this one is the special tree?" Mary inquired as she shifted her gaze around the forest. "They all look special … and incredibly huge."

"Yes, they are all special but this one even more so. This is the one that has the power to heal. This is the one with the gift."

"The sweetness … it *is* the strongest here," Paul added.

Fionna could hear the satisfaction in Paul's voice. They all stared at the tree.

"Water is dripping from its bark," Paul exclaimed as he walked towards the tree. After a couple of steps, he stopped and looked over his shoulder towards the forest.

Fionna knew what he was looking for; she could still feel their presence. The fairies were watching them, hidden in the shadows. They didn't completely trust the humans and probably never would. She couldn't blame them; history was fresh in their minds. "Yes, that is the essence of life," she said, without really knowing how she knew. "That is what we are bringing back to the children."

"In the Children's Ward?" Paul whispered.

She nodded.

"Why?"

"They are very sick … this will make them better."

Paul looked at Susan and then back towards the tree.

Susan shrugged her shoulders.

"You saw those children," Fionna continued, sympathetically. "Don't you think those children deserve a second chance?" She pointed to the tree, "This is all part of *their* plan."

Paul walked to the edge of the deformed base, squatted on the back of his heels and held the palms of his hands a few feet away as if he were warming himself by a fire. He carefully watched the streaks of clear liquid that reflected the afternoon sunlight as they ran down the side of the tree. The small droplets grew in size and sparkled as they accumulated along the edge of a piece of bark that curved out away from the tree. When the drops lost their battle with gravity, they dripped down into an indented bowl-like growth in the burl-like wood at the base with an audible thud. "So, this is what we're here for," he solemnly announced.

"Yes, this is what we need to take back."

"You mean, we hiked all the way out here for some droplets of water that accumulate on a tree!" Susan quipped. "I think I saw a couple of trees a few dozen miles back that way that probably would have worked just fine." She motioned her thumb over her shoulder in the direction they had come.

"Evidently, this isn't just any tree," Mary jumped in. "Smell!" She took a deep breath. "This is the only one that smells like the Garden of Eden."

Susan also inhaled deeply and held the breath in her lungs for a moment before she slowly let it out. "I guess you're right!" She smiled.

"These trees are more special than you will ever know. This tree has the power to heal. We're here to save the ancient trees," Fionna lectured. "But first, we need to save the children in the hospital."

"Like I'm constantly trying to tell our environmental friends I run into, these trees are already protected," Susan chimed in. "They don't need to be sat in, chained up, or spiked with nails. They are protected within the boundaries of the parks."

"Not all of them!" Mary protested.

"There are still ancient ones, just like this one on private lands." Fionna agreed, the desperation obvious in her voice. "They will soon be cut down if we don't do anything. You see, only a few remaining trees like this one have the power to heal. It's the essence of life that the tree so freely gives that we will take back to the hospital." Fionna felt determination building within her as she looked back to Paul for confirmation and strength.

Both Mary and Susan followed her gaze to Paul.

Paul nodded.

"Unbelievable," Susan whined. "She seems to have you boondoggled, too. Rain water from an old tree will save the world … unbelievable!" Susan walked over and stood next to Paul.

"And the flowers," Paul nodded to the droplets, "how do you account for the smell?"

Susan knelt and placed her cupped hands, palm up, under the path of the next droplet. Everyone silently watched in anticipation of something special.

Fionna heard the droplets of water hit Susan's palm. Immediately, Susan jerked her hand away and stared at it in disbelief.

"My goodness!" Susan exclaimed as she stepped away from the tree and plopped down onto the forest floor.

"What's wrong?" Paul's asked as he moved to Susan's side.

"It isn't just water, is it?" she murmured as she held out her hand. "It tingles! It's very, very strange!"

They all stared in awe and disbelief at Susan and the ancient tree. Fionna developed a lump in her throat as she suddenly realized the importance of the quest on which they were about to embark. She knew that, from that moment on, there was no turning back. Many hopes were resting on their shoulders. She strained her ears, for a moment, she thought she heard the trees chatting in the gentle breeze.

Act 5: Remedy

Chapter Fourteen

The Hospital Visit

When Paul arrived at the double doors to the Children's Ward, he sighed audibly. His legs and feet would go no further. When he reached out for the door, his arm suddenly felt heavy, his shoulders sore, his throat and mouth dry.

He felt as if he were in a place he should not be and one more step would force him down a path of no return. The struggle between right and wrong dominated his restless nights and left his mind weary and unsettled. *They needed to do the right thing but were they doing the right thing?* Thoughts screamed in his head.

Only the day before, all four of them had found the ancient tree that would change everything. They collected the fluid that dripped from its ancient bark with a glass vial and packed it carefully into his pack. He remembered Susan's reaction when she first touched it, her sudden belief and support of what they had been asked to do. He couldn't resist the temptation to touch it himself. He remembered his surprise, the incredible warmth and tingly sensation it brought to his hand and arm. Then, there were the fairies … the fairies, the minuscule mythical creatures of children's stories. Even they were depending on the humans to succeed. *Were they trying to play God?* The thought was forced … it felt wrong. *Or were they instruments?*

Then, there were the children. They would be given a second chance at life that had dealt them a tough hand. *How could that be wrong … how could it be wrong to give these children a second chance! But what if the liquid merely worsened their condition, hastened their end? What if … the force they assumed to good was really evil? What if …* At that moment, it came together. He was doing the right thing. He hadn't worn his park uniform; today, he was like everyone else but *special* because he had been given the opportunity to make a difference. He felt Fionna's gentle touch on his shoulder.

"Is everything okay," she softly whispered.

Her green eyes revealed soft, tender concern. There were many things he wanted to say to her but they would have to wait. Instead, he gave her an encouraging wink, "Couldn't be better." Paul felt a strange relief. His legs no longer felt like lead, his shoulders no longer sore, but his throat remained dry. He was crossing ground he never dreamed he would.

Fionna patted her purse. The sound of glass against glass echoed loudly in Paul's ears. He looked around to see if anyone had noticed but the hospital personnel didn't give them a second look. They continued to scurry back and forth like squirrels scrounging goodies for the winter.

What Fionna had wrapped in the bottom of her bag was going to change the lives of so many. If this really worked, within a week, the hospital would be in chaos; specialists would be called in; the media would be swarming around the patients and staff alike. They would ask questions, scrutinize the sign-in logs, search for the miracle cures and choose the easiest answers for situations they couldn't explain.

As he pushed open the double doors of the Children's Ward,

Paul heard the theme song from Barney, the purple dinosaur. It seemed to match the dinosaur prints on the walls, the love they carried with them and the unusual world of magical cures they were about to enter.

To his left, halfway down the hall, a woman sat on a couch thumbing through a magazine, oblivious to their arrival. Bobby, the same little boy he met before, sat next to her, wearing Ninja Turtle pajamas and slippers. Their first meeting suddenly seemed so long ago.

Bobby looked up and turned in their direction. It took only a moment for an ear to ear grin to stretch across his face. "Fionna!" His gleeful voice echoed down the hall. He was up off the couch and down the hall towards them before his mother knew what had happened. Her protective protest fell on deaf ears.

Fionna dropped to one knee and opened her arms. The boy didn't waste any time closing the distance; he dropped whatever he held in his arms and fell into Fionna's warm embrace. The boy closed his eyes and wrapped his arms tightly around her. Paul saw tears in the corners of the boy's eyes. The lump he felt from his earlier visit was back in his own throat.

Paul saw the boy's mother get up from the couch and start walking over to them. Beyond her, the nurse at the front desk looked in their direction. He recognized her middle aged, overweight features as well; it was Sally, the same woman that worked the reception desk the last time he was there. *So much for the stealthy approach!* he mumbled to himself.

"I knew you would come back!" The young boy spoke quietly in a gleeful tone. "I knew you would come back!"

"Yes, we're back," said Fionna. "I told you that we would return."

Paul knew exactly what she was thinking. He knew they were there to do the right thing.

The boy opened his eyes wider and then quickly narrowed them as he looked directly at Paul. He released his grip around Fionna's neck and spoke in a tone of surprise, "But, you're the ranger...!

"Yes, he is. We are both here," Fionna smiled.

Coming out of the shock, Bobby took two steps forward, wrapped his arms around Paul's waist and squeezed tightly. The boy's actions took Paul completely by surprise and he had to take a couple steps backward to catch his balance.

"Everything's okay," Paul whispered as he patted the boy gently on his shoulder.

The scene made Fionna laugh. "You've got to be on your toes around here."

"I am sorry," Bobby's mother interrupted with noticeable embarrassment. "He is quite emotional these days."

All three of them looked in her direction. "I don't know what has come over him," the mother continued, "he usually isn't like this."

Recognizing Fionna, the mother reached up to shake her hand but Fionna gave her a hug instead.

"Yes, I have come back to visit, and brought a friend." Fionna gestured to Paul.

"Remember, mom, he's the park ranger that gave me the trading card." Bobby released his grip and pointed directly at Paul as if he had just correctly answered the million-dollar question. He stepped back towards his mother's side as he continued to point.

The boy's mother stared at Paul, "You look much different out of uniform ... thank you so very much for coming!"

Paul nodded his head, and grasped her extended hand. Beyond her, he saw Sally, in her bright pastel smock, stand up from behind the counter and walk in their direction.

"Fionna ... is that you?" Sally's voice boomed down the hall. Everyone turned to greet her.

Fionna met her halfway from the reception desk, “Yes, I have come back to visit.”

Sally wrapped her meaty arms around her and gave her a great big hug, lifting her off her feet and spinning her around. “My goodness, the prodigal daughter returns.” She laughed, “I am so glad you have come back, the other children have been asking about you.” She held Fionna at arms’ length away and looked her up and down, smiling. “You look good … how are you feeling these days?”

Fionna waited until she regained her balance before she spoke. “I’m fine; I brought a friend,” she nodded at Paul.

“So you brought the park ranger. Hey, Jean, the prodigal son returned as well,” Sally yelled back to the woman at the front desk. “I told you he would.”

A tall, slender woman in a floral print smock with a stethoscope draped over her shoulder stepped out from the nearby office and made her way towards the group. She looked pleased to see everyone.

Fionna accepted her embrace. “Honey, we’ve been thinking about you quite a bit around here. I know a few young boys and girls who are going to be absolutely ecstatic once they catch wind of who is here.”

“May I go see them?” Fionna pleaded.

“Honey, you can go see whomever you like. They have been doing nothing but asking about you!”

By the expression on Fionna’s face, Paul suddenly knew what Fionna she was up to. Everyone who could interfere was now in the reception area; there was no one to stop the momentum. It was now or never.

“Could Bobby go with Fionna to show her around?” Paul saw the doubt in the mother’s eyes. “He’ll be the hero for the day … a great opportunity!”

“That’s fine with me,” Jean said. “Sally, any objections?”

“I think that would be an excellent idea,” Sally agreed.

“Mrs. Johnson, what do you think?” Jean asked.

Bobby's mother shrugged her shoulders as she momentarily stared into her son's pleading eyes. "Well, I guess it'll be okay."

Bobby gave his mother a big hug and ran off into Fionna's arms.

"No rough housing!" she called out to him.

"Okay mom!" He yelled back without turning around.

Paul watched them walk away, hand in hand, past the reception desk, then down the hallway and towards their destiny with the rest of the children. When he refocused his attention on the others in the reception area, he realized that everyone else in the room was doing the same thing. The pressure was now on him; he had to keep three people entertained for the next ten minutes. If he failed, their quest would end before it ever started.

Chapter Fifteen

Sharing the Gift

Fionna gripped Bobby's hand and led him down the hall to the first curtained partition on their left. She found herself breathing heavily as she pulled Bobby along faster than he wanted to go. She needed every second she could get. Once inside the room, she carefully peeked back down the hall. She smiled nervously when she heard Paul's boisterous voice above the background of a catchy *Sesame Street* tune. "Good luck," she whispered, then slowly pulled the curtained door shut behind her, making it a point not to draw any attention.

She peeked around the end of the curtain one more time but the adults continued to talk, oblivious to her intentions.

Relieved, she turned around and saw Bobby staring at her, an inquisitive look stretched across his little face. "But there is no one in here, this is my room!"

"Bobby, remember I said I was coming back with a special gift?" she whispered, gently patting her purse.

"Did you bring me a toy?"

"No, Bobby, not a toy, something much more special. I brought you something that will make the cancer go away forever!"

He looked at her in disbelief and took a couple of steps backwards out of her reach. His eyes clouded over with disappointment and mistrust.

Fionna reached into her purse, carefully pulled out a vial of clear fluid and held it out for him to see.

"What is that, holy water?" his voice was on the verge of anger. "My mother already tried that and it didn't work."

"Shhhhh, not so loud, Bobby!" she fought the frantic tone in her own voice. "I got this from the forest … with the fairies help; it came from an ancient tree." While as a patient in the Children's Ward, she had confided in Bobby about getting lost in the forest, seeing the fairies, and learning about her family heritage. She made him promise never to tell anyone. "Do you remember the stories I told you?"

He nodded.

"Bobby, they weren't just stories. Everything I told you was true." She made an ***X*** across her heart with the tip of her finger. "Cross my heart and hope to die, that what I tell you is not a lie."

He moved a little closer, nervously rocking from side to side.

"Bobby, I have never lied to you." She spoke slowly and clearly so he could easily follow along. "Remember, I told you I was going to return with a special gift?"

Bobby nodded. She could tell he was thinking about everything she said. "Look." She opened her purse and tilted it so he could see the glass vials that were clinking together.

He stepped a little closer, raised to his tipi toes and peered in.

"I brought these for all of your friends; I want all of you to get better. You want everyone to get well too, don't you?"

He shook his head *yes*.

"Bobby, are you listening? look at me, this is very important …" Fionna felt the time ticking by and started to squirm.

Slowly, Bobby nodded his head again.

"Bobby, I need your help to give these to all the other little boys and girls to make them better. Do you think you can help me with that? Are you ready?"

When he agreed, Fionna said, "We'll start with you first." She unscrewed the lid and handed him the opened vial of the magical cure. "In order for it to work, you have to believe. Do you believe Bobby?"

"Yes, I do!" His voice was sincere.

"Then drink … and ask for it to cure your sickness."

Bobby's eyes grew big as he drank all that was in the small vial. "It tingles," he giggled.

"Yes, that tells you that it's working."

"It is working!" He threw his arms around her neck and gave her a big hug.

She had to peel his little arms from around her neck. "We don't have time … we must hurry. How many other boys and girls are in the ward today?"

"Seven, I think, counting me."

"Good, we need to be quick to get to them all today. We don't have much time."

"Okay!" Bobby started to walk out from behind the curtains but she quickly grabbed his arm.

"We need to be quiet about this, remember?"

He nodded his head and put his finger up to his lips.

She playfully rubbed her hand on the top of his head. "Okay then, follow my lead."

Bobby nodded.

Fionna cautiously poked her head around the curtain. The others were still involved in conversation beyond the front counter. "Here we go … act natural." She walked over to the next curtain-lined cubical where a six-year-old girl was lying in bed, her big blue eyes staring up at Fionna. Her skin looked yellow under the hospital's florescent lights. Next to her sat a kidney dialysis machine that constantly hummed as it did the job of her failing kidneys. Catheter tubes led from her arms, a nasal canula hung from her nose. Fionna felt her heart sink. Jennifer's condition had worsened.

Despite everything, the child smiled.

"Fionna, do you have a gift for me too?" They had to strain to hear her faint voice. "I promise not to tell anyone, no matter what they do to me."

"Yes, we do!" exclaimed Bobby. He reached into Fionna's purse and removed one of the vials before Fionna knew what had happened. He unscrewed the lid and held it steady while the girl drank it.

"Tingles, doesn't it Jennifer?" Bobby noted.

The girl nodded. "Thank you!" She squeaked.

"You're welcome Jennifer, you're so very welcome." Fionna made sure she retrieved both the bottle and lid.

Four beds away a ten year old boy slept. White bandages covered his head, chest, left arm and leg. His breathing was labored and heavy, a noisy machine sat next to him keeping him alive. The victim of a house fire. He had been luckier than his two brothers and younger sisters who had perished.

"Manuel!" Bobby's loud whispering voice broke the uneasy silence.

It took a moment before his brown eyes met theirs.

"Hey, Bobby … what's up?" His voice was raspy and faint. He had also suffered from smoke inhalation.

"Fionna brought us a special gift." Fionna held up one of the glass vial and shook it ceremoniously.

"I have been dying … for a drink of water. How did you know?" His breath was long and drawn out. "Hey Fionna … you came back!"

"Manual I said I would." She moved closer to the edge of the bed. “And I said I was going to bring you a special gift. Can you keep a secret?” The tone of her voice confident.

He looked at the vial in her hand, “What’s that?”

“This vial contains magic water.” She teasingly shook the glass container. “If you believe in it, it will cure you of your sickness.”

He laughed sarcastically and motioned his free arm towards the bandaged portion of his body. “If you haven’t noticed … I’m scarred all over. How is a little water … supposed to change that? How can it … get rid of the ugliness? It won‘t just … wash off, I tried.”

She caressed his free hand. He squeezed her hand in return.

“If you believe, it will happen,” she whispered into his ear. “I would not be here if I didn’t believe. What have you got to lose?”

He tightened his embrace and then gently pushed her away.

“Did angels give this to you?” he asked as he wiped the tears from the sides of his bandaged face with the fingers of his right hand.

“Not quite angels,” she stammered, “more like the spirits of the forest.”

“They probably work for the angels!” he added.

“Yes, they probably do!” she had never thought of it that way before. She was Catholic but her family only went to church on Easter, Christmas, and Ash Wednesday. Her eyes drifted around Manuel’s room. On the counter shelf next to the sink were pictures of his entire family smiling back at the camera; sadly, it was the last photograph that they would ever take together again. Next to the family portrait was one of Jesus and the Virgin Mary standing together, while tongues of fire danced divinely above their heads. She knew that Manuel believed in miracles. During mass, when Fionna was a little girl, she remembered hearing that God worked in mysterious ways, *but through fairies … ancient trees?* When she refocused, she caught Manuel slowly examining his bandaged hand in front of his face.

"I want to be normal again," he whispered. "You know … it has been six months … since the fire. What I would do for a second chance."

She took off the lid and handed him the vial, "This is truly a gift from the ancient ones. You have to believe and you mustn't tell a soul."

He gently took the vial in his hand and looked it over for a moment before asking, "Not even my mother? I have to tell my mother!"

She could tell that Manuel did not want to keep any secrets from his mother. "Well, maybe not right away. You will know when the time is right to tell her."

He nodded and smiled, as if a tremendous relief had been lifted from his little shoulders. He poured the liquid sloppily into his mouth, some of it spilled down the edge of the bandages.

His eyes suddenly grew big.

"It tingles, doesn't it?" Bobby remarked.

"Yes, and it tastes … very good."

Fionna collected the empty vial. "We must go; we don't have much time. Remember your promise?"

Manuel smiled and turned his eyes toward the miniature alter that graced his wall, made the sign of the cross and started mumbling the words to the Hail Mary, a prayer she hadn't recited herself for a very long while. The words materialized in her thoughts and flowed from her heart. She found herself softly reciting the prayer along with Manuel. She was captivated by the moment.

Bobby's grip on her arm, pulling her back to the task they had before them.

"Remember, you said we have to hurry!" he whispered. "I think Jean and Sally are starting to look at us funny."

She looked down at her watch, five minutes had passed and they had four more children to see. She fought the sudden feelings of panic and then peeked through the opening in the curtain. Bobby was right; they seemed to be less interested in what Paul had to say and more interested in what they were doing behind the closed curtains.

"Act like nothing is different," she whispered to Bobby and then walked out, waving happily toward the nurses; Bobby mirrored her movements. The women returned the wave and focused their attention back to Paul who looked relieved. So far their plan was working. They casually walked to the next occupied bed.

"Do we have to stop here?" Bobby asked. He no longer smiled.

"Yes, we are here to help everyone, even Gina. I know some times she is hard to get along with but she needs our help just as much as everyone else."

Bobby looked towards the floor and shuffled his feet.

"I know she might be a pain in the backside from time to time."

"Yeah, try all the time," Bobby moaned.

"Come on." she nudged him along in front of her.

They stepped around the curtain to meet a young dark haired nine year old girl sitting up in bed busying herself with her *Game Boy*. The hand held game sounded off as she aggressively worked the keypad with her fingers, shifting her upper body from side to side. Gina was caught in one of her favorite pastimes.

Fionna smiled; the young girl hadn't changed; she still spent hours on that game. She played when she was bored, she played when she was happy and she played when she was upset. Sometimes the nurses had to take the game away at night so the others could get some sleep.

Fionna was about to speak but the girl beat her to it.

"I see you standing there," Gina's hard voice was laced with sarcasm. She never looked up from the game.

Fionna suddenly remembered why she wasn't liked by the other children. She seemed to enjoy making everyone else's lives miserable. "Gina, it 's Fionna and Bobby, how are you doing?"

"How do you think?" She stopped just long enough to gesture to everything in the room before she went back to playing the game. "I'm still here. You got out, why would you even come back?"

Fionna suddenly didn't know what to say. The speech she had prepared was suddenly lost, totally erased. There was no way she was going to talk this girl into doing anything she didn't want to do. She thought that maybe Bobby was right; they should use their time helping the other children who wanted to be helped. Regretfully, she started to turn around and leave.

"So, have you made it to level six yet?" Bobby asked.

Bobby surprised her.

Gina quickly looked up at him as she continued to work the keypad with her thumbs. "Not yet, but I'm almost there. I would be there sooner if people around here would stop bothering me."

"Fionna brought you a special gift." Bobby snapped at her. He was tired of pretending to be nice. "She brought all of us a special gift."

Gina stopped pushing the keypad and stared up at Fionna. The game continued to play itself.

"Yes, I brought everyone a special gift," she said, patting her purse.

"So, what did you bring me?"

"A cure for sickness."

"Oh yeah!" She snorted. "Something that will make everything go away, right? Fix everyone's problems. Right! They don't even know what my problem is. How can you fix something if you don't even know what's broken?" she said feebly, finally expressing some emotion.

"Do you remember our conversation about …?"

"You being lost in the woods … remembering strange things,"

Gina interrupted. "When you left, you said you would come back! Now you're back...whoopee! Of course, I remember. I'm not stupid!"

"I said that I would bring a special gift."

Gina shrugged.

"Well, I did. One for everyone here." Fionna patted the purse again and the vials clinked together.

Gina turned quickly towards the sound. "Well, let's see it then!"

"Let's make a deal first."

Gina wrinkled her nose at Fionna. "Make a deal? I don't have to make deals with anyone." She shook her head, showing her stubborn streak. She stared at the game, her thumbs finally motionless.

"Maybe not, but if you want this surprise, you'll have to make a deal with us." Both Fionna and Bobby nodded in agreement.

"So, what if I don't play along with the two of you."

Fionna leaned closer to her and rested her hand on the side of her bed. Gina leaned back as if challenged and looked down at Fionna's hand. "I am giving everyone something that will allow them to leave this place once and for all. Do you like staying here?"

Gina shrugged her shoulder and shook her head, "It is okay." She wasn't convincing.

"Really, somehow I don't think I believe you."

"I 'm tired of playing this stupid game … it won't even let me go to level six." She tossed the device on the bed towards her feet and crossed her arms. "I 'm tired of being in this stupid hospital. How does being with everyone else who's sick supposed to make me better?"

"Like you, they are here to be treated."

"It's a waste of time," she pointed in the direction of the other patients. "Don't they know that? Nobody gets better around here."

"I did," Fionna reminded her.

"You were never sick. The treatment here's a joke."

"No it isn't!," Bobby spoke up. "We are all getting better, just you wait and see." He stuck his hand into Fionna's purse and pulled out one of the vials.

Fionna fought the urge to stop him.

"This gift from the trees will make you better. Just you wait and see. It will make us all better but only if you believe it will."

Gina stared at the vial in Bobby's hand.

"And you have to promise not to tell anyone."

"So, what's it going to be?" Fionna asked. She watched Gina closely. She could see the little gears turning.

Gina's eyes began to water. "Do you think, it would help … even me?"

Fionna gently picked up Gina's hand and held it tightly. "It will, I promise." She saw Gina's eyes searching hers. "I said I would come back to help every child here, right? And here I am, like I promised." Fionna saw that she was finally getting through to the young girl. "It will only work if you believe … do you believe?"

"I have no choice."

"You mustn't tell anyone how you got better. Do you understand that?"

She nodded.

"Then it's a deal." Fionna nodded to Bobby, "Give it to her."

Bobby quickly unscrewed the lid and handed Gina the vial. "Remember, you promised."

"Yes, I know," she grumbled. She held the vial up to the light and stared at it a moment, "It's clear." She sounded skeptical.

"And filled with magic."

"Hurry up and drink it," Bobby complained.

"Don't tell me what to do; you're not my mother."

"Gina, please, we haven't got much time," warned Fionna as she peaked over her shoulder and towards the front desk.

Without saying another word, Gina drank the entire vial in one gulp.

"It tingles, doesn't it?" Bobby confirmed.

Gina nodded. Her eyes were filled with tears.

Bobby snatched the empty bottle out of her hand. "Remember, you promised."

She wrinkled her nose at him.

Fionna smiled at her as she stepped past the curtain. "It's a gift from the trees." She whispered as she left the enclosure.

Fionna and Bobby walked directly across the open hallway towards the next row of waiting beds on the other side. She flashed a quick smile and a wave as they crossed the open space between the two rows of curtains. Both nurses waved out of habit but their faces reflected their curiosity. She did not have much time left. She looked down at her watch. Gina had taken five more minutes. The clock was ticking.

Fionna met the welcome set of the smiling twin's. The curtain dividing the two adjoining rooms was open. The two girls with matching hairless heads were in deep conversation.

"Fionna!" their voices echoed in unison. Though they wore different colored pajamas, their facial features were almost identical.

"Samantha … Alexandra, it is good to see you both." She hugged each one of them. "How are you feeling?"

They shrugged their shoulders and exchanged weary glances. She knew the prognosis wasn't good. She didn't have time to hear the depressing details, nor did she really want to.

"We're still here!" Samantha, the one in green, exclaimed.

"And I came back …" Fionna added.

They looked at each other and giggled. "Do you have something for us as well?" Samantha asked.

"Yeah, like a gift from the trees," Alexandra, wearing pink, smiled.

"There is no keeping secrets around here is there?" Fionna teased. "I see we've been eavesdropping, haven't we?" Fionna put her hands on her hips and pretended to be annoyed.

Both Fionna and Bobby grinned.

"Yeah, it's really cool!" Bobby said.

"We promise we won't tell." Samantha said. She crossed her heart and exchanged looks with Alexandra. "We both promise."

"And we believe it will help us to," Alexandra added.

"Well, I can't ask for more than that." Fionna reached in her purse and pulled out two vials. She handed one to Bobby to give to Alexandra, while she gave hers to Samantha. Both drank quickly. Alexandra snorted as she giggled. Fionna laughed so hard she almost choked.

"I think it's working already," Samantha clapped her hands loudly.

Fionna hushed her with a finger to her lips, "We don't want the bosses down here, do we?"

Bobby collected the bottles and handed them to Fionna. She shoved them into her purse.

"We have to go; mum's the word right?"

Fionna and Bobby stepped into the hallway and walked in the direction of the front desk. They were twelve minutes into their mission and had one more patient to go. This time they didn't even look at the adults down the hall. She didn't want to give anything away. They pulled back the drapes to find the little Mickey, a five-year-old boy sitting up in his bed looking at a picture book. She sighed heavily when she looked into his face, dark circles surrounded his eyes. An EKG machine pulsated with the rhythm of his heart. A nasal canula draped across his face and attached to his nose. She remembered why he was there. He had a faulty valve in his heart; he was waiting for a heart transplant. It was good that small hearts were hard to come by but not good for the child who needed it to survive. Even though his condition was getting progressively worse, he had never given up hope.

“Fionna, you came back! Did you bring me my present like you promised?”

She knew that the staff definitely heard him. She had to move quickly. “Yes, Mickey,” she whispered, as she took a small brown teddy bear out of her purse and gave it to him.

He took it in his hands and squeezed it tightly into his chest.

“Mickey, there is something else, something very special but you can’ t tell anyone about it.”

He looked at the teddy bear in his hands.

“No, it’s not that, it’s this.” She pulled the vial out of her purse. “I don’t have much time to explain, you must drink this and your sickness will go away. But, you can’t tell anyone about it.”

“How come?”

“Because, they wouldn’t understand. It’s a present for a special little boy.”

He stared at her strangely.

“Oh, no, they’re coming,” Bobby whispered loudly. “There coming.”

Fionna heard the approaching footsteps on the hard linoleum. She suddenly felt weak. “Remember the stories I told you about the forest?”

Mickey nodded his head.

“Remember the special gift I told you I was going to bring,” she said, speaking quickly.

He nodded again.

“This special gift is from the trees, they want me to give it to you. They say it will make you better.”

He smiled and reached for the vial.

She quickly unscrewed the lid but in her haste, she dropped the lid onto the floor and it bounced under the bed.

"Hurry!" Bobby whispered.

She helped the child drink it all down quickly. "Don't tell anyone, this is our little secret, right?" she lectured as he finished it off.

She saw his eyes get big as she quickly shoved the empty vial into her purse. "Not a word," she repeated as she held her finger up to her own lips. Mickey mirrored her action.

"How's it going in here, you guys have been awfully quiet," Sally said as she curiously eyed everything in the room. Sally could read guilt etched across Bobby's face.

"Look what Fionna gave me!" Mickey exclaimed.

At first Fionna's thought her heart was going to stop, but She sighed heavily when she saw Mickey waving around the teddy bear as if he had just won the most important prize in the world.

"Aw, that is so cute." Sally gave Fionna a wink. "That was very nice of you."

Fionna hoped the worst was over.

Chapter Sixteen

Discovery

"Well, we need to be going," Fionna said, looking in Paul's direction and gripping her purse so tightly that her knuckles turned white.

"But you just got here," Sally said as she eyed her up and down. It was obvious to her that something was different. Bobby looked guilty of something; he looked down towards the floor and avoided eye contact with her, *very unusual for Bobby*, and Fionna couldn't wait to get out of there for some reason. *For someone so happy to be there one moment and now couldn't wait to leave the next was indeed very strange*. Mickey tightly hugged his gift; *a dozen professional wrestlers couldn't have taken it away if they tried*. "Did I miss something? Is there something you need to tell me?"

"Like what?" Fionna asked, trying to look surprised.

"Like the looks on your faces for starters … it 's like you all just committed the crime of the century."

Bobby and Fionna tried to laugh it off but it only made them look guiltier.

Sally stepped away from the bed to get a better picture of the whole scene. Nothing looked out of place until she followed Fionna's guilty gaze to a small black object on the floor. It was a screw-on top to a glass vial. Sally grunted as she bent over and reached under the bed to pick it up, keeping her eyes on the object long enough to reach it with her fingers. Her eyes flashed the signal … *you're busted!* Her knees popped and creaked as she used the railing of the bed to pull herself back up. She toyed with the black plastic lid as she stared at everyone in the room. Fionna's first instinct was to take off running, but she didn't. Bobby turned paler and his eyes became huge. *Bingo!* Sally thought. *But what are these kids up to?* "Well, am I going to have to ask again or are you voluntarily going to tell me what's going on around here?"

They stared in silence. She could almost see them making up the stories as the seconds ticked by. *This should be good.* "Well, would you rather tell me or Jean. You know how understanding Doctor Jean is."

Bobby nodded.

She waited a few moments to let the threat sink in. She was always the more lenient of the two, letting minor infractions go by unreported. "Well," she looked at Fionna who had pulled her purse closer to her chest. Sally held up the lid for her to see. "Does this look familiar to you?"

Fionna nodded, downcast.

"Fionna honey, what do you have in your purse?"

"It's holy water," Bobby blurted out, trying to save Fionna. "We blessed them with holy water!"

Sally glanced at Bobby and then shot her gaze back to Fionna.

"Holy water? Fionna, is this true?"

"Ah, yes...it's holy water...."

"Honey, what's this all about?" She motioned for Fionna to hand over her purse.

Fionna slipped the purse off her shoulder and reluctantly handed it to Sally. As the bag was transferred, the glass vials clinked against each other. Sally opened the purse, seeing seven empty glass vials.

"Seven … one for each child here today."

Fionna nodded in agreement.

Sally thought the gesture was so real, so sweet. "Oh honey, come here." Her huge opened arms easily fit around both Fionna and Bobby and she gave them a gentle squeeze. "So, you have come back to bless them with holy water. That is so very sweet of you. I know how you feel; I have wanted to do that many times myself, but I'm afraid it might take more than holy water to help these children. Fionna, you can't just come in here thinking that you are going to save everyone with holy water … not everyone here is Christian. They don't all believe that holy water is going to help."

Fionna looked up at her. "But, if they believed it could, wouldn't it help?"

"My dear child, faith does heal many things. It all works in a strange way as they say. But, you are not the first person to bring holy water into this wing of the hospital, and I know you won't be the last." The vials clinked against each other as she handed Fionna back her purse. "Just a minute, Fionna." She took a few sheets of tissue from a box and stuffed them into the purse among the empty vials. "No point in your having to go through all of this again now is there! This tissue should help to keep things a bit more quiet."

Fionna smiled her thanks.

"Please let me know the next time you want to come in here and bless everyone."

Fionna nodded. "I promise."

"Okay then, now that is settled …" Sally smiled at everyone in the room.

"Sally, I really must go," she nodded towards Paul who shot her a worried look. "My ride is waiting."

Sally looked in Paul's direction. "Honey, did Paul put you up to this? He knows better."

"Oh, no," she shook her head, "he doesn't know anything about the holy water."

"Are you sure?" she narrowed her inquisitive eyes.

"Oh, I'm sure alright." Fionna turned to the boys. "Goodbye Mickey, Bobby … remember what I said." She gave Bobby a hug. He returned the embrace and began to cry, "Bobby, it'll be okay … trust me. I have to go now." Fionna fought her own tears.

Sally had to smother Bobby in her arms so Fionna could leave.

"Thank you, Sally, for everything." She wiped away her watery eyes. "Sally, do you believe in miracles?"

"Yes, honey, I do." She did believe in hope; it was one virtue that no one could ever take away from the children.

"So do I," Fionna smiled, turned and walked down the hall towards Paul and Jean.

Sally watched Fionna walk down the hall to join the rest of the group. There was something strange about the lighting, she thought. There appeared to be a faint, glowing sensation around the young woman. At first, Sally thought it was the florescent lights or the way the shadows fell in place. But then the light seemed to follow her down the hall. When Fionna stood next to Paul, Sally felt the hair on the back of her neck stand on end, and goose bumps run the length of her neck. The glowing aura engulfed Paul as well as they stood there among the others. She shrugged it off; her imagination was getting the better of her or *could it be that there was something more to them than met the eye?*

Chapter Seventeen

Grandma Elisabeth

Fionna beamed up at her grandmother. She wanted so much to tell her everything, but had to wait until they were alone. Supposedly, her grandmother knew about the fairies in the forest, yet she said nothing. *Did they also make her promise? Did she take an oath?* Fionna had waited impatiently for Grandma to return from her trip to the East Coast. Twice, her flight was delayed due to unexpected snow. The first time was in Boston; the second, in Denver. Now, she was finally back in Springville, the town named for the many creeks that once produced a magnificent redwood forest. According to Grandma Elisabeth, who was born and raised in the area, the timber town had grown more over the last five years than it had over the last twenty. Fionna remembered her Grandma complaining about the recent addition of the town's third traffic light as if it were a major inconvenience.

She looked absolutely adorable with her long gray hair draped over her flannel-covered shoulders and her green eyes accentuated by her knowing smile. She slowly hobbled over to the couch where

Fionna was sitting quietly. With a heavy sigh, she started to lower herself next to her granddaughter.

Fionna quickly stood up and helped her grandmother settle into the couch.

Grandma Elisabeth patted her gently on her knee. "Now, tell me about that great big smile. Honey, what have you been up to while I was away? If I didn't know any better, which I do, I would have to say that it is something bigger than both of us."

Fionna nodded and cautiously looked across the room to make sure that her mom was still out of earshot. The last thing Fionna wanted was for her mother to hear.

"So, we have another secret, do we?" Elisabeth grinned. "You know how I do love secrets."

Fionna forced her words out in a whisper, "The strangest things happened to me while you were gone."

Elisabeth leaned in closer to hear, "Yes, my little angel got herself lost in the forest." She reached up and affectionately grabbed Fionna's folded hands. "I was so worried when I received the phone call. But somehow I knew that you would be all right." She gently patted her hands again. "Those were three long days. The longest I have had to experience in quite a while. But, I did not lose faith. Oh, no."

"Grandma Elisabeth, something strange happened to me while I was lost."

"Oh?"

"The things I'm going to tell you, well, you have to promise not to tell anyone else."

"Well, I don't know …" she sounded a bit puzzled.

"You have to promise … they said that I could only tell you and ranger Paul."

"Ranger Paul, isn't he the one who found you?"

"Yes, I've already told him but he also experienced strange

things in the forest when he was looking for me. He said something mysterious had led him to me."

Grandma Elisabeth narrowed her eyes and leaned back into the couch.

"Do you promise?"

"Yes, I promise."

Fionna's face blossomed. "I had a dream," she whispered, "a wonderful dream that our ancestors came from Ireland."

"Yes honey, that's no secret."

Fionna nodded, "One of my grandmothers left Ireland during the potato famine and came to America."

The elderly woman nodded, "Yes that sounds about right. It was a long time ago."

Fionna shot a quick glance over her shoulder; her mom was still talking with her father in the kitchen. "She brought something special with her; something many people don't believe exists." Fionna studied her grandmother's face. "She brought fairies. She brought fairies to America … it was *your* mother who brought them to the ancient redwood forests here."

Grandma Elisabeth nodded politely as if she were talking to a confused child. "Yes, I remember the story and that is what it was, just a story passed down in the family for years."

"Why didn't you tell me?"

"I had just about forgotten about them until you mentioned it. I remember my mother telling me something about fairies when I was a little girl but they were just stories, things to pass along down the line." She shrugged.

Fionna couldn't control her smile anymore. She slowly shook her head, "They aren't just stories anymore!"

Grandma Elisabeth reached up and touched the side of Fionna's face as she examined her closely. "My dear, did that bump on your head shake you up a bit?"

Fionna carefully pulled her grandmother's hand down to her lap and squeezed it gently. She knew her grandma would understand once it was all explained. After all, the fairies were right about Paul. "Your mom set them free in the forest; they were very thankful for what she had done. They love the ancient redwoods. They no longer made their presence known; they were safe, they were free. She promised not to tell anyone what she had done. Years went by but now they have become concerned about losing the ancient trees." She summoned her courage and continued.

"I didn't just get lost in the forest, I was sick. The further I went, the sicker I was. We were lost … all five of us. We took a shortcut. We were stuck in the middle of a bad storm. There was lightning and cold rains everywhere. We were scared; we thought were going to die. But that's when I smelled the flowers; they drew me to the log that crossed the canyon."

Her grandmother gently rested her hand on Fionna's shoulder.

Fionna felt compelled to continue, "I heard Gaelic voices. I heard music. I remember Paul finding me. It was during this *dream*, when everything came to me. Everything about the trees, the fairies … I was supposed to tell you everything."

"Oh my, Fionna, the dreams you have."

Fionna shook her head, "No, they are not just dreams, I've seen them, the fairies. They're real." She pointed towards the window. "Paul has seen them too. If you do not believe me, you can call him yourself. He'll tell you the same thing. They want us to help them save the ancient trees that aren't protected in parks."

"How are you supposed to be able to do all of this?"

Fionna smiled a devious smile and glanced sidelong at the kitchen. All was still clear. "We've already done it!"

Her grandmother gave her a quizzical gaze, "But … how?"

"The trees gave us medicine; we in turn gave it to seven children in the hospital I stayed at. If anyone deserves a miracle, it is them!" She added defensively.

"Did the hospital staff just let you walk right in and administer this medication?"

"Well … no, we kind of had to sneak it in to them." In the retelling, it sounded dishonest and wrong.

"Ranger Paul was in on this, too?"

"Well, I needed his help; I asked him to help."

"And he willingly did?"

"Grandma, it was the right thing to do. We did what we had to; those children weren't going to get any better. Now with our help they will."

"My dear child!"

"You have to trust me. The children will get better and there are fairies in the forest, you'll see. Our family has been called upon to do the right thing. Don't you see, it's our calling … it's why we are here," Fionna pleaded for understanding.

Grandma Elisabeth stared silently out of the window for a moment before she spoke. "Are you sure it will work?"

Fionna nodded.

"And Paul is okay with this?"

"Well, not at first, but he is now."

Grandma returned her gaze to the window. "I know I'm going to regret this," she remarked as she glanced quickly towards the busy kitchen. "But for now, we will not tell your mother. I don't think she could take this on top of your accident and all. The poor woman has worried enough."

Fionna felt her grandma gently squeeze her hand. The contact felt special. It felt as if things were going the way they were supposed to.

"I won't let you down, I promise."

Grandma Elisabeth nodded, "We can't afford it to go any other way."

"There is one more thing."

Her grandma looked exhausted. "Honey, what now?"

"Can you give Mary and me a ride to the park the day after tomorrow?" She nodded her head towards the kitchen. "I don't think mom is going to be quite as understanding."

"Why do you need to go back to the park so soon?"

"I need to tell the fairies what we've done. We need to know what they want us to do next."

"Mary knows about the fairies?"

"Yes, I think she might have seen them during our last visit."

"Promise me you will be safe."

Fionna traced an imaginary ***X*** across her chest. "It's very safe; the rangers have marked a safe trail for us. We've already hiked it once before."

"Okay then, we can have a picnic in the park. I am not the fastest driver, you know, so it will take some time; old ladies travel at a speed of their own. But seriously, some day soon, we will have to tell your mother everything."

"Yes, I know, I just want her to be ready." Fionna smothered her grandmother with a hug. "I love you, grandma, you're the best."

"You know it."

Act 6: Enchantment

Chapter Eighteen

Back to the Forest

The two blue and pink raincoat-clad figures stood out against the greens and browns of the winter rain-soaked forest as they weaved their way along a fern shrouded path. A gray fog hugged the tops of the towering trees this Valentine's Day, sprinkling them with constant drip and drizzle. They moved silently but quickly. Fionna in the lead, Mary following closely behind; both determined, both on a mission.

A raven sounded and Fionna stopped and searched for the direction of the bird 's call. Mary had to place her hand on Fionna's shoulder to keep from running into her. "You need brake lights," she pointed out.

"We're close," Fionna whispered, "very close."

When Mary squeezed Fionna's hand, she found her grip wet and clammy; the two hours on the trail were beginning to show. Mary nodded and wiped the rain soaked sweat from her face with the back of her hand. She too had heard the muffled cry of the raven over the dripping sounds of the soft rain but she couldn't tell from which direction the calls had come. She felt her heart pounding in her chest as her eyes searched for the bird. Fionna's hospital visit was still fresh in her mind. Any day now, seven children with a variety of ailments would miraculously become cured. *They would declare it a miracle but was it? Were mythical creatures capable of performing miracles? And if they found out whom or what was responsible, would they still embrace the gift? It was indeed a gift.*

Nothing had happened yet and that was the reason they were here, searching for the fairies. Fionna swore they existed but Mary had only seen movement, silhouettes darting through the forest. The silhouettes could have been birds as far as she knew, turned into fairies by her active imagination. But then there was the smell of the sweet flowers that she could never find. *Were the forest fairies responsible for the flowers?*

"*Tic, tic, tic, tic, tic, tic, tic, tic, tic.*" The winter wrens scolded as they sneaked in for a closer look. Green and brown was everywhere. Mary suddenly realized how much they were out of place in the forest; every animal could see them. They were like walking, colorful billboards.

She watched a series of small branches bounce in her direction, as if something small was moving in for a closer look. She smiled when she saw the tiny wrens peeking out at them with a tilt of their heads.

"*Rrraaawww, rrraaawww, rrraaawww, rrraaawww, rrraaawww.*" The call of the raven echoed above the soft rain and winter solitude. The birds were almost directly overhead, sending the wrens retreating into the vegetative cover. Mary backed into Fionna as she scanned the treetops. The physical contact brought her comfort; she was glad she wasn't alone.

They first heard the sound of the wind distinctly whistling through each of the birds powerful wing beats. It was most likely a mated pair that weaved their way towards them. Ravens fascinated

Mary; they were one of the few animals in the wild that mated for life. They were intelligent birds that had been known to live up to seventy years in captivity and unlike most of the other animals in the forest, they successfully adapted to human influence. They were opportunistic, huge and powerful.

Their black silhouettes skillfully swooped under some branches and dodged others. With a sudden shift in their wings, they pulled higher into the air and back peddled their wings as if caught in a river's eddy. The birds circled around above them several times, their curious dark, intelligent eyes never leaving the girls, as they scrutinized them from above. "*Rrraaawww, rrraaawww, rrraaawww, rrraaawww, rrraaawww.*" With that, the ravens abruptly flew away slowly in the direction they had come. "*Rrraaawww, rrraaawww, rrraaawww, rrraaawww, rrraaawww.*" They sounded again as if trying to hurry the girls along.

"How can this be?" Mary called to her friend. The birds' behavior unnerved her. It was as if they were trying to communicate. "It's almost as if..."

"They want us to follow!" Fionna cried as she turned and bolted off after the birds. "Hurry," she yelled over her shoulder to her friend.

Mary was entranced, refusing to take her eyes off the two birds that now seemed to fly just fast enough to stay ahead of them.

Forced herself to lean forward, Mary's legs had to adjust to keep her from falling over. Surprisingly her upper torso followed. She couldn't believe it. The ravens were leading them down the path and into the shadows.

The raven's call echoed in the forest. Mary willed herself forward after Fionna and in pursuit of the ravens, in pursuit of their destiny.

♦ ♦ ♦

A strange sort of joy flowed through Fionna. She was back in the forest. Strangely, the moist air, the misty rain, the coolness were all part of what she liked best. She was going back to see the fairies, to let them know that she had accomplished what she had set out to do. The Gaelic phrase, *Óna crainn … From the trees …* echoed in her thoughts. The gifts now flowed through seven children. She knew it worked; each talked about the tingling sensation after they drank what she had now grown to call simply *holy water*. She could clearly see the expressions on their tender faces. The thought made her smile. She shot a quick glance over her shoulder to make sure Mary was still with her, then increased her pace.

Her thoughts faded to the children. She found Gina's desire to get better the most compelling. The child listened intently to everything, despite what she led others to believe. She wanted so much to get better; she wanted the doctors to pinpoint her illness. She dreamed of being like everyone else. At least with a diagnosis, she would know what she was dealing with. Fionna understood her anger and confusion.

The twins, Alexandra and Samantha, not only shared the same features and mannerisms, they also shared the same life threatening cancer. They understood each other and their desire to overcome it.

Despite everything that had happened to Manuel, he still believed that a powerful force was guiding him down a predetermined path. Skin grafts could improve his looks; they could mask the devastation the searing flames had caused. But, the scars on his soul would take time. His unswerving faith! He still prayed, he still believed in God. He still believed in miracles. He still believed there was a chance that things would get better. He prayed for the souls of his departed brothers and sister. He prayed for his mother. He prayed for himself. Fionna admired his strength.

Jennifer was willing to do anything to lose her dependence on a machine to filter her blood. She had been waiting for a matching donor for the last six months and every day she felt herself spending longer hours in dialysis. Every day challenged her belief that someday she would be like everyone else.

Mickey was waiting for a donor heart. Surprisingly, he took everything in stride. He was the youngest in the children's wing. He had lived with heart problems most of his life. Incredibly, a smile never seemed to leave his face.

Then, there was Bobby, her favorite. His cancer was supposed to be in remission, but he confided to her that the monster within him was still growing, still feeding off his weakening body. He felt weaker every day. He had embraced the story of her adventure in the forest. She felt a kindred spirit. She also felt the pressure to succeed, to bring the gift of healing from the fairies and the ancient ones and distribute it among the needy, among the children in the hospital.

She felt a twinge of anger. She had done her part. It was now up to the fairies and ancient trees to hold up their end of the bargain.

Her pace quickened and the ravens responded with an increase in their wing beats. The whistling of their wings echoed ever louder.

Her lungs burned and her muscles strained as she panted heavily. She crashed along through the path of towering ferns, knocking the drops of moisture from the saturated fronds as she pursued the pair of ravens. The desire to help drove her along, her friend hot on her trail. A few minutes into their pursuit, she skidded to a stop; the two ravens sat on a low branch, blocking their path.

"Rrraaawww, rrraaawww." The forest absorbed the sounds of their raspy, shrill calls.

Fionna glared narrowly at the two birds. The large black ravens held their ground, or in this case their branches, about thirty yards away. They nodded their heads, dropped their broad shoulders and moved their chests in her direction. The shaggy feathers of their throats stood out away from their heads with every low, drawn out croak.

"What are they waiting for?" Mary panted.

Fionna had forgotten that Mary was standing directly behind her. She glanced at her out of the corner of her eye, afraid to turn away from the two guides. Instead of bending over at her knees, gasping for air as she was, her friend stood upright and rested both of her hands on top of her head to help herself breathe easier.

"Look at them," Mary whispered.

The largest raven emitted a low, drawn-out gravelly sound as it swiveled its entire body in a direction toward their left, almost as if it were pointing. As Fionna stared at the bird, it cocked its head and fluffed up its shaggy throat feathers. Its eyes seemed to grow in size. When Fionna tilted her head in the same way, the ravens shook their heads as if in disgust.

"What is wrong with them?" Mary asked. "It's like being in some kind of enchanted forest or something."

"Criminy! Do they hav' te' dra' ye' a picture?" The loud voice bounced from the shadows to their left. They ar' doin' the best they can … them is only birds, after all, ravens at that!"

Fionna smiled in recognition. It took her eyes a moment to spot the plump, silhouetted figure of the silver bearded fairy. He spied at her from behind the moss-covered bark of a young Douglas fir tree about ten yards away. "Séamus!" she exclaimed joyfully. She took a couple of steps closer to him.

"*Dia duit tráthnóna Fionna (Jee-ah ghwich thraw-no-nan)*, Good afternoon, Fionna," he said as he bowed his head.

"A good afternoon to you too, Séamus."

Séamus floated out from behind the tree and into the dim, overcast light. His wings glowed like silver in the mist and light, gentle rain.

Mary blankly stared at the shadow, her mouth open and her eyes big.

"This is my friend, Mary," Fionna reached over and touched her friends shoulder, causing Mary to jump.

"*Tá fáilte romhat Máire (taw fawl che row-at Maw-ir-uh)*, Welcome, Mary," the elder fairy greeted Mary as he bowed his head again.

"Then, it is true … there really are such things as fairies … I thought … can I touch you?"

"Another non-believer, hav' we?"

Mary grabbed Fionna's arm, pointing at the primeval being.

"Ye' know, it's not polite te' point." The fairy smiled.

"I'm sorry … but, I just …" Mary quickly dropped her arm to her side as though she were standing at attention.

"Sea (Shah) yes … ye' thought that fairies wer' mythical creatures. That the forests just took car' of themselves!"

"Rrraaawww, rrraaawww," the ravens sounded off.

"*Táim buíoch díot (Taw-im bween-ukh Jee-ut)*, I am grateful te' ye'." Séamus waved them off with a quick flick of his stubby fingers. Both ravens took to the air with a flutter of wings, obviously pleased with themselves. They flew over their heads, banked into the trees and then out of sight. Their calls faded into the forest drizzle. Fionna waved goodbye.

Mary watched as the tiny man hovered above a moss-covered log, crossed his pudgy, muscular arms and landed gently, less than ten-yards away. His body vibrated as he shook the moisture from his wings and long sleeveless coat. The woven redwood fibers hung down to his knobby, wrinkled knees like a medium length skirt. He stepped out of his woven, grass-like sandals and dug his oversized toes into the moist, rich green moss.

"Ahh," he exhaled, "the rain makes it perfect fer' me little toes."

"… but, you're a fairy!" Mary stammered, disbelief still stretched across her face.

"Yer' friend Máire her' doesn't miss a thing, does she," he laughed. "A real hawk fer details."

"We did it … we gave the children the *holy water*," Fionna announced as she took two steps forward.

He interlaced his thick fingers behind his back, military style. "*Holy water*? Ye' wer' supposed te' give em' the stuff from the trees," the diminutive creature grouched.

"We did … just as we were supposed to," Fionna responded more nervousness in her voice than she intended.

"So, yer' calling the gifts *holy water* now, ar' ye'?"

"We can' t just call it what it really is … they would never understand"

"*Tá, agus fáilte (Taw ug-us fawl-che)* …Yes, of course. Right ye' ar' then te' do that. Most humans could never understand the likes of fairies nor the enchantment of a forest outside of children's book." He nervously tapped one foot on the moss and buried the toes of the other beneath it. "*Sea (shah)* … yes, humans ar' funny that way. Even when they see, they don't believe. Typical." He gazed off into the shadows and spoke with deep concern. "Will hav' te' work harder. We ar' running out of time. Even as we' stand an' speak, the ancient ones still fall. If somethin' isn't done an' done quickly, soon, the only ancient ones will be a handful left in parks."

The hammering of a pileated woodpecker against an old tree echoed in the distance, drawing Fionna's attention to the far away sound. She knew the bird was still a recognized symbol of the ancient forest and one of the largest woodpeckers in North America. Biologists called them indicator species, a plant or animal species that survived better in a certain type of habitat. Few were left, soon to be added to a growing extinct species list, a distressing fact she didn't want to happen in her beloved forest. The red-feathered scalps were treasured as traditional regalia by First Nations People that called the forests their traditional home. They treated the woodpeckers as sacred. To her, the sound meant that the forest was still wild, still full of ancient trees.

A sudden whistling through the tops of the trees caused them to sway in uneven directions. Fionna shuddered but the unnerving chill ended as suddenly as it began. She watched silently as the chaotic movement of the trees returned to uniformity. The mist continued to accumulate at the tops of the trees; the raindrops grew in size and intensity. She closed her eyes and let the droplets sting her face.

"Tis' been done."

She looked over to see Se'amus extending his short stubby fingers in the direction of the surrounding trees. "The earth has spoken, now we wait te' see what the humans will do." He chuckled to himself as if he told the punch-line of a joke she couldn't hear. She strained to hear him over the pouring rain. "I believe, how do ye' say … the ball is in yer' court. The actions of the humans will determine our next step."

Fionna wanted everything to go right, but she knew that was seldom the case when dealing with people. By the words and actions of the ancient trees and the fairies, the seven children would get better. They deserved to get better; they would benefit from the exchange but would the forest benefit as well.

She turned away and gazed off into the cool downpour. Uneasiness settled in the pit of her stomach. Her thought raced to the culture that went about their daily lives on the outskirts of the forest. It made her skin itch. *Would everyone taking from the forest realize that their behaviors needed to change? Would they be willing to change? Was a miracle enough to encourage them to change their ways? Would seven miracles be enough to do it? Would it take ninety-three more to sway them? Or a personal visit from the fairies themselves?*

"*Tar ar ais, le do thoil (tor er ash, led heuyl)* … please come again."

The fairy was no longer there. Only Mary's sad eyes looked back at her. Fionna knew their thoughts were the same. Their journey had only begun.

Chapter Nineteen

Granting a Wish

Sally stood, leaning lazily over the crossword puzzle positioned on the outside edge of the nurse's station counter next to a card and an open, half eaten box of assorted Valentine's chocolates. Supporting her face with one hand, she rhythmically tapped the eraser of her pencil against her lower lip with the other. No matter how hard she tried, she couldn't get the catchy beat of the pop song out of her head. It was late and she was covering for another nurse who called in sick for Valentine's Day.

"Shirley, what has nine letters, begins with I, the third letter is a C, the fifth letter's a D and it ends in T. It's an occurrence." Sally stared at the page as she bent toward the other nurse on duty.

Shirley scratched the letters on a piece of paper, stared at the word a moment and then looked up with a smile. "Try … *i-n-c-i-d-e-n-t*." She spoke slowly, waiting for her friend's eyes to light up with discovery.

"I-n-c-i-d-e-n-t, why didn't I see that!" Sally spoke her thoughts aloud.

"Because you're too busy playing dentist!" Shirley laughed. "You're going to end up hurting yourself if you're not careful!" She teased as she paged through a magazine to pass the time.

"What?" Sally shifted her attention from the crossword puzzle to her friend Shirley.

"The pencil," she nodded and pushed herself away from the magazine. "I have never seen you this nervous; what's up? Waiting for the perfect Valentine's gift from the hubby?"

Sally looked at the pencil in her hand and stopped moving it around. She didn't realize that she had been tapping herself with the writing utensil. She looked back at Shirley and smiled. "I wouldn't want to poke my eye out or something like that and have to be admitted to the hospital. Now that wouldn't look good, especially on Valentine's Day."

"Yeah, you might get stuck with Doctor Heckler and Mr. Claude."

They both laughed.

"Seriously, you seem awful nervous these days … did you switch to decaffeinated coffee or something?"

Sally knew her friend meant to be funny, but she was right; she hadn't gotten a good night sleep since Fionna's last visit to the Children's Ward.

As if reading her thoughts, Shirley remarked, "I heard Fionna was here a couple of days ago. She is such a sweet girl."

Sally nodded, "Yes, she dropped by for a quick visit. She brought park ranger Paul with her."

"How is she doing?"

"Okay, I guess, but she was behaving a bit strange the other day." She decided to keep the part about the strange lights around Fionna to herself.

Shirley raised her eyebrows and leaned forward. It was obvious she loved gossip.

"You know," Sally chuckled as she leaned in and spoke softly. "She sneaked in several vials of holy water during her last visit."

"Holy water? So, that would probably explain Gina's morale change. Her sarcasm just hasn't been the same." Shirley shook her head, "Holy water, huh … why didn't we think of that before!"

"Yes, gave it to several of the patients."

"So what did Doctor Jean have to say about all of that?"

"Nothing; I didn't tell her. There are some things that are better left unsaid, if you know what I mean. No foul, no harm done. Just a concerned teen."

"I know what you mean; she's definitely by-the-book Jean," Shirley snickered again. "She would have probably had you run a bunch of tests."

"No doubt."

"Fionna asked if I believed in miracles."

"What did you tell her?"

"What do you think … that I …" She flashed back to the look in Fionna's eyes. "It was how she asked … so filled with hope." She could feel Shirley's eyes searching her face for more. She didn't feel comfortable talking about it so she looked down at her watch to avoid discussion. It was 10:15 p.m., time to make their rounds. Seven children occupied the ward for the night and all were supposed to be asleep. "It's time to check our little angels."

Shirley started to get up and reached for the clipboard but Sally motioned for her to stay seated.

"No, that's alright, I've got it!" she picked up the clipboard. "I need to stretch my legs," she groaned, "to work off the day's chocolate!" She gently rubbed her enormous belly.

Shirley smiled.

Sally took two steps then abruptly stopped. She heard a high-pitched ringing in her ears and felt a chill ripple through her body. "Did you feel that?" She asked.

Shirley looked up, “Feel what?”

“I don’t know, it was like ….”

The whole room suddenly shook with a boom and the floor began to buckle and roll. Sally struggled to keep her balance and with clipboard still in hand, she grasped the edge of the counter. She gripped it with her fingers as she fell against it; the counter groaned under her weight. Her ears filled with screams but it took her a moment to realize that the blood-curdling screams were her own. The walls, ceilings, and floors creaked, popped and moaned. Objects were tossed about and fell off the shelves. She watched the half-empty box of chocolate slide down the counter top and spill across the floor. Strange eerie sounds filled the air.

“It’s an earthquake!” Shirley screamed, her voice terror-stricken. She slipped out of her chair and crawled beneath the leg space of the counter.

The seismic waves rolled beneath the linoleum floor. Sally lost her balance and fell onto the floor hard, crushing chocolate candies as she knocked the wind out of her lungs with her elbow. She gasped for breath as she instinctively covered her head with her arms and tried to tuck herself into a ball. Objects struck her harmlessly about her body, but a sharp pain throbbed through one of her arms. She cried out, grabbed her arm and squeezed her eyes shut. There was no safe place like doorways or tables within her reach. She again heard screams and cries among the chaos. *The Children*, she suddenly remembered.

No sooner had she opened her eyes, the hallway lights blinked a couple of times and then went out. “No!” she yelled. Almost as if in response, half of the emergency lights came back on for a moment before they too flickered and went out as well. “For the love of God!” she screamed. The tremors stopped as suddenly as they started but the hospital was plunged into a black abyss. Sally caressed her throbbing arm, crawled towards the desk and struggled to pull herself up using one arm. She strained to make her legs push her the rest of the way upright.

Behind her, the desk drawers were being frantically yanked open and rifled through and she was momentarily blinded by the bright beams of the flashlights. She averted her eyes and hung onto the edge of the counter with her good arm. Good, now they at least had some light to work with.

"Sally, you okay?" Shirley asked, as she created silhouettes in the beams of both flashlights.

Sally accidentally bumped her left arm on the edge of the counter and cringed. She clenched her teeth to hide her pain. "The children!" she whimpered as she grabbed her throbbing arm. "We need to check on the children!"

Shirley stared at her for a moment before she offered the second flashlight. Sally reached across the counter and snatched one of the flashlights, fumbling with it until she held it tightly in her grip.

"Your arm, it's hurt!"

"Just sprained I think … I'll take the left side and you take the right."

Shirley nodded and hurried in the direction of the children.

"I'm coming," Sally fought the panic that was building within her. The power had gone out and the backup generators had failed to stay on, a first. Two children relied on machines, one for her kidneys and the other for his heart. *The machines have their own battery backup*, she kept telling herself. The spark of hope gave her courage. She stumbled along, the children's cries and screams getting louder. Sally hurried in the direction of Jennifer on the kidney machine and Shirley, towards Mickey and the heart machine. *This could be disastrous!* The thought made her shiver.

The beam of the flashlight illuminated the open curtain to Jennifer's room and the back of Bobby's pajamas. He stared at the silent dialysis machine. Sally shifted the beam of her flashlight to the now silent machine. It no longer beeped and hummed, the little light no longer flickered telling everyone that it was alive, well, and working.

Sally tripped over something on the floor, scrambled for balance and just missed Bobby as she fell against the edge of the bed that had been moved sideways towards the entrance. She winced at the pain in her elbow and almost dropped the flashlight. The beam of light illuminated Jennifer's terrified face, then the silent machine.

Jennifer screamed as she pointed to the silent machine, "She promised … I don't want to die!"

Bobby silently stared, disbelief clearly imprinted across his face as he pointed towards the silent machine.

The nasal canula oxygen tubing had been pulled loose and the I.V. that once carried filtered blood now dangled from Jennifer's arm. "Oh my goodness!" she whispered under her breath. It took a moment for Sally's nursing instincts to kick in and for her to take action. She scrambled around the edge of the bed and over to the dialysis machine. She shoved the flashlight under her arm, frantically flicked the power switch off and on and then checked the outlets. There was no change. *This can't be!* She was overwhelmed with a feeling of helplessness.

She scrambled back towards the bed, reached for Jennifer's struggling arms and reattached the oxygen tube. She knew the oxygen worked from the big tanks in the room next to her bed; the valve was manual, the power outage would not affect that piece of equipment. But then, she noted that the other end of the tubing had been yanked clear of the oxygen tank. It hissed like an angry snake. "Bobby, help me move the bed closer to the machine."

Bobby just stared at the machine.

"Bobby, please!" she yelled as she gripped Jennifer's hand with her good arm and gave her a gentle squeeze. Jennifer returned the embrace and looked into Sally's face for reassurance, "It's going to be all right; we are here with you."

"The machine … it's …."

"I know, it will be okay, the machine only helps you. You are the one that does all the work," Sally strained to keep her voice calm, not to rush her nervous words. "Bobby, sweetheart, please help me push the bed closer to the wall." Her voice was sterner this time, finally finding her inner strength.

Bobby snapped out of his trance and pushed the bed closer to the now silent machine.

Adrenaline surged through the room as the bed moved on its own; *after shock*, Sally realized.

Bobby remarked, "She is going to be okay. It is just like Fionna said it would be … we are all going to be okay."

"Yes, Bobby, everything is going to be okay." She released Jennifer's hands and plugged the oxygen tubing back into the canisters' attachment.

"The air, it's working!" Jennifer announced.

"Sally!"

A bone-chilling scream from across the room startled her. The other flashlight beam was peeking beyond the curtains of Mickey's room. "Oh, my God!" She had forgotten about the electronic heart machine that his tiny heart depended on. She felt a sharp uneasiness in the pit of her stomach. She handed Bobby the flashlight. "Stay here, I'll be right back. Mickey needs me!"

Bobby nodded, accepted the flashlight thrust upon him and pulled it tight to his chest; no one was going to be able to pry it out of his hands.

"Sally, come here quickly!" shattered the uneasiness, the panic notable in Shirley's voice.

"Bobby, you're in charge!" She patted him on his shoulder as she rushed past the drapes and towards the beam of Shirley's light. She brushed past the open curtain and in the direction of Mickey's bed. She could only imagine the worst. Little Mickey's heart had worsened to a point where he relied on a machine from time to time to keep him alive, while they waited for a donor heart to be found. She entered the room and just about ran over three little girls, whose amazed expressions were mirrored across their faces.

"The machine doesn't work," the cry filled Sally's ears, "and neither does the backup …"

"The kidney machine isn't working either," Sally yelled back.

"It's okay, my heart is still *beeping*!" Mickey said with a smile as he pointed to the quiet machine with his little hand. He held his new teddy bear tightly in his arms. "I don't need it any more … am I better?"

Shirley tossed Sally the second flashlight and stumbled along in the direction of the front desk and telephone. She recognized the strange look on her friend's face; she was sure it was on hers as well.

Sally felt little hands grip her tightly about her arms and legs. She had to grip the edge of the bed to keep her balance as she looked down into four sets of inquisitive eyes. She allowed the three girls to squeeze in closely to her as she reached up to embrace Mickey's little hand.

She heard Shirley on the telephone. At least the phone lines still worked; they were not cut off from the rest of the hospital. "We'll be okay now," she told the children as the girls snuggled closer.

Mickey looked up at her and smiled, "I'm not worried, it is just like Fionna said."

Chapter Twenty

The Miracle

Though it took less than five minutes to restore power to the children's wing and another thirty more to control the chaos in the building, it seemed like a lifetime to Sally. Her throat was parched; her injured swollen wrist throbbed painfully every time she moved it. The sounds in the room were distorted as they mixed with her rapid heartbeats. Her legs were tired and sluggish, as if she had been trudging through soft sand. Every so many feet she had to fight the urge to stop, rest and regain her balance. Everything but the children moved in slow motion. They circled around her, quickly darting back and forth. Sally struggled to make it from one side of the room to the other. Her constant pain in her wrist kept reminding her of reality but her maternal instinct pushed her onward. She found the smell of the sweet chocolates smashed into her clothing oddly comforting.

Her friend cradled the telephone against her ear as she frantically dialed an outside line and hung up when there was no answer. Finally, Shirley's trusty cell phone made it through. *Hang tight, help is on the way* was the answer. Until then, they were going to have to deal with emergencies on their own. They were lucky and she knew it. Though the machines and oddly enough their backup had failed, the children were alive and well. Actually, they were better than that. She hated to use the word loosely but it was like a miracle had taken place. The obvious signs of illness were no longer visible.

Mickey's heart was beating stronger than it had since he arrived months ago. There were no indication of a faulty valve. She couldn't believe her ears through her own stethoscope; no matter how many times she checked, the results were the same. His heart was exceptionally strong and rhythmic, like the heart of an athlete. He was rambling excitedly about the gift from Fionna. When he wasn't talking, he was loudly singing his favorite songs off key with an incredible smile on his face.

The sight and sounds of him made her remember the *holy water* that Fionna had snuck into the hospital; others had done the same thing before. She would have done it herself if she thought it would have made a difference. She had seen so many children come and go through those double doors, not all of them under their own power and not all of them ever made it back home.

Many people grew sick and died. When it happened to adults, it was interpreted as an unfortunate turn of events. But when it happened to the children, it was looked upon as a crime against humanity. *Why would a creator, with unlimited power, let such a thing happen to the children?* She had been wrestling with those thoughts her whole career, never really accepting things as they were. Some battles the children would win, but most they would lose. She felt hope growing inside her … for the little boys who always smiled, for the twins who always laughed, for the boy who believed, for the boy who cared, the girl who watched and for the girl who no longer seemed to be angry at the world. They grinned from ear to ear, as if they had secrets of their own.

Her thoughts were pulled away from Mickey and drawn to the needs of the others. She scurried over to Jennifer to find her dancing on the floor like a graceful ballerina, no longer in her bed that had been her home for so long. No longer hooked up to the life-giving dialysis machine that filtered her blood of toxins. But without the aid of the machine, she would slowly poison herself with her own bodily functions, *wouldn't she?*

Jennifer struggled to free herself from Sally's hands. She was adamant; said she didn't want to be connected to the dialysis machine … didn't need it any more … would never need it again. Incredibly, Jennifer's color was good; she no longer looked jaundiced, her yellowish tone had been replaced by pink. The lethargy and depression had vanished. Tied to a machine was a place she no longer wanted to be; she wanted to be free. In bewilderment, Sally gave in to her and moved on to the next child.

It was the excitement in Manuel's voice that gave her another chill and sent her running to his bedside. White bandages were strewn onto the floor and draped over the side of the bed.

"Look, it's disappearing!" he was on the verge of tears. "Look, it's a miracle, the Holy Mother has given me a gift!"

She grabbed his flailing arms with her good arm and examined them closely. It was unbelievable; a couple of days ago she had changed the bandages and the scars from the skin grafts were obvious. Sally stared open mouthed at his arm; she felt a chill surge throughout her body. The scar tissue on his arm had all but disappeared. "Great mother of God!" *Could Manuel have been right?* It was the blessing of a miracle that comprised his constant vigil.

Neither she or Shirley could believe what they were seeing. The children danced and sang. Even Manuel was out of his bed joining them. Bobby grabbed her good arm and pulled her along, the biggest smile she had ever seen etched on his face. An incredibly happy feeling overwhelmed her as she allowed herself to be pulled into the dancing circle. She danced until her aching muscles forced her to sit and try to understand what had happened. While it was only Mickey who talked about Fionna's gifts and Manuel's miracles, the others shook their heads. They knew something that they weren't about to share with her. Although Sally was aware of the holy water incident, she couldn't believe it worked. *What a Valentine's!*

Doctor Jean burst into the room panting heavily, her eyes wild in disbelief. Her stethoscope was barely hanging from her long, skinny neck. She had hurried as quickly as she could to the Children's Ward but was detained along the way by other tasks. She expected to find disaster but instead found unbelievable celebration. The children were out of their beds. Some were sitting on the floor, others danced around without a care in the world. They all seemed to be incredibly happy. "What on earth is going on here … why are children running amuck?"

Sally jumped out of her chair and pointed, but nothing came out of her mouth. She hadn't totally recovered from her own disbelief. She didn't know where to begin.

"My goodness … Jennifer, Michael, they're no longer hooked up to life support!"

"They don't appear to need it anymore," Sally shrugged her shoulders with control and confidence. "I can't seem to talk them into sticking needles, I.V.s, and wires back into them." She grabbed Jean's arm with her good one to slow her down as she attempted to pass. "Jean, Jean … I don't think it's necessary anymore … really! We checked them out … they are stable, everyone of them." Sally gave her a big smile.

Jean looked stunned.

Shirley nodded in agreement. "Sally's right, they are stable, incredibly stable," Shirley's voice reflected her astonishment.

"All of them?"

"Every single one of them," Shirley pointed to Manuel. "The

scars on his arm are hardly noticeable, I haven't checked the rest of him but I'm sure you'll find a notable change." Her voice was calm, her emotions in check.

Jean narrowed her eyes as if searching for the proof.

"Jennifer," Sally jumped in, her smile now replaced by wonder, "has the skin color indicating a properly functioning kidney. Michael's heart beats like an Olympic athletes. And if there is a pattern in all of this," she gave the others a knowing look, "I'll bet you will find the rest in remission if not completely cured."

Jean plopped loudly into the empty chair next to them. She looked from one child to the next as they went about their play. A couple of the children waved hello. She returned the wave without thought, her mind still racing through the possibilities. "We will have to do the tests right away!"

"Yes, of course, but they are only going to confirm the obvious. I don't know how to say this or whether or not I believe it myself."

Jean shot her an inquisitive look.

Sally cleared her throat before she spoke, "I do believe we have just witnessed a miracle. Seven of them to be exact." The pride and confirmation in her voice surprised her. But there was no other explanation for the experience. It was the thought of Fionna, the innocent, comatose sixteen-year-old that the rangers found in the forest and brought to the ward to recover, that made her wonder. She was sure now that the child was different, there was no doubt about that. All the children had taken to her; even Gina, the little girl who didn't like anyone, had spoken affectionately about Fionna. *Oh, what had that child done?*

Jean cringed at the word *miracle.* "It can't be, there are no such things as miracles," the scientist in her coming to the fore front. Almost as an after thought, a smile embraced her features.

Chapter Twenty-One

A Job to Do

Pepper firmly gripped the doorknob with one of her sweaty hands and turned it slowly until it was free of the latch, while sliding her glasses securely back onto her broad nose with the other. She felt her heart pounding in her temples and beads of sweat dripping down her back. She hated the butterfly feeling in her stomach but, more than that, she hated being summoned to the Editor's office, like she was a child sent to the principal's office for punishment.

For that matter, she *hated* the editor, Mr. Williams. Well, *hate* was a pretty harsh word, *disliked* was more appropriate but *misunderstood* was even better. A short, overweight little man, motivated by greed and power, he bellowed about everything. No matter what she did, or what lengths she had to go to get a story, the man was never satisfied. Of course, there were those he liked, the ones that could do no wrong; like Phyllis, his aged private secretary who perched birdlike at a desk on the other side of the two heavy wooden doors. Rumors flowed that the senile old woman was actually his devoted mother with whom he still lived. He was unmarried and she was pretty sure she knew why.

"*Well, here goes nothing!*" Pepper whispered to herself. She pulled herself together, shook her short, salt-and-pepper colored hair out of her eyes and forced the biggest smile she could muster.

She then firmly pushed open the double doors and walked in a steady, controlled gait in the direction of the reception desk to her right.

The desk chair creaked to attention as the elderly, gray haired woman flinched. She looked up in surprise, her hazy blue eyes searching for recognition as she busied herself by shuffling paperwork from one side of the desk to the other. As her memory cleared, her eyes narrowed, partially hidden behind round reading glasses that had slid down to the end of her nose.

Pepper held her satisfied smile, the grooves deepening across her broad tanned face. She had caught the receptionist nodding off again. As she hurried up to her desk, the sudden stench of lavender perfume filled her lungs and made her cough. Obviously, the woman had bathed in it.

"Good morning, Phyllis," she coughed again.

"Oh, hello, Pepper..." the pasted-on smile had returned to her face, "didn't hear you knock." Her dark penciled-in eyebrows stood out comically against her white hair and pale skin.

"I didn't knock."

"How was your vacation … you're not catching a cold, are you, dear?" Pepper couldn't tell if the woman was genuinely concerned or pleased by the thought of her impending illness.

"No, no, vacation was great," she lied. Her thoughts momentarily flashed back to her trip to Orange County for her high school's twenty-six year reunion planning meeting. The thought caused a sigh and she watched as Phyllis raise one of her penciled-in eyebrows sensing a bit of tabloid controversy. Like many of the good news women of her era, she definitely had a knack for digging until she found dirt she could use. In this case, most likely against Pepper.

Oh, what a waste of time that was, she remembered...

... She had blown off the last twenty-five years of her high school's reunions galas. But, for some strange reason, she decided that, at forty-four years of age, divorced, with no children and still employed for the moment, it might be interesting to help prepare for this year's silver plus anniversary. She wanted to see what she had been missing. She hardly remembered the people on the committee, or for that matter, most of the people in her high school graduating class. She recently dug out her high school year book, blew off the dust and tried to match names with faces. As she thumbed through the album, she was surprised that some of it started to come back. The people on the committee had been popular girls and guys and, of course, people that she hadn't paid much attention to nor they to her. She kept track of two friends, the ones she had gone off to college with in Northern California. It was one of them who suggested they help improve the reunions. But, like the story of her life, her friend dropped out at the last minute, leaving her alone, frustrated and committed to an event in which she had absolutely no interest.

As usual, she had arrived a couple of minutes late to the meeting at an attractive suite at one of the expensive hotels in Newport Beach. She felt out of place as she navigated the great, Louis IV mirrored halls to the soothing tempo of *Beethoven's Fifth*, while looking for suite 111-L. Eventually, she found the black numbers and letters on a shiny, gold-colored nameplate alongside two intricately carved wooden panels on the double doors. "It's 24k, no doubt," she commented on the reflective nameplate while using it as a mirror to brush back her hair. To her embarrassment, the heavy oak door moved easily and silently out of her way, unlike the ones in Phyllis's office. She unsuccessfully scrambled to keep them from swinging outward and banging noisily into the walls as they opened.

Her eyes wandered aimlessly around the huge, elegant room. It reminded her of a scene from the seventeenth century, like crossing the threshold and taking a step back in time. It was period decor right down to the bulky furniture, the velvet curtains and the grand piano that sat by the window with light reflecting off its freshly waxed finish.

Someone cleared their throat impatiently, forcing her attention back to the four people in the room. Everyone had stopped talking and were looking her up and down. She forced a smile and tried to hide her embarrassment as she scrambled to pull the doors back into the closed position.

"There, good as new." Pepper forced a breathless smile.

The three women gave her a curious look. They had painted nails, salon-curled hair, two-piece, pin-striped business suits, attractive makeup and an air of snooty, confident arrogance. They were in their element, whereas, Pepper was way out there somewhere. The gentleman, on the other hand, gave her a warm, welcoming smile. He looked familiar ... a middle-aged model with blond hair and blue eyes, six-foot-four, toned physique, and impeccable suit.

"You're late," scowled the most thoroughly preened of the three women, as the other two offered inquisitive stares.

Says who? Pepper's thoughts raced. If they didn't approve of her Birkenstock sandals, long silk tie-dyed dress and white embroidered hemp blouse, she didn't care. She felt a lot more comfortable than they looked.

"I couldn't find a parking spot," Pepper lied. The other two women nodded along with the man, an excuse to which they could relate.

"You must be Pepper," they recited in unison.

She nodded, "In the flesh!"

“Well, then,” one of the women gave her an impatient look, “would you like to have a seat so we can get started.”

She felt a sudden dislike for the woman at the head of the carved, mahogany table. She worked her way over towards the big table, but was relieved when the man offered her a chair.

“Thank you.” said Pepper.

“Hello, Pepper, I’m Mark … Mark Jones.” He extended his hand and gave a little laugh, “I was the …”

“Prom King,” she offered. “Yes, I remember … it has been awhile.”

“Yes, it has, you remembered?”

She nodded, but she hadn’t really. She didn’t have the heart to tell him that she had cracked open her old yearbook and did her homework. *Oh, how long ago high school had been!*

“This is my lovely wife Amelia … you probably remember her.”

“Yes, nice to see you again.” There was no substance to her hand shake. Pepper felt like she was inconveniencing the woman by being there.

“You were the Prom Queen.” Pepper forced a smiled. “You got married? Wow.” She didn’t know what else to say. It was a very small town, marry your high school sweet heart. The thought fascinated her.

“Yes, that was a long time ago.” Amelia forced a smile in return.

The other three ladies introduced themselves, but Pepper forgot their names as soon as they said them. None of them seemed real and sincere. *So much for being a people person today.* That’s when she realized that the piped in music in the hallway had stopped. It was like entering another world.

She decided to give them a chance at least.

Evidently, the group was staying in the expensive hotel and had been there for a couple of days already. Their commute consisted of an elevator ride after their manicure, followed most likely by a pedicure, a brunch of some kind and a casual stroll to the great hall of the early Nineteenth Century. Successful in their careers or their marriages, they offered themselves on the altar of obligation; they were giving back to the less fortunate. Pepper felt extremely out of place.

Pepper had not attended any of the past reunions and now she knew why. She had heard that some ended in drunken brawls or snobby competitions. The big fight one-year was probably from sheer, ridiculous boredom or the unearthing of old wounds. Sadly, that reunion was probably the most entertaining, no thanks to the legendary Mrs. Jones. Pepper could see herself clobbering the Homecoming Queen over the head with a full bottle of champagne, just for the heck of it.

Mrs. Amelia Jones, Homecoming Queen of nearly twenty-six years ago, took her role very seriously. Pepper's suggestion to try something new and different ended with Mrs. Jones countering with "The reunions have worked so well, I don't see the point in changing what isn't broken!" or "Maybe if you had attended at least one of these you would see what we mean!" Her annoying sing song voice wrung in Pepper's mind. What bothered her even more was the fact that the other members of the committee just went along, even Mr. Prom King Jones proved to be spineless, most likely kept in his place by his better half. Plans were supposed to be a group effort, but she made five, the odd person out. As far as she was concerned, the others were meant for each other. They had been absent from her life too long for her to really care. They were from two different worlds. Mark, on the other hand, nice, handsome, and well proportioned …

The nasal honk from Phyllis dissolved Pepper's trance.

"Are you feeling okay, dear?" She leaned forward and narrowed her eyes. "Are you sure there is nothing about your trip you want to share … to get off your chest?"

"Oh … no, no it's just the strong scent of flowers." She tried not to breathe in too deeply as she spoke, "It's the lavender that hit me."

"You like it?" Phyllis flashed a toothy smile with perfectly straight white teeth. *Obviously not her original set.* Thought Pepper.

"It was a gift from … Mr. Williams." She awaited Pepper's answer with arched eyebrows.

The perfume or the teeth? Pepper turned a snicker into a cough. "It's very pungent." She quickly changed the subject, "So what's up with the old man?" She nodded in the direction of Mr. Williams' office.

Phyllis wrinkled her forehead even more than usual in disapproval. "Oh, Chuck is a little under the weather today; he needs someone to swing by the hospital and interview one of the doctors, they are excited about their new x-ray machine."

Chuck! Am I the only one around here who calls him Mr. Williams? Pepper felt her smile fade. She was a people person, not a machinery guy. The last thing she wanted to do was interview someone about a boring piece of machinery. She had to think fast. "What about Harvey, the gadget geek, I thought he liked doing all of those boring technical follow-ups?"

"He's sick."

"Sick? What about good ol' Bill? He doesn't mind …"

"High school sports," the woman replied, curtly.

"Doesn't he know he's too old to play high school sports?"

Phyllis just stared at her, obviously not appreciating her sense of humor.

"Diana?" Pepper continued.

"Day off, won't be back until tomorrow."

"For heaven's sake, can't the story wait until then?" She pleaded, her smile long gone.

"Evidently, not, I'll let Chuck know you're here."

She spoke into the intercom in a disgustingly sweet voice that Pepper barely heard.

"Peppermint," the angry voice boomed from beyond the closed wooden doors. "Where have you been, you're late!"

"It's Pepper," she sighed under her breath. She stood there for a moment staring towards the doors.

"Hurry up and get your tail in here. Time is money, you know … my money!"

"Yeah, time is money!" Pepper mumbled under her breath as she rolled her eyes back towards Phyllis. She forced a confidante wink as she felt her stomach tighten.

Phyllis nodded her head in the direction of the double doors, "He will see you now." She obviously found satisfaction in Pepper's discomfort.

"You think!" Pepper turned and walked towards the door. She stopped when she heard Phyllis remark, "I must warn you, he is in a foul mood today."

"Is he ever not!" she said without turning her head to give Phyllis the satisfaction of seeing her face.

Phyllis shrugged and went back to the useless shuffling of papers on her desk.

Pepper swallowed and knocked on the huge doors. She knew better than to barge in on the man who signed her paychecks.

"Peppermint, get in here already!"

"Pepper she mumbled as she turned the knob and pushed one of the doors open. The odd mixture of leather bound books, stale cigars and a forest scented air freshener assailed her nose. It reminded her of an underused library. She stepped around the worn, red and black rectangular Navaho rug that covered the forest green tile. She thought it a crime to step on such a beautiful object. She could never understand why he would leave such a priceless object on the floor to be walked on. Beyond the rug sat a huge, heavy oak desk. Her eyes quickly scanned the room. Nothing had changed since she had been there last. In fact, nothing had changed since she had started working for the paper seven years ago. Off white walls, dark furniture, a huge bookcase filled with hardback books. A working model of a steam donkey sat in a Plexiglas case, a miniature of the machine used in logging operations during the 1880s to pull heavy logs out of the forest. Above it hung yellowed black and white photographs of the machines in action throughout different forested locations in Northern California and Southern Oregon. There were other framed pictures from the early twentieth century … timber fallers in baggy pants and suspenders, pin-striped shirts with rolled up sleeves stood next to men in three piece suits, holding felt derbies in their hands. They stood proudly as they stared into the lens, awaiting the flash of the camera that would record that moment in time. Behind them rested an incredibly large coastal redwood that must have been at least 1600 years old. Above the gnarly base and approximately ten feet above the forest floor, a triangular wedge-like cut had been removed from its base exposing the darker, rot-resistant heart wood, the very reason its species had been selectively chosen. Below the cut, balanced on a section of the tree's burl-like base was the blade of a double buck saw that extended out beyond the width of the tree. Two burly timber fallers sprawled inside the massive cut were scowling confidently at the camera, for that moment, masters of their universe.

Near the model sat another, a late nineteenth century detailed replica of a four-mast schooner that once hauled the logs down the rugged coast to the San Francisco Bay. Certificates and awards hung in glass frames on a special wall to her right. The office reflected his family history. He had inherited the paper business from his father, who had inherited from his.

"Please have a seat."

Please? She looked back at the pale skin and baggy cheeks of the balding man behind the desk. His gray, two piece suit matched the decor of the room perfectly. She was surprised to see him smiling.

He gestured toward the chair that sat in front of the desk with his ham hock fingers.

"So, did you have a nice vacation?"

She paused for a moment, but just as she was about to answer, he broke into his usual rhythm. "That's good, that's good, so then you should be all rested up and ready to go!"

"Well, I guess …"

"Excellent, excellent! I have an assignment for you."

"Phyllis mentioned that …" She pointed over her shoulder in the direction of her desk.

"Then it is settled … he is expecting you this afternoon."

"Who? What?"

"Marshal … Doctor Marshal. This is going to be some good press for us." He leaned back in his huge leather chair. "You see, we donated some money towards the purchase of their new x-ray machine." He spoke quickly and confidently. "They needed a new machine and well, …it's a good tax write off and all that stuff. That hospital has been around for a long time. My father used to give donations for equipment all the time."

She nodded. His mood seemed a bit more up beat and she wasn't about to give him an excuse to be his usual self. "So, your family has been giving to the hospital for years?"

"Oh, yes, you keep the doctors happy, they keep you healthy, if you know what I mean." He laughed as he patted his chest with his open palms.

Some things never change, she thought.

"He will be expecting you at 1:00 this afternoon at St. Francis Memorial Hospital." He narrowed his eyes to make a point, "Be there on time, will you!"

She knew it would be useless to argue. "Okay, I will meet the good doctor at 1:00." Her voice sounded less enthusiastic than it did when she first stepped into his office.

"Marshal …," he raised his eyebrows.

Oddly, Pepper thought she saw a twinkle in his blue eyes.

"Doctor Marshal is single you know. Doctors make good money these days." He slipped the words out as he slid some papers across his desk and busied his hands organizing them.

"What!" She cleared her throat, suddenly taken back by not what he said, but what she thought he meant.

"And while you're there, maybe he can give you something for that cold of yours. I want to put your article in tomorrow's paper so let's get her done. Time is money …"

"Yes, I know … your money! And by the way, I think I can find my own dates," she retorted.

"Well, I thought..."

She stood up and frowned over her glasses at him. "For your information, if I wanted a date, I am fully capable of finding my own, thank you very much." She wrinkled her nose at his apparent nervousness. "I will be fine. I will interview the wonderful doctor, write an exceptionally interesting article on the stupid laser machine …"

"X-ray machine …" he corrected.

"X-ray machine and have it ready to go to the printers by midnight. Slam dunk!"

He nodded as he avoided eye contact, "Uh, good!"

She turned, walked half way across the room and stopped and turned around. "And for the record my name is Pepper not Peppermint and I can find my own dates thank you very much." She turned, headed out the double doors and shut them loudly behind her without looking over her shoulder. She could feel his eyes following her out. Strangely, he had been right. She hadn't had a decent date in a while. Everyone in the office seemed to know that. In a strange way, she was actually looking forward to the doctor's interview. She smiled at Phyllis as she walked past her desk. The secretaries mouth was hanging half open, a surprised look on her face. *Priceless.* This time she didn't have to work at it.

Chapter Twenty-Two

Seeing is Believing

The excited phone call from Sally, the hospital nurse, made Paul's heart skip a couple of beats. He clumsily set the receiver back in place, leaving his hand on the telephone and gazed quietly at the color photograph hanging on his office wall.

The picture was the one he had taken of the mammoth, ancient tree that dripped what Fionna called the *essence of life*. He squinted into the rich green and earthy brown background for anything unusual. The tall ferns funneled his eyes into the thickly furrowed, reddish-brown fibrous bark. The tree was symmetrical except for the huge base that bulged close to the ground like the bottom of a melted candle. Its strange growth was a distinct sign of its age and it ranking within ancient redwoods. It was special, unique among the rest but it was not the only one in the grove that reflected signs of old age and ancient wisdom. The fact that it was in a part of the park that he had never been to before also added to its mystique.

He tried to imagine fairies fluttering around its base or wiggling their thick toes into the spongy moss of a downed log nearby but failed. This he had seen but his mind wasn't quite ready and or willing to accept the world of myths, legends and fairytales as fact. It had only been two weeks since the bizarre scene presented itself and caught him off guard. It went against everything he was taught, everything he thought and believed in. His belief system had shifted through multiple paradigms.

He tried unsuccessfully to relax and relieve the tension in his neck and shoulders but he could not pull his eyes away from the photograph or his hand from the receiver. He remembered the joy of finding Fionna and the unusual circumstances that followed.

As in many traumatic events, the rescuer was idolized for his feat, whether it was as simple as being in the right place at the right time or going beyond what was expected of him. He had only done his job. He had located a missing hiker and completed what every search and rescue person wanted to do, return him or her to their loved ones, alive and in one piece, and when the job was done, proudly walk away and move on to the next.

But he couldn't, something would not let him. At first there were the moving shadows … fairies? Then, voices in the forest … fairies? The sweet smell of flowers … the ancient trees? And, finally, the incredible face to face meeting with the fairies themselves. Real, honest to goodness fairies. Everything he had ever learned about the subject was wrong. And if that was wrong, *what else that he grew up knowing could be wrong?* He lived in a cloud of confusion that he shared with his fellow park ranger, Susan. Once a major skeptic, she had now swung the other way but she didn't know what to make of the whole mess that she blamed him for getting her into. She was dealing with it one step at a time. It was their little secret, one she wished she was not a part of. He wasn't quite sure how the phone call he just received would affect her. He wasn't so sure how he was going to handle it himself. Then, there was Fionna, the wild card, the teenager they had found … or rather were led to in the forest.

Evidently, based on the statements of Fionna's family and friends, Fionna had changed. Some said it was like part of her was still lost in the forest; others said a forest spirit had stolen her soul and was now using her to convince the human race to save old growth forest habitats. From what Paul had seen, their statements might not be that far off the mark.

Upon awakening from her coma, the young woman had incredible insight into things she had never known before. Her story wasn't all that much different than some of the others he had heard. About people who woke from comas or survived incredible accidents to find their minds supercharged with facts, figures and theories. Unfortunately, their abilities were frequently short lived. Gifts or curses, it was all a matter of interpretation.

At any rate, Fionna was no longer the timid teenager she had once been. She exuded unique confidence and an incredible desire to help. Paul was unsettled as well. It was as if he too had unfinished business to take care of … an empty void to fill.

First hearing of her recovery had pleased him and he could not resist the urge to reconstruct her bizarre story and shine some light on the strange uneasiness that had grown within himself. He had seen and heard things in the forest that he couldn't explain and somehow knew she had the answers. But he was absolutely not ready for what he had learned. Although her message was bizarre, he believed her, instead of writing her off as a teen who had hit her head a little too hard. Against his better judgment, he let her talk him into the strange plan to heal the patients in the Children's Ward. *Fairies in the forest, we need to protect them and the ancient trees!* Fionna's frantic voice echoed in his head. He realized he still had a white-knuckled grip on the phone and released it.

And now it had come true. It was incredible; seven children

were no longer sick, miraculously cured. The Children's Ward was upside down. Sally was trying to tie Fionna's visit to the event and, by the tone of her voice, he thought that she included him as a possible miracle worker as well. Evidently, the hospital was keeping the information under wraps until they could figure out exactly what really happened. Sally wanted to meet him at the hospital in private. Although he intended to go, he had no idea what he would say. Somehow, he didn't think telling her "*a fairy in the forest gave them something to heal the children.*" would set the record straight. He dreaded the visit but, at the same time, he was looking forward to seeing the children who were once on their deathbeds now excitedly running around. The amazement of the medical staff and families would be an added bonus. He decided to ask Susan to come along for support. If a second person confirmed his wild story, maybe others would believe.

He was still concentrating on the photograph when he saw it. An icy tingle raced down his spine and out through the tips of his fingers. There, hidden among the earth tones of the vegetation was a face. Paul slowly raised from his chair and shakily made his way towards the photograph. Not once did he take his eyes off the picture for fear of losing what he had seen. He stopped in front of the photo and rested his hands on the wall, one on each side of the forest photograph. It was as if he were keeping whatever it was that he seen from escaping. It was still there, right there! The beads of cold, nervous sweat tickled as they glided down his temples.

The big dark eyes, broad forehead, distinguishable thin mouth and obvious nose peered out from the tangle of surrounding ferns. Paul moved his head from side to side and took turns closing one of his eyes. *Why didn't I see that before?* To his surprise there was another face, this one smaller and darker, further back, almost hidden. He frantically searched for more.

"What on earth? Paul, are you feeling okay?" The voice made him flinch but he quickly recognized it as Susan's.

He stepped away from the picture and locked into her worried gaze. She stood within arm's reach, her hands resting impatiently on the edge of her hips, beneath them her leather gun belt.

"Are you doing that wall thing again?" She nodded to the photograph. "First, you stare at that thing like some kind of art critic and then you behave as if you'd seen a ghost or something. I came because you said you got a phone call and I find you braced on the wall in another world."

Paul saw the worry and concern on her face and by the tone of her voice, he could imagine what she saw in his. He tried to reclaim his calm, confident voice he knew he had hidden somewhere inside. "It has begun! Susan … Fionna did it! And there is nothing we can do about it now." The blank stare he received from his fellow park ranger was expected.

"Did what?"

Paul pointed to the phone. "That was Sally, the hospital nurse … she wants to meet me … us, this afternoon." He raised his eyebrows. "The children, well, they are no longer … sick." He found himself speaking in short sentences, he didn't know if it was for her benefit or his own.

Susan nervously looked over her shoulder to make sure the office was still empty, which it was, the other ranger wasn't due in until later on that afternoon. "What?" She barked back in a harsh whisper. "How can that be?"

Paul thought he saw the color drain from her face. "The seven children in the Children's Ward are no longer sick. The place is in disarray. The doctors and nurses don't know what to do!"

"Why did Sally call us? She doesn't suspect us, does she? Those children didn't say anything did they … you said they promised." There was a tinge of panic in her voice.

"Not us … she called about Fionna."

"So, why does she want to talk to us?"

Paul shrugged. He repeated the whole conversation he had on the phone, making a point not to leave anything out. The more he listened to himself speak, the more he started to worry. He wasn't sure if he had missed Sally's subtle hints the first time or if it was Susan who was making him paranoid. *Had they done anything wrong? After all, holy water was … holy water. Practicing medicine without a license was one thing, but administering holy water … it wasn't against the law to bless people, was it?*

"So, you think Sally is going to believe you when you come right out and say, *the fairies in the forest made you do it!*"

The way she exaggerated her voice made Paul laugh. He didn't mean to laugh, but it made him feel better; it helped clear his thoughts.

"This is no laughing matter," she scolded. "I, for one, like my job." She paced back and forth a couple of times, running her fingers through her hair. She appeared to be in deep thought. Then she abruptly stopped and slapped the sides of her pants. "*Geeeeeeees*," she exhaled in frustration. "How did I ever let you talk me into doing this … stupid idea of yours in the first place?"

"I didn't!" He pointed towards the enlarged photo on the wall. "I believe it was them."

"What?" She looked back at the photograph in disbelief. "A stupid picture of the forest … oh yes, a stupid picture of an old tree, yeah … that's going to do it. Yeah, it's got me convinced," she uttered sarcastically as she rolled her eyes toward the ceiling.

"It's what's in the photo that matters." Paul stepped up to it and placed his finger just below the first figure he had seen. "You asked me what was wrong earlier, whether or not I had seen a ghost, remember?" He tapped on the photo confidently. "Well, maybe not a ghost but in this case, the next best thing. Look!" He motioned towards the photo. She reluctantly walked over. "Look, there, right there!" He emphasized again hardly being able to control his excitement. She followed the finger with her eyes and then squinted into the photograph.

Paul watched her closely; he knew exactly when she saw it. Her eyebrows almost seemed to jump off of her forehead and her mouth would have dropped below her chin if it weren't attached. "My God, it's them, it's them! How did you ..."

"Lucky I guess; I didn't notice it until after the phone call."

She carefully scrutinized the photograph."

"There's a second one, over here." He pointed. Her eyes quickly followed. He could also tell when she found the second.

"Are there any more?"

"Why, isn't two enough?" He shook his head. "We're going to bring this with us this afternoon."

"You're not planning on showing this to her are you? You really think these blob-shots are going to convince her?"

"Show it to her," he shook his head, "not unless I have to. And do I think these are going to convince her?" He examined the photo again. "She believes in miracles you know, and if she believes in that, why not this." He smiled at Susan. "Something convinced the biggest skeptic I know!"

"Well, let's get going. Time's a-wastin'."

Chapter Twenty-Three

The Inquisitor

Paul and Susan paused at the double doors to the Children's Ward and gave each other an supportive glance. They had said hardly a word to each other during the forty-minute drive north to the town of Springville and the parking lot of St. Francis Memorial. Paul was pretty sure they were both thinking the same thing. *Let's get this over with!* Susan slapped him playfully on the arm that held the rolled up photograph a little harder than she had intended. The sound echoed in the hallway and numbed Paul's arm. "Take it easy there, Wonder Woman," Paul forced a laugh as he attempted to rub out the soreness.

"Sorry about that!" Susan mumbled through her clenched teeth as she casually glanced around the busy hallway. "It's my ninja training." To his surprise, no one appeared to give the two-uniformed park rangers a second look, a behavior that Paul thought very unusual indeed. *But then again, if two rangers were seen slapping each other around …*

"Coast is clear, you first," she said as she gently pushed him toward the doors.

Paul paused a moment to clear his thoughts.

"You're not telling me that I hurt a big strong ranger like you?" She shook her head in a mock display of disgust. "Age before beauty," she sighed.

"Beauty before wisdom."

"Get in there before I punch your other shoulder … remember, you're the reason we're here."

"Point taken," he nodded, rubbing his shoulder to tease her further.

"Oh, for heaven's sake, men can be such babies sometimes!" she exclaimed as she brushed past him, pushed open the double door and strutted confidently down the long hall towards the reception desk. Paul dropped his arm and followed; playtime was over, it was now time to get serious. He nervously rolled the photograph tube between his fingers, well aware of its importance. Eighties rock echoed louder than usual down the long reception area. For now, *Barney* was something of the past. The thought made him smile. There had indeed been some changes around there. He noticed that there weren't any parents hanging around either. He glanced at Susan but she wouldn't have noticed the changes since this was her first time there. She was focused on the blonde head sticking up from behind the front desk and counter. Paul recognized Sally. He felt his heart pound a bit faster as he walked quickly in an attempt to beat his partner to an introduction. He wanted things to run smoothly.

Paul tapped on the counter.

Sally flinched noticeably and gave them a surprised look, "Oh, I didn't hear you come in." They could barely hear her over the sounds of the rock group *Queen*.

Susan tilted her head towards Paul and mumbled only loud enough for him to hear, "Obviously."

"We're a little early," Paul admitted as he playfully kicked Susan lightly against the back of her calf.

She kicked him back harder against the side of his knee. "Ninjas!" She mumbled over her breath.

He cleared his throat to cover the minor discomfort and shot her an annoyed glance.

She shrugged her shoulders defiantly and looked at Sally as if nothing had happened.

Sally rose to her feet and turned down the music; the room suddenly became much quieter. "It got too quiet around here without the children … thank you for coming Paul. As you can imagine, I have a few unanswered questions," she gestured with her good arm towards the empty beds down the hall behind her, "and, I imagine, you do too!"

Paul reached over the desk to shake her hand but hesitated when he noticed that one of her arms was in a sling.

She read his thought. "Oh, I had a little accident during the earthquake."

"Earthquake?" Susan interjected.

"You must be Susan Sheatham?" Sally smiled and extended her good arm to shake Susan's hand, then Paul's as well. "I really appreciate your taking time out for us and dropping by so soon. I really don't know where to begin. But somehow, I think you do!" She paused a moment to let her words settle in. "Please, have a seat; we need to talk."

Paul and Susan walked around the edge of the counter and took seats. Sally quickly joined them. At first they sat there and stared at each other as if each wanted to know what the other had to say, but no one wanted to be the first.

"So, all the children are gone?" Paul stated the obvious. "Seven, weren't there?"

He nervously tried to swallow but nothing happened. He opened his mouth to speak, but nothing came out.

Sally's scowl melted into a smile and she wiped away a tear that trickled down her cheek with the back of her hand. “Incredibly, they are all cured, every single one of them! I suppose you don’t know anything about that, do you?”

Paul toyed with the laces on his boot, while Susan examined her nails.

Their reticence opened the floodgates and the words flowed freely from Sally’s heart. She talked about Fionna and the holy water. The moderate earthquake that was centered off the coast, and how it temporarily knocked out the power at the hospital. How every child’s health had improved. How Manuel’s sudden recovery had been the most incredible of all. How the tests had proved what she could not bring herself to believe. The children no longer suffered from the ailments they had when they arrived and that, with no other logical explanation, they had witnessed multiple miracles. “Unless there is anything you can add!” She sipped her coffee and watched Paul closely over the top of her cup.

Paul was going to wait for the right moment to speak, even if it took all afternoon.

“I confronted Fionna,” Sally uttered.

Paul suddenly strained to hear her every word.

“She said the strangest things.” Sally continued, her voice steady and filled with admiration. “She made me promise to keep a secret … and for some strange reason I accepted. It was like, you know … the right thing to do.” She set down her cup, looked off as if seeing Fionna’s face in the distance and returned to Paul, “Maybe it will help if I tell you what I already know. Fionna admitted that the *holy water* was responsible for the miracle … that the *holy water* came from the forest … the ancient redwood trees.” She laughed nervously, “That the fairies told her where she could find it?”

Paul started to say something but Sally held up her hand and stopped him before the words could slip out of his mouth.

“What am I to believe; I watched the results walk right out

of this place." She pointed towards the door, "I have never seen a happier group of kids. Can you believe it, they all covered for her. One by one, they looked me in the eye and told me they had no idea how they became healthy. They just shrugged their shoulders but they all agreed that a miracle was responsible. It was Mickey who shared the bit about the *holy water*, bless his little heart, and Fionna confirmed it." She shrugged, "Based on what I have seen here, how can I argue with that? I guess there are such things as miracles.

"The hospital administration is pulling their hair out trying to figure how it happened. How an earthquake lead up to a miraculous cure of seven children with a variety of illnesses. I made a promise not to share," she nodded towards the door, "and I keep my promises; I am a woman of my word. It is obvious to me that what I witnessed is definitely not what one would call normal. You found her in the forest. I'll bet the two of you know more about this than you're letting on …"

Paul took great pride in reading people; his line of work had taught him well. She appeared honest and sincere; he felt he could trust her. She had always kept the children's welfare in mind in everything she did. He looked deep within himself and asked what he should do. Evidently, to his surprise, Fionna had already pulled the 'F' card, revealed the plan and mentioned the fairies.

Susan's look pleaded for him to keep quiet. "She already knows but just doesn't understand," Paul whispered, indirectly asking for her permission to continue.

Susan wrinkled her forehead, as if in deep thought. "I guess a little knowledge can be dangerous. You're right; she already has part of the picture, it makes sense to include her. Show her your picture, maybe that will shine light on the subject."

"Picture?" Sally could not hide her anxiety.

"Sally, do you believe in fairies? That ancient redwood trees have the power to heal? That teenaged girls have the power to bring it all together?" Paul queried profoundly.

Sally gave him a surprised look; she wondered if he was having fun at her expense.

Paul slipped the rolled photograph from its protective tube, slipped off the rubber band and unfurled the large picture across the counter top. Susan helped hold down the edges, while Sally moved closer for a better look.

"Tell me what you see," Paul instructed. He watched her closely as she scanned the picture.

"An old tree? What exactly am I looking for?"

"Look beyond the tree, beyond the obvious." Paul slowly moved his index finger until it stopped just below the face, then tapped the picture three times. He watched Sally's eyes suddenly grew in size, her face contort to an astonished expression.

Her mouth dropped open. "My gosh, is that what I think I'm seeing?"

"Well, that all depends if what you're looking at is what you think your looking at," Susan mumbled loud enough for her to hear.

"Do you believe in such things?" Paul asked.

"I really don't know what to believe … it's the twenty-first century, there aren't supposed to be things like this around..."

"Yes, I know, myths and fairytales … no one in their right mind is going to believe a word of it." Susan laughed, "Hello, shrink, here I come!"

"It is true," Paul said. "As incredible as it may sound, they are indeed there. And, from my understanding, have been there since the late 1800s."

Without breaking her concentration on the photograph, Sally plopped down noisily onto one of the vinyl chairs. It creaked under the strain of her weight. "So, everything Fionna said is true?"

"Yep, afraid so." exclaimed Susan.

"Well, as far as we know … yes. I don't know how to explain it, but I guess we're part of the plan now."

Sally stopped staring at the picture. "Please tell me how it started, how you got involved."

Paul looked to Susan for her support. She nodded in agreement.

"Oh, what the heck, the more the merrier!"

He cleared his throat and began at the beginning.

Chapter Twenty-Four

The Interview

"You must be Peppermint Jensen," the young nurse at the contact desk smiled. Her voice flowed in a pleasant, Southern, sing-song twang.

"It's Pepper," she corrected with a forced smile. *After all, it wasn't her fault*, she told herself. The responsibility fell on Mr. Williams … aka, Chucky, her boss for nearly seven labor-intensive years, who still hadn't taken the time to know her name. Evidently nor she his first name either.

"You're right on time." The nurse handed her a plastic covered visitor badge and asked her to sign in on the clipboard that was slid in front of her.

Pepper scratched her name on the paper before she glanced at the visitor badge in her hand that read, ***Peppermint Jensen …Visitor***. She sighed before she put it on.

"Welcome, Pepper … sorry about that," she nodded at the badge, "but that was what I was given."

Pepper shrugged; there wasn't much she could do about it now anyway.

"Doctor Marshal is expecting you, he asked me to call him as soon as you arrived." She reached for the intercom phone with her immaculately groomed pink painted nails and pushed the intercom button with the eraser of a pencil. "He will be down to meet you."

Pepper looked self-consciously at her short stubby nails. No matter how hard she tried, she could never dream of matching the nurse's. Her lifestyle prevented it. She liked it when she was in control of her destiny and she no longer wanted to wait around. "No, that's all right," she looked down the hallway. "If you tell me where his office is, I'll save him the trip."

The nurse looked up at her surprised. "He really won't mind coming down, as a matter of fact, he …"

Pepper cut her off, "Actually, I really don't mind the walk. I insist. This will give me an opportunity to see the hospital along the way. I promise, I won't get lost!"

After a slight pause, the nurse recovered, "Well then, I will let him know you're on your way."

"Thank you." For that moment, Pepper seemed pleased with herself; she once again felt in control but she knew better.

The nurse pointed towards her left, "Just follow the signs to the *Administrative Wing* down the hallway on your right. Go through the double doors and look for Room 25. It will be on your right. Doctor Marshal will be expecting you."

"Sounds easy enough," Pepper nodded, adjusted her glasses and was on her way. She liked the flip-flop sound of her Birkenstocks that echoed down the waxed, linoleum floors. The place smelled like she expected a hospital would, sanitized. She weaved in and out of the green, gown-clad staff as she made her way to the *Administrative Wing*. Most acknowledged her existence with a quick glance, some with curious stares, and others with welcomed obliviousness. Those were the ones she rather preferred. She felt the fewer people who gave her a second look, the better. She noticed with growing interest and building mistrust that she was the only person in the hospital wearing a visitor's badge pinned to her white hemp vest. She slipped her hand over her badge as she continued to walk. She could hardly wait to lose it.

She momentarily stopped at another intersection and scanned the alphabetized list of hospital destinations; the one she was looking for was at the top of the list, ***ADMINISTRATION WING***. She read through the other five just to make sure. ***X-RAY***, with an arrow pointing in the opposite direction, would also be one of the destinations of the day so she would end up walking the length of the hospital after all … more to see, more to do, more things to entertain herself with. She never really liked going to hospitals, a pleasure right up there with visiting ones dentist or psychologist, both of whom had consumed plenty of her quality time. One was because of her notorious sweet tooth and soft enamel and the other was related to an earlier, unpleasant divorce which also led to more of the first. In both cases, it was like pulling teeth. She giggled to herself then looked furtively around to see if anyone noticed.

She heard voices and the sounds of people approaching and casually placed her hand over the bulky badge. She stared straight ahead and acted as if she was still reading the sign, knowing that if she looked even the slightest bit lost or confused, some do-gooder would feel obliged to assist her. The hospital was full of them; they were all there to help in one form or another. And that, no doubt, would lead to more questions, more confusion. She wasn't there to answer questions; she was there to ask them.

The conversation between the two nurses became suspiciously quieter as they approached. She wouldn't have thought anything of it but it was their hushed cautious tones that drew her attention. She couldn't help herself, she was a reporter, she had a nose and, in this case, an ear for gossip.

She glanced at them, making a point not to move her head,

tried to appear oblivious to their presence. The taller woman wore standard green scrubs, while the shorter wore a unique, pink colored smock with a flowered print. What she heard captured her interest and ignited the inquisitive torch she carried within. She felt her body go ridged as she fought her reaction to turn and face them. She clearly heard the words, "Children's Ward … miraculous cures … administration … keeping it quiet …" This was much better than donations for a new x-ray machines and a family legacies.

When the two nurses got closer, they stopped talking all together and eyed her suspiciously. Pepper finally turned towards them, fleetingly looking at the pink gown and instinctively searching for a name tag. **Shirley Garcia** was stenciled in black letters. "That is a beautiful uniform," Pepper exclaimed. "How do you get away with wearing that while everyone else has to wear that god-awful green?" She pointed to the taller woman's attire, knowing she wasn't making any points.

The taller woman just stared at her.

Shirley smiled, "Oh, I work in the Children's Ward; we get to dress a little more colorful. It helps the children feel a bit more … at home."

The thought of children having to stay in the hospital caused Pepper a momentary twinge. "Is the Children's Ward out that way?" Pepper pointed in the direction they had come. "It must be quite different dealing with children in a dreary hospital."

"Yes, it can be demanding at times …" Shirley's eyes revealed some discomfort before she turned away and pointed in the direction they had come. "It's basically at the end of the hall. But, there aren't any children there right now."

"No children, then where are they?" Pepper asked innocently. She noticed the wary look the taller woman gave Shirley … perhaps a warning to keep silent.

"The ward is currently vacant," the taller woman spoke as she noted Pepper's hand that still covering her visitor badge.

"I'm Doctor Jean Excelsior, is there anything I can help you with ….?" She made an obvious attempt to look for her name.

Pepper fought to keep her poker face, not wanting to appear inquisitive about the ease in which the good doctor changed the topic. There was obviously something about the Children's Ward they didn't want her to know.

"Oh," a pleasant booming voice caught them all by surprise. "You must be Pepper!" He made an obvious point to pronounce it right.

That was a fast correction with the name. she thought. *Nice!*

A tall, handsome man with thinning blond hair extended his hand. "I'm Doctor Robert Marshal, but you can call me Bob."

She gave his large, cold, moist hand a firm shake and then unconsciously looked at her own hand.

"Oh, I'm sorry." He quickly wiped his hands on the sides of his green smock. "I just came from the bathroom … I mean, I just washed my hands, didn't dry them off well enough. I'm saving paper towels." He nervously stuck out his hand again for examination. "See, just water."

If you say so. Pepper looked at his hands and raised an eyebrow. Though he was a bit goofy, she took a sudden liking to his simple, honest nature. *Probably one of those save the whale types.*

"I see you have met some of our fine hospital staff," he nodded to the women. "Jean, Shirley, this is Pepper Jensen, she works for the local paper."

"*The Eel River Sentinel*," Pepper corrected. She thought she saw the color fade from their faces and the strength drain from some of their grips as she reached out to shake their extended hands. Doctor Excelsior's hand was cold and clammy like she had just washed her hands as well. Pepper felt a sudden dislike for Jean.

"She is here to do a story on our new x-ray machine," Doctor Marshal's voice boomed. "The proprietor of the *Eel River Sentinel*, Chuck, I mean Mr. Williams, sent her to write the article."

She watched as the expressions of the two ladies faces suddenly changed from concern to one of relief. Pepper's growing suspicions deepened … something was definitely more complicated that an x-ray machine.

"It's great to have the machine, it works much better than the old unreliable one." Shirley smiled. "We never really knew how safe the older one was. It was a flip of the coin whether it was an x-ray or a microwave."

Pepper joined her laughter, while Doctor Marshal gave Shirley a disapproving look.

"Well, it's true," Shirley stammered along. "The equipment is probably older than me and I'm no spring chicken!"

This one Pepper liked.

"Well, got to go before I get myself in more trouble," Shirley reached out and shook Pepper's hand goodbye. Doctor Jean gave a nod before the duo headed off down the hallway in the opposite direction. They spoke in low whispers and Pepper had no doubt that they were talking about her.

"How about a tour?"

Pepper pointed to her visitor badge. "I seem to be the only one wearing this."

He looked embarrassed. "I'm terribly sorry about the miscommunication on the name. Well, the name badge is policy. Every one at the hospital has to wear one."

"Really?" She raised her eyebrows. "They just don't all seem to be as huge as mine."

"Like your more important … a special guest!"

"Well, I hadn't quite looked at it like that before. To me it was more like … *who do we have here!*" She forced a laugh. "I believe you have been badly misinformed, I prefer not to even be noticed. Besides, this seemed to make the staff nervous like they thought that I was here to check on them or something."

"I'm terribly sorry … As long as you're here with me, I won't make you wear it if you don't want to." The doctor suddenly seemed concerned that he might have offended her.

Pepper decided to leave the silly visitor badge in place, not wanting to hurt his feelings or break policy.

"Not a problem, I guess I will just have to wear it then." She couldn't believe it; she was strutting around wearing an ID badge like it was some sort of corsage given on a first date. "Lead on."

They talked as they casually walked, mostly about the success of the newspaper, Mr. William's friendship and welfare, and about the hospital and with an occasional question about her slipped in. She found it hard to believe that they were talking about the same Mr. Williams … aka Chuck. He asked her questions she normally wouldn't answer but for some reason she did. What she learned about the doctor, she liked.

He was a widower in his early fifties; his wife died of cancer five years earlier. How ironic for a doctor's wife to die from the nondiscriminatory disease like cancer. A man with the power to heal rendered helpless when it came to someone he loved. She could sense the guilt he clung to as he spoke.

His office was typical with certificates and degrees gracing an entire wall. There was a photograph on his desk of two young men, his sons. Both were grown and had young families of their own. Although the doctor's faith in medicine had been shaken by his wife's death, he buried himself in his work to chase away the demons. She wanted to ask about their relationship but hesitated; it was really none of her concern. Time was the best healer. She felt comfortable around him. It made her nervous, but she liked it.

They took the scenic route, if there were such a thing, through the hospital, walking down corridors that had no significance to her visit as if he were trying to stretch their time together. Normally practical and to the point, she did not mind; she rather enjoyed it.

She giggled over things that she was glad no one else was around to hear. They walked by the Children's Ward twice but she fought the urge to ask him to go in.

"Hey, Pepper," the recognizable voice interrupted her mood. She looked up to see the lanky, bearded man wearing a white, short sleeved T-shirt under his black leather vest, the words 'PAPARAZZI' embroidered in red and white across the back. His thinning hair had been pulled back into a graying ponytail, hung down to the middle of his back. His once thick, jet black hair was no more. It was better than a comb over she had to admit, but there was a time when a man had to acknowledge the facts, that some hair was better off cut short or removed entirely. His frayed blue jeans were cut off just above his knees; leather sandals adorned his huge feet. "There you are, I've been searching this whole hospital for you! The old man sent me over to rip some shots … thought it would look good with the article." He held up the camera from around his neck as if for proof, then flashed a couple of quick shots of her and the good doctor standing close together. The flash temporarily blinded her, causing her to step backward onto the doctor's deck shoes.

"Sorry," she mumbled under her breath to the doctor as she glared back at her co-worker and ex-husband, Matt Medena. He was the last man she wanted to see standing there at that moment.

The cameraman smiled and shrugged his shoulders as if he had read her mind. "Chuck sent me; he wants some stills of the nuke."

"Chuck! Well then, just take pictures of the machine, not me!" she retorted. "Okay, you think you can do that?"

"Roger that, no pictures of the Pepper!" The man's smile revealed a couple of missing front teeth. *Those were new.*

"That's a new look for you. Took a few too many pictures did you?"

Mat nodded his head. "It was worth it though!"

Pepper let out a heavy sigh and annoyingly gestured to the

photographer "Doctor Marshal, this is Matt Medena. Matt, this is Doctor Marshal."

Matt bowed his head as if about to be knighted.

"Matt is the newspaper's version of a paparazzi."

The doctor warmly extended his hand and offered a firm shake.

"He is affectionately called M&M, which some interpret as Mad Medena."

"Or, Magic Man," Matt bragged as he held up the camera.

"Whatever, but, mad or not, he does take some pretty good pictures from time to time."

Matt gave her a thumbs up.

"So, where is this nuke?" Matt smiled. "I've got many miles to travel and lots of sleep to get caught up on."

"X-ray machine, you mean?" Pepper rolled her eyes and shook her head. Things were just fine until he showed up. She made sure he noticed her disappointment. "Mr. Williams didn't tell me that he assigned a photographer."

"I asked Chuck if I could tag along and he said it was an excellent idea."

"Chuck … since when did you start calling him by his first name?" she squinted into his dark eyes. *There it was again, another side to her boss that everyone else knew but her.*

"Since you have been calling him Mr. Williams, I guess?"

The doctor cleared his throat to get their attention. "The *nuke* … is just down the hall, this way. Please follow me."

"Right on!" Matt nodded his head and smiled. "Lead on, Doc."

Doctor Marshal turned down the hall and walked in the direction of the x-ray room.

Matt leaned towards Pepper and whispered in her ear, "Your boyfriend's cool."

She shot him a drop dead look. “He’s not my boyfriend.” She then abruptly turned and stormed down the hallway after the doctor.

Matt shook his head, unconvinced, and followed.

Chapter Twenty-Five

Circumstantial Evidence

Pepper quickly caught up with Doctor Marshal, hoping to create distance between her and the lanky cameraman. But when she looked back to her disappointment, she found his long stride had quickly closed the gap, the hyena smirk still smeared across his face. Matt's observations were right; she did indeed like the doctor. She concentrated on controlling her breathing and tried to relax. If Matt had noticed, the doctor might have as well. After all, they were both men and, apparently, their minds all worked the same way.

For the moment, she was glad the doctor hadn't spoken or turned and looked at her. There was no doubt in her mind that he heard Matt's comment and only needed to look into her eyes to confirm it.

It was then she saw the sign hanging from the ceiling of the hallway above the double doors, its raised black letters standing out dramatically against the white background … ***Children's Ward.*** She instinctively stopped and stared. Her pulse increased as her thoughts shifted once again to the two women she had met earlier in the hallway.

Matt had to brace himself with his hands to keep from running into her. “Jeez, Pepper, how about signaling next time!”

She grabbed his bicep and firmly pulled his ear down to her lips. The quick movement caught him by surprise. “Take pictures if we go in there,” she nodded towards the closed double doors.

“What?” Matt looked towards the doors and then up at the sign.

He started to open his mouth but she motioned with her index finger for him to be quiet. “Just do it,” she added.

He nodded, knowing Pepper well enough to recognize the urgency in her voice.

She released her grip as she called out to the doctor. “Doctor Marshal, uh … Bob?” her voice tapered to an exaggerated sweetness.

The doctor spun around and smiled; it was obvious that he liked the way she said his name. “The x-ray room is down this way,” he pointed down the hall, “that’s the Children’s Ward.”

Pepper was unmoved. “The Children’s Ward … can we see it? I’ve heard such good things about the place.”

Matt bobbed his head in agreement. She was surprised at how well he was playing along. The moment was strange; it was the first time that they agreed on anything in a long time.

“But the children aren’t in there right now,” the doctor responded, playing down his concern.

“I would still like to see the place, if we can,” Pepper shrugged her shoulders as she turned on her sweet charm.

She watched the doctor consider the double doors, his mind in deep thought.

She hurried his decision, not giving him the time to think. He was the third person in this hospital who behaved strangely when the

Children's Ward was mentioned. Now she wanted to see inside more than ever. "We won't take up more than a moment of your time."

The Doctor glanced at his watch before he spoke. "Well, I guess a quick stop won't matter." He walked back towards them.

Pepper sighed in relief; bubbling with success, she moved towards the doors.

The doctor held open one of the doors for her, while Matt pushed open the other door for himself.

As she walked down the long hall to the reception area, she was drawn towards the counter at the end but her journalistic instincts were geared to examine every part of the room. The atmosphere was relaxing, almost as if she were no longer in the hospital. The aroma of sweet flowers filled the room and the pastel colors on the walls and floor were warm and inviting. "This is very nice," she observed.

The doctor nodded in agreement. "We have been housing children in this ward for the last five years," the doctor talked as they strolled through the ward. "It has only been recently vacant for about a week or so."

"A week ago … they all left at the same time … where did they go?"

The doctor shrugged his shoulders before he spoke. "They no longer needed the facility." He smiled mischievously, "They went home; there was nothing else we could do for them here."

"Home?" She felt the pitch in her voice change.

"Yes, it is where they should be." He silently looked around the interior of the room before he spoke again.

Pepper knew enough medical terminology to assume that "all we could do for them" meant the children were terminal and had been sent home to spend their last days but that was not the impression she'd gotten earlier from the two women in the hallway.

Doctor Marshal continued, "A hospital, even as nice as this one, is no place for children. We try to make them feel comfortable during their stay but as Dorothy would say, 'There's no place like home!'"

Both Matt and Bob recited the last phrase together in unison.

Pepper shifted her gaze in between the two of them. *Were all men really the same?*

"Yeah, that *Wizard of Oz* stuff applies everywhere!" Matt snapped a couple of shots of the reception area but then focused his attention on the front counter. "Looks like this place isn't totally empty."

When Pepper looked towards the counter, she saw three people, two in beige uniform shirts and a third in a colorful hospital smock. A look of sudden surprise permeated the room, as if each group noticed the other simultaneously. The two officers appeared to be interviewing one of the nurses. All of Pepper's instinctive curiosity was aroused as the Children's Ward mystery suddenly grew in proportion. If she had heard the conversations in the hallway correctly, there were alleged *miraculous cures*, which seemed to have rendered the facility empty. And now, officers interviewing witnesses? It was adding up, the *administration wanting to keep it all quiet … the nervous Doctor and now the investigating deputies?* The thoughts made her suspicious mind spin. Excitement surged and she looked at Matt for reassurance. He, in turn, raised an eyebrow, as if fighting the urge to ask questions himself. Without saying another word and to the doctor's dismay, Pepper and Matt both strolled toward the other trio, camera at the ready, with the doctor reluctantly loping right behind.

♦ ♦ ♦

Paul felt tightness within his stomach drift up towards his throat when he saw the three determined looking individuals approaching the counter, one wearing a hospital smock and the other two in casual attire. His gut instinct told him that they were not average visitors.

The woman's badge stood out like a billboard and the expression in her eyes searched for anything she could grasp. He gave Susan's chair a warning kick and whispered, "We've got company!" From her expression, he knew that she felt the same way.

"Do you know these people?" Paul asked Sally.

She squinted down the corridor. "One is Doctor Marshal, our head administrator, but the others …" she shook her head.

Susan announced, "I do believe it's time to go." She grabbed her Stetson off the counter as she rose to her feet.

"We will talk with you later," Paul said as he rolled up his photograph and shoved it into its protective tube. He held the tube firmly in his sweating hand.

"Hello," the doctor stammered, extending his hand. "I don't believe we've met."

Paul accepted his clammy hand, noting that the doctor appeared as nervous as he.

"I'm Doctor Marshal, head administrator for Saint Francis Memorial." He offered his hand to Susan who reluctantly accepted it. "We didn't mean to interrupt. Anything I can do for you deputies?" He shot Sally an inquisitive look.

Sally took control. "They come regularly to see the children."

The doctor seemed relieved. "Oh, yes, the children; sorry, but they are no longer here, deputies."

"Really!" Susan grunted as she pretended to look around, surprised.

The doctor gave her a strange look.

Paul saw the woman stare at his nametag, as if she were committing a name and face to memory.

"So we were told," Susan agreed. "It's too bad, we were really looking forward to seeing them."

Paul fought the urge to reward her sarcasm with a swift kick.

"We appreciate visits from men and women in uniform," the

doctor continued, "the children love to see you guys ..." He nodded apologetically to Susan, "and gals."

Susan gave him a half smile for his quick correction although she objected violently to the title. "We guys and *gals* are actually park rangers." She pointed to the patch on her sleeve and then held up her green felt Stetson, "We work in the woods."

"Park rangers ... I stand corrected." The doctor noticed Paul's gaze shift back toward the woman on the other side of the counter.

"Oh, this is Pepper Jensen," the doctor exclaimed, "she works for the *Eel River Sentinel*, our local paper."

Paul felt a sudden chill surge through his entire body. He hoped the woman hadn't noticed, but knew that she did. "Kind of cold in here." He tried to recover.

"Not really, Ranger Behaan," she remarked confidently, which seemed to unnerve him. The woman had already committed his name to memory. Not only that, she had even pronounced his name correctly. "Where did you say you worked?"

"In the park, in the forest, by the river, with the animals about an hour south of here," Susan jumped in, her sarcasm evident.

Pepper flashed Susan a natural smile, "That's the huge redwood park, isn't it? I love that place; it's so beautiful. It's good to know that there still are some of those marvelous trees left for us to enjoy."

Paul swallowed loudly. Did she know something, *but how?*

Pepper quickly flashed to one of her concerns. "I can't believe the way the private timber companies have been slicing down those precious trees."

Susan nodded silently; it was obvious that the last thing she wanted to do was talk politics with the reporter. "Yes, we're lucky that there are still thousands of acres of beautiful, ancient Douglas fir and redwood forests protected within the park," she added. It was apparent that this was a subject near to the reporter's heart and if it diverted her attention from the missing children ... so be it.

“Do you get those tree sitters out your way?”

“Does the pope go to church?” Susan laughed. “Yeah, they flock to pay homage before they go out to do battle.”

“Do they try to sit in your trees? I mean the ones in the park.”

“Well, we explain that the park trees are already saved and they seem to accept that.”

Pepper nodded, “You probably get stuck in the middle of it all, don’t you?”

“Like a piece of cheese in a P.J. sandwich.”

Pepper laughed.

Paul closely observed the two of them like he was watching a tennis match. He hoped the conversations would end quickly.

“Miss Jensen is writing an article about our new x-ray machine; her paper was gracious enough to make a serious donation towards its purchase,” the doctor offered.

“Actually, it was Mr. Williams …” she looked at Matt, “Chuck who donated … I’m just here to cover the story.”

Paul suddenly felt as if a great burden had been lifted from his shoulders. She wasn’t here for the miracles, after all.

“Pepper, we must be going,” The doctor nodded towards the two rangers, “It’s a pleasure having you visiting the hospital. I’m sorry you missed the children; they kind of … unexpectedly left.” He cleared his throat, “Unfortunately, I am sure the Children’s Ward will be filled with more children again soon enough.”

Pepper reached out and shook both of the ranger’s hands. Paul felt her strong grip. The doctor, the reporter, and the cameraman turned and walked down the long hallway and then out of the double doors. Paul and Susan silently watched them leave. “I think she knows more than she’s leading us to believe,” he said when he was sure the group was out of earshot.

“What was your first clue, Sherlock?” Susan’s voice rang with annoyance.

"You seemed to hit it off with her very well, sarcasm and all." Paul patted her on her shoulder.

"Yeah, on the other hand, I think you crashed and burned, Ranger Behaan." She laughed, "I like her...she's got redeeming qualities, but I wouldn't trust her."

Paul and Sally gave her a surprised look.

"After all, she is a reporter," Susan leered down the now empty hallway. "And I doubt she just happened to stumbled upon the Children's Ward because she wanted to visit the c-h-i-l-d-r-e-n.... somehow, I'll bet she knows. I don't think we have seen the last of her.

"And you call me paranoid!" Grumbled Paul.

"What are we going to do," Sally queried nervously, "if she finds out?"

"She may indeed," expressed Paul in heavy thought. "We can only do what we can. It seems that Fionna is the only one who has a grip on what is going on around here. We appear to be pawns on the board and Fionna is the chess master."

Susan rubbed the bridge of her nose. "How ironic; destiny left in the hands of an imaginative teen. Things could be worse, you know. The fairies could ask her to do something else and it wouldn't take long for us to be in the thick of it."

Susan was right; this phenomenon wasn't coming to an end, it was just beginning. Paul dared not think about what could happen next.

Act 7:
Change

Chapter Twenty-Six

Following the Path

Fionna walked briskly through the forest with Mary on her heels. Although the morning air was cool, it had been four days since the rains had contributed to the magnificent splendor. They skirted around the crater-like root holes that provided emerald pools for frogs and salamanders. The spider-like arms of the massive root balls of the old logs testified to their once incredible height. Like many places in the forest, ferns, ground cover, and young trees established a foothold on the nurse logs, allowing the cycle of life to continue. As the older trees grew in size, the underbrush thinned and more light filtered through the upper canopy that towered well over three hundred feet above their heads.

The strange quietness was still present in the winter forest but the uneasiness they felt earlier was gone. They bounded off the public trail and stepped into the recesses of the forest with no fear of being lost or thoughts of running into whatever might make this dark forest its home. She knew where to go. Energy drew her to the gnarled, ancient trees hidden within the forest's interior. This was, after all, her fourth visit to the grove.

Fionna wished her mom could have come along but that wasn't the case. If she even guessed what they were up to, she would have exploded. Her mom worried about Fionna's being even near the woods. She still hadn't fully recovered from the thought that she could have lost her daughter forever. Fionna had tried once before to get her mom to drive her back to the park, but the answer was *absolutely not!*

She didn't like having to lie to her mom about going back to the forest, a place she now truly loved. She had to make a deal with Grandma Elisabeth, who had been driving her to the park every time she asked. Although her grandma shared in the excitement, unfortunately, her health would not allow her to venture far from her parked car.

An uncontrolled excitement pounded in Fionna's chest as thoughts raced through her mind. Today, she would learn about her next step, the next piece of the puzzle she needed to put into place. The thought made her feel a little uneasy. It was no longer just her; at last count, there were several adults and seven children and their families unwillingly pulled into this bizarre turn of events. If the word of the crazy miracle got out, thousands of other people would join in … some happy, some not so. Right now, she wouldn't exactly know what to say. She needed guidance from the trees and inspiration from the fairy elder.

There was a spring in Fionna's step and a perpetual smile on her face this beautiful morning. She had completed her first challenge. Incredibly, it was the eldest of the trees that directed her actions through Se'amus. Now, it was her responsibility to direct the actions outside of the forest. The results had been more than she could ever imagine. The children had shown more than signs of healing, rekindled sparks of hope and understanding. They were ecstatic, their worlds were brought back from the brink of despair. She came to tell them that she had done as they asked, to be relieved of her duties. *What else could they possibly need her to do?*

Fionna picked up her pace, brushing past the bright green fronds as she weaved in and out of the shadows. It no longer scared her; in fact, it filled her with a strange sort of wonder. Not long ago she was a shy young woman, drawn to her fate by the warmth in her caring heart and by the sensuous aroma of irresistible orchids. *Oh, how that seemed so long ago, the forests would never be the same.* Her life was different; she was empowered, emanating from every cell of her body, taking over her every need and desire.

She was grateful for Paul's support and confidence. She trusted him with her safety and her new found secrets. After all, it had been he who stumbled on her in the rain and the mist and taken her to the safety and comfort of the hospital. He had already helped her once and she was sure he would help her again if asked. There was a sense of peace about him. He was a man who had accepted the responsibility of protecting the forests and the people who visited and, like her, he was *selected* by the forest to be its guardian. Other than Fionna, he was the first to smell the flowers and see the fairies. Then, there was Susan, the other ranger who was somehow also pulled in to help. She, on the other hand, was not quite as charming but she had a caring side buried deep under a protective outer shell.

Fionna walked briskly, well aware of Mary's presence on her heels. She occasionally looked back into the smiling eyes of her friend who had supported her from the beginning. Words were not necessary because the message was clear … their roles were not over, and they were going back.

The distant sound of a raven stopped them in their tracks. The birds were back.

"We're close!" Mary panted knowingly.

Fionna searched the horizon in the direction of the approaching, raspy call. She felt her friend's comforting squeeze on her shoulder. "There!" She whispered as she pointed off in the distance to their right. "The bird is coming to greet us … they already know we're here!"

"*Rrraaawww, rrraaawww, rrraaawww, rrraaawww, rrraaawww,*" The call of the raven increased in sound and power as it echoed loudly and flapped in their direction.

Fionna shivered as a familiar tingle ran the length of her neck as they waited for the raven to arrive. She knew the bird was looking for them, to direct them to the ancient one that stood waiting in the nearby forest. She could almost feel the trees' uneasiness, their concern for their future. For everyone's future.

It felt urgent.

She heard the raspy call again just before she heard the broad wings whistle through the still air like a huge, ominous black omen of something bad to come. The raven swooped below the upper canopy and into view. With a slight turn of its head, it made a minor flight adjustment and headed directly towards them.

"*Rrraaawww, rrraaawww, rrraaawww, rrraaawww, rrraaawww,*" it sounded again as it made a quick circle above their heads before settling on the end of a broken branch. "*Rrraaawww, rrraaawww, rrraaawww, rrraaawww, rrraaawww.*" The call had a quicker cadence as the harbinger bobbed its head, raised the feathers on the back of its neck and dipped its broad, shiny shoulders.

Its obnoxious greeting appeared to be the raven's way of saying hello as it insulted the person under its breath. It cocked its head sideways and stared at them with limpid, dark eyes. Its behavior was unnerving but Fionna knew the bird was merely her guide. Although the creature was on a mission, it still didn't like troublesome humans.

"That's got to be the same bird," Mary's voice broke the strained silence.

"Yes, it's the male, come to greet us."

"Where's the other one?" Mary surveyed the surrounding forest. "Maybe she dumped him for being so loud and rude."

The raven sounded off again but continued to remain on its perch.

"Wonder why he hasn't taken off or made us chase him through the forest like last time?" Fionna whispered as she prepared for the tiresome sprint.

"Maybe it's being sporty by letting us catch our breath first before it runs us into the ground."

Fionna raised an eyebrow at her friend who was starting to remind her of Ranger Susan.

"Well," Mary shrugged, "that's what I would do to break up the boredom … isn't that what they did last time! That raven and I, we might not be so different after all!"

Suddenly, without another sound, the raven diverted its attention off to their right, nodded its massive head, blinked its expressive dark eyes and dived directly at them. They dropped to their knees and covered their heads in anticipation of an attack from the suddenly deranged bird. Mary screamed in surprise as she hit the forest floor, but Fionna couldn't get any words or sounds to leave her lips. Narrowly missing them, the raven pulled sharply up and disappeared among the trees, screaming as it went. When they turned in the direction of the fleeing bird, all they heard was the whistle of its powerful wings fade into the forest and then a distant call, the last of the insults.

"What is wrong with that bird. It went crazy on us." Mary shook noticeably. "Now, that was freaky! I take back that part about our having anything in common."

"What wer' ye' expecten'," the familiar Irish voice boomed out of the shadows. "Criminy! Ye' can't go around insultin' the ravens an' expect 'em te' sit there an' take it, now do ye'?"

They both quickly turned towards the sound of the voice, rising to their feet and instinctively moving closer to one another. Fionna shaded her eyes against the glare as she squinted into the light. The sound of his voice had energized the air.

"Yer' lucky he decided not te' take a piece of yer' hair as a keepsake." The voice boomed again. "Them ravens aren't as dumb as they look."

"Séamus?" Fionna suddenly found her voice.

Mary gasped as the elder fairy stepped out from behind the huge ferns and shuffle-stepped awkwardly into the open. The long, sleeveless bark robe hung to his baggy knees. A long pipe drooped from the corner of his firm mouth and his beard stretched from his chubby face to his pot belly. "Dia duit ar maidin, Fionna … Máire. (jee-ah ghwich er may-jin.)" He bowed his head in greeting.

"Good morning to you, too," Fionna returned the gesture." Do you always sneak up on people like that?" she asked, settling on the end of a log.

"No, sometimes we hav' a little fun … knock on the trees, whistle, make scary noises in the darkness an' toss a few rocks from the shadows." The fairy grinned mischievously as he slipped off his sandals and climbed onto the opposite end of the log. "A big hairy fello' has been getin' all the credit fer' that mischief," he pointed his stubby arm in the direction the raven had disappeared. "But 'tis more fun te' sick the ravens on 'em; Ravens ar' the masters of fun, ye' kno'."

"The children are all cured," Fionna exclaimed proudly; she couldn't wait any longer to share the news.

The elder fairy nodded his head and smiled. "'Tis true, the children hav' been given a special gift."

"Are there others out there …," Mary pointed to the surrounding shadows, a slight panic in her voice. "Are we being watched?"

"Yes, they ar' keeping a close eye on the two of ye'. Na síogaí (na shee-ohg-ee) don't trust humans. They learned that centuries ago."

"But, you are here in front of us!" Mary exclaimed.

He sighed deeply and gave Mary an emotionless stare. "Sea (shah), ye' only see me because I let ye'. An' I only let ye' on behalf of the ancient ones." He forced a tired smile, "Ye' hav' been chosen. When we ar' done, we will each disappear back inte' our own separate worlds. Mine is here, an' yours is out ther'."

Fionna felt sorrow fill her heart; when all was done, she would probably never see them again. To her surprise, Séamus gave her a warm, understanding smile. It was almost as if he had read her thoughts.

"We ar' part of the forest," he gestured with his stubby arms. "As long as the hills an' the valley floors ar' filled with ancient trees an' the streams quench the mighty thirst of the forest, the air that we breathe will be sweet," he wiggled his toes affectionately on the moss covered log. "An' if there ar' places people can go te' listen te' the solitude, our presence will always be felt. Ye' might not see us, but ye' will always feel us."

Fionna was comforted by his words. She nodded; it was so simple and to the point. As long as the forests were protected, so were they.

"Now, you hav' been asked te' do somethin' else."

The girls perked up and listened carefully. Fionna felt her heart race; this was the very reason they had come back.

"Ye' hav' been asked te' release the secret … te' tell the other humans."

"What?" Fionna suddenly felt confused. She had been trying to keep everything a secret and avoiding sharing her unbelievable encounter. Trying to keep the healing powers of the fairies and the ancient trees to herself. *To share now would put her right smack in the middle of the chaos. What would people think of her? What would they think of her friends that she had pulled into this strange mess with her?* She suddenly felt a sense of total panic. "But, they will know where the power comes from … they will feel the need to come and take it! You don't understand, they will …"

The fairy held up his hand as if he had an uncanny ability to read her thoughts. "Tis' what has been asked of us by the ancients. In order te' protect the ancient forest, the humans need te' kno' its importance. Once they understand, they will kno' the trees hav' greater worth left alone than cut te' the ground. 'Tis is the only way."

Fionna shook her head. "You don't understand, this will only make them want to cut down more trees. Humans do not think that way!" She leaped up, clenched her fists and threw her arms in the air in frustration. Immediately, the angry sounds of buzzing wings permeated the glade and she turned to see five fairies darting towards her from the direction of the shadows with an attack demeanor and their faces scrunched in mistrust. Fear surged through her entire body. Panicked, she stumbled backwards, nearly tumbling over Mary, who screamed in terror.

The elderly fairy flew straight up with lightning speed and put himself between the charging fairies and the two teens. He knotted his fists and flexed his stubby arms.

"Ní hea, ní hea! (nee hah) …no!" boomed like thunder all around them. The agitated fairies stopped just out of arms reach of the two frightened, cowering young women but their wings still buzzed as they hovered like a flock of hummingbirds, moving from side to side, up and down as if they were taking a closer look at a flower. Fionna felt the eerie chill make its way down to her toes; she could feel the hate radiate from the tiny beings. There were both men and women, all looking at her with disgust. It was at that moment that she realized that it would take a very long time for the differences between them to be resolved and maybe it would be best to leave them as soon as possible.

The fairies starred silently at each other as if they could communicate without saying a word.

With a wave of the aging fairy's arm, the flock slowly broke away and moved back into the shadows. Each giving the teens a look that said, *we're watching you, mess up again … bring harm to us or our leader … that it is by the grace of the trees and the fairy elder that you are left unharmed.* Fionna began to wonder if it were more than just nature that had a hand in the disappearances of missing hikers and recreationist. The thought made her shiver and she fought the urge to run from the forest and to never return.

Se'amus fluttered back to the moss covered log and let out a tired sigh as he eased down. "Tá brón orm (taw brone ur-um.) … I am sorry, they wish to hav' no part of dealing with humans. An' as ye' can see, they ar' very protective of what is theirs." He gave the hidden fairies a distant look for a moment before he focused his attention on the girls.

"I wasn't going to hurt you!" Fionna exclaimed, her voice quivering with disappointment.

"Sea (shah), yes, I kno', but they ar' all on edge … being forced te' give ancient secrets te' the thankless humans."

"We're not all thankless humans," Mary blurted out defensively.

"Ní hea (nee hah.), no ye' ar' not."

"But, we, the teenagers …" Fionna stammered.

"Sea (shah), yes, children ar' appreciative. We hav' never found fault with the children. They see us for what we ar'. Not for what they think we ar', believe us te' be, or what they think they can get out of us. Tha' is why ye' hear stories involving children."

Fionna glanced back into the shadows.

"Ní hea (nee hah.), no, they would never hurt children."

His soothing voice was working a little magic of its own. Fionna felt a strange sort of relief; she released her white knuckled grip on Mary's arm.

"Ye' hav' to get the word out; ye' hav' te' tell the humans that it is the trees that cured all them children. That the ancient trees need te' be protected … the forests need te' be protected."

Fionna said, "I read an article that said a few years ago, some scientists discovered that the yew tree, a small, slow growing tree that also grows around here in the forest, had elements that could be used in the fight against cancer. Not long after that announcement, the yew trees became harder and harder to find on public lands. Evidently, people were going into the forests and cutting them down to sell them on the black market. The trees suddenly became gold mines. The only thing that probably saved the trees was the scientists, who out of desperation synthesized the element … to recreate it. You see … it is what humans will do once they find out. That's why we can't tell them about the trees!"

Mary nodded in agreement as they both gave him desperate looks.

He looked at them and smiled. "My dear sweet children." He held out his hands and gestured for them to come sit next to him.

They hesitated at first, as they looked over their shoulders, still unsure of the reactions of the other fairies.

"It is alright, I hav' spoken, they will not bother ye' again … today."

Today! The meaning of the word rang in Fionna's thoughts. *What about tomorrow?*

They cautiously sat down next to him. Mary kept a concerned eye on the edge of the shadows, not quite sure whether she trusted the temporary truce.

"Fionna, do ye' kno' why ye' hav' been chosen?"

Fionna paused before she answered. "Because my Great, Great, Great Grandmother brought the fairies over from Ireland?"

Séamus smiled and patted her gently on the shoulder. "Sea (shah), yes, but 'tis more than that. Your ancestors believed in the na síogaí (na shee-ohg-ee), the fairy folk, they understood us. They cared more about us than any other humans."

"Did you know them?"

"Sea (shah), yes." He looked passionately around the forest. "Ye' remind me a lot of them. Like ye', they cared passionately about fairies an' humans. There was nothing that they wouldn't de' te' protect what was right. They say, that every century, there comes a human who will make a difference." He looked at her gently and smiled, "That, my human friend, is ye'! Ye' ar' the chosen one … chosen by the likes much greater than me."

Fionna stared blankly at him; she didn't know what to say.

"The forest is now our home. We grew up in a forest much like this. Immortal, ye' say we ar', but 'tis where, when the time comes, I will return te' fairy dust." He gazed into her eyes. "We will become part of the forest an' be reborn in the trees an' the ferns. Ye' see, we aren't much different, those trees an' us. We ar' more alike than ye' can imagine. There was a time when ye' humans felt the same way. There wer' proper behaviors, sacred areas, herbs used for curing … the forest provided an', in turn, the forest was protected."

Fionna watched him closely; his every word was sending chills down her spine. He spoke like an elder of the Sinkyone people, the first nation that once made the ancient redwoods forest, in these very mountains, their home. He talked of understanding, responsibility and the determination of people to live with respect for the land. *Maybe they were related.*

Se'amus gently caressed her hand as he continued to speak. "Ye' ar' the one we trust; ye' hav' proven that already. We hav' trusted ye' thus far, as ye' well know, it is a feat we find very difficult te' do. Now, ye' must trust us; we believe 'tis the only way. 'Tis desperate times. There ar' unprotected forests out there with ancient elders that hav' asked fer' our protection. I feel their cries." He pointed to the shadows. "They feel their cries fer' help. Ye' hav' already experienced their concern. They behav' like scared children. They don' see how humans, the very ones who ar' causing the concerns, how they can be the key te' solving the problem." He sighed heavily, "Sea (shah), yes, though they ar' not young, they lack the vision."

He focused on Fionna again. "Ye' an' yer' friends ar' that hope. Ye' will carry that message te' the humans. I know that most of them really do care. Sea (shah), yes," he nodded. "I hav' watched them as they travel through the forest. I saw the caring in their hearts. Sea (shah), I do believe that once they learn that the ancient trees offer more than beauty an' solitude, they will fight te' protect them as well."

Mary began to speak but the elder cut her off with a wave of his hand.

"Sea (shah), yes, I know there ar' some out there that will do what they think they need te' do. Every society has 'em. They will be a problem at first, but we believe they will be short-lived." He smiled. "We hav' Paul an' Susan on our side; they will not let anythin' happen te' the ancient trees in this forest. They hav' sworn an oath te' protect the forests an' hav' done a good job in that. There ar' other Pauls an' other Susans out there in other forests. They will step up when they ar' called." He patted them both on their shoulders. "Ye' must hav' faith; isn't that what ye' told the children in the hospital? That they needed faith fer' the trees' magic te' work?"

Fionna nodded her head and smiled as she thought about the children's little faces. She felt warm beginning to build within her heart and radiating out through her arms and legs. And she began to smell the flowers. "Yes, that is true. It worked because they believed it would." The discovery was noticeable in her excited voice.

"An' it would not hav' worked if ye' hadn't brought it te' them an' convinced them te' believe that it would. Now ye' must do the same with the new message. Many ar' depending on ye'r success."

Fionna found it hard to explain, but a strange energy flowed through her entire body. One look at Mary told her she felt the same way. Fionna suddenly no longer felt alone on this impossible quest.

The elder fairy unfurled his wings and slowly took flight, rising high above their heads. They watched in quiet amazement as if they were participants in an unbelievable fairy tail.

"Go n-éirí an t-ádh leat! (guh nye-ree un taw laht.) Good luck! Remember what we hav' talked about. It is yer' faith that wields the strongest power. Go mbeannaí Dia duit (guh man-ee jee-ah ghwich.), May the gods bless ye'... now go, do what is right!"

At that, the air was filled with the buzzing of wings as the rest of the fairies left the shadows and joined Séamus high above their heads. They no longer looked down upon them with hate and disgust; they gazed down upon them with wonder and support. Strangely, Fionna noted their support and their love for the forest around them. The winged forest protectors were more like children than she ever imagined. Her throat became dry and her eyes began to water, she fought the urge to cry … not from sadness but from joy, an unexplainable joy and determination that now burned deep within her heart.

Chapter Twenty-Seven

Family Council

Fionna, her mother Anna, and her Grandma Elisabeth sat quietly on the living room sofa, nonchalantly sneaking glances at each other. Each was still in their flannel night shirts on this quiet morning; they all looked as if they had just awoken from a restless sleep. Both mother and grandma held coffee cups in their hands; Fionna fidgeted nervously with her fingers. It was obvious that each had something weighing heavily on their minds. Faint bird calls could be heard through the closed windows and thinly insulated walls. Fionna was glad that the robins seemed to be taking advantage of the break in the series of winter storms that relentlessly pounded the North Coast.

Fionna sat next to her mom, staring deeply into the Navajo rug that lay in the middle of the hardwood floor. She wracked her brain on how to start, where to begin, what to say. She forced a quick, supportive glance at Grandma Elisabeth. After all, it was because of her that the three of them were here now. Until this point, Grandma Elisabeth had indeed kept her promise, as requested, not to tell her mom about their going back to the forest, about the fairies. But now, after some thought, grandma insisted that it was up to Fionna to set the record straight. That it was up to her to tell her mother the *truth.*

Grandma Elisabeth held her mug firmly as she sat on one side of Anna, Fionna on the other. Elisabeth leaned forward, a knowing smile on her lips as she nodded toward her daughter. Anna stared off into emptiness in deep thought, as she normally did each and every morning. Savoring her every sip with her delicate hands securely cupped around the oversized coffee cup, inhaling the rich aromas as if it were a delicacy.

Fionna nodded in Grandma Elisabeth's direction. *I can do this!* She told herself. Grandma was right. It was up to her to set things straight, to tell her mom the truth. In a way, she had been suffering from her own guilt. It was unfair to put her grandma in the middle. Fionna tried to speak, but it wouldn't work. She hated the fact that her emotions were tying her up again.

"Is something wrong?" Anna stared straight ahead as she spoke.

Fionna could hear the concern in her mom's voice. "Uh … not really, there is, well just that … uh." She sighed loudly; the words just weren't coming together the way she wanted them to.

Anna stared at her from over her steaming cup. "So, what's with the sudden loss of speech?" Her eyes narrowed as if probing Fionna's thoughts.

Fionna looked away from her mother and to her grandmother for encouragement. Grandma nodded, lowered her coffee cup to her lap and motioned with her free arms for her to relax. It helped a little, but it would take more than a friendly smile and a nod to jump start her confidence.

Anna lowered her cup to her lap. "Is there something going on that I should know about?"

"Well, there is this … thing that I've been doing. Well, actually, it's kind of what we've been doing." Fionna pointed to her grandma. "Well, actually, it involves the park rangers, Mary, grandma and me." She counted them off on her fingers.

Grandma Elisabeth nodded in agreement.

"Like what?"

"Well … I have …" Fionna couldn't believe it. Her voice had almost disappeared. She hadn't felt this nervous in a long time. "It's all good!" She squeaked nervously. She couldn't believe how guilty she was making herself sound.

"Fionna … what are you trying to say?"

She heard the worry and concern in her mom's voice. She looked to her grandma for help.

"I believe what she is trying to say is that I have been driving her to the park," Grandma Elisabeth spoke in a calm, controlled voice.

"You've been doing what? To the park?" The nervousness and concern was evident in the voice. "You know I don't want her going there. Mom, for heavens sake, we almost lost her in that forsaken park! The last thing we want is for her to try to do it again. She might not be so lucky next time. The rangers won't always be there to help!"

"I realize that you're upset, but …"

"Upset!" she raised her voice. "You bet I'm upset; you haven't even scratched the surface of how upset I am. You weren't here when we received the news." Her shrill voice echoed loudly in the room. "She was missing for three days and in a coma for over a week because of that forest. Why on earth could you ever think of taking her back there?"

"I asked her to," Fionna said, her voice had suddenly returned and her confidence intact.

"Honey, but why …" Tears had begun to form in her mom's eyes.

"... Because I had to, because it was what I was asked to do. It is what I was meant to do." Fionna twisted in her seat, emotions running high.

"Go on, dear," Grandma's gentle whisper filled their ears. She placed a hand on her daughter's shoulder. "Anna, please listen to what she is going to tell you. I too didn't believe it at first but I have no reason not to now. I might be an old woman but I know when someone is telling me the truth and, trust me, she is speaking the truth."

Her mom started to speak but Fionna cut her off with a wave of her hand. "This is the very reason why I have waited until now to share this." She saw the focus in her mom's eyes. It gave her strength to continue. "I don't know how to explain it. I haven't totally understood it myself and there are things that we will probably never understand."

Her mom nodded as she slipped one of her hands off her cup and touched her daughter's fingers. Fionna grasped them tightly.

"I haven't told you everything that had happened to me in the forest." Fionna tossed her head towards the window. She felt her mom's grip tighten. As she had done earlier with her grandmother, she talked about being sick in the wilderness and the sweet fragrance of flowers drawing her into the canyon to her disappearance ... to her time in the hospital and awakening from the coma with the strange knowledge that she now possessed. She spoke, to her mom's disbelief, about the fairies in the forest and the desires of the ancient trees. She finished with what they had asked her to do. Fionna told her mom about the children in the hospital and that she was responsible for the changes in their lives.

Her mom only stared at her in disbelief.

"It's all true, every word of it," exclaimed her grandma. "It will soon be all over the news. Seven children miraculously cured, compliments of the trees. The public won't be hearing about the fairies anytime soon though; that part has to remain a secret."

"Fairies … mom, you have never talked about fairies before. Surely, you don't believe in that nonsense," Anna exclaimed.

Grandma shrugged her shoulder. "Yes, that's true … until recently anyway. I thought fairies lived in the imagination of children and Irish folktales. But I guess I was wrong. I'm sorry!" She laughed, "Evidently, the forest is jam packed with them."

"Have you seen them?" Anna stared at her mother.

"No, I'm too old to be running around in the woods."

"But you have taken Fionna to the park?"

"Yes, I took her and Mary to the park but I waited near the car." She pointed to Fionna, "They went back into the forest."

"I was safe … I didn't go alone. I trust Mary with my life," Fionna said, "and have."

Anna stared at them silently for a moment. Fionna could read the confusion in her eyes. It was obvious that she was struggling with everything she had heard. "Mom, what do you want me to say?"

"I don't know. It's so strange. What am I supposed to think?"

"You need to trust me, mother … you have to trust me on this one. Do you trust me?" Fionna pleaded. She stared into her mom's emotional eyes. "I have to go back. I need your blessings to go back."

Chapter Twenty-Eight

Finding the Truth

Pepper sat on the brightly colored, tattered and squeaky vinyl bench in the booth for six, hidden in the corner of the mom-and-pop restaurant. She fidgeted nervously with the salt and pepper shakers on the table. She owed her nickname to this nervous habit, not from her now salt-and-pepper-colored hair. She thought about how different she was from the man sitting across from her. Just as the salt and pepper dispensers appeared the same on the outside, they were totally opposite on the inside. Even though they worked for the same newspaper, they weren't even close to being on the same page when it came to solving the hospital mystery or for that matter when it came to anything else. She couldn't even believe that at one time they had actually been close friends. It was hard to say who was responsible for the change, who was the one who went his or her own separate way, Irreconcilable differences were the verdict.

There, they sat landed there by an anonymous phone call the night before directing them to the time and place. Promising them an exclusive, the answers to the hospital miracle. Pepper was beside herself. She couldn't believe it, the secrets of the hospital miracles would finally be hers for the recording. She would be the first to share the facts. It was going to be the article of the year. She would show Mr. Williams her underestimated potential, her inherent worth. *No more silly write ups for Pepper Jensen*, her proud thoughts echoed in her head. She reached for the glass of water in front of her with her shaky hand and noisily gulped down half its contents. She set the glass noisily on the table and stared at her trembling hand a moment before she tightened it into a fist to stop the shaking. She shot a quick look across the table to Matt Medena to see if he had noticed.

To her dismay, her eyes met those of the tall photographer. He snorted a sarcastic laugh, supported the left side of his face with his open hand and then returned to his silent stare out the window. His right hand nervously fiddled with the strap on his camera sitting on the table in front of him. His nonchalance angered her but she reeled in her emotions and tried to hide her true feelings. "This is a big story, you know!" She barked off nervously in her defense. "This is an opportunity to set me apart … to set *us* apart," making a halfhearted attempt to include him. She continued to study his emotionless features, wanting him to say something, yet hoping he didn't.

Matt clinched his jaws annoyingly. She knew she was going to regret what he was about to say.

"This is just another *story* for you, isn't it?" The coolness in his voice caught her by surprise. It was the first time he had talked since they had arrived.

"What?"

"These so called miracles … you couldn't just leave them alone, could you?"

"But, the people …"

"No, not the people, you … You can't just let nature take its course, you have to mess with everything, don't you? This is what they mean about history repeating itself. Some people just don't seem to get it."

She nervously reached for her glass but stopped halfway and stared at her hands. They shook again. She started to interlace her fingers but instead pulled them apart and slid them under the table.

"I sure hope you aren't planning on taking up religion now after all these years." There was crudeness to his quiet, pointed words.

She suddenly found her voice. "What is wrong with you? The past is the past!" She struggled to keep her conversation to a whisper as she studied his eyes. When he didn't respond, she looked around the room to make sure that no one else was close enough to hear. To her relief, the restaurant was practically empty. When she spoke again, it was louder than before. "You don't like me very much, do you?" She couldn't believe she had actually asked that question. "What we had together is history … ancient history. It was a mistake; opposites may attract, but sometimes not for the better."

He stared at her a moment, slouched back in his seat and crossed his arms. "That is not what this is about and you know it! But just for the record, history does repeat itself."

She shot him a confused look. *How did this conversation ever end up about sharing personal feelings with a man she no longer liked?* "So, what is this *really* about?" She tossed her hands in the air in disgust. "We are not here to discuss your personal opinion, nor a past relationship. If I wanted it, I would have … what am I talking about, I don't really care for your personal opinion. Your personal opinion means nothing to me...n-o-t-h-i-n-g. You have been assigned to take pictures, nothing else but taking pictures." Her voice now loud enough to attract the server's attention. "I ask the questions and you take the pictures, end of story!" She grabbed her glass and gulped down the rest of her water, pounding the empty glass heavily down onto the table, jiggling the ice and rattling the silverware. She then crossed her arms and settled back into the seat, giving him a dominating glare. "We are not here to discuss a failed relationship."

Matt smiled and shook his head. "You will never change."

"More water?" the waitress' concerned voice interrupted the tense moment.

Pepper almost jumped out of her seat.

"Is everything all right?"

"Oh, yes, everything is fine!" Pepper ran her fingers nervously through her short hair. Her face was flushed and she could imagine her cheeks glowing a nice shade of pink. *Of all people, how did this meeting bring her into conversation with her ex-husband?*

"She's just a little nervous. Meeting a special client." Matt forced a smile.

The waitress nodded. "Water?"

"Yes, please."

They both silently watched her pour the water and walk away.

Pepper glared out the window, one of her hands partially covering the side of her face.

"It is about, like … the reasons we are here today," Matt stumbled as he attempted to explain.

She continued to stare out the window as if she weren't listening.

"It's about your thinking you need to butt into people's lives. It's about your opinions … It's like your search for the Holy Grail." He talked with his hands, his long delicate fingers gracefully painting the picture.

She looked at him. There was a noticeable grace to his movements. She didn't remember his talking with his hands before.

"Haven't you thought about the fact that maybe these kids should be left alone? Haven't they gone through enough already?" There was a ring of concern in his voice, something else she hadn't noticed before.

"Aren't you the least bit curious?"

He stared at her a moment before he spoke again. His voice was less accusatory, more sentimental. "Yes," he nodded, "I am … all seven children at once! Wow, that doesn't happen every day, you know. You saw the doctor's concern for the children. We talked to all seven of the children … and what have they told us?" He paused for Pepper to answer.

"That it was a miracle …" She mumbled.

"Yes, every one of those children agreed it was a miracle in one form or another."

"Yes, but they were hiding something," she added. "It was written all over their faces. You heard them, they were protecting someone, tell me you didn't feel it!"

Matt nodded, "Yes, they were being protective, but they were also happy. Free of their ailments. Free to start their lives over."

"That nurse, Sally … she knows something, but she isn't talking."

"Yes, she did. Remember, she talked about Fionna blessing the children with holy water."

"Get a grip, you really think holy water was responsible for the miracle," she queried, her sarcasm obvious. "Evidently, that ward had been blessed and re-blessed more times than anyone can count. Now, why should it work all of a sudden … seven times at once?"

Matt shrugged. "Accumulative effort? It's not what I believe, it's what they believe. It's what actually took place." He slid back in his seat and eyed her suspiciously. "You don't believe in miracles, do you?"

"No, I don't!"

"Ye of such little faith. That could be your problem right there."

She leaned over the table and poked her finger in his chest. "Don't you start pulling that holier than art thou attitude with me."

Matt grinned and changed the subject, "I hope you're not just using the good doctor."

His words seemed to take the steam out of her words. She gasped as she leaned back into her seat. She actually liked the doctor but she also wanted the story. For that matter, there might be a thing or two she still liked about her ex-husband. All she could do was shrug her shoulders.

"I believe it's show time … it looks like we have company," Matt nodded in the direction of the door and straightened up in his seat.

Pepper felt her heart jump as she saw the six people search the room and bring their eyes to rest on their booth. She recognized two of them as the park rangers and knew who the other two girls were. It was the whole crew. She nervously grabbed her glass and gulped again.

"Relax, it will be alright." Matt mumbled in an attempt to comfort her. "Still don't believe in miracles?"

Chapter Twenty-Nine

A Reporter's Dream

"There they are," Paul nodded towards the couple in the far corner booth. His voice echoed in the reception area of the diner. "It's very unlike reporters to be late; especially, when they think they smell a story," he added with a hint of sarcasm.

"You've got that right," Susan laughed, trying not to look in their direction. "Let's just stay here until the others show up. Remember, be careful what you say; in their minds, there is no such thing as off the record! Remember, they are the e-n-e-m-y." She raised her index and middle finger on both her hands to emphasize her words. "And these aren't air quotations, they are fangs or horns, both will work in this case."

Paul laughed, "Do I detect a bit of pent-up aggression?"

"No, recessed memory!" exclaimed Susan.

The muffled laughter and the rattling of the miniature cowbell that was attached to the glass entry door caused the two rangers to turn in the direction of the noise. Fionna and her friend Mary entered; behind them, wearing uncomfortable frowns, were her very concerned mom and her curious grandmother, Elizabeth.

Fionna saw the rangers right away and it took only a moment to notice the curious expressions on the two other individuals staring in their direction from the booth in the corner. There was no doubt in her mind that they were the reporters they were supposed to meet. She smiled at them and offered a delicate wave with her petite hand. *How could they possibly be the enemy?*

The reporters reluctantly returned the gesture and Susan looked at Paul and shrugged.

"Hello, Mrs. Brien," Paul extended his hand to Fionna's mom.

"Oh, hello, Ranger Behaan," she casually pushed his hand out of her way and gave him a great big hug. "It is good to see you again. I can't thank you enough for everything you have done for my daughter. She can't seem to stop talking about you."

"Well … uh," Paul blushed.

Susan smirked deviously.

"And you must be Susan?" Fionna's mom directed her attention to Susan.

"Yes," Susan nodded. "Nice to finally meet you, Mrs. Brien."

"Oh," she laughed pleasantly, "you can call me Anna … Mrs. Brien is my mother." She gestured to the shorter, elderly woman who was smiling back at everyone.

"Nah," the elderly woman's scratchy voice cut in proudly. "You may call me Grandma Elisabeth." As she nodded slowly and respectfully towards the rangers, her long gray hair slid off of her shoulders and into her face. She looked up, pushed her hair back onto her shoulders. "I think I'm overdue for a hair cut."

Fionna watched as they returned the greeting.

Anne turned towards Susan and extended her hand, "You are just as Fionna described." Anna gave her a hug as well, which Susan took in stride.

"Really? I hope it's all good."

Grandma Elisabeth hobbled over to greet the both of them. "I am so honored."

"No, I do believe the honor is all ours," Paul laughed.

Susan nodded in agreement.

Grandma Elisabeth softly whispered something Gaelic into their ears as she gave them both a hug. They both looked at her inquisitively but didn't say anything.

Paul tossed his head toward the awaiting individuals in the booth. "So, Fionna, are you ready for this?"

"Yes, I am," she said calmly. Fionna felt a strange calmness overwhelm her, inner strength building. Her nervousness dissipated. She walked directly over to the edge of the awaiting party's table and stopped. She looked to see if the rest of the group had followed. The fact that both Paul and Susan were suspiciously eyeing the rest of the occupants of the restaurant as they approached made her shake her head in amusement. Fionna stared at the reporters for a moment before she leaned over and extended her hand in friendship. She could see their nervousness in their uncomfortable smiles. The tall man looked as if he had honestly looked forward to their meeting. The female reporter on the other hand …

"My name is Fionna," she said, "And these are my friends … Paul, Susan, and Mary. I also brought along my Mom Anna and my Grandmother Elisabeth."

Pepper and Matt slid to the end of the booth to shake hands.

"I believe we met before." Matt offered as he slid out of the booth and firmly shook both Susan's and Paul's hands first. He then greeted the rest warmly. Fionna took a sudden liking to Matt. He had a disarming smile that made her feel at ease. His height towered above everyone there. His voice was sincere, his eyes twinkled with excitement. Fionna liked the feel of his energy.

"Do you mind if I take some pictures?" He held up his camera passively. "I'm the team photographer. And that woman there," he pointed, "is the reporter." He laughed.

Pepper reluctantly joined the laughter.

Fionna thought it was comical the way both Susan and Paul looked at each other before looking at her. "I don't see why not, but I don't think the pictures in this diner will be very interesting."

Matt laughed. "You're probably right, come, please have a seat." He gestured toward the booth.

Fionna slid in next to Pepper who moved closer to the window. Mary slid in after her.

"After you," Susan gestured for Matt to retake his seat.

Matt stuffed his lanky frame back behind the table.

"So you actually fit in there?" Susan laughed.

"Just about," Matt seemed to be the only one there who appreciated her sense of humor. "That's as long as no one needs to leave in a hurry."

"Elisabeth, Anna, please," Paul helped them both into the booth after Susan. Paul then grabbed a nearby chair, and sat down at the open end. "Everyone cozy?"

Fionna and Matt were the only ones who nodded.

"Order anything you'd like, the paper will pick up the tab," Pepper finally found her voice, calm and control once again dominating her nervousness.

"That could be a mistake!" Susan joked as she picked up one of the menus and scanned through it.

Pepper cleared her throat and then looked at Paul. "I want to thank you for meeting with us. This is such an important story."

Anna raised an eyebrow.

"Don't thank me," Paul gestured to Fionna. "It was the young woman right there who made this possible. I'm not so sure I agree with this whole mess but she seems to think this is what is needed, sooo … here we are." He shrugged. "Now, why we are here? Well, that is another question entirely."

Pepper looked at Fionna, surprise spreading across her face. She took a tape recorder from her purse and slid it toward the middle of the table. When she noticed everyone staring suspiciously at the black recorder, she asked, "Do you mind if I record our, uh … interview?" As if she needed to explain more, she added, "It helps me to get everything right."

"That would be a first," snorted Susan without taking her eyes off the menu.

The table filled with Matt's deep, muffled laughter. "I think I'm beginning to enjoy this."

The others joined in.

Pepper even found herself cracking a smile.

"Pepper, do you believe in miracles?" Fionna asked out of the blue. She studied Pepper's reaction closely. She thought she saw her jaw tighten and her forehead wrinkle.

"Well, I'm not so sure what you mean?" she answered cautiously as if carefully choosing her words. "I know some people believe that … miracles," she hesitated as if it were difficult even to say the word, "have been known to happen in history and were usually credited to Saints and men and women in religious circles, but …"

"You don't think they could happen today?" Fionna queried, "Why not?"

"Because, it hasn't … they don't." she stammered. "I know that when things can't be explained, we tend to make up ways to comprehend what we just don't understand. It's not your fault honey; it's human nature. My gosh, sweetheart, this is the twenty-first century; miracles don't just happen, how could they?" Pepper gestured with her hands and looked around the table as if it were all so very clear.

The group, including Matt, stared at her. The waitress collecting orders finally interrupted the moment.

"I think I'm changing my order to the New York steak," Susan announced, without batting an eye. "Do you have any caviar?"

Matt laughed and hid behind the menu as Pepper shot him a disapproving look.

As the waitress walked away, Fionna whispered, "But, what if you're wrong. What if I could prove to you, beyond a reasonable doubt, that miracles really do happen? What if I told you that the conditions were perfect. That people believed and a special power did make it all happen?" She watched Pepper's expression closely.

Pepper was biting her lip to keep quiet.

"What if all of this were done and the proper formula was followed … Why couldn't it happen?" Fionna shrugged.

"Because, it can't happen … It just can't. Things like that don't just happen!" Pepper flopped back against her seat. "If they did, you would read about them all of the time; they would be common knowledge."

"But they do!" expressed Mary. "You're just not listening!"

"Oh, really!" snorted Pepper.

"Seven beautiful children in the hospital are no longer sick," Fionna continued. She struggled to maintain composure. "They are back home now with their families and friends. Their hearts are whole again; the cancer no longer eats away at their souls. Their kidneys once again remove the toxins from their bodies. The scars burned into their skin into their hearts are gone. They are free because they believed they would be."

Pepper sighed and gave her a confused look.

Fionna was surprised that the words flowed from her heart. "It was more than the holy water from the trees that cured those children."

Pepper raised her eyebrows. "Holy water from the trees?" It was obvious she spoke louder than she had intended.

"Sea, óna crainn," the Gaelic accent rolled confidently off Fionna's tongue.

Grandma Elisabeth sat up straight in her seat. It was obvious that she was fighting the urge to speak. The smile no longer caressed her aging face.

"That is where I collected the essence of life. I found it when I was originally lost in the ancient redwood forest. It was a gift from the ancient ones." Fionna couldn't stop herself; the words just seemed to keep coming, one right after the other. She regretted saying some of them, but it was too late, the damage had been done.

Everyone stared at Fionna intently as she spoke, as if mesmerized by her every word. Paul slowly nodded; she could see the surprise in his face. The voice in her head and the spirit in her heart encouraged her to continue. All of their secrets were being released.

She told them of her backpacking trip with friends into the forest, how the winter storm had started her down the path, and how getting lost had taken her to the base of the ancient ones, the huge, deformed trees that were well over 2,000 years old. How the park rangers had found her, how once awakened from her deep sleep, she knew what she needed to do, what needed to be done. That she was fifth generation Irish American, that her Great, Great, Great Grandmother had rescued the ancient fairies from Ireland's dying countryside well over 150 years ago.

"Fairies!" Pepper laughed. "Your kidding, right?" she looked around the table for support. "There are no such things as fairies! There are no such thing as little green, bearded midgets running around the forest protecting pots of gold."

"No!" Susan exclaimed. "It seems to me that maybe you're not listening. Hello!" She rapped her knuckles on the table. "She is not describing the midget on the Lucky Charms' cereal box. She is talking about winged little people who have the power to turn the likes of you into an ugly toad."

Matt burst out laughing.

Pepper shot him a look that could kill.

Susan snatched the photo tube from Paul's hands and slapped it noisily onto the table. "Then, maybe, you need to take a look at this!" She popped off the end of the tube, slid out the rolled up photograph, noisily knocked the ketchup and mustard, salt and pepper shaker out of the way and spread the enlarged photograph across the top of the table. She held down the edges of the photo as she hastily pointed out the little figures in the background. "So, what is that? And that? And that? I suppose they are all a bunch of blobs that just happened to look like little fairies. What are the odds of that, huh?" She huffed as she shook her head. "Lucky Charms...leprechauns."

Pepper stared dumb-founded at the shadows, her eyes moving from figure to figure.

Matt's huge torso shadowed the photograph as he leaned over it, squinting as he scrutinized the shadows. "There are four of them."

Fionna also leaned over to examine the photo more closely. "Matt, do you believe in fairies?"

Matt shook his head. "Right now, I don't know what to believe. I do know that there is more to this world we live in than what meets the eye …" He looked up at Fionna and smiled. "Or the imagination."

Fionna nodded.

Pepper shook her head as she backed away from the photograph and crossed her arms in disapproval. "This doesn't prove anything … shadows in a photograph don't prove anything."

"I beg to differ. We have seen them." Paul nodded towards the enlarged photograph as he leaned forward. "Pepper, listen, I know it all sounds crazy, believe you me, I know … been there, done that myself, but it's true."

"If you say so," Pepper raised her eyebrows, her arms still tightly folded across her chest, disbelief in her eyes.

"We have all seen them," Mary added. "They are out there in the forest. Don't ask me how it is possible but it is true!"

Pepper narrowed her eyes.

"Don't believe in fairies, do you?" Fionna asked. She read the smirk on Pepper's face.

"Why should I believe in myths and legends, why should I believe in fairytales? Why should I believe any of you?"

"Because you asked us to tell you what happened, that's why. Because you are the one who asked us," said Mary. The disappointment was evident in her voice. "We all came down here because you asked us to."

"Fine … interview over. You will probably get a lump of coal for that one! After all, the press is still, the press," Susan sighed. "But, a free meal, after all, is a free meal."

Matt pulled his head away from the photograph as if coming up for air. "This picture is somewhat remarkable. The figures are life like but, of course, I would have to study it under different circumstances." He looked at Susan and Paul for approval.

"Here, knock yourself out." Susan thrust the empty cardboard picture tube into his hand. "We do want it back though."

Matt nodded appreciatively and accepted it.

"So, let's say for the practical purposes of this scenario … Why would fairies want to cure anyone, for that matter, why children?" Pepper asked.

"It wasn't the fairies that wanted to help the children … it was the ancient trees," Fionna said. "The trees are trying to save themselves. They are desperate. They don't know what else to do." She shrugged.

"And the fairies?" Pepper quizzed, egging her on.

"They are helping the trees because without the forest, the fairies would have no place to live," Fionna continued.

"Of course!" Pepper quipped.

"If something isn't done soon, the few remaining ancient trees will only be in parks. Every time one of those are cut down, the power is distributed among those who are left. The remaining ancient trees are trying to protect themselves. They want us to save the ancient ones that aren't protected in parks. They believe that if humans know the ancient trees can heal, they will protect the ones that are left."

Pepper stared at her. "If everything you say is true, then there shouldn't be a problem with my photographer and me seeing these fairies and mysterious trees for ourselves. You do understand where we're coming from, don't you … this whole fairytale thing is hard to swallow."

Grandma Elisabeth loudly cleared her throat until everyone was quietly looking at her as if something were wrong. "I have been sitting here patiently listening to this whole conversation," she shook her head. "I realize that I am just an old woman, who some may believe has outlived her usefulness, but I have lived on this earth longer than anyone else in this room. Wouldn't you say so?" She looked around for effect, shifting her gaze from person to person. She frowned at Pepper to get her point across. "I do believe I have seen a few miracles in my time and if you are lucky enough to see your late eighties like me, so will you. My grandmother first told me about the fairies when I was a little girl, about half your age," she said to Mary and Fionna. "I never did see the fairies outright. They were always in the shadows but the voices. Such beautiful voices. Once I heard music … flutes, bagpipes and drums … I never did find out where it came from." She laughed. "They always seemed to stay a couple of steps ahead of me. Like trying to reach the end of a rainbow."

"That's that leprechaun thing!" Susan smiled. "Sorry, Elisabeth."

"I might not have seen them outright," Elisabeth continued, "but I did believe that they were there. Oh, yes, they were there alright, hiding in the shadows. Tossing rocks, leading me astray … tricky rascals they are, you know! What I'm trying to say is that these people have no reason to lie to you; they'd just as soon keep everything as quiet as possible." She looked around the table. "But, there are some secrets that, even against all efforts, don't remain so. They do what they do because they were asked to do so. These brave young men and women are responding to a calling, much like the one my Great Grandmother did back in Ireland during the potato famine. She brought the fairies to the New World so they could start a new life. Now, we have been asked once again to make a difference." She let her eyes drift to Pepper's. The sternness was gone; she now pleaded for understanding. "I believe you too have been asked to help."

Fionna could still read the doubt hidden behind Pepper's masked surprise. "Pepper, I will take you there."

"I wouldn't take that woman anywhere!" Susan exclaimed. "She doesn't deserve to know!"

"No, she has a right to see them!" Fionna exclaimed. "Seeing is believing. Once in the forest, she will surly understand."

Chapter Thirty

Doubt Not

"They really *are* here!" Fionna whined. She shifted her desperate gaze and gestured with her arms toward the ancient forest around her. "Maybe they just aren't ready to be seen by so many of us." Her voice wavered in frustration. Even the ravens had not made an appearance.

Paul nodded in agreement. "They have probably never seen this many humans gather at one time in the heart of their world. I, for one, wouldn't be all that happy to see the likes of us."

"That's ditto for me as well!" Susan shrugged as she carefully searched the edge of the misty forest. "Maybe, just maybe, they agree that the media is out in too much force today."

Pepper unsuccessfully faked a smile. She couldn't believe it; Susan's demented charm and wit had bested her. She had met her match in the field of sarcasm. She could admire this woman later but, right now, she wished the good ranger would somehow lose her way or run out of manic charm. She wished her no ill will; she just needed space, lots of space. When the mood was right, when they were back out of the forest, back safe at the trailhead, she would join Susan's banter once again. But right now, she wanted it to be over, to be dry and comfortable.

She hoped it wasn't too obvious that she had regretted her decision to take the journey into the shadows, but she knew the group had noticed. It was in the look they gave her; it was in the tones of their patient voices. It was only Susan, with her uncanny ability to sense weakness in her fellow man or woman, who decided to make her trip into the interior more entertaining for herself. The fact that Matt seemed to enjoy Susan's company only compounded Pepper's discomfort, making things even worse.

She sank into deeper thought …

The first hour of the trip had kept her in awe; she had forgotten how beautiful the ancient forest really was. The deeply grooved, cinnamon colored bark of the huge redwoods blended nicely with the lush green ferns. The rich pleasing aroma of the late February forest and the quiet soothing sounds offered peace. She thought that if there were a way to market the essence of the forest, she would like to be the first in line to try. She was a capitalist at heart, a no-nonsense businesswoman. She had backpacked and hiked in her younger years but as her life changed, so did she. She told her friends she had lost touch with the earth tones of her past and had fallen in love with the bright synthetics of the present. So far, she hadn't seen any bright colors in the forest. Matt, on the other hand, seemed to be completely in sync with his earth tones.

Since her meeting a couple of days ago with the very same crew that surrounded her now in the heart of the ancient redwood forest on this drizzly winter day, she hadn't known what to think. The three hours that it took to hike this far had strained her sore muscles and pushed her to the edge of her endurance. She cursed her sedentary life, wishing that she had kept herself in better shape. She also wished she had broken in her new boots before she wore them on this trip. A rookie mistake. She felt the hot spots on her tender, wet feet and knew each one was the start of a blister. She fought the discomfort as she limped along, not daring to tell anyone else.

It was Paul who noticed and dealt with the soon-to-be medical emergency. It was Susan who lectured on the potential problem. They were both right but she wished they had saved their speeches for another time, a time when her heart was into it, a time when the mind was capable of and willing to use that information. She thought of the rangers' strange partnership. How they were both confident and yet so different. How they complemented each other. How their actions to preserve the wild areas had actually led them to this very moment. She had no reason to doubt their stories. It was obvious they had nothing to gain and much to lose from their involvement. She admired their traveling through the forest with ease and comfort. She, on the other hand, was in an alien world.

She thought about Matt. He too seemed to be at ease in the forest. His tall lanky figure towered above them, yet he was dwarfed by the immensity of the ancient scenery. He constantly snapped his camera as they traveled, capturing the beauty of the moment, burning them forever into memories, unchanged by time. Matt had a gift for photography, which he wielded with an unyielding passion. She thought it strange that the satisfied grunt and confirming nod after his every shot no longer bothered her. In a strange way, she found satisfaction, knowing that each one captured the essence of the moment. She wondered if they could ever get back together as friends outside the realm of work. Like her, he had never remarried. Unlike her, he embraced the childlike notion that fairies might actually exist. Deep down, she was glad for him but she couldn't see it for herself.

She admired the way Mary stuck by and supported her friend through the incredible ordeal of the search and the aftermath of her coma-induced visions. Mary had a no nonsense confidence about her and made it clear that she knew the meaning of true friendship, one that Pepper envied.

She flashed from her own discomfort to Fionna and Mary's now famous trip and Fionna's sick and delirious condition. Her being lost for three days, comatose for weeks, her incredible story, and now her involvement with the fairies. Fairies, indeed!

The young woman seemed sincere and confident about the experience. Pepper had no reason to doubt that Fionna believed what she believed but she had to question the existence of such creatures. *Fairies in the forest … ancient trees that heal?* She couldn't get the idea of fairies out of her mind. As prep work she read everything she could about the mythical creatures. She couldn't believe how much she actually found about something that didn't exist.

To her, fairies lived more in the minds of children than in the realm of reality. These immortal, humanlike, mythical beings with beautiful wings seemed to inhabit many societies. According to her research, they ranged in size from *very, very tiny flower fairies* to *great stone divas … fairies that controlled the wind.*

Surprisingly, the Irish believed the *Tuatha De Danaan*, the People of the Goddess Dana, was part of a previously conquered society who were driven into hiding when the Celts invaded Ireland. The pagan gods of the *Tuatha* were skilled in building and magic. They were forced underground destined to live in tombs and mounds they built. Overtime, as the Irish myths and legends spread, the *Tuatha* grew smaller and smaller until they turned into fairies. She found it incredible that some superstitious people in Ireland still believed that these mythical beings lived in the mounds. Some cultures believed that fairies were the souls of the dead who never made it past the gates of heaven but were not evil enough to be engulfed by the caves of hell. Wandering the *Netherland*, trapped between realms only to be occasionally seen by the likes of humans.

The thought made her shiver. She longed for the comfort of her cozy home and the warmth of a cup of coffee. However, she liked the thought of their being angels that had been cast out of heaven with some falling into the sea and others onto land, where, if left alone, they would live out the rest of their existence caught between two worlds.

The Welsh believed them to be an invisible race of spiritual beings *living in a world of their own*, so it was said. They were *Gods in their own right, spirits of nature that have grown smaller over time*, possessing magical powers, gifted with the ability to change the seasons, the weather and aspects of nature. They moved swiftly, became invisible at will and had the ability to blend into the woods. Dressed in green, they lived on hills, underwater, in woody dells and used caves and hollow trees as doorways to other worlds. They ate fruit, made shoes and bows, stole household items, and enjoyed music, laughter and dancing. On many occasions, they were observed dancing under the moonlight. But it seemed that, most of all, they enjoyed playing tricks and fighting, always at war with insects and reptiles.

If fortunate enough to encounter their sensitive side or lucky enough to be chosen or have the earth's greatest treasures revealed to you, watch out. You could be gifted with a touch of magic, relieved of your pain and suffering, or taken into guardianship to help you grow in love and wealth. It could be a curse or blessing to be taken into confidence as a human into the fairy realm. Legend said to approach the fairies with true belief and understanding, an open mind, presents of fresh flowers and heartfelt laughter.

Of course, there was a lighter side in the information she found. That, in the fairy world, *every flower, leaf and blade of grass had a story to share*. That streams sang and the wind whispers ancient secrets into the ears of those who would listen. That any sudden changes in the forest was a message, an invitation to join them. All you had to do was look for them at the forks in the road, where the streams divide and where the hedges border a clearing. All you needed was to be *attuned* and that each tear that was shed in laughter created a new opportunity to see a fairy.

Though rarely documented by humans, there were a couple of *tried and true* ways offered to accomplish the goal: to find a four leaf clover and lie down quietly in a field and await the dancing fairies or to find a stone with a hole that water had naturally bored its way through, look through the hole and be gifted with their presence. It was believed they appeared most frequently on the *high days*, *Beltane* (May's Eve) of the Celtic calendar, when they gathered to fight. Or during Midsummer's Eve when they celebrated …*what* the legends did not say! On *Samhain* (November's Eve) when they danced with ghosts and loudly mourned the coming of winter.

She read that there were ways to protect yourself from the mischievous fairies. Evidently, fairies had a bad reputation for stealing infants and replacing them with *changelings* … a child secretly exchanged for another in infancy. To protect against them, all you needed to do was place the father's pants over the cradle or hang an open pair of scissors above it. All done safely, of course.

The best place for seeing fairies was at the ancient lakeside settlement *of Lough Gur*, Ireland's most important archaeological site, believed to be the portal to *Tirna Nog*, the land of eternal youth. Then, there was Scotland's *Isle of Skye* situated off its west coast, affectionately called *The Misty Isle*, a special place among the largest in the chain of islands. And, of course, a place called the *Shiehallion Mountains*, in the Highlands of Scotland, also known as the fairy hill of the Caledonians and believed to possess magical powers. Last, there was Eskasoni Reserve of Nova Scotia and, of course, she could now add the alleged fairies and the enchanted ancient redwood forest of Roosevelt Redwoods.

Strangely, after the meeting at the restaurant, she found herself smiling more and looking at things a bit more intuitively. But her trained, factual mind still couldn't accept the concept of fairies. In the restaurant, once she was out of earshot of the *believers*, she willingly gave in to an uncontrollable fit of laughter. It had provided comfort. She imagined her tears of true laughter creating opportunities for her to see fairies and laughed again until her stomach hurt. Matt's scolding about her attitude and behavior couldn't change her mood. Now, oh, how much she wished the joy of laughter could pull her out of her present mood, if only for one brief moment …

At this point, they had been in the forest for about three hours and had tramped over many miles to reach what Paul called the *heart* of the forest. Along the way, she watched the trees grow in size, the thick moss and lichens stretch farther down from the trees. She didn't like the way the shadows darkened and danced in the cooler air. She didn't like the way her damp rain gear felt against her skin. She shuddered, more from nervousness than from the chill in the air. She spent more time looking over her shoulder and into the faces of the others for comfort than in the direction they were traveling. She wanted to ask the others if they also had that strange feeling of being watched but she thought better of it. That was something she didn't want confirmed.

This forest was like no other she had ever seen. She dreaded reaching their destination but, at the same time, wished they were already there. When it was announced that they had finally arrived, she was relieved but could not shake the uneasiness flowing through her body because the feeling of being watched was now stronger than ever.

They silently turned their heads and searched the forest as if they were waiting for something to arrive. Pepper strained to hear the forest sounds over her desperate breath. The deafening mist that condensed on the upper branches and ground cover dripped rhythmically onto the forest floor. The gray light made the shadows that much more mysterious and somewhat frightening. They stood quietly for what seemed like hours before Fionna called out into the forest.

"Séamus!"

Still silence followed. Fionna called again. Everyone stared intently into the surrounding mist.

"Séamus … is that you?"

Uncontrollable anger flowed through Pepper. She couldn't explain it and she couldn't help herself. She had been set up and made a fool of.

"Maybe they are not seeing visitors today," she sarcastically remarked, glancing at Susan. "Maybe, just maybe, they have prior engagements … maybe with the *trees*."

"Now is not the time," Matt motioned for her to be silent. "We are here for a story …"

"Oh, yes, it is … high time," Pepper snapped. She couldn't stop now. They weren't going to make a fool of her.

The others stared at her in disbelief.

"I have just hiked three hours through the darkest forest I have ever been in just to get to this point … and what do we find? Nothing!" She hissed, her words absorbed into the rolling mist. "We're here looking for *fairies*, for heaven's sake …" She shifted her angry stare to Matt, "... little winged midgets who supposedly, based on this imaginative young lady," she pointed at Fionna, "claim to have the power to …"

"Pepper! That's enough!" barked Matt.

"You're so gullible," she retorted, "you always were and probably always will be."

Matt gripped her bicep firmly to keep her quiet.

Pepper struggled for a couple of seconds before she freed her arm from his grip and took a couple of steps backwards out of his reach. "Ouch. Don't you ever do that again!" She thrust her finger in his direction. "You got one thing right … enough is enough!"

Unexpectedly, a piece of rotting wood about the size of a silver dollar struck her loudly in the shoulder and bounced off into the ferns. She angrily jerked in the direction of the others. "Who did that?" she demanded. "*Who* did that?"

The group, Matt included, stared at her strangely for a moment before speaking. Intensity electrified the air.

"Did what?" Susan asked through narrowed eyes. "You surely aren't accusing me of …"

"Oh, you know what! Someone just threw something at me." Pepper narrowed her eyes as they fell on Susan. "And I'll bet I know who the culprit is …"

Just at that moment, a second chunk of wood coming from another direction bounced off Pepper's pack. She spun around angrily and stared in the direction of the dense shadows. "Don't do that!" she screamed. She desperately squinted into the mist before she turning back toward the others. It only took a moment for her to process the fact that no one in the group could have thrown the wood chip from where they were standing. She pointed towards the surrounding forest and tried to speak but to her surprise, nothing came out but a gasp of air. She felt the energy drain from her body as she staggered backwards into Matt.

Only Fionna smiled, recognition on her face, as she stepped forward in the direction from which the sticks had been thrown. "Séamus?"

"No, don't!" The words finally slipped out of Pepper's mouth, the pitch high and cracked.

"It's all right," Fionna whispered. She patted her delicate hand on Pepper's shoulder as she passed. "There are no such things as fairies, remember!"

Pepper, along with everyone else, watched as Fionna faded into the mist.

It was then they heard the faint buzzing of wings, the mist parted in the direction Fionna had disappeared and one of the shadows moved close enough to be recognized as a human-like form. It hovered about five feet above the forest floor.

"No way!" Matt's incredulous whisper echoed. The eerie silence was filled with his joyous laughter as he took slow steps after Fionna, his hand holding his camera close to his chest.

"No!" Pepper gripped his arm to stop him. She didn't want to be left behind. *Not here, not now.* He was the only one she felt comfortable around. This could still be an elaborate hoax carried out at their expense. In that moment, she reluctantly decided that wherever Matt went, she was going to follow. Matt shrugged his shoulders, instinctively swung his camera in front of his face and took another couple of steps forward.

"I wouldn't do that if I were you," Susan's voice of reason echoed from behind them. "Not if you cherish your expensive camera."

Pepper stared straight ahead, allowing herself to be reluctantly dragged along side Matt.

"Good heavens!" Matt exclaimed. Pepper felt his whole body go tight and ridged.

It was only a matter of seconds before another piece of branch suddenly whistled out of the mist and shadows and bounced off the extended lens of Matt's camera with a loud *pling*.

"Good grief." Matt quickly covered his camera with his body as he stumbled backwards, catching himself before he fell. Instinctively he pulled his camera back up to his face again but quickly lowered it, protecting the lends with his free hand.

"I told you," Susan calmly lectured. "They don't take kindly to trespassers, especially the paparazzi type."

"What happened?" Pepper asked, looking at Matt and then

Susan. She sensed the sudden change in Matt's behavior, the sudden change in his emotions.

As Pepper waited impatiently for the answer, seconds melted into minutes that vanished into timelessness.

"They're here!" Matt offered a muffled laugh to regain his composure. "They're in the shadows all around us," he whispered.

"What?" Pepper heard her own voice quiver. "Who is here?" she asked as she moved closer, gripped him tighter around his arm and stared into his face. "Who is here?" She demanded again. "Talk to me." She felt a strange fear seep through her every muscle and every joint like the mist around her. *Why would a big man like Matt behave this way … what did he see?*

"Fairies … the forest is full of them," Matt answered finally.

She let the words bounce off her at first. Though that was the reason they were there, Pepper thought their imaginations had gotten the best of them all. Their minds were running out of control.

But then she saw shadows glide through the mist. Shadows weren't supposed to do that. Matt's comment echoed in her ears and flowed down the entire length of her tingling body as one of the shadows moved close enough to reveal its dwarfed, humanlike form. She began to smell sweet flowers. Oddly, her fear began to subside. The mist no longer hid secrets. The impractical no longer seemed to be so. Legends and myth collided headlong with truth.

"Oh my …" she laughed. She was at a loss for words.

Act 8:
An Understanding

Chapter Thirty-One

Obligation

Fionna stepped out of the clearing and into a maze of abundant ferns as she cautiously splashed through the cool, drizzly mist, leaving the rest of her group behind. After about a half dozen steps, she paused and looked back. She shuddered as a strange feeling of emptiness wormed its way into her heart. The shadows of her friends moved unnaturally against the giant curtain of gray and green, the murmur of their voices indistinguishable from the rhythmic drips of the saturated forest. She felt so distant from them, so alone. She fought the desire to flee the shadows and rejoin the safety of the group. *No*, she told herself, *I have to do this … I'm supposed to do this.* She sighed deeply and forced herself to turn away from the security of the narrow trail, stepping deeper into the forest and brushing the droplets from the oversized ferns as she passed. She felt a new wave of coolness as the moisture and solitude evaporated more of her cherished warmth. She knew she wasn't alone; she could sense the presence of other creatures hidden in the mist, their eyes watching her from the shadows. What once frightened her, however, gave her only a minute of discomfort. She was never totally at ease in the forest and knew she probably never would be. She had grown up among cinderblock walls, paved streets, buildings of all shapes and sizes, and vehicles everywhere she looked, traveling here and there. People were everywhere. That was her norm but this place of emerald and brown was far from her norm or normal, for that matter. To her, it was an alien world but for the fairies it was home, it was all they knew. A place they would do anything to protect.

She could still feel the contempt and mistrust that permeated the shadows, primarily because she was much more sensitive to things around her than she had ever been before. *What harm could a young woman do to them? How could I ever make them understand that I would never try to hurt them. They are the ones who called me here to help.*

Soon, the sight of her friends and any sign of human presence, except her own, were gone. She now felt truly alone.

"Séamus, please come out," she heard the fear in her voice and knew that they could as well. She also heard the muffled flutter of wings over the rhythmic drizzle and spied shadows darting in and out among the silhouettes of the ancient trees. She didn't have to be told what they were; their presence usually made her nervous but, today, they induced a strange inner fear. She was well aware that there wasn't any love lost between the humans and the fairies. History had proven that time and time again. Though neither trusted the other, attempts had been momentarily made to set aside their differences and, on occasion, one side helped the other. As history once again repeated itself, she struggled to make sense of the whole process. Deep down inside, she wished this ordeal would end. She wished it had happened to someone else, that she could once again be just a shy, teen-aged girl struggling to fit into a world that seemed ever different to her.

"Séamus!" She squeaked again in a harsh whisper. The shadows moved closer, using the ferns and trees for cover. She heard the Gaelic whispers of their tempered, sing-song little voices over the drizzle and now over the buzz of their wings. She could hear some of them quarreling angrily among themselves. She knew that her presence alone, this deep into the forest, had angered some of them but she had no choice. She did what she was supposed to, she brought the reporters as requested. *Why don't they understand that?*

She followed the wing whistling sounds with her eyes as a larger, darker figure darted through the shadows. She felt a spark of hope and some comfort. She knew it was him, the leader of the fairies once again showing up to protect her, to set things straight, to share his charm.

She watched him come into focus, stop and hover above the hedge of ferns less than five yards away. She saw him search the forest with a focused gaze before his eyes fell on hers and he smiled.

He seemed exceptionally cautious today, not like his usual confident self. She gave him an inquisitive stare.

His eyes softened as he slowly fluttered to the ground just out of arms reach. "So ye' hav' come back?"

Fionna nodded, her nervousness obvious.

As if just noticing her uneasiness, Séamus waved away the hovering fairies, sending them back into the shadows. The sounds of dripping rain replaced the muffled sounds of their wings.

"Tis' is all very strange te' them as well. This contact with humans …" He gazed into the forest again. "It can't be doin' them much good. Makes them nervous."

"Makes *them* nervous?" Fionna's squeaked. "I think you have that all turned around."

Séamus shot her a strange look, "Sha (Shah), Yes, I guess it would make the humans a bit nervous as well. The trees make the request an' 'tis us who carry it out." He nodded to one of the mist-shrouded silhouettes of a massive tree. “After all, ‘tis their forest an’ ‘tis by their grace that we ar’ allowed te’ live here.” He paused a moment to let his statements soak in. “Let us walk.” He motioned his arm deeper into the ancient forest.

Fionna desperately glance back in the direction of her friends.

“They will be fine,” Séamus laughed mischievously. “The fairies will keep them company. Especially that female with the short hair.”

“Pepper?”

“Sha (Shah), Yes, especially the one ye’ call Pepper.” Séamus laughed.

Fionna knew only too well what that meant. She looked at him with pleading eyes.

“Did they not come her’ te’ see fairies?” Séamus smiled. “Come on, they will be fine.”

Fionna still froze in her tracks as she considered both directions; it was as if her legs no longer wanted to move.

“Trust me, they will be fine,” He gave a toothsome smile.

Trust me! she thought. In a way she did; it was the rest of the fairies she didn’t trust. Their mischievous behavior, their misdirected anger and the mistrust she had felt from them. After all, they were fairies. A strange lot.

“Come.” For the first time, Séamus reached out to her with his hand. It caught her by surprise. He wiggled his stubby little fingers as he smiled, “We hav’ a tree elder te’ meet.”

She slowly reached out, cautiously touched his hand and then quickly pulled it away as if she were petting a snake. She wrinkled her nose.

Séamus laughed. “What do ye’ think I’m going te’ de’ te’ ye’?”

“Sorry.” Fionna suddenly felt embarrassed. “It’s just that …”

“Yes, ye’ hav’ never touched a fairy before today. Ye’ will get over it.” He wiggled his fingers again. “Come now, we ar’ already late.”

She stared at his hand and willed her arm in his direction. She heard her breathing increase and felt her heart pounding in her chest as she anticipated his touch.

Just as she was about to embrace his hand, he snatched her wrist in his gentle grip and began to tug her along.

Before she had time to protest, she found herself being escorted quickly through the ferns.

We haven't much time echoed in her ears.

She looked down occasionally to see the top of his bald head as he weaved easily in and out of the giant ferns. While he walked under the ferns, they slapped against her chest and face, leaving her dripping with moisture. She allowed herself to be transported along by the little old man who was less than half her size. His firm grip held hers in place. It reminded her of a Labrador retrieving a delicate bird in its powerful jaws and delivering it, without a bruise, to his master.

They traversed a maze of ancient trees, shrouded in a mist that snuggled among the huge bases gave them an eerie appearance. She felt her fear and nervousness fade with every step. Being with Séamus gave her the strength she needed to overcome her fears.

When they finally stopped, Séamus released her hand and stepped back from one of the trees that Fionna immediately recognized as the one that had given her the *holy water* nearly two months earlier. "This is the tree …" she quivered, "the one that gave …"

"Sha (Shah) Yes, the gift," he spoke proudly.

She nodded as she looked respectfully towards the tree.

"I thought ye' might hav' wanted te' see her; I know she wanted te' see ye'."

"*Her*? See me?" She looked back at Séamus. She knew he could read the surprised expression on her face. "I thought that trees were both genders …that..."

"Oh, ye' humans, ye' ar' always trying te' make like ye' understand things ye' know nothing' about. Of course they do, we all do. There is a bit of, what ye' call, man an' woman in all of us …

in every livin' creature on earth. Unbelievable!" He shook his head and gave her a bewildered look. "*She* is the dominatin' spirit that lives in the tree, just like, *she* is the dominating spirit that lives in ye'. Don't ye' humans kno' anythin'?"

"Evidently not; how is it that you seem to know all of this?" Fionna quizzed.

"We hav' come te' know tis'," he said plainly, "unlike what ye' hav' been..."

Fionna interrupted his lecture. A sweet fragrance filled her nose and lungs. "Do you smell that?" She turned her head, trying to locate the delicate aroma.

Séamus smiled.

It took Fionna only a moment to find its source. "It's coming from the tree! It's the same … I smelled this before."

"Indeed ye' hav', indeed ye' hav'."

She gazed at him, halfway between amazement and surprise before she refocused he attention back to the tree.

Séamus cleared his throat as if he were going to give a speech. "Ar' ye' expecting the trees te' talk te' ye'?"

Fionna raised her eyebrows. Strangely, in a way she was. After all, that was what she expected to happen in an enchanted forest. For the trees to move around, to elude their enemies by pulling up their shallow roots and making their way to safety, deeper into the mysterious shadows of the dark forest … much like Treebeard, the tree elder of the Ents, in Tolkien's *The Lord Of The Rings*. She found herself thinking about fairytales more often. If fairies were true, well, then....

"We fairies can move about to avoid danger." His voice was almost a whisper. He nodded sorrowfully to the trees around them. "But, the ancient ones ar' her' te' stay; this has been their home fer' thousands of years. With yer' help, they will probably be her' fer' a thousan' more."

She heard the admiration and respect in his voice. There was no doubt that the fairies respected the trees that were the soul of the forest in which they lived.

"If thes' trees wer' te' disappear tomorrow, it would be an incredible loss te' the entire forest."

She could hear the sorrow in his crackling voice as he looked at the base of the huge tree with tender respect. She followed his eyes as they crept up the length of the tree and into the shroud of mist.

"It would be an incredible loss te' yer' human world." His eyes showed sorrow, his voice louder and to the point. "Why de' humans feel the need te' cut down every livin' tree? Do they not care fer' their future? If the tree is bigger than themselves … why de' they feel the need te' cut 'em down …" There was a slight pause before he continued to speak. "I understan' the need fer' the trees …" He pointed his stubby finger into the mist. "They understan' the need te' take some of the trees, but why take all of the ancient ones? They ar' what keeps the forest in balance; surely humans must kno' that by now. The humans with the long dark hair, who ran freely through this forest, surely kne' that. They made offerin's. They respected the tree elders; they respected their own elders. But now, we rarely see those humans. The ones that we de' see now no longer look as they once did. We can no longer tell 'em apart from the ones that take what they please." He squinted as he spoke, "Ye' should surely now understan' why we feel the way we do?"

Fionna nodded in agreement. She hadn't really looked at things that way before.

At first her mind raced to understand what Séamus was saying. But then, her thoughts cleared and her knowledge seemed to emanate from within …

History recorded the awestruck Europeans' reactions when they first set foot in the North American Wilderness. Most feared the unknowns of the New World. The First Peoples, who called this wilderness their home, also feared the arrival of these Old World humans. As it was always recorded throughout history, fear led to misunderstandings and self-righteous attitudes led to hate. In time, concepts and ideas from the Old World populated the New World and resources were soon conquered and exploited. Whatever frightened or baffled them was soon rendered harmless. A belief spread that everything placed before them was theirs for their taking and those who didn't the gifts didn't deserve them. Hidden shadows were discovered, rendered safe and turned into places where shadows could no longer frighten the human imagination.

Thanks to a handful of humans who cared enough to save the ancient trees, there were still mysteries that stoked the fires of imagination. But the fear of the unknown still reminded them of their ancient past. In the end, however, they needed the wild places like these to sooth their primitive psyche. Awestruck by the massiveness of the forest wilderness, some humans managed to save blocks of land, left in their natural state as a reminder of the time when their forefathers had stumbled upon their likeness.

Fionna knew that the grove of ancient redwoods that she stood in front of at this very moment was now a remnant of what had once covered nearly two million coastal acres, extending from just beyond the Oregon border, south to southern Monterey County. Of that, only about three percent of the ancient redwood forest was left standing, most protected in National and State Parks. Protected only as long as the American people and the people of California wished it to be so.

On private timberland, the only ancient trees guaranteed protection were those within the protection of streambeds and waterways. For those that still resided in inaccessible areas, it was just a matter of time before the fallers took them down and the helicopters removed them to the mill.

In the West, there were other pockets of ancient forests, consisting of fir, spruce, cedar, pines, and hemlocks, that still resided on lands managed by the National Forest Service and Bureau of Land Management. Some of those forests were designated wilderness areas, places to be left in their wild state. But, most were subject to the whims of bureaucrats who seemed not to understand their importance....

Séamus' voice interrupted her thoughts. "Now we hav' humans that seem te' think that everythin' her' is fer' them te' take whenever they feel the need," his voice was gruff and protective. "We ar' surely doomed as a kingdom an' as a forest if the humans de' not change their ways."

"I have already told you that the lands here are protected, the ancient trees here are protected," she found herself arguing, trying to prove that not all humans were a harm to the forest.

"So ye' hav'," he acknowledged. His voice seemed to have calmed down a bit. "But, ther' ar' other groves of trees an' other forests that need te' be treated with the same respect. When they realize the importance, they will need te' de' the same fer' those as well."

Fionna nodded. She agreed his feelings about the ancient trees but there was a whole world outside of the forest that Séamus knew nothing about. A place she thought that he would never understand. She lived in a town that, for generations, had relied on the harvest of timber for their livelihood; the community's economic development was tightly woven into the board feet per year that the forest would yield. Despite the laws that protected the spotted owl and the marbled murrelet, both federally protected birds associated with ancient trees, the ancient groves on private lands had dwindled to only a few. In California, there were laws that strictly enforced and regulated the harvesting of timber and took into consideration factors like types of soil, riparian corridors and percent slopes, laws that frustrated the timber industry as well as the environmentalists. One accused the other that the laws were either too strict or not strict enough. She watched and listened to their clashes on the news. She had friends on both sides of the issues. She wondered what they would say if they knew what she had done or was about to do. There was plenty of second growth to harvest; the ancient trees were indeed special. That is what the people needed to know.

She coughed, took a breath and found the sweet aroma more powerful than ever, drawing her towards the ancient tree. When she looked back towards Séamus, she saw his face embraced in a contented, encouraging smile. As she stepped closer to the tree, warmth replaced the cool drizzle on her face and hands. She felt her heart race, her confusion fade and her thoughts clear. Within arms reach of the swelling buttress, she stopped. The tree stood before her like a heavily furrowed, cinnamon colored wall, the base like a melted candle. To her, it no longer looked like a tree. She followed the furrows in the bark with her eyes, watching them blend and then disappear into the mist. When she looked around for the elder fairy, she was surprised to see that he was no longer standing there. She frantically searched the mist. The drops that fell from the gray fog dripped noiselessly from the ferns and onto the forest floor. She was on the verge of panic but the warmth on her hands and face worked its way into her mind. Among the fragrant aromas were the earthy smells of the forest. Every deep breath brought comfort.

She turned back to the massive tree that stood before her; she no longer felt alone or abandoned but drawn to the tree. Stepping within inches of the base, she noted that she no longer felt the droplets on her face or the coolness of the afternoon. She closed her eyes and breathed deeply, letting the fragrant air dance in her lungs. She smelled the fibrous bark of the tree and the organic rich soil about her. This time she didn't cough.

"May I?" she spoke in a calm, controlled voice. Feeling it was okay, she reached out with the both of her hands and slowly placed them on the tree, caressing the bark with her fingers. At first nothing happened but then, suddenly, she felt the soothing warmth flow through her entire body. There was incredible joy and understanding and then she began to cry.

Chapter Thirty-Two

Media Blitz

As Paul walked past his desk, his legs seized and his body came to a screeching halt. The book he was carrying slipped out of his grasp and came crashing noisily to the hardwood floor. A strange silence followed. His fingers and toes tingled; the chill that started in his lower back flowed to his extremities. He fought the urge to look at the dreaded object that lay open on top of his desk. A strange, familiar fear settled in the pit of his stomach. Without turning his head, he took a quick glance. Earthy tones of green and brown covered half of the folded newspaper and he recognized it immediately as a photograph of the ancient forest. He swallowed the lump in his throat, slowly turned his head and stared. There it was, running along the top of the page in bold letters:

EEL RIVER SENTINEL Sunday, March 11th.

Feeling slightly faint, he supported himself with both hands on the edge of his desk as he stared down at the newspaper in disbelief.

His legs felt as if they could no longer support his weight. He had guessed right, the day he had dreaded was now upon them.

An ancient forest setting filled two thirds of the page. Dwarfed by the massive trees stood five recognizable silhouettes. He found himself first, then Susan. Though thankfully out of uniform, they both appeared somewhat at ease as they stared off into the forest. He moved closer to the photograph and closely examined the rest of his party. Mary and Fionna were both looking disappointedly in Pepper's direction, while she, in turn, was staring back at them, her face cloaked in her characteristic smirk. There was no doubt in his mind that they were in some heavy conversation at the time, most likely talking about Fionna. He refocused on Susan and himself. It took him a moment to realize they were looking in the same direction. He felt a strange nervousness again flow through him. He scanned the photograph back and forth, looking for something out of place. He gulped loudly when he did. First, he found one, then another.

"No!" His voice crackled in disbelief, his hands clenched tightly into fists as he focused on the photograph. The figures weren't much different than the ones that he found in the photograph that he had taken. Things had suddenly become more complicated. Trees were one thing, but fairies; well, they were something totally different. If he found them, he knew others would too. Their discovery would make things much more complicated. He narrowed his eyes for a closer look. There was a third. Their little faces stared back at the cameraman from the shadows of the ferns and moss.

"I don't believe it!" he said aloud.

A dreadful feeling surged through him again. He felt his stomach knot and his throat become too dry to swallow. The echo of his quickening heart pounded away in the back of his mind. Beads of icy perspiration dripped down his brow and his face flushed as he willed his eyes from the picture to the words.

Óna Crainn Ancient Secret from the Trees-Ancient Trees Responsible For Hospital Miracles.

by Pepper Jensen

He jerked his head up and desperately looked around the empty office before reaching for the paper with shaking hands. He paused a moment, almost as if afraid to touch the print, as if touching it would make it real. Finally, he unfolded the entire length of the paper and lay it across his desk.

His knees were still weak, as he slipped noisily into his chair and slid himself up against his desk. At first, he stared at the jumble of words; it took a moment for them to come into focus. With great reluctance and dread, he rubbed the spots from his eyes and began to read.

Pepper wrote about Fionna's getting lost in the forest, about the rangers finding her and her recovery in the hospital. She spoke passionately about the seven children of the ward, their families, their disabilities, and their miraculous recoveries. He looked up from the words and gazed curiously once again at the photograph. He glanced at his own oversized forest print hanging on the wall and back to the one he held in his hand. The fairies in his print seemed to stand out against the forest setting but the ones in the article were barely noticeable. Surprisingly, one of the fairies appeared to be in both photographs. He smiled when he thought of the coincidence. He returned to the article with less anxiety and a greater interest.

The article described the redwood trees' magnificent ability to heal those who believed it possible. She spoke of the need to protect the ancient trees, to alter timber harvesting practices and to protect more than just the trees. She challenged the readers to take a trip into the forest and discover for themselves the secrets that lay within. As he read on, he felt the concern well up from within as he envisioned a huge influx of people invading the forest sanctuary. It was the same reason the park staff never told anyone the exact locations of the world's tallest trees.

To his relief, not a single word was mentioned about the fairies or about the park ranger's involvement with them, Fionna's hypothetical past or, most importantly, the whereabouts of the ancient trees.

He slowly folded the Sunday paper and slid it away from him. He settled back into his chair and rubbed the palms of his hands across his eyes and face as he let out a heavy sigh. A strange roller coaster of emotions pulled his mind through highs and lows. The secret was out; the Sunday edition would make sure of it. Now, all they could do was wait.

"Now what?" He exclaimed as he stared at the picture on the wall of the ancient trees and fairies. His voice sounded so different. "What's our next move?"

"Hopefully, not out of this office. I have grown somewhat attached to my desk … and some of the people that I share my work space with," a familiar voice echoed in the room.

Paul turned around so quickly he almost fell out of his chair. He was relieved to see that it was his fellow ranger. "Susan!"

"In the flesh, for now." She forced a laugh. "It's good to see that I still have that effect on men."

Paul smiled, glad she was there.

She stopped when she reached the edge of his desk.

"I'm very surprised that I didn't see the fairy word mentioned once." Susan nodded down to the newspaper on the desk. "That crazy park rangers weren't running after them in the forest with butterfly nets … It could have been *devastating*. I wouldn't have put it passed her!"

"I know what you mean."

"The woman does have a heart after all. A small one though, but it appears to be growing." She held up her thumb and index finger and closed one of her eyes. She gave him a knowing smirk.

Paul scooped up the newspaper and held it out for her to see.

"Nah, you can have it. I've got a couple of those already." She smiled as she gently pushed the paper back towards him.

"See the photo?"

"Yeah, couldn't miss it, covers most of the front page. Must have cost them a pretty penny for the big color print …"

"No, it's not just the print; it's what's hidden in it." He nodded at his own photograph.

Paul watched the concern grow in her expression. He tapped his index finger on one of the fairy-like shadows and watched the color fade from her face.

"No, she didn't?"

"It appears that she has either knowingly or unknowingly played the *Fairy* card. Things are about to get interesting."

The sudden ringing of the telephone made them both jump. They silently stared at the phone.

"It's your desk," exclaimed Susan who continued to focus on the phone. "I've got my own phone, remember."

"Yeah, right."On the fourth ring, Paul picked it up.

"Hello?" He almost didn't recognize his own squeaky voice.

"Is this the ranger's office?" the voice quizzed.

"Yes, this is Ranger Behaan, how may I help you?"

There was a strange silence before the voice spoke again.

"You're the one that rescued that girl, aren't you? I read about it in the paper."

Paul cleared his voice as he looked up at Susan. He could tell she was reading his thoughts.

"Yes, I am one of the people who found the girl. What can I do for you?" Paul motioned for Susan to move closer to the phone receiver.

She slid her face next to his.

There was an eerie silence on the other end of the phone as Paul waited. It was the caller who broke the uneasy silence.

"Have you seen the photo in the Sunday paper?" the man's voice was calm and inquisitive.

"The one with the article?" Paul found himself dreading the call already.

"Yeah … I know you're going to find this strange, but … that man and woman in the photo … well, there appears to be three little faces staring back at them from the forest. I do believe those people see the little faces as well."

A dreaded uneasiness overwhelmed Paul. He and Susan stared helplessly into each other's eyes.

"Are you sure they aren't just shadows or something," Paul continued. "I have seen it many times before; they even have a term for them, blob shots, I believe." Paul tried to play it down.

"No, they're little faces. Three of them to be exact; don't you see them?"

Paul detected a strange tone in the man's voice. There was momentary silence while the person on the other end obviously thought about what to say. And Paul was unsure whether or not he wanted to hear. He roughed up the paper so the man on the other end would think he was examining the photograph. "No, all I see are shadows that I can turn into anything I want."

"Look three inches from the center of the left margin." The anxiety was noticeable in the man's voice.

Susan followed it with her finger. She nodded to Paul and mouthed the words, *the same ones.*

"No, I just see strange looking shadows," Paul cleared his throat.

"Can I meet with you?" the man quickly cut in. Then, with conspiratorial desperation, he added, "I have other pictures you might want to see."

"Other pictures?" Paul shuddered; he felt as if the room had just dropped twenty degrees.

"Yes, I have two others taken in Roosevelt Forest."

"Taken in this park?"

"Yes," he spoke calmly. "One I took on a backpacking trip into the interior over ten years ago and one, recently."

Paul nervously gripped Susan's shoulder. "Where did you take the most recent one?" He heard the squeaky panic in his own voice.

There was a strange silence before the man spoke again. "Do you believe in fairies, Ranger Behaan?"

"I believe many things are possible," Paul answered as he tried to recover.

"Well, then … would noon tomorrow work for you, Ranger Behaan?"

"I didn't get your name."

"Sorry, Ranger Behaan, my name is Clint, Clint Smith."

"Okay, I guess I will see you at the park office at noon tomorrow."

"Yes, thank you for your time."

The phone went dead.

Paul found himself holding the phone in his hand and staring into Susan's questioning eyes.

A phone rang again; this time it was Susan's line. Paul interrupted the uneasy silence. "And, so it begins!"

Chapter Thirty-Three

Na sléibhte (shleeoo) - The Mountains

Paul drove his patrol vehicle faster than usual up and down the parkway, avoiding the curious stares of the visiting public. He hoped they would assume he was in route to something important. It wasn't the first time he had driven fast to clear his mind and it probably wouldn't be the last. Susan sat quietly alongside him, silently staring out the passenger side window, her thoughts obviously wrapped in a faraway place of their own. They needed time to figure out their next move without interruptions. But, more importantly, they wished to be left alone.

The fact that they zoomed past the public without giving them a second thought brought Paul some comfort. He was so wrapped up in his own thoughts that it took him a while to realize that there were more people than usual out and about on this beautiful spring-like day. His mind refused to put two and two together. He didn't want to consider the possibility that the Sunday edition of the local paper had anything to do with the people that flocked to the forest.

His mind raced feverishly through all of the scenarios. Each one ended poorly for the park and devastatingly for him. *Why me … why us*? He recognized the signs and symptoms of feeling sorry for himself.

He had received two more phone calls since the one from the mysterious Mr. Smith. He wasn't even sure if that was the man's real name. The others only wanted to confirm the healing power of the redwood trees and why the Park Service was keeping it a secret! He sidestepped around the issues; after all, he told them, fresh air and beautiful scenery were known to heal just about any ailment.

It was Mr. Smith, however, who was causing him the greatest concern. An anonymous man calls about mysterious faces he noted in the background of a forest photograph recently published in association with miraculous cures of children. The man allegedly saw little faces in a couple of photographs he had taken himself. Little faces that he most likely believed were attached to little bodies. What was Paul to say to this man when they met face to face tomorrow. *Yes, you did see something special. Yes, there are such things as fairies and they do live in the ancient redwood forest. Yes, I have seen them and talked with them myself. Yes, my employer does let me carry a gun. And by the way, the fairy folk prefer to be called na si'ogai', but it's really the trees that are calling the shots. The children were cured because the ancient trees wished it to be so.*

The thought brought a needed smile to his face. He was glad to be temporarily rid of the stuffiness of the enclosed office to help air out his thoughts. At least, out here in the forest, they could hide among the visitors. Fortunately, noon tomorrow was still a long way off.

"Do you notice anything unusual?" Susan asked without taking her eyes off of the passing trees. Her voice snapped Paul out of his trance.

"What?"

"See anything different?" Her voice had that *I told you so* quality about it.

When he turned, he found Susan's expressive eyes drilling holes into the side of his head.

"Different?"

"Yeah, different. Like a bunch more vehicles parked along the shoulder of the road, much more than usual. Like the people themselves seeming a little more excited than usual to be here."

"What?" Paul looked around. He swerved down the parkway as he tried to catch quick glimpses of the other drivers.

"Paul, if you're going to insist on gawking at where you've been, instead of focusing on where you're going and the road in front of you, I'm going to insist that you pull over before you ruin both of our days."

Red faced, Paul slowed the vehicle. "You're right, maybe we should park."

"Maybe," she raised her eyebrows to emphasize her sarcasm. "But not too close to those vehicles."

Paul spotted a place along the shoulder of the parkway that was wide enough to park and let the vehicle roll to a bumpy stop. He left the engine idling.

"I hope this meets your specifications," he teased.

"Yeah, for now."

They rolled to a stop thirty yards from a small, paved parking lot filled with vehicles. At first nothing seemed out of the ordinary. A few people stood around their cars, staring up at the obscured tops of the tall trees, while others paced back and forth posing for pictures. He had seen this type of typical tourist behavior thousands of times before. To him, it was a reminder that summer would soon be upon them.

"They couldn't fit another vehicle in that parking lot if they tried," Paul laughed. "Looks normal enough to me; why don't we find a place that is a little less ... visited." Paul threw the car back into gear and checked over his shoulder for traffic.

"No, wait!"

Paul was alarmed at the urgency in her voice as she rolled down her window and firmly gripped his arm.

"Turn off the engine and look." She nodded in the direction of the grove of ancient trees.

Paul did as she ordered. He reluctantly followed her gaze, scanning the photographers and then the visitors in the parking lot. "What exactly am I looking for?"

"Not the parking lot, *eagle eyes*, in the forest just beyond ... by those big trees ... there."

Paul's glance drifted into the forest until it fell upon two wheelchairs visible through the gaps in the trees. The chairs' tenants in suits and dresses were struggling with the wheels as they rolled around the ferns and the bases of the smaller trees. "They are off the trail ... what do they think they're doing?"

Susan shrugged her shoulders; her eyes never leaving them. Paul was surprised to see that she was now watching them through 10X power binoculars.

"Take a look the person in the lead." She handed him the binoculars and pointed out into the forest.

Paul took the pair from her and searched until a tall, overweight human figure came into focus. The sunlight reflected off the sweat on his balding head. His wide, dark tie stood out against the rolled up sleeves of his white shirt and pressed seams of his dark pants. The man raised his hands towards the big tree as if giving praise. In one hand he held a small book that Paul recognized as a bible; obviously, the man was an evangelist. Other wheelchairs began to arrive and spread in an arch around others who were standing around the tree.

Paul faced Susan and was surprised to see that she now had a more powerful set of binoculars trained on the group. He smiled; it was very like Susan to be one-up. He shook his head and reexamined the scene through his smaller binoculars.

The bible-holding man faced the gathering group and began to speak.

Paul and Susan nudged against each other for viewing space within the open window. The sounds of the passing traffic and the distance from the group made it difficult for them to hear what the man was saying.

"I think I'm going to get a little closer," said Susan without taking her eyes off the action. She quietly stepped out of the vehicle and into the forest. Paul nodded agreement and made his way out of the vehicle. Susan had already disappeared into the forest before he stepped foot off the pavement. He moved quietly through the ferns, keeping the larger redwood trees between him and the droning voice of the large man. He glanced to either side as he quietly moved but he no longer saw any sign of Susan. He grumbled about not following her boot impressions in the redwood clover on the way in.

The booming voice of the preacher stopped him dead in his tracks. He was close enough to hear the man's excited voice clearly. The preacher praised their beliefs, why they were there, how the unity of their prayer would put an end to pain and suffering. He peered around the left side of one of the trees in front of him. Among dozens of people, he spotted an elderly woman wearing a bright blue, long dress, seated in a wheelchair and holding the hand of a well-dressed elderly man next to her. The man patted her hand in a comforting way as he quietly whispered words in her ear that Paul was too far away to hear. *Husband and wife*, Paul thought. Beside the couple, in a wheelchair of her own, was a delicate looking young girl in a pink, knee-length dress. Freckles spread across her face and a pink, lacy ribbon held her red hair in pigtails.

Directly behind her stood a middle-aged woman, *mother and*

daughter, Paul decided. The elder woman firmly held both of the girl's arms in her hands, aggressively stretching them up into the air and high above the young girl's head. The girl screamed in agony, tears streaming down her cheeks and a slightly demented smile stretching across her face.

Paul was mesmerized as the preacher rambled on in an inspiring tone, intermixing words and Amen's, fluctuating between highs and lows, whispers and screams. He couldn't help but be inspired himself, wanting the trees to do what they did best. It was a scene much like a river baptism or a bible belt revival, not what you would normally expect to see in a grove of ancient redwoods.

The chanting prayers raised to a feverous pitch, the tempo increasing with deep rhythmic assents. The preacher stepped towards those in the wheelchairs and encouraged them to come forward with a gentle motion of his hand and a knowing, caring smile. The older woman began to cry softly, then loudly in pain and anguish.

Others in the audience began gently helping her out of her chair and onto the forest floor beneath the large tree. Her husband at her side firmly held her hand, encouraging her to her feet. The elderly woman screamed in pain and almost collapsed, but the others caressed her and half-carried, half-dragged her towards the glowing preacher. He stepped backwards into the forest, encouraging them to follow.

Paul stepped from behind the tree where he had been hiding to watch. He was no longer concerned about concealing himself from what was taking place. As he began to move closer, he noticed the assortment of burls and proboscises that protruded from every side of the rich, red bark of the tree and how the deeply furrowed bark and base of redwood bulged like a melting candle before it rose into the upper canopy. This was indeed an ancient redwood.

Louder cries of joy, praise and deep rhythmic prayer drew his attention away from the tree and back to the gathering of people beneath it.

They carried the elderly woman over and placed her at the base of the ancient tree. She desperately held onto her husband's hand with both of hers. Her face expressing her joyful anguish. Her husband moved closer and feebly knelt alongside. Others joined him, placing one of their hands either on her shoulders, back and head, the other against the side of the humongous tree.

Next, a middle-aged man and two younger boys hurriedly carried the young girl over to the same location. *The father and brothers,* Paul thought. The mother was still holding the young girl's arms uncomfortably high above her head. The young girls arms were stretched up in the direction of upper branches. Though the young girl cried out in discomfort they continued.

Others made room for them when they reached the base of the tree; they quickly huddled around them and fell to their knees, bowing their heads. Each person placed one hand on the tree and joined hands with the other, engulfing them in the semi circle. The preacher's voice boomed over the chanting, crying crowd for a few moments before the entire group went strangely silent.

Paul stared, taken aback by what he was watching in front of him. They no longer looked like a group of individuals gathered around the base of a tree. They appeared to be a different organism entirely, a jumble of arms and legs, a writhing, colorful growth at the base of the tree. For a fleeting moment, they appeared to be one.

Before Paul realized it, he was a mere ten yards away.

He felt a breeze and *then* the sweet smell of a familiar orchid. A strange tingling chill flowed to his fingers and tears ran down his cheeks *or was it drops of mist falling onto his face* from the upper canopy of the tree.

When the group untangled, Paul found himself still staring, unable to move. He knew something had happened; he could feel it. But how could it be. The ancient trees with the power to heal were in the heart of the wilderness, not within walking distance of the road.

The people slowly rose to their feet, stunned. They helped each other up and dusted the duff and soil from their clothing. They began to talk, first quietly among themselves. They were oblivious to his standing there, motionless.

Paul watched intently as the last of the people rose to their feet; soon, the only ones left on the forest floor were the two individuals removed from the wheelchairs. A couple of people stepped forward to help but the preacher shooed them away. They reluctantly did as he asked. The preacher knelt down next to the elderly woman first. He placed one hand on her shoulder and the other on her forehead. He lowered his mouth next to her ear and whispered.

Paul was too far away to hear what the man was saying.

The elderly woman twitched, opened her eyes and turned her face towards the preacher. She looked lost, confused. It looked as if it took her a moment to regain her bearings.

"Rise to your feet," the preacher's confident voice echoed in the clearing. He extended one of his beefy arms for her to grab and gripped her arm with the other.

Without giving it a second thought, the once frail, elderly woman allowed herself to be assisted to her unstable feet, hanging on to the preacher's arm. She stood there a moment, held up by the preacher, her legs trembling under a weight they hadn't felt for years. She looked down at her feet, up towards the tops of the trees and then into the preacher's eyes. She mumbled something Paul couldn't understand and then burst into a convulsion of tears. The preacher motioned for others to help her away from the tree. The woman's husband quickly hobbled to her side and embraced her in his trembling arms. He burst into tears. Others helped escort them away.

Paul scrutinized everything with a look of disbelief and confusion. He gazed between the departing group and the group that remained, with the preacher. The young girl's family anxiously hugged each other on the sidelines as the young girl, who had been removed from the wheel chair, still remained motionless in a fetal position on the forest floor beneath the tree.

Hope glimmered in the preacher's eyes as he walked up to the girl and carefully kneeled down beside her.

Paul moved in closer.

Everyone suddenly became silent. Paul stood among the group, watching intently like the others.

The preacher gently placed one of his hands on top of the girl's head and placed his other on the girls arm as he had done with the older woman.

"Get up, rise to your feet." His voice echoed in the clearing.

To Paul's amazement and as if on cue, the little girl's eyes fluttered open. Instead of looking confused and disoriented as the elderly woman had, she looked up into the preacher's face and smiled. The beads of water that dripped down her face were not tears. She looked toward her family, to the preacher and then up towards the top of the ancient tree.

"Get up, my child," The preacher ordered.

Paul found himself willing her to do so as well. His heart pounded in his chest in anticipation.

She pushed herself up from the ground until she was in a sitting position.

The preacher began to help lift her but she pulled her arm away and refused his help with a shake of her head. Taken aback, the preacher took a couple of steps away and watched with growing excitement.

Paul watched her closely as she stared up into the upper canopy with a knowing gaze. He had seen that look before. He shuddered slightly at the thought. He held out the palm of his hand and watched the droplets of mist grow into a puddle. From the corner of his eye, he saw the little girl crawl up the bench-like base of the tree. She held her mouth open, her eyes closed, her face in a joyous expression as she turned it upwards towards the falling mist and the top of the tree. He watched her open her mouth, lick her lips, and swallow, and then with growing strength, she pulled herself to her feet.

The others stared in open mouthed amazement as she finally made it to her staggering feet, still holding onto the side of the tree. The preacher again attempted to help her but she waved him off with an irritated grunt.

The preacher looked on, confusion etched across his face as he watched the young girl continue to stare blindly into the top of the trees. Many of the crowd followed her lead, while others began to talk quietly among themselves, anticipating witnessing another miracle.

Paul ended up standing alongside the preacher as if he were drawn to that very spot at that very moment. The preacher looked at him, surprised, took a step back but did nothing to stop Paul from moving closer to the girl. Paul stopped about ten feet away from her, his heart pounding in his chest and the aroma of flowers growing stronger. Beads of sweat mixed with the drops of condensing mist on his forehead. No one else appeared to have been touched by the mist but tear-like droplets rolled down the girl's face as it did his own. He was sure the preacher must have noticed.

Suddenly, the girl opened her eyes and turned her head towards Paul. Her quick movement surprised him, making him jump. Her eyes lit up with recognition.

She took a deep breath and slowly let go of the tree, balancing her arms along her sides. She looked worriedly at her trembling legs for a moment and then back to Paul. Her face lit up with a smile.

Paul returned the smile.

And she began to walk. With each short, staggering step, she closed the distance. The others stared some were speechless, some crying, others singing praises for the miracle. Her family hugged each other, fighting the urge to run to her aid.

Paul stood with outstretched hands, waiting in excited anticipation for her to reach him like a child taking her first steps. The preacher's words of encouragement echoed from behind him.

When she was within arms reach, she fell forward into Paul's awaiting arms. He gripped her tightly and held her close. Her body was so frail and tiny. There was a strange kinship he could not explain. He did not know why but the scene was charged with emotion. He felt the weight of other arms pressing against his shoulder and back, surrounding him and praying loudly.

Paul wasn't expecting that.

"Thank you!" the little girl mumbled in his ear. She must have read the confusion in his face and whispered, "They told me …" She pointed up into the trees, tears of joy trickling from her eyes. Then, she burst into a torrent of streaming tears as she hugged her family.

Paul backed out of the huddle and stepped away from the ancient tree. He watched the group swarm the girl. Another gentle hand was laid on his shoulder and when he turned, he saw the preacher with his hand extended.

"Reverend Jones."

Paul embraced his hand with a firm shake. "Ranger Behaan."

The reverend nodded toward the elderly woman, Paul looked in the indicated direction, his hand still held firmly in the man's grip.

"When her son died," the reverend explained in an emotional voice, "she ceased to walk. Compounded with age and the lack of desire to do as she once did, she lost the ability. Now confined to a wheelchair, she prayed to be whole once again."

Paul silently nodded.

He then gestured to the young girl. “Her dreams of being a ballet dancer were shattered by a bicycle accident that left her paralyzed from her waist down. Her desire to be given a second chance was the strongest of all.” The reverend focused on Paul, his eyes peering inquisitively as if he were searching for answers. “You are the one … in the paper!” His voice reflected reverence as he continued to hold Paul’s hand.

“Yes, that would be me.”

“I mean, thank you …” The reverend dropped his hand back to his side. “God does work in mysterious ways.” He looked up nervously into the trees and raised both of his arms into the air.

Paul followed his gaze, suddenly wishing that he were anywhere else. “These trees are like no others.”

The preacher nodded, cleared his throat and asked, “How long have you known Hannah?” He took a handkerchief from his pocket and wiped the perspiration from his forehead.

“I think we just met.”

The preacher looked confused. “But she acted as if she knew you!” There was another pause before he spoke again. “How did you know to be here?”

Paul shook his head. “I kinda’ work here.“He read the uneasiness in the man’s voice.

“The mist fell only on Hannah … and you!” He pointed.

Paul shrugged his shoulders. He knew why but didn’t think the man would understand.

“What did she mean by *they told me*?” The preacher stepped further away from Paul as if he suddenly thought he needed to increase the distance between them.

Paul saw the fear of the unknown building in the man’s eyes. In the preacher’s world, there was good and there was evil. And from the way he stepped back … “Like you said, God works in mysterious ways." He looked to the trees as if for support. "These ancient trees can serve many purposes."

"Yes, the article in the paper alluded to it."

"Is that why you're here?"

The preacher gave a stiff nod.

Paul took a deep breath. "The article in the paper left out quite a few things, things that the average person would not understand."

The preacher gave him a strange look. "Like what?"

"Well …" Paul stopped talking and turned when he heard footsteps. He was relieved to see Susan walking towards him.

"There are some things that need to be explained," Susan's voice echoed in the clearing as she came to a stop alongside them. "And then there are others that should be left alone. But what the good ranger here is trying to tell you is that most minds aren't open enough to comprehend them." She nodded to the man. "So far, it seems that the simple mind of a child doesn't have a problem with the facts. Only adults do."

The preacher narrowed his eyes.

Susan reacted to his gesture with a knowing smile. "It's the trees that cure people in this forest, the ancient ones. Whether guided by a higher power or not, it's not up to us to determine. All I know is that little fairies protect the trees. And friends of mine are being asked to do the impossible."

He stared at her in disbelief.

"Call it a miracle, if you will but if it weren't for these trees, none of this would have happened today. Cured by a child's belief in the impossible."

"Or by the grace of God." the preacher added.

"To be honest," Susan continued, "I am blown away by what I have seen over the last few months."

"It's a gift," Paul pointed as Hannah stumbled along clumsily on two legs, her family and friends close at hand, arms extended.

“A miracle for those who believe. You brought them here, believing as much; maybe there is a bit of a trusting child within all of our own hearts.”

The preacher looked at his congregation a moment before he turned back to the two rangers. “Then, maybe it is also you who does the Lord’s bidding.” He stepped forward and extended his hand, “May the Lord bless you and keep you safe! Evidently, whether you know it or not, you must be special servants of the Man upstairs.” He looked up into the bright sunlight. “You have my utmost respect and my prayers.” He bowed his head to them, turned and walked back to the rest of his group.

His congregation quickly engulfed him.

The preacher looked back at them one last time and nodded before he disappeared into the group.

Paul returned the nod.

“Well, *Dalai Lama*,” she patted him on his shoulder. “Let’s get out of here before they want you to feed the hordes lunch from scraps of bread and leftovers.”

Paul laughed.

“I’m serious … there is something very weird going on around here and I’m not going to stick around long enough to find out what it is!”

They walked in the direction of their vehicle. Paul suddenly felt better about their mysterious mission to save the trees. Maybe people believing in the existence of fairies won’t be as bad as he thought.

Chapter Thirty-Four

Need to Know

Paul sat at his desk, nervously tapping the eraser end of his pencil rhythmically on top of his *Standard Diary*, a hardbound journal in which he recorded his day-to-day activities. The hollow sound of the drumming helped set his mind at ease; it helped him think. He had long ago lost interest in the meticulous shuffling of assorted paper piles from one side of his desk to the other. Digging through his junk drawer containing bits and pieces of memorabilia he had acquired throughout his career, only dragged his mind back to the oversized color photograph, back to the mysterious forest.

He stared at the blank wall that once held the framed forest photograph with the three faces staring knowingly back. He brushed the toe of his boot against the picture to reassure himself that it was still well hidden beneath his desk. The last thing he wanted to do was to encourage Mr. Smith, the man expected to show up due at the ranger station any minute, to push the fairy issue.

He looked at his wrist, then remembered that he had no watch.

He hadn't worn one for the last couple of years. He shot a quick glance to the clock on the wall; it was five minutes until noon. He had taken down the photograph, only to end up second guessing himself and putting it back on the wall two times already. The empty space stuck out like a neon sign flashing, *Guess what's missing!* If anyone seriously looked around his office, he would be sure to notice that something was indeed missing from that very spot. Overtime, he covered every possible bit of wall space with other photographs and certificates.

He sighed. "If the man saw little faces in every forest photograph he looked at, maybe it would be easier to explain them away as blob shots or shadows, a natural phenomena in any dark forest." He spoke loudly to the empty room as if trying to convince himself. He thought his voice sounded smooth, convincing and rational.

He slid his chair back, reached under the desk and pulled out the framed photograph one more time. Holding it at arm's length, he examined it once more. It always amazed him that a photograph was actually made up of a series of well placed dots. Up close, the color spots formed amorphous shadows, making it harder to see the details. He had enlarged to eight times its original size to emphasize the details when viewed at a distance.

Paul cocked his head from side to side as if critiquing a work of art. He then got up, walked over to the wall and once again hung the photograph on the nail. He took three huge steps back from the picture, crossed his arms and closed his eyes. "Okay, here we go." He let his breath out slowly. "Maybe, he won't notice." Seconds later, he opened his eyes and looked at the photograph again.

Almost instantly, he shook his head. "Who am I trying to kid!" The three faces were clear. There would be no doubt they were forest fairies.

It was then he heard the knock on the door. The man was right on time. Paul felt nervousness starting to build; the more prompt the individual, the more serious the contact.

Overwhelmed, he paced back and forth a moment before he hurried over to the photograph, snatched it off the wall and aggressively shoved it underneath his desk. As a second thought, he slid his chair with his foot to hold the photo in place. He walked toward the door, glancing toward his desk one last time before he opened it.

The man before him caught him by surprise. Paul knew his bewildered facial expression had given him away. He felt the beads of perspiration building along his temples. Casually, he attempted to brush them away with the back of his hand as he focused on the man's gentle, blue eyes. Paul felt the tension in his whole body begin to drain; there was a strange calmness about the man. In his left hand he held a folded paper bag, which Paul knew contained the photographs he had spoken of.

Based on their earlier phone conversation, he expected a middle aged man; probably an occasional park visitor who stumbled on his discovery by accident while viewing old pictures. But, before him, there stood a tall, stocky, elderly man who appeared to be in his sixties. A delicate, knowing smile spread across his weathered face. His white and brown thinning hair was pulled into a ponytail with a beaded, black, blue and white band that hung across his right shoulder. A picture of four colorful turtles graced the front of his dark blue, long sleeved T-shirt. There was a hole in one of the knees of his faded, well worn jeans. A worn pair of Birkenstocks graced his otherwise bare feet.

"Ranger Behaan?" The voice was calm and confident.

"Ah … yes."

"I am Clint Smith; I called yesterday." He extended his right hand.

Paul accepted the proffered hand, always one to judge a man by the firmness of his grip. "Yes, come in please."

Clint nodded and stepped into the room. His eyes shot around the room as if he were trying to read the man he had come to visit by what was reflected on his walls. Paul was not surprised when the man's eyes came to rest on the empty space on the wall near his desk.

"You're on time," Paul tried to break the uneasy silence.

The man nodded. "I have to confess, I could hardly wait to talk with you. I have been counting the hours since …"

Paul didn't have the heart to tell the man he hadn't felt the same way. "Would you like to sit down?"

The man nodded and Paul rolled the chair from behind Susan's desk, parking it near his own. "This one is pretty comfortable; they seem to be making chairs better all the time."

The man sat down and placed the folded paper bag on his lap.

Paul turned his chair around, sat and leaned the backrest against his desk. For the moment, he had forgotten all about the picture that was stuffed under the desk behind him.

The man's eyes continued to search the pictures and plaques that hung from the walls. His eyes came to rest on the photograph of Paul kneeling among a patch of budding marijuana stocks. "Is that what I think it is?" The excitement was noticeable in his voice.

Paul followed his gaze. "Yes, a dope garden."

"Do you guys find many of those?"

"Not as much as we used to. Most of the grows are done indoors these days." He pointed to the helicopter pictures. "During flyovers, we have seen an increase in green houses on adjacent properties. Why scurry around the brush or up and down steep hills looking for springs and south facing grow sites when you can grow it in the comfort of your own green house." Paul had to stop himself from rocking nervously back and forth in his chair. "Are those the pictures?" Paul pointed to the paper bag in the man's lap.

Clint looked down at his hands for a moment. "I just want you to know that I'm about as normal as the next guy."

In a regular contact, that statement alone would have piqued Paul's curiosity. His definition of normal had changed over the years.

"I like to take pictures," Mr. Smith continued, the anxiety noted in his voice.

The second statement got Paul's imagination going as well.

"I didn't notice anything unusual until later." The man continued. "I wouldn't have thought anything of it but then I saw the news paper. I'm actually not that great a photographer, most of my stuff either finds its way into my photo albums or into the round file. It's a hobby I picked up after my wife passed away. It helps keep my mind on other things."

"I'm sorry for your loss."

"I didn't tell you that for you to feel sorry for me," he expressed firmly.

Paul leaned back in his chair, he could tell immediately that the man regretted his response.

"I'm sorry … I didn't mean."

"It's alright!"

"That was then, and this is now," the man continued. "It was during my long walks into the forest that I started documenting my trips." He cleared his throat. "It's a way of sharing what's out there with those who may never have the opportunity to see."

Paul nodded. He was beginning to like this guy; he didn't strike him as someone who wanted to exploit the fairies. He seemed more like someone who wanted to do what was right.

Clint slowly pulled a photo album out of the folded paper bag, gently opened it and laid it on his lap. He paged through it for a moment until he found what he was looking for.

Paul watched the man wrinkle his eyebrows as if second guessing his decision to share his secret.

Paul responded with a knowing nod. "I appreciate your taking the time to share this with me."

Clint nodded.

"Where did you take these?"

"Along the wilderness trail that leads towards the valley on the north side." Clint still held the album firmly in his hands.

"Pretty country out that way; doesn't see that many visitors. It's a bit off the beaten path, close to where the photograph in the newspaper was taken."

Clint nodded. He turned the album around so Paul could see.

Paul rolled his chair closer to Clint's and leaned forward. His eyes scanned the color photograph protected behind a plastic sleeve. An ancient redwood tree covered most of the frame; an elderly woman sitting against the bulging base of the tree smiled back. Surrounding her were giant ferns. Paul searched the shadows but nothing jumped out as being unusual.

Paul looked up and gazed into Clint's face. He found his eyes studying him closely. "Your wife?"

"Emily." He nodded; there was reverence in his voice.

"She looks very content among the trees."

"She loved the redwood forest … she loved our walks."

Paul nodded and shifted his eyes back to the photograph.

"She was the reason I went back to that spot." Clint flipped to the next picture. A similar forest scene filled the page. "This was taken just to the left of that tree. Tell me what you see?"

Paul quickly scanned the photograph for anything that would catch his attention. All appeared normal. He then carefully searched it from left to right with a scrutinizing gaze. Nothing looked out of the ordinary. Everything appeared as it should.

"Forest and ferns," he shrugged his shoulders and looked up into Clint's smiling face.

Clint nodded as if he had passed the first test. He reached down and systematically flipped the page to the next photograph and then leaned back as if to study him carefully. "Now, tell me what you see!"

Paul nodded and examined the photograph again. This time the color photo covered the whole page. He recognized the similarities and landmarks in the earlier photo right away. It only took a moment to find the humanlike shadows in the bottom left corner, tucked in among the towering ferns. He moved his face closer to see better. The shadows took on faces, torsos and arms. He could almost make out what could be eyes. A strange, nervous tingle rolled down his neck and the middle of his back. He flipped back to the previous picture and then back to the enlargement. He repeated the process several times, increasing the movement until he finally let the album fall open on the enlargement. To his surprise, the shadow stood out even more. The lighting was almost identical but the mysterious shadows were non-existent in the first. Paul looked into Clint's smiling, inquisitive face.

"What do you think? What did you see?" He bubbled with enthusiasm as he leaned forward.

"Humanlike shadows."

"Shadows, yes … but they are too small to be human." He reached for the album and flipped to the next page.

Paul directed his eyes to the next photograph. This time, his wife was standing in the patch of ferns. Though the lighting was different, the landmarks matched the two earlier photographs. Paul flipped the page back to the one with the mysterious shadows and then back to the one with his deceased wife. "When were these taken?"

"About ten years ago … do they look like fairies to you?"

Paul noticed the desperation in the man's eyes. "They surely don't look human." He flipped back to the photo of Clint's wife smiling out from the ferns and then shifted his gaze to Clint's. "What did she think?"

Clint stared down at the photograph for a moment before

he spoke, his eyes never leaving the picture. "She said they were fairies."

Paul felt a lump build in his throat. "Did she see them?"

"Yes, several times … but I didn't believe her. I just thought they were shadows." He shrugged, "How was I supposed to know. I use to tease her about it." He forced a smile, "Boy, that used to bug the heck out of her. And she always talked about the sweet smelling flowers, too..."

"What?" Paul felt a familiar chill race through his body.

"Flowers … more like orchids, I believed she called them." He jabbed his thumb in the general direction of the forest. "She used to smell them out there in the wilderness. I, on the other hand, never smelled them, nor saw the fairies." He wiped his eyes with the back of his hand.

Paul struggled with the urge to confess his own encounters. The thought of others being in contact with the fairies surprised him. "How often did she see the … I mean smell the flowers?"

"Every once in a while, about as often as she said that she had seen the fairies. From what I could guess, one led to the other … Ranger Behaan, are you all right?"

Paul stared straight through the older man; he was back in the forest, back among the fairies. He immediately changed the subject. "You said you had a second photograph?"

Clint nodded, "Indeed, I do." He reached forward, flipped to the next page and pointed directly to the shadow.

Paul's eyes anxiously followed his finger to a shadow on a branch in a younger tree. The photo was dark; the shadow was one of several that had been created by the angle of the late afternoon sun. But, like the others in the previous photos, it had human-like qualities. With a little imagination, one could almost make out a face, torso and arms. Like the others, the figure was much smaller than a human's.

Without the first, he would have written off the second as a curious shadow. He didn't know what to say to the man.

"I have to confess," Clint spoke up, "this photograph was not taken by accident. I saw it in the tree and snapped the picture. I was so excited that I didn't even think about taking another one. Strangely, I could never find that same place again." He shook his head, "My wife was right. I wish I could tell her that." He sighed.

That statement alone gave the photograph more credibility. Paul was well aware of the fairies' ability to confuse and disorient the unsuspecting. Or was it a gift for him in her memory. Paul wanted to tell the man all about his own experiences with the mythical creatures but, at the same time, he needed to keep his feelings and emotions separated from those of the man before him. It was a self-defense mechanism he had learned throughout his career. "Clint, those are incredibly interesting; please tell me exactly why you wanted to share these with me. Weren't you worried about what I would say, what I would think?"

Clint laughed. "Yeah, I was. Walking into the station and telling the rangers that there are fairies in their forest … It would be worse than me coming in here and telling you that I had just seen Bigfoot!"

"That actually has happened before." Paul interjected. "Well, if fairies exist, then maybe so does the big fellow." It was seasonable logic.

He laughed nervously. "I could see how that would do wonders for someone's reputation but for an old man with nothing to lose …" He stopped laughing. "For some strange reason, especially after seeing the Sunday paper and all, I decided to talk with you. I know this may sound silly but I got the feeling that somehow you would understand."

Paul nodded. "What do you want me to do?"

"I want you to protect these things … I don't want them getting hurt." He raised his hand. "I know this all sounds crazy, but with the trees curing people and everything, the obvious fairy shadows on the front page … They need to be protected! That's all that I'm saying."

Paul nodded. He suddenly knew what to do. "Clint, I have something I would like to show you." The figures were so clear in his photograph, there was no doubt that they were anything except fairies.

Clint looked at the empty space on the wall and then at Paul.

Paul shrugged his shoulders and smiled. He turned around in his chair, reached under his desk and removed the framed picture. He stared at it a moment before he handed it over to Clint. He carefully watched the man's reaction over the top of the picture.

Clint anxiously leaned forward in his chair as he gently took the photograph from Paul. His eyes opened wide as he quickly found the figures. His mouth opened and his face contorted in emotion as if he had found the answers he had searched for his whole life.

"Emily …" Clint's body convulsed with each heavy sob. Paul knew he had done the right thing.

Chapter Thirty-Five

Coming to Grips

Pepper took another draft from her soda and stared into Matt's face, as he looked silently out of the diner window and off into oblivion. She wished it were a beer that she held in her trembling hand but her dearest camera man Matt talked her out of it, saying there would be plenty of time later for her to feel sorry for herself, plenty of time later to make other mistakes that she could spend the rest of her life trying to forget.

She was on edge. Worse of all, it was what she had done that made her feel so angry; it was what she had written that cast shadows across her tired, sleepless eyes.

She wanted to write a story that would set her apart from all the others; one that would give her fame, recognition and the respect she felt was owed her. Evidently, however, ancient trees with the power to heal were more than what the average person could accept. Instead being recognized for a dynamic piece of work, which she had indeed written, the letters to the editor raved of fairytales, children's stories and deception on the part of the *Eel River Sentinel.* Had she admitted to its substance as being nothing but fiction, she would have received the support she had been looking for. After all, people did love good fiction with a happy ending. But, by insisting it was factual, she had started her journey down a long, dark road.

She begged Matt to meet her at the same diner where they had occasionally met in the past, the one where they had recently met Fionna and the rangers. It was where they had spent time when their relationship was still new, back when they still danced to the beat of the same drum. She felt reassured when he accepted like their friendship was beginning to grow again. The man in front of her seemed so different. He had gotten thinner around the middle and more wrinkles graced his face; though his hair was still long, it was now tipped with gray and thinning by the day. A wiser and older Matt, one now more fun to be around stared back. She wondered why she had to wait so long to see. *Why hadn't she noticed before?*

Pepper took another long, stiff drink of soda. Frustrated, she gulped loudly and set the glass down noisily on the table of the quiet diner. To her embarrassment, moments later she felt the carbonation doing its work, escaping her throat and echoing loudly across the room. She looked around her, embarrassed. She hadn't made such a disgusting spectacle since adolescence. "Oh, sorry, I didn't mean to …" She covered her mouth as she blushed.

"Right on, Pepper!" Matt laughed loudly. He gave her a wink, drained the last of the soda in a big gulp and then gave the loudest belch she had ever heard.

To her surprise, the older couple on the other side of the diner didn't even give them a second look.

"Yeah! Haven't heard you do one of those in a while," he whispered loudly. "It's good to know you still have it in you me-lady." He playfully bowed his head. "To be unladylike when the need presents itself. To let emotions, not thought, rule your heart." He laughed again and patted her on her shoulder.

His touch felt warm and welcoming. She laughed along with him. His new found charm was disarming. "Can't say I planned the carbonation thing."

"That's the neat thing about life Pepper, no matter how hard we plan, something or someone else always seems to have a plan of their own."

She nodded, even though it felt strange to do so. She was actually agreeing with this man with whom she had argued so much in the past, the man that now felt like her only friend left in the world. She reached across the table and held one of his hands in the both of hers. It was warm and comforting. She felt the tears building in her eyes.

"Now, now, Pepper; it will be alright!"

"I'm sorry!" she said as she released his hand to wipe the tears from her eyes. "It's just that, well, the paper …what they said."

"Listen to me, Pepper … you wrote the truth." This time, his hands gently caressed both of hers and pulled them across the table and closer to his chest, his calm voice reflecting his sincerity.

This was definitely not the man she remembered, but he was one she would like to get to know.

"People might not want to hear the truth; they aren't ready for the truth. Just you wait. In time they will run out of logical explanations for things that they won't be able to explain. People will come to the forest because they believe and they will be rewarded for it." He chuckled, "If you remember, it wasn't that long ago when you scoffed at the ideas of fairies running around the forest. Let alone trees that heal."

"But, you were willing to believe even then."

He nodded his head. "Yes, I wanted to believe. I wanted there to be more to this mundane world that we live in." He paused a moment before he spoke again. "A strange thing happened to me that day, when I first felt their presence."

"The fairies?"

"Yes, it was like … fear being overcome by satisfaction. It was like just knowing that they existed gave me strength. Pepper, just like the ancient redwood trees may cure those who believe … the Na síogaí may also come to those who believe …"

She shuddered. She knew that Matt felt it as well because he looked at her even closer, as if trying to read her thoughts. His concern was evident. She remembered the others who had come to the forest to seek the very thing he so elegantly explained, to partake in the miracle. A few at first but then hundreds. People talked about how the trees were just as she had described in the article; powerful medicine for those who were willing to believe. People were soon decimating the delicate environment of the ancient forest. To her dismay, they hadn't treated the forest with the respect it deserved. In their excitement, they trampled; they took without a thought of the outcome of their actions. The rangers were working overtime to save what they had sworn to protect. They were forced to keep the people on the trails and out of the trees; in other words, they had to keep the people from loving the forest to death. Left unchecked, that was surely to be the outcome. Fionna's frantic voice still echoed in her ears from her early morning phone call. *Do something … they are trampling the forest. They don't understand.*

"Your article told those who …" Matt started to say.

"My article opened the flood gates," she exclaimed. "They do not understand the delicacy with which the forest was created. I have to slow them down … I have to make them aware."

"Heavens no Pepper...you can't tell them about the fairies! They, they … will *not* understand." He released her hands and stared out of the window. "You can't imagine what people will say if … what they would do."

"I know, I know. The fairies are safe for now. I would never put them in that position."

He turned back towards her, "Only if the people stay out of the wilderness will they remain protected." He crossed his arms and sat back in his chair. "If only we hadn't published that picture."

"Yes, but you didn't know … neither of us did until …"

"I know, I know; why didn't we notice until it was too late?"

She shook her head. "Maybe we weren't meant to." After a moment of silence she again felt a warm, comforting feeling worm its way into her thoughts. She recalled gray, finger-like clouds embrace the upper canopy of the ancient trees. A soft mist drifted to the forest floor, collecting into beads that twinkled in the light on the bright green ferns and lush moss. Rays of filtered sunlight illuminated the deeply grooved, cinnamon- colored bark behind it. The echoing drones of the tree, red and yellow-legged, frogs harmonized with the flutelike sounds of the thrushes. The vision brought a smile to her face.

"Pepper, there is that devious look again. What are you thinking?"

"I need to write … I must write again. I have to appeal to their emotions. Only then I think I will be able to make them understand the importance of accepting the outcome of their actions."

Something clicked in her mind as she looked into his eyes. "Matt," she questioned nervously, "do you think we have a chance to start over … you and me?" She wanted the answer to be *yes*.

He nodded.

She quickly jumped out of her seat and wrapped her arms tightly around his neck. "Yes!"

The elderly waitress politely cleared her throat. Neither of them had seen the woman standing there, nor knew for how long. In her hand she held a half-filled pitcher of caramel colored liquid. "Would you like some more soda?" She rattled the ice and smiled. They returned an embarrassed smile. More soda might just be what the doctor ordered.

Chapter Thirty-Six

Reaching a Balance

Fionna's mom dropped the folded newspaper onto the kitchen table and set her green Saint Patrick's Day steaming coffee cup down next to it. She crossed her arms and plopped into her worn chair. The ends of her shoulder length, brown hair glowed red in the low angled sunlight that streamed through the full-length window next to her. It was quite a contrast to the cozy blue bunting robe and fuzzy slippers she wore on her feet. She stared out the window at the fluttering birds gathering just outside. They hopped noisily from one branch to the next in the early morning light. She could hear their gleeful chirps from inside the quiet room. She loved watching the little birds, especially the wrens. They always seemed so carefree, dancing around with excited chatter as they greeted each other. At times like these, she wished she were a little bird. Their lives seemed so much simpler, so much easier. Eating when they were hungry, drinking when thirsty. Singing their beautiful songs as they absorbed the comforting rays of sunlight or huddled together for warmth on a chilly spring morning. Then, there was their ability to fly with grace and freedom, a feat they made look so easy. They did not have to deal with inexplicable miracles, useless holidays, daunting newspaper articles or understanding things that were better left alone.

Since her daughter's disappearance in the forest, her recovery in the Children's Ward, and the bizarre days that followed, life had not been the same. She wondered if it would ever be the same again; if they would ever return to the innocent times when the only worries Fionna had were making good grades, fitting in, finding friends and wearing the right clothes. Fionna had changed overnight; her smiles were now forced. She walked with a newfound confidence but also as if she were carrying the burden of the world on her narrow shoulders. She told passionate stories, incredible stories of what their grandmother had accomplished back in the old country, a feat that was very much a fairytale in itself. As time went by, Fionna shared more and more; sometimes, it scared her mother to learn what was bottled up in her daughter's mind. She talked of her involvement in changing the lives of seven children, how she needed to broaden people's awareness, to save the ancient redwood trees … that, she said, was the most important thing in the world to do. That those environmentalists who sat in the trees were doing it all wrong. They were destroying the very thing that they wished to save and protect. Their naïveté and arrogance were sending them down the wrong path. That what they were doing would, in the long run, force others to cut down the trees at an alarming rate. That being up in the tree was disrespectful to the ancient tree itself.

Anna wiped the forming tears from her eyes and snuffled her sobs. Hers weren't tears of sorrow; they were more tears of joy, regret and admiration all wrapped up together. She gripped her cup tightly to warm and busy her nervous hands. She shook her head as she stared at the stereotypical leprechaun that danced through a patch of four-leaf clovers under a rainbow and across her porcelain mug.

Holidays were so off the mark. But, yet, here she was, flaunting her piece of green … *to avoid a pinch!*

Incredibly, even Grandma Elizabeth had something to say about the family history. Things that she hadn't shared with her own daughter while she was growing up. Anna knew her Grandmothers were from a generation of desperate Irish immigrants who fled their motherland and made their way to America to start over. They were proud of that. Living among millions of other Americans of Irish decent, Fionna was the fifth generation to be born on American soil. They were mainstream Americans now; their Irish heritage mixed in a typical American melting pot of French, German, Dutch and First Nations. Like millions of others, they proudly displayed their heritage on Saint Patrick's Day in March, then put it away like Christmas ornaments in January.

She was surprised to hear that Fionna's story matched that of her mother's. In her vague recollection, there was the young girl who smuggled the fairies over from Ireland back in the 1840s. Again, it was part of the family history that her mother neglected to share with her when she was growing up. It hurt to think about it. When questioned, her mother only shrugged her shoulders. *They were only fairytales, meant to entertain children …*" she said. "*All but forgotten until Fionna had her experience.*" She had glared at her mother in amazement and disbelief. "Don't encourage her!" She had scolded. "The poor child has enough to worry about." She thought her little Fionna had been still suffering from the concussion.

It was Fionna's grandmother who had been taking her to the forest, driving her south to the park. Several times now Fionna had asked her to go with them, to see for herself that everything she was talking about was true. But she declined, making up excuses, dreaming up reasons why she couldn't. How foolish she thought; she didn't want to contribute to the fantasies.

But then there was the newspaper article, what her friends and the rangers had shared. *They couldn't all be crazy!* She slid her hand gently across the newspaper and traced the bold print of the headlines with her index finger.

She knew what it said without reading it. She felt another lump of pride welling up within her. Fionna had changed the lives of seven children with her faith and she was now changing many more. She struggled to understand.

She thought about her daughter's new passion for the forest, about her desire to protect the ancient redwoods, about her new friends that also shared the very same passion. She was so proud of Fionna. They were calling what she did for the children a miracle. "How did she do it?" she whispered out loud.

Gifts from the trees ... she heard her daughter's voice echo loudly in her head, almost as if she were standing right behind her. She turned abruptly, expecting to see Fionna standing there, but found herself alone in the quiet, dimly lit kitchen. She shuddered. Her mind was still playing tricks. She grasped the warm coffee mug with both hands, brought it to her lips, closed her eyes and inhaled the pleasant aroma to calm her nerves. She took a sip of the steaming coffee and placed the mug off to the side. It was too hot to drink; she would have to wait for it to cool.

She shifted her attention to the Saturday paper she had retrieved from the front walk earlier. This was her ritual, getting up early to enjoy the quiet mornings before the rest of the clan arose noisily to start the weekend. First, breakfast and then what ever came up before noon; after that, the time was spent in whatever the family decided to do. Lately, that involved spending a lot more time at the redwood park. But, for her, it was spending time waiting for Fionna to return from her secretive wilderness. Fionna had invited her to tag along but she had turned down the offer each time. Fionna announced that *today was to be different*. Her mom dreaded hearing those words. Their lives had already been different for months and she wasn't sure she was ready for something else. She reached down and unfolded the paper to expose the headlines.

Saturday March 17th.

Saving the Ancient Trees … Is Everyone's Responsibility. What we do to the trees, we do to ourselves.

by Pepper Jensen

Below was another color picture of the ancient forest but much smaller than the Sunday before. That photograph had caused quite a stir, according to Fionna. This one was a shot of a young girl standing next to her a discarded wheelchair and embracing one of the massive trees. She stood confidently, an incredible smile embellished her youthful face.

Anna had planned to skim the article but found herself consuming every word, every phrase, as if magic were being released through every sentence. The more she read, the more she wanted to read, the better she felt about herself, and the better she felt about the forest mystery. It was as if she were finally understanding her daughter.

The article beautifully described the young girl's belief that the tree had cured her paralysis and how it was her faith in the tree's ability that did it. That *we, the people*, who took from the forest needed to give back and to treat the land with proper respect, noting that the ancient trees were more special than we could ever imagine. The reporter spoke of how the forest had changed her, awakening her inner spirit and renewing her belief in the miraculous.

Anna reached for her warm cup and took another quick sip. The coffee had cooled enough for her to take a few noisy gulps. It instantly warmed her insides. She sighed in pleasure; it tasted better than she expected.

"That good, huh?" Fionna's queried from behind her.

Anna turned to see her daughter's smiling face. "You're up?" she unsuccessfully fought the surprise in her voice.

"You're reading the paper? Is the article there?" Fionna's excited voice filled the kitchen.

"Yes … come here and see for yourself!"

When Fionna stepped closer, her mother hugged her tightly.

"I'm sorry," Anna said, "for not understanding, for not wanting to understand."

"But, mom … it's all right …"

"No, it isn't!" she held Fionna tightly in her arms. "It wont be alright until you take me with you to the forest. I think that's the only way I'm going to understand what you're going through. Why have I been so blind?"

♦ ♦ ♦

Fionna had to catch her balance as her mother's embrace just about pulled her off her feet. She returned the unexpected hug. She was surprised to see her mom on the verge of tears, asking for a second chance to understand something Fionna herself could hardly explain. She had tried many times before but the bizarre tale was a bit too much for her mom, usually making her angry or frustrated. Now, surprisingly, the situation was suddenly different, there was hope. Fionna looked over her moms shoulder and down onto the open newspaper that laid sprawled across the table. Pepper's name in bold print graced the headlines. Her words had struck again; probably blessed with a little fairy magic of her own, she had been able to capture her reader's emotions with every word.

Fionna recognized the young girl in the picture as the one Paul and Susan had told her about; she was the one who was paralyzed but could now walk. Fionna knew it was the young girl's faith that had made a difference; her willingness to believe in change, to believe in the unseen forces of nature.

As she broke from her mother's bear hug, Fionna was surprised to see that the woman was crying. Anna tousled her daughter's hair, pushing the bangs out of her eyes, and announced, "Today, you and I are going to this wilderness of yours."

Her mom hadn't tried to smooth Fionna's hair since she was a little girl. As expected, the bangs sprang back to where they were before. The curls around her face never seemed to cooperate. Her mom tried twice more out of nervousness but then gave up. Fionna readjusted her, St Patty's Day, green silk butterfly pendant over the unruly patch of curls.

"Looks like we need to cut your bangs," her mom laughed as she guided her daughter to one of the kitchen chairs. "Sit down, please; there is something I want to say."

Once seated, however, the words came slowly and with difficulty.

Finally, Anna broke the silence. "I'm so sorry I didn't believe you … I thought, well … after hitting your head and all that your imagination had gotten the better of you."

She pointed to the newspaper. "These people say that it was the trees that helped them. But it is still difficult to accept."

"It wasn't just the trees, mom," Fionna rested her hand on her mom's shoulder. "It was the fact that they believed in the trees. They believed in what the forest could do for them. I couldn't have done what I did without believing that the trees were capable of healing people." She lowered her voice, "I couldn't have done what I did without the help of my friends, the trees and the fairies."

She noted the same doubt creeping back into her mother's expression.

"Mom, I know you are having trouble understanding what I'm saying but it will be clear once you join me in the forest. The answers you're looking for are in the forest." She heard the excitement in her voice. "The fairies depend on the trees … the trees are very special." Fionna folded her hands in her lap and stared out of the window as if in deep thought. "The ancient trees have been living and dying in these forests for thousands of years. They can't just get up and walk away when they are frightened. They have given life and shelter to all the animals that call the forest home. Even the First Nations, the First Peoples, knew that; they respected the trees, they respected the needs and wants of the ancient ones, the old growth trees."

"Over the last 100 years, we have not given the ancient forest the respect it deserves … we have taken from it without any concern for its future, for our future. Yet, when so few of the ancient ones are left, it is they who still give to us, regardless of what or how we treat them. It is up to us to protect them and the fairies! It's pretty incredible isn't it; over a hundred years later, grandchildren are asked to once again help protect the fairies … to make things right. To protect the ancient forests, the home of the fairies. The cures for human ailments. You see, it's all connected … were all connected!"

"Yes honey, it is … pretty incredible." Anna's sobbing was making her words hard to understand. "I am so sorry … I just didn't know. Today, we go to the forest."

Fionna nodded. "Grandma Elisabeth, too?"

"Yes, Grandma too!"

Chapter Thirty-Seven

It Is Our Profession

Entranced, both Paul and Susan sat silently, surrounded by an ancient forest, overlooking the fern lined, moss covered canyon thirty yards below. The roar of the cascading rapids filled their ears; the ions generated by the crashing water energizing their spirits. They casually dangled their legs over the vertical rocky face with their behinds safely wedged in smooth, serpentine impressions that seemed to be carved for that very purpose. They fearlessly swung their booted feet rhythmically back and forth as they sat, supporting themselves with the palms of their hands. Behind them on the rocky ledge lay their daypacks, stuffed with food, water and the other items they needed to do their job of protecting the redwood wilderness.

The spot was where they went to think, to relax, to enjoy an area of the wilderness that very few knew existed. A place where few would venture. Paul knew that if this place were turned into a regular destination for the average visitor, it would lose its special quality, the energy that flowed across the surface of this rocky outcropping would dissipate.

Paul knew of other places that were hidden in the darkest shadows of the ancient trees or in the deep, moist recesses of the mountain's secret caves or associated with special rocky outcroppings similar to the one they now enjoyed. All were believed to be sacred by the Sinkyone People, the first people who inhabited this section of the redwoods. He protected the sites with his silence, shared the whereabouts of these places with very few people.

He inhaled the smells of conifers, moist organic soils, exposed rock and the rosy fragrance of Susan's perfume.

"What are you grinning about?" Susan asked in a tranquil voice without turning her head or diverting her eyes. She crossed her boots and continued to swing her legs.

"What makes you think I'm grinning?" Paul stopped swinging and sat still.

She turned towards him and smiled, "Because you have been ever since we entered the forest today."

Paul nodded. "I guess I can't help myself. Especially with everything that has taken place over the last few months."

"Yeah, I know what you mean. Who would have ever believed that things would have ended up as well as they did," she stopped swinging her legs, sat up and crossed her arms. "I just don't get it. Yes, I know, I'm not supposed to … that spirits and angels work in mysterious ways and all!" She raised her eyebrows at his mischievous smirk. She responded by slapping him on the shoulder with lightning quickness.

The open hand slap was heard clearly over the sound of the creek below.

"Hey, what's that about?" Paul protested as he reached over to massage his shoulder. He frowned, pretending that it hurt even though he knew it was merely Susan's way of showing affection. Growing up as the only girl and the youngest with three older brothers, she had learned to hold her own.

"That's for getting me into this mess in the first place."

"What mess?"

"Oh, say, gee, now where do I begin!" Supporting her chin with one hand and her elbow with the other, she looked towards the tops of the trees across from them and pretended to be in deep thought. "Something about a search, miracles, fairies, ancient trees, the media, hordes of park visitors wanting to trample the resources to death …" She paused for a moment. "You know, it was really strange how Pepper and Matt were able to do a little magic of their own."

"Does this mean that you still hate reporters?"

"Don't you think hate is a little strong?" she challenged.

"Dislike, avoid, run away from …" He counted on his fingers.

She shook her head. "Who … Pepper? Nah, she's awesome. I know she can't help herself, it's what she was taught in journalism school … get the story at all costs; give the readers something they can sink their teeth into. And, if it's not juicy enough …" She shrugged her shoulders.

"So now were blaming the school of journalism … that's a different approach!"

She ignored him. "They add more sauce. It takes a certain breed like Pepper to be a consistent reporter. And you can bet your bottom dollar that she is. I don't know how she did it; her words painted the pictures, guided the readers, calmed the visitors. She helped reduce the impact on the forest."

Paul nodded, "I thought we were in real trouble there for awhile. People were taking everything. Trampling the ground cover just to touch the giants. They even came at night, thinking they wouldn't be seen."

"Yeah, nothing like working long night shifts with the ninja."

"Plus an incredible amount of overtime as well and pulling rangers from all over the district to help with twenty-four hour coverage for weeks at a time."

Susan raised an eyebrow. "It was like the fairies passed a spell over everyone who had read, seen or heard about the articles. Which, evidently, included everyone who entered the park," she whispered. "I hate to say this, but it seems a lot quieter than it should be!"

"The last time I saw any of the little people was when we were all together weeks ago." He paused for a moment and then returned her gaze. "I still feel them though. Every once in a while I think I hear their music, their Gaelic sing-song little voices, see a darting shadow out of the corner of my eyes or take a rock in the back."

Susan smiled.

The hammering of a woodpecker echoed off the rock face.

"But now, all I smell are roses." He wiggled his nose in her direction.

"Trust me, it's good that is all you smell when you're around me, especially after I've been hiking miles under the sun in the woods."

They laughed.

"I'm glad that Matt and Pepper are willing to give their relationship another shot … come to think of it, do you think the fairies had anything to do with that?" Paul gave her a quizzical glance.

She stared at him a moment before she threw her arms around him and kissed him gently on the cheek. "Happy St. Patty's Day!"

She had caught him by surprise. In all the years they worked together, she had never done that before. He stared at her, speechless.

"Now, that was for being my friend." She snickered as she roughed up his already messy hair. "Beyond that, you're not that lucky, bud. You're just not my type."

Act 9:
The Gift

Chapter Thirty-Eight

A Gift from the Heart

Fionna squeezed her mom's hand tightly as they sat quietly on a rotting log for what seemed like hours. She closed her eyes and used her other senses to feel the forest come alive around her. She knew that everything she heard, smelled, touched, saw, tasted and felt meant something; the constant annoyance of the buzzing insects, the scolding of the Steller's jay, the rhythmic orchestra of frogs; the curious chatter of the Douglas and flying squirrels as they closed in to investigate their presence; the sweet and haunting sounds of the thrushes, wrens, and chickadees; the distinct calls and taps of the northern flicker and the pileated woodpecker echoing off of the trees. It was in the hoots of the spotted owls as they searched out their mates in this ancient wilderness. It was the distant, faint calls of the bald eagle and the ones of the passing ravens, which she strained her ears to hear. It was the ravens, the messengers of the fairies, that she was supposed to meet. For them, she waited.

The air was warm; the sun was shining, its rays causing the greens to glow, the browns to lighten and the shadows to all but disappear. She thought about that winter day, so many months ago, when it all started, when she had been chosen to help protect the ancient trees and preserve the fairies secret. She wasn't finished but had gotten off to a good start. Of course, nothing would have worked if it weren't for the help of her friends and if it weren't for the support of her family.

Then, she heard the distinctive sounds that caused her nerves to vibrate with excitement.

"They're coming!" Fionna exclaimed excitedly as she looked in the direction of the sound. She gave her mom's hand a big squeeze before she releasing it and jumping to her feet. Her mom followed her off the log in one big leap. Fionna could see the worry in her mom's eyes. "It's okay, mom, they're friends."

"What? Who?"

"The Ravens."

The distant calls of the ravens were much different than the ones she heard earlier. They almost sounded excited. She wished she could understand what it was that they were trying to say. The direction of their boisterous calls meant that they were heading straight for them, silencing the forest in their path. She heard their wings whistling through the wind before they came into view. The rays of sunlight glowed on their jet-black feathers as they swooped down. They flew through the upper canopy, weaving in and out of the ancient branches with the grace of dancers. When they saw her, their calls became a louder, more excited pitch as they circled a few more times. They landed on a low, moss covered branch about seventy feet above her. They squawked, stretched their necks, rocked their bodies, puffed out their breasts and dipped their heads in excitement.

Anna watched in surprise as her daughter welcomed the duo.

Fionna giggled happily as she returned a *squawk* and a couple of nods.

The birds began to *cluck* and *coo* as if they were delivering a message. Fionna wasn't so sure but it didn't sound like the usual scolding she received from the pair every time they appeared. This time it was more like a welcome, like they were actually pleased to see her. That, in itself, was very odd; she wondered if they were up to no good.

She smiled briefly at her mother before returning her attention to the birds. "They seem to be in good spirits today." She was glad her mother didn't seem as frightened as she had before.

"Well, hello, what are you up to?" Fionna cupped her hands alongside her mouth and yelled loud enough for the birds to hear over their own noise. To her surprise, the birds became silent and stared down with intelligent eyes. They tilted their heads in jerky movements as if studying her. She could almost see their minds at work. She spoke to them again, this time in a softer, more respectful voice. "How are you doing today?" She motioned her hand towards Anna. "I brought my mother."

To her surprise, they clucked and cooed, making a variety of oddly human sounds. She laughed playfully. She wasn't exactly sure but she thought they were mirroring her gestures. She stared at them stunned … *could they actually understand me?*

"They are talking!" Anna whispered.

Fionna nodded.

"They thanked ye' fer' yer' mutual respect," the powerful, Gaelic voice boomed from the forest around her, catching her by surprise. She flinched as her mom almost fell to the ground in surprise.

The ravens made an annoying sound that sounded like uncontrolled laughter. Fionna turned and shot them a surprised look.

Séamus was quick to scold them in a raven-like tongue. The ravens squawked as they rose into the air with heavy beats of their wings, flying high above their heads in an ever widening circle. Fionna took a few steps out into the moss and fern lined clearing.

Her mom followed closely behind, her eyes searching the forest shadows for the source of the voice.

Fionna squinted into the sunlight as she listened to the whistling of the powerful wing beats slowly fading with each growing circle.

"Honey …" her mom's frightened voice raise to an eerie squeak as her hand gripped Fionna's shoulder. Something was close.

Fionna turned to see Séamus standing wide-eyed only a few feet away, staring deeply at her mother, his face etched into an unnerving smile, the likes of which she had never seen before. Behind his back, his short, stubby muscular arms held a bundle of moss.

"They ar' making sure no snoopin' fairies or pesky humans ar' where they aren't supposed te' be."

Fionna nodded. She couldn't take her eyes off of the bundle of moss.

"I av' some thin' fer' ye'," noting what he held in his hands and then Anna. "But, first, who is this beauty?"

Fionna followed Séamus' eyes to her mom. She had forgotten, for the moment, that she was there. "This is my mom …" she exclaimed. "Mom, meet Séamus, the king of the fairies."

The diminutive creature took a couple of cautious steps forward, then abruptly stopped when he saw Fionna's mom backing away from him. She was trying to pull Fionna backward by her shoulder but Fionna shrugged away.

"Nice te' meet ye', mom. I can see the family resemblance. I guess the likes of fairies takes some getting' use te'," he laughed. "I'm glad ye' decided te' finally come. Fionna must be happy as a lark that ye' have come. Welcome. I guess there really ar' such things as fairies."

All Anna could do was nod. She no longer tried to back away or to look for a place to hide.

"There is nothing to worry about, mom, he won't hurt us."

"That is true, ye' ar' our guests today. But, tomorrow … that may be different!"

Fionna laughed. Her mom forced a smile.

"Now, that's much better," Séamus said as he winked at Anna.

He pulled the moss-covered bundle in front of him and then scanned the forest through squinting eyes. When he was satisfied that all was clear, he carefully set the bundle on the forest floor and tilted his head. He held one of his stubby fingers up to his lips and cupped his other hand to one of his oversized ears. He tilted his head again in every direction, searching for sounds.

Fionna followed the gaze into the forest and strained her ears, curious about the reason for such secrecy. To her surprise, the forest was quiet. It suddenly dawned on her; outside of her mother being there, this was the first time that Séamus and she had ever been truly alone. At that moment, there were no other fairies around.

He nodded as if satisfied, carefully stooped over and picked up the moss-covered package again. He paused a moment as if in deep thought, started to hand the bundle to her but abruptly stopped.

Fionna couldn't help herself; she quickly reached out with excitement but Séamus was no longer there.

She heard her mother gasp.

When she saw Séamus again, he was about ten yards away, standing alongside a root ball of a huge ancient, fallen tree. In his arms, he still held the package.

"It is a gift fer' ye', a very special gift indeed. There aren't the likes of them around here." He spoke with great reverence and respect as he nodded towards the package. "There is so much ye' hav' done for us, there was so much we hav' asked of ye'. But ye' hav' done it an' done it well; fer' this we owe much gratitude." He laughed. "Though ye' may be the size of a girl, ye' hav' the heart of a fairy and the strength of an ancient tree." He paused for a moment to wipe his runny nose with the moss-covered bundle. He winked in Anna's direction.

Fionna found her tears swelling. When she looked at her mom, she saw she was crying as well. Fionna knew that this day would come and dreaded it from the start. She had grown to love her friendship with the fairies and her visits into the very heart of this ancient, enchanted forest. Saying goodbye was not something she wanted to do. She sniffed her nose, wiped her eyes and forced a smile. "We don't have to say goodbye, you know! I can always come visit you in the forest … can't I?"

"Of course ye' can. No, this isn't goodbye!" he sounded surprised.

She gave him a confused look.

"It's just, well, I've never had that many human friends. I didn't think I could ever feel this way about a human. I know how the fairies musta' felt about yer' Great, Great, Great Grandmother. At first, they weren't se' happy te' see her either. But, in time, they came te' love her, too!" He looked embarrassed, as if caught in an unexpected emotional state. "I must be getting soft in my old age."

"How old are you?" Fionna asked spontaneously.

He blew his nose noisily onto the moss and smiled. He then wiped his nose and eyes with the back of his hands and then stared into the air for a moment. "I don't think I know; it has never been an issue. Ye' see, fairies ar' immortal, ye' kno'. We can live forever if left alone. But, if our worlds ar' destroyed or taken away …" He shrugged.

Fionna gave him a surprised look.

"No, I'm not the oldest fairy in the world." He laughter boomed in the clearing and echoed off the trees. "I'm rather young." He winked again in Anna's direction. "But, unfortunately, I am the one with the responsibilities." There was a change in his voice.

The three were quiet for a moment as they listened to the rhythmic singing of the frogs. It was one of those moments when time stopped, as if something special were about to happen. It was Séamus who interrupted the silence.

"An' now fer' the gift." With a nod of his head, he motioned Fionna to where he stood alongside the towering root ball. The tree lay on its side, its finger-like roots extending more than fifteen feet into the air with ferns and moss growing in the pockets of soil that still clung to the gray, aging wood. Its immense size dwarfed them all. Beneath the roots was a huge crater that could have been six feet deep, surrounded by ferns and filled with clear, emerald colored water.

Fionna walked to within arm's reach of the fairy elder before she stopped. She knew better than to reach for him. This time, she would control her excitement, as she listened to the pounding of her heart echo in her ears. *What kind of gift would a fairy give a human?* She clinched her fists nervously as she looked eagerly at the moss-covered package.

"Fer' ye' te' hav' this gift, ye' must find it on yer' own." He smiled affectionately at her mom and then at her before he turned his gaze towards the pond. He rose from the ground and slowly hovered above the winter root hole. "I will lose it an' this is where ye' may find it."

Fionna's eyes followed his every movement as she tried quickly to piece it all together. When he was just above the water's surface, the moss covered bundle splashed into the frigid water and sank quickly to the bottom of the six-foot hole.

"Oops!" He pretended to be surprised. "I meant te' de' that!"

Aghast, Fionna watched it sink to the bottom. A stream of tiny bubbles floated to the surface and then disappeared.

Séamus drifted high above the pond and settled onto one of the moss and fern covered fingered roots that extended from the downed tree above the rain filled root hole. "Now, ye' may find." He laughed as he pointed to the pond, crossed his arms and smiled.

"She is not going in there!" Anna shrieked.

"I do believe the choice is hers an' hers alone."

Anna started to argue but Fionna quieted her down. "He is right, you know."

Séamus shrugged in agreement.

Fionna stared up at him in disbelief. "Why did you do that? Why in there, why not just leave it hidden in the ferns over there?" She pointed to the clearing.

Séamus shrugged his shoulders again. "Would ye' prefer I placed it at the top of one of these trees?" He looked up to emphasize his point. "I can't just out right give it te' ye', where would be the challenge in that? That is not the way of the fairies."

"No, I guess you're right," she whined. "A simple solution would never do now, would it?"

"Ní hea (nee hah), no, that would never do."

Fionna crept to the edge of the pond, blocking the low angled sunlight with her hands as she searched for the bundle. It only took her a few seconds to see where it lay. With Séamus's help, as expected, it had found its way to the deepest part of the hole. She touched the water with her hand. It was cold. The thought of swimming made her shiver. She stood there for a moment as if contemplating a means of retrieving the package without getting wet. She knew Séamus wasn't going to make this easier. After all, fairies never made things easy for humans. They couldn't help themselves. Applying misery and discomfort to humankind was what they did best. She left the pond with determination. She would show him who would get the last laugh. She searched around and quickly found some branches that were long enough to reach the bundle. She gave Séamus a knowing smirk and went to work trying to fish the package out of the pool with the end of two sticks, manipulating them around like chopsticks.

Out of the corner of her eye, she saw Séamus settle down loudly onto the roots and give out a loud audible sigh as if he were going to be there a while. She tried to ignore him but felt she wasn't doing something right. *Surely, he doesn't actually want me to go swimming for it, does he?* She prodded and poked with the stick but only managed to pull the moss off the gift and stir up the pond's murky bottom. In frustration, she tossed the sticks back into the forest, sat down noisily on the ground with crossed legs and stared at the pond, as she waited silently for the water to settle.

Her mom comforted her with an arm over her shoulder. "It's okay, dear. The water will calm."

"Maybe, ye' should just go in ther' an' get it." Séamus said. "Ar' ye' goin' te' stay out here all night?"

Anna gave him a dirty look.

"I would watch what I was thinking if I were you!" Séamus scolded. "Ye' must not meddle in things ye' don't know and understan'. I know ye' mean well but leave this te' me. I beg ye' te' trust me. If Fionna trusts me, why can't ye'?"

"Are you serious?" Fionna exclaimed in disbelief. "Do you know how cold that water is?"

Séamus smiled, "Yes, but only at first"

"Only at first! Fairies!" She waved her arm at him in frustration and continued to stare intently into the water, swatting at insects that came too close to her mouth, eyes and ears. As the water began to clear, she looked on in surprise and then panic as she noticed that the pieces of moss had torn free of the gift and were now spread along the bottom of the pond, revealing nothing. "It's gone … there is nothing there!"

"No, it's there a'right." He didn't move a muscle; he still sat back, relaxed. His attitude frustrated her more. He was obviously enjoying this. "Tell me what ye' see that shouldn't be there."

"What?" she heard the anger and frustration in her own voice.

"What de' ye' see that is out of place?"

She attempted to calm down and focus beneath the surface of the water. The moss stood out the most. When she first saw the pieces of green moss, anger began creeping back but she shifted the disappointment to her own actions, regretting pulling it apart. She then saw the molded brown maple leaves from last fall that paved the bottom of the pool. She imagined them quaking in the cool autumn breeze, their golden colors absorbing the last of the warm sunlight before they gave in and allowed the breeze to carry them to this resting place. She envisioned the rains filling the pond, gently at first but then turning into a non-stop torrent. Her thoughts flashed to the thunder and lightning, the misty clouds and the sheets of rain. Her backpacking trip, her friends and the aroma of sweet smelling flowers. To her surprise, the movement of an orange and brown newt casually crawling among the dark brown leaves along the bottom caught her attention. Amazed, ,he watched it slowly work its way across the leaves and dirt and toward a tan stone. The color of the stone was very different from the other earth tones along the bottom of the pond. "There is a strange stone," she said excitedly.

"Well then, what ar' ye' waitin' fer', bring it te' me!" demanded Séamus in his playful voice. "That pond will dry up before it gets any warmer."

Fionna knew what she needed to do. Without giving it much thought, she quickly slipped off her boots and socks, pants, coat and shirt. Clad only in her underwear, she located the tan colored rock with her eyes and slowly lowered herself into the cold water. She felt the coolness bite into her skin as the goose bumps raised across her body. Despite the discomfort, she pushed on, easing further into the cold water. At first, she felt as if her skin were on fire, then she suddenly understood the meaning of fire and ice. The further she slipped into the water, the less the coolness seemed to matter. She moved slowly in order not to disturb the bottom or make ripples on the water's emerald surface, keeping her eyes focused on the submerged object. Soon, she could no longer feel the bottom beneath her bare feet. She moved her arms back and forth just under the surface to keep her head above the water and flutter kicked with her legs, making sure she didn't push down toward the bottom. With her head above the cold water, she made her way directly above the submerged object. She took a couple of deep breaths, dropped her head below the water's surface and pulled at the water, forcing herself towards the dark bottom. The coolness bit into her face as the pressure and chill grabbed her ears, causing a tingling headache like eating ice cream too quickly, as the air rushed out of her lungs. She blew bubbles to relieve the discomfort but found that her lung capacity had shrunk. She panicked and scrambled back towards the surface. When she broke through, she gasped for air.

She didn't even take the time to look for Séamus; after a couple of deep breaths, she plunged back to the bottom again. By then, she had stirred up enough murk to obstruct her view of the bottom. Without swimming goggles to help her see the details, she relied on her sense of touch. She headed directly to where she had last seen the object and began carefully to grope around for it. She systematically moved her hand along the leafy bottom, dragging it back and forth through the moss and other debris. She felt the brief softness of a moving object and knew it was the newt that she had seen only moments earlier in the vicinity of the gift. She was out of air, yet she pushed on for a few more seconds; she wasn't sure she would be able to find this very spot again. At that moment her numb fingertips bumped into a hard object. She grabbed it and ran her fingers across it. It was stone and fit perfectly into the palm of her hand. There was something unusual, however, a smooth hole went all the way through the middle.

Without wasting another second, she scurried toward the surface light. When she burst through, she gasped for breath and coughed as she stared down at the stone that she held tightly in her grip. It was tan and rough to the feel and she knew right away it was a piece of sandstone. In the middle was a smooth hole that went all the way through the rock. She stuck her finger through it again; it was smooth as if water had been flowing through it for thousands of years. It felt good in her hands. She panted heavily, treading water, as she looked up from the stone and searched for the giant root ball on which Séamus had been sitting ever so casually. She was surprised to find him directly above her, soaking wet and fluttering silently in the air. Water dripped off his smiling face. The sight of him made her laugh.

To her surprise, Séamus appeared to be laughing right along with her.

"I see ye' hav' finally found it."

He motioned for her to go over to the side. She swam over and stumbled clumsily up the pond's shallow side. She stopped to catch her breath and regain her balance. Something didn't seem right, her legs suddenly felt tired, unable to support her weight, and her chest hurt.

"Be careful there! Ye' need to wait fer' yer' land legs te' return. Ye' wer' in that water fer' quite a spell."

She felt the familiar grip of her mom's arms around her waist and allowed herself to be pulled to her feet. The warmth felt good.

"Look how cold she is; how can this be. She wasn't in the water for more than a couple of minutes." Anna exclaimed. She looked at Séamus for an explanation.

Fionna looked down at her arms and legs and was surprised to see that they were red, water logged and itchy if she had been in the water for hours. She vigorously scratched her legs as she looked over her mom's shoulder and into Séamus' caring eyes. The look on her face said it all.

"Ye' went on a journey te' retrieve the magical stone."

Anna looked down at the pond, while Fionna examined the stone. She could hardly feel it in her numb hands. She lifted it towards her face to get a better look. It smelled of the pond and the forest; it looked as if water and time had carved it. She flattened it on her trembling palm and clumsily slipped her index finger into the hole. It was then she noticed her teeth chattering and trembling that ran through her entire body. There was no way a few minutes in the pond would have made her that cold. She shot Séamus a questioning look.

He nodded. "Ye' hav' taken a journey … an' hav' been rewarded with that magical stone which ye' hold in yer' hand." He spoke tenderly and with great respect.

She returned her gaze to the stone. "But, thhhhereee …. is a hhhhoooole in it." She shivered. "Hhhhooooww long was I in thhhhhere?"

"Fer' a while. Ye' wouldn't stop until ye' brought it up." Séamus smiled. "Ye' hav' truly earned it, my little friend. The stone belongs te' ye' now. Do ye accept our gift?" Séamus waited for her answer.

She looked suspiciously at the stone for a moment, then to her mother's curious eyes and back to Séamus. She smiled as she pressed the stone between her hands and pulled it to her chest. "... I do."

Séamus nodded, satisfied. "Then, it is yers' Fionna, it will always be yers'."

At that moment, she felt the tingling in her hands and spreading throughout her entire body. She no longer felt cold; her skin was no longer red, waterlogged and shriveled. It no longer itched. Even her underwear was dry.

"Like yer' Great Grandmother and your Great, Great, Great Grandmother before ye', ye' will always be considered a friend of the Na síogí."

She felt a strange, joyful feeling overwhelm her as she held up the tan piece of sandstone, drawn to the unusual symmetrical hole in the middle.

"This is a magical stone, created over time by the flow of water. They say that if ye' ever want te' see *na síogaí*, all ye' need te' de' is te' hold it up like so." He simulated the action with his stubby little hand, "Look through the hole, wish te' see the fairies, an' there ye' ar'!" He giggled, "Because ye' know how hard tis' te' see fairies around' her'.".

"Thank you so very much!" Fionna reached out with her delicate hand but to her surprise, Séamus slowly flew backwards, twice the distance away and landed on a downed log. She gave him a puzzled look.

"Why don't ye' try the stone." He nodded anxiously to the gift. "It hasn't been used in a while."

Fionna looked at Séamus, to her mother, and then to the stone.

Her mother nodded in encouragement.

She closed her eyes and took a couple of deep breaths. She fumbled with the stone for a moment, running her fingers over its smooth shape, sliding her fingers into the strange, water sculptured hole. Keeping her eyes closed, she raised her arms like she would a camera. Concentrating on fairies, as Séamus had instructed, she slowly pulled the stone up to her eye and stopped when she felt it against her face. Holding it there silently for a moment, she concentrated even harder on the existence of fairies. She heard her own deep breathing and felt the pulse of her racing heart in her ears. She opened her eyes, gasped and almost dropped the magical stone.

"Are you alright?" Anna quizzed. She was oblivious to what her daughter was seeing through the magical stone.

Dozens and dozens of fairies emerged cautiously from the shadows all in their earth tone colors of the forest. Their silvery wings moved about the shadows. They no longer looked at her with angry stares; they no longer gestured as if they meant her any harm. They looked at her with respect. She held the stone tightly against her face in her trembling hand. She couldn't believe it.

Anna looked on, trying to see what had surprised her daughter. "What do you see?" she demanded.

Both Fionna and Séamus ignored the question.

"Lower the stone now an' let 'em get a good look at ye'," Séamus's voice echoed in the clearing.

Fionna's heart raced as she slowly lowered the stone. To her surprise, the fairies were still there. The little ones hid behind the bigger ones, many keeping a safe distance away. It was the guards, those who had harassed her and her friends during their visits to the forest, that stopped just out of arm's reach. The one that bothered her most stood the closest. Instead of glares of anger and mistrust, she thought she saw a twinkle and a delicate smile of friendship.

"Fionna, what is it?" her mom asked again.

"There are fairies everywhere; it's incredible!"

Her mom twisted around in vain but Séamus was the only fairy she could see.

One by one, the fairies bowed their heads as if saying thank you. And, then, one by one, they slowly disappeared, fading into the shadows. The forest absorbed the buzzing of their wings. Soon, Séamus was the last one left standing.

"This isn't goodbye, ye' kno'..." With those words, he bowed gracefully towards them. She returned the bow and when she raised her eyes, he was gone. All she heard were the soothing spring sounds of the forest. His sneaky disappearance brought a smile to her face. Séamus was indeed a *na síogaí* and fairies … well, they couldn't help themselves; after all, they were fairy folk. Mythical creatures that inhabited enchanted forests.

About The Author

Robert Leiterman is currently a park ranger on California's North Coast. His unique experiences and his vivid imagination has inspired him to share the richness of the North Coast environment in an educational, but yet entertaining way. He enjoys being with his family and spending time in the outdoors. He is also the author of other books in print.

The Bigfoot Trilogy:

The Bigfoot Mystery – The Adventure Begins
ISBN: 0-595-14175-7

Yeti or not, Here we come! – Bigfoot in the Redwoods
ISBN: 0-595-26561-8

Operation Redwood Quest – Search for Answers
ISBN: 0-595-30513-X

Other natural history related books:

Great Valley Grassland Adventure
ISBN: 0-595-20302-7

GOJU QUEST – A Martial Artist Journey
ISBN: 0-595-34185-3

Either One Way or The Otter
ISBN-13: 978-0-595-38218-7

Óna Crainn
An Ancient Secret – From the Trees